THE
DECISION

CHRISTINA ROST

Scrivenings
PRESS
Quench your thirst for story.
www.ScriveningsPress.com

Published by Scrivenings Press LLC
15 Lucky Lane
Morrilton, Arkansas 72110
https://ScriveningsPress.com

Printed in the United States of America

Paperback ISBN 978-1-64917-293-8

eBook ISBN 978-1-64917-294-5

Editors: Amy R. Anguish and K. Banks

Cover by Linda Fulkerson www.bookmarketinggraphics.com

This book is dedicated to my husband Steve, my best friend and the love of my life. I also dedicate my creative journey to my three children, David, Eric, and Katelyn. I hope you're inspired to reach for your own dreams and pursue them with determination and perseverance.

THEME VERSE

"Have I not commanded you? Be strong and courageous. Do not be frightened, and do not be dismayed, for the LORD your God is with you wherever you go."
Joshua 1:9 (ESV)

CHAPTER ONE

Uganda

S tepping down off the rickety truck, Ava Stewart pinched her eyes shut and swallowed back the acrid bubbles clinging to her throat. The oppressive humidity and the crater-filled roads did little to quell the storm brewing in her skull—and in her belly. Traveling to Uganda during the fall rainy season had been a bad idea. Ava sipped from her water bottle and sighed. The tepid liquid brought relief but not satisfaction. *I'd do anything for a glass of ice-cold mint tea.*

High-pitched cackles and a barrage of feathers shot through the air. Ava eyed the culprits and scowled. A rowdy group of scruffy chickens scratched and stomped at the muddy dirt, hoping to spy anything to peck. *What am I doing here? I'm a city girl.*

Two adolescent girls brushed past her, kicking a twine-wrapped ball, laughing and batting at each other for the next shot. Another girl, smaller than the others, struggled to keep up. When her foot caught on a protruding rock, she tumbled to the ground.

Ava bolted forward. "Are you okay, sweetheart?"

The little girl glanced up. Her wide brown eyes were glossy with tears, and Ava's heart ached. *Mommy misses you, Evelyn.* Taking a deep breath and releasing it, she pushed past the memory of her daughter. "Looks like you've got a scratch." She motioned toward the little girl's knee, now ruddy with blood, and frowned.

The girl sucked in a quick breath and Ava drew her attention back to the child's face. Pointing to the gash, the girl sniffled as a handful of tears twisted down her dusty cheeks.

"I have something that might help." She dug through her bag until she found the wad of bandages she'd packed for the trip. Finding one with an ombre of pink and purple flowers, she smiled back at the little girl. "Would you like one of my special stickers?" As if Ava were a magician pulling a rabbit out of her hat, the colorful bandage brightened the girl's expression. Splashing a bit of water on the cut, Ava dabbed the wound with a tissue and threw her a wink. "Need to clean out the dirt." She pulled the paper from the bandage and gently covered the girl's knee. "All better."

The girl stared wide-eyed at her leg and grinned. Then, bouncing to her feet, she wrapped her arms around Ava's neck.

The child's hug melted her heart as longing filtered through the creases of her soul. *I miss my little girl.*

Releasing her arms, the girl stepped back, darted through the group of chickens, and skipped across the open field.

Ava took in a couple of long, cleansing breaths as she stood. *You're here to help, not wallow in your grief.* If she thought too much about the irrational decision she'd made to travel thousands of miles from her tidy, comfortable home in Dallas, she'd be tempted to sprint back to Kampala and jump on the next plane to DFW.

Don't make any extreme decisions in your grief. Her therapist's words sprang into her mind like an out-of-control bouncy ball.

Ava pinched her brows together. "Too late."

"You have some time before our transportation arrives." A booming voice pulled her from her thoughts, and Ava glanced up. After picking up two more local doctors, they needed to transfer into a larger, roofless truck—hopefully one with better suspension.

Charles, the village pastor and leader for today's trek, pointed to the two grass-roofed huts and smiled. "Maybe take a minute. Stretch your legs."

Ava followed the group, grateful for the promised relief from the jarring roads.

"The sun's finally breaking through." Sharron, a pediatric nurse from her church, sidled up next to her and nodded toward the parting clouds.

"Yeah, but even with all this rain, it's still so hot." Ava squinted. Her designer sunglasses did little to darken the glare from the peeking sun.

Sharron chuckled and motioned ahead toward one of the shelters. "Smells like they're cooking up something delish in there."

Ava grimaced as Sharron trotted away and vanished inside the simple, four-walled building. When the sharp scent of aromatic spices assaulted her nose and throat, she darted for the nearest copse of trees. Placing a hand over the soft pooch of her belly, her stomach spasmed until that morning's breakfast splattered across the muddy ground and her new pink running shoes. *Please, God, don't let this be what I think it is.* Ava shoved her sunglasses on top of her head, then yanked a wet wipe out of her bag and swiped the cloth across her lips.

"You okay?" A hand landed on her shoulder and squeezed.

She stilled. Hearing the low timbre of her friend Colby's voice, she pleaded for the dusty ground to open and swallow her whole. "Yeah—yeah, I'm good." The words came out shaky, and she lifted a palm to steady herself against the trunk of a tree.

Colby's hand dropped from her shoulder as a shudder of frustration rippled through her. *I should have never come here.* Another flutter of uneasiness stirred in her belly, and she kicked at the tree trunk like a spoiled child. *It's nobody's fault but your own.*

Colby sighed, yanking her out of her pity party. "Ava," He paused. "I know you're going through a tough time right now." Another pause. Nobody—not even a good friend—had the right words to rub out the sting of grief.

Ava shook her head. "Don't say it." She couldn't handle any more well-intentioned expressions of comfort. She'd fled Texas, angry at her husband, angry at God—well, angry at everyone—and if a few thousand miles couldn't bring relief, then she didn't know what could. *Get it together, Ava. Two weeks. You just have to get through two weeks.* "I'll be fine. I think I just got a little car sick."

Colby stood there for a breath of a second, and she didn't doubt he was questioning her sanity. No sane person buries her husband, then a few weeks later jumps on a plane to Uganda.

Intense emotions are normal. Take some time to heal.

Ava wanted to scream—or laugh. She'd not even bothered to tell her therapist where she was going. Why? Because she didn't want anyone to stop her.

"Just make sure you're drinking plenty of water." The gentle tone of Colby's voice circled through the air as tears gathered in her lashes.

She nodded, afraid to speak. A moment passed before he patted her shoulder, then dropped his hand and shuffled away. Releasing a sigh, she reached into her bag, pulled out a ginger drop, jerked off the wrapper, and plunked it onto her tongue. *God, if You care anything about me—never mind.*

After a quick swipe of her brow with the back of her hand, she turned, slipped on her sunglasses, and focused on the bumpy, red dirt road they'd driven in on. It was lined with umbrella trees, sprigs of tall wispy grass, and a handful of other low-hanging vegetation she couldn't name. Everything about this country felt unfamiliar to her—the food, the people, and the insects. Ava shuddered, then dusted off her hands on her pants. *The insects.* Some creatures she'd come across, she'd only seen at the Dallas Zoo behind thick glass. *The zoo. Our first date.* The sentimental image darted across her mind. She jerked back as if someone had slapped her in the face. *Don't go there.*

Ava pinched her brows together. *What I wouldn't give for one more day.* She kicked at the ground again, this time the tip of her shoe hitting hard against a buried rock. She groaned and crinkled her toes in pain. However, the ache was nothing compared to the raw, gaping hole in the center of her heart.

A buzz of activity pulled Ava's attention back to the group she'd traveled with.

"Time to load up, everyone." Their translator for the day pushed through the crowd and clapped his hands. "Our replacement vehicle has arrived." The airy lilt of his voice sent a ripple of laughter across the diverse group of missionaries.

The battered vehicle rolled in front of them, and Ava cringed. So much for added luxury.

"It's not glamourous, but it does the trick." Sharron, who'd shimmied up next to her holding a skewer of unidentified meat, flashed her a grin.

Ava wrinkled her nose and studied their new ride. The

truck's green paint was faded and the large dent in the side gave the impression it had been through a fight scene in *Jurassic Park*. "If you say so." She forced a smile and watched Sharron hoist herself into the open bed of the truck. Each side had a plank of wood to sit on and raised backs to give it the illusion of safety and comfort. "No roof or seatbelts?"

Sharron motioned for her to get in. "Not today, city girl. Not today."

She looked down at her long skirt. She still hadn't grown used to wearing one, but etiquette called for it, and admittedly, the light fabric kept her cooler than jeans. Gripping the side of the truck, she considered the most lady-like way to get in.

"Are you ready for your first shot clinic, Mrs. Stewart?"

She glanced back at Colby and frowned. "Mrs. Stewart makes me sound ancient."

He chuckled as he wrapped his hands around her waist to give her a gentle lift.

Stepping up into the truck, Ava straightened her threadbare Texas Rangers baseball cap and settled onto the bench across from Sharron. She had no medical experience but she'd volunteered to keep track of supplies and help with the children's Bible camps.

Colby hopped up into the truck with the ease of an athlete and plopped down next to her. Ava rolled her eyes. Her muscles ached all over, and today she moved more like someone on injured reserve than a woman of thirty-two.

"Okay Ava Marie, are you ready to entertain kids and hand out lollipops?"

She forced a happy expression. "I think so." The truck lurched forward, and a myriad of ruts and bumps in the uneven road rippled through her body. Glancing over the side of the truck, she swallowed back the burning liquid coating her throat. *Why can't they have smoother roads?*

Twenty minutes into their trip, Colby nudged her shoulder. "You look a little pale. I'd like to give you a brief check-up when we get to our next stop."

Her stomach tensed beneath her T-shirt. "No need. I'm fine." She plastered on a smile and looked up at the sky. It had rained all day yesterday, but today it felt like a sauna. "You'd think the sun wouldn't be so scorching after all the rain we've had." She'd only been in Uganda for seventy-two hours and had already used nearly half of her bottle of sunblock and her can of bug spray.

Colby slid off his medical jacket. "Here, put this on." Underneath, he wore a light blue T-shirt that said *Got Meds?*

"Don't you need it?" She slipped her arms into the sleeves and sighed. It took just a few seconds to feel the relief of having her bare skin covered by the airy fabric.

"Nah, not right now." He smiled big and pointed to his shirt. "I promised Arabella I'd send her a selfie of me wearing this. This will help me follow through."

Ava grinned, recalling his niece, a spunky teen she'd once taught in Sunday School. "Teenagers and social media, you've got to love them."

He laughed. "Right."

As she rubbed the sweat off her forehead, she studied the open terrain. The sporadic trees dotted the landscape with their bushy arms reaching up and out toward the sun. The pose emulated a dispersed crowd in silent praise. She envied them.

"The scenery is beautiful." Ava waved her arm past the road but didn't hear Colby respond. After a few seconds, she turned away from the moving topography and glanced at him. Something about the way the muscle in his jaw rippled made her heart stall. "Colby?" As she said his name, he reached out and grasped her arm. "Is something the matter?'

Her words barely passed her lips before the truck lurched to a stop. She tried to shift her body to get a better view of the road. Before she could, the truck spun its tires into reverse and almost catapulted her off her seat.

"Ava, this doesn't look good." He lowered his gaze and the fear in his eyes shot a cold bead of sweat across her forehead. The truck lunged to another stop. Ava's body slid hard into Colby's, and he released her hand and wrapped his arms tight around her. "We need to get off this truck."

The revving of several engines in the distance drew closer, and Colby looked past her to the road again. To calm her racing heart, she tried to concentrate on the tiny droplets of sweat traveling down his temple and sliding into the dark stubble of his beard.

"God, help us." Ava's whispered plea was snuffed out by the shouting between the driver and the passengers. Her ears strained to pick up on the one-sided English clashing with the native tongue as the voices rose in an anxious crescendo. "Colby, what's going on?"

Colby didn't answer. A tremor rolled down her spine while the engine beneath them throttled and roared, permeating the air with a thick fog of throat-burning fumes. Bracing her back against the splintered wood, Ava's mind fought to distinguish between her body trembling and the vibration of the truck's clunky metal shell. "Colby?"

The driver slammed through the gears, and Sharron prayed aloud. The cacophony of sounds made her heart pound as nausea swirled in her belly.

"Dear God, please help us." Sharron's petition deepened into a husky whisper.

Colby jerked his head to the right, and Ava followed his gaze. Beside them hung dense brush and low-hanging trees. Off to their left stood an open field. He glanced back in

Sharron's direction, and seemed to weigh an unseen dilemma.

"They're armed." Colby's voice lowered to a guttural hiss. "If something happens to me, tell Arabella I love her."

Before Ava comprehended Colby's words, he moved her to the back of the truck. The truck turned to the right and idled.

"Get low and stay out of sight." He leaned in closer. "When the trucks are gone, head south to the village."

"Wait! What?" Ava's chest tightened. "What about you and Sharron?"

"I'll get Sharron. If we all get off at once, we'll cause a scene." Colby nodded toward the copse of trees. "We're close enough to the trees now no one will notice us jumping off."

Ava didn't have time to argue before Colby nudged her off the tailgate. Her body propelled forward, and the truck spun out from under her jamming its engine into high gear.

"Colby!" She stumbled through a thick curtain of brush and landed on her knees with a thud. Trying to pull herself up, Ava grabbed onto the thick vines curling along the hill like gnarled, dirt-covered fingers. "Help! Colby!" Beyond her line of sight, the truck engine roared to life and sped away.

"No!" In a panic, she took a stumbling step up the slope. As she slipped into the mud, she lost her balance and clawed her fingers into the bushy leaves. "Don't leave me." Ava's plea dissolved into the humid air. Seconds later a loud blast rocked the ground, and she lost her footing. Dropping to a crouch, she crawled behind a low-hanging tree with branches bent over and hugging the ground. When a second explosion sent a tremble beneath her, Ava dug her shaky fingers deeper into the wet earth. "Dear God, help me."

Peeking around the tree, Ava squinted past the natural barrier of foliage, hoping to see the truck or any of her friends. For several seconds, she saw and heard nothing. Then, like a smudge from an artist's graphite pencil, grey smoke fanned out across the sky.

"Oh, no." As tears rolled down her cheeks, she begged God for His protection. She didn't want to die like this—in a foreign land, alone.

CHAPTER TWO

22:05 Southwest of Lake Bisina, Uganda

Special Operator Blake Martin flipped up his night vision goggles and let out an exasperated breath. "Looks like the intel's correct."

His partner, Jacob Armstrong, cursed and spat on the ground. "What did you see?"

"They have a scout about one hundred and fifty yards out."

"Are they here to cause trouble?"

"Not sure." Blake glanced out over the moonlit terrain. From this vantage point, he could see for miles. "But we need to move these people."

After days of unrelenting rain, the rivers in central Uganda had widened and pushed life-threatening levels of water into Lake Bisina. Now stranded groups of villagers who'd grabbed all the belongings they could carry were like sitting ducks.

"Roger that," Jacob answered before he took off down the hill.

A day ago, they'd received intel about a group of rebels

causing havoc among the locals. With villagers displaced from flooding and crops ruined, it was the perfect storm for the bad guys to make their move.

Blake flipped down the goggles and watched the scout, dressed to impersonate a wandering farmer, climb into a truck full of heavily armed men. After a few minutes, three of the men leaped off the back of the tailgate, threw up a few hand signals, then fanned out in different directions. Flames of irritation shot through Blake's veins. There was nothing agricultural about this group—these men were up to something.

The vehicle turned the corner and headed their way. His gut told him these were the men they were looking for. Men who had kidnapped adults near this area to test out a new deadly drug and trafficked kids to fund the project.

Jacob and he, under the banner of a humanitarian mission, were here to collect intel, not start a war. However, if this group of men wanted to cause trouble, they'd need to engage.

He had about three minutes to make a decision.

Blake pushed away from the hill and took off toward the river where Jacob organized the people and loaded them and their belongings onto the backs of battered trucks and mopeds. Blake's plan? Move the families east, over the grassy embankment, and out of sight. After that, he and Jacob would circle back, use the night to their advantage, and shadow the unwelcomed visitors to get a read on their intentions.

"Don't let these kids out of your sight." Blake handed two younger kids to Jacob. There's no way he'd let this group of innocent people lose any children on his watch. "I'll catch up with you after I secure the perimeter."

"Copy that." Jacob hollered his response over the rumbling engines.

The trucks sped off, and before Blake fell too far back, three lanky teens ran toward him shouting. From what he could decipher from their panicked pleas, a family of three was left fishing down by the inlet.

Blake's neck muscles twisted into a knot like an angry snake. Night fishing. It made sense. Now swelled from the rains, the lake carried an abundance of fish for the locals to feed their families. He lifted his eyes to the ebony sky, and several heavy droplets of water pelted his face. The torrential rains were both a blessing and a curse for those who relied on the elements to survive.

Blake ordered the teens to catch up to the trucks before he slid down the rain-soaked hill. Mud splattered across his face and arms, and he whispered a prayer of gratitude for the earth's natural camouflage. After he landed on the saturated ground, Blake closed his eyes and allowed his hearing to take over.

Rushing water.

Rain.

The flapping of a bird's wings.

But no voices.

Flipping down his night specs, Blake crept closer to the water. Scanning the embankment, he growled softly. Too late. He took a few more steps, and the sludge suctioned onto the heels of his boots. Keeping his gaze level, he checked for a pulse on the two bodies lying face down in the mud. Nothing.

A stormy wind moved across the water, and along with it, a child's whimper. He searched the tall grass and sent up a silent petition, asking for a break in the rain. Twenty feet ahead of him, a little girl, with a shaved head and a raised jagged scar over her right cheek, stood sobbing in the stream. The child's eyes opened wide when she caught sight of him. *It's okay, little one.* Blake surveyed the edge of the river before bringing his finger up to his lips to quiet the frightened child.

He took another step forward and strained to listen for any other sounds beyond the pouring rain. Between the trees, a shadow moved. Steadying his weapon, he aimed. The girl stopped crying and turned toward the shadow. He curled his finger around the trigger. *Steady.* As the pad of his finger pressed, the shadow lunged and yanked the child out of the water. Blake adjusted but could not execute a clean shot. The girl's shriek sliced through the tepid air, and an icy shiver traveled down Blake's spine. *There are more of them.*

Something shifted in the trees behind him. Pivoting, Blake peered through the verdant haze filling his goggles and searched for movement. A branch creaked. Holding his breath, he zeroed in on the direction of the sound. Inhaling slowly, Blake shifted to the right. As he exhaled, an arm shot out from behind a tree and thrust a needle into his bicep. His muscle flexed, forcing burning liquid through his veins like an out-of-control wildfire.

His vision blurred. Two forms moved out of the shadows and raised their weapons. *What did they inject me with?* Blake struggled to keep his firearm level as he battled the disorienting effect from the jab. Releasing a frustrated growl, he threw out a hand toward a gnarly tree trunk and fought to hold himself upright.

One of the men paced in front of him and fired off a litany of questions in Swahili. "What are you doing here? Are there others with you? How long has the American military been here?"

They didn't come across as hardened killers. Only amateur soldiers who'd been given vague orders.

When he didn't answer, the man leaned into his face and yelled again. Blake's heart pumped faster as he blinked past the haze and tried to unravel the distorted words. From what he could gather, this wasn't going the way they'd planned. He echoed their sentiment. Whatever they'd shot into him made his mind feel like it bobbed in black tar.

I'm running out of time. Blake's weapon slipped through his hand while searing heat drove through his body like a bullet train. His eyelids drooped. *Keep it together, Martin.* His partner would come for him, but by the time he did, it might be too late.

As he grasped for the knife fastened to his thigh, the man jammed a second injection into his neck. Clutching at the tree bark, Blake begged his body to combat the red-hot lava binding to his muscles and clouding his mind. Losing the battle, his hand scraped down the tree, and in a split second, his vision went from blurry to black.

CHAPTER THREE

Ava peered out over the dusty ledge of her prison window. She'd been in this village one week. Seven days of hard rains and little food. How much longer did her captors plan on keeping her here?

She swiped the back of her hand across her eyelids, then blinked. Nothing help. Her vision still blurred from fresh tears and chemical smoke. Lifting on her tip-toes, she rested her chin on the ledge and leaned her head on the two rusty iron bars, hoping to catch a glimpse of any activity in the village.

Each morning they burned their refuse, and the inky black swirls of noxious fumes already twirled through the sky. She angled her face, hoping to inhale a short breath of clean air. All she got for her efforts—the smell of animal waste and burning rubber. Ava held her hand up to her throat and attempted to swallow past the dry irritation coating her windpipe. Unable to find relief, she groaned. She needed water and clean air. For now, she was conserving what she had of one and praying she'd find the other.

Taking a few turns around the tiny room, Ava slid her

fingers lazily along the crumbling mud walls. Already warm to the touch, the heat in the small room wrapped around her skin like a blazing kiln. Shaky and exhausted, she lowered herself to the floor and tucked her knees under her chin.

Hours after the explosion, a group of armed men found her, soaked from new rain and hiding in the brush. She contemplated running, but the weapons slung over their shoulders suggested it wouldn't have done any good.

"Are you a doctor?" The taller, muscular man asked her after she stood, wobbly on her legs.

Ava looked down at Colby's medical jacket. Quivering nerves pooled in the pit of her stomach. "Not really." She fingered the coat nervously and scrutinized each man standing around her. Were they an answer to her prayers? Or just another layer to her nightmare?

"Were you with them?" The short man with little to no teeth nodded up the embankment.

A tingle walked down her spine as her mind conjured an image of what might be left of the truck. "Is there ..." She paused, unsure of how to ask and uncertain if she wanted the answer. "Is there anything left?"

They all shook their heads.

"No, no, there are no supplies left." The younger of the four spoke up, then added, "There is nothing left."

Ava swayed. The tall man reached out and grabbed her arm. In a knee-jerk reaction, she yanked away from him.

He held up his hands and leered at her. "We won't hurt you." He exchanged a look with the other men and smirked. "But you *will* come with us."

Ava wiped several tears from her face and glanced back at the crude, cut-out window. How much longer could she endure them believing a lie? A lie that, so far, had kept her alive. Trying to rein in her dispirited thoughts, she sent a silent plea up to heaven to renew her strength and provide a way back home.

Before Ava lingered long on her melancholy feelings, the bulky prison door opened with a reverberating bang. Two guards barreled across the threshold, dragging a limp man between them.

"You fix this." The rotund guard with sweat pasted across his forehead pushed the tip of his boot onto the body they'd thrown at her feet.

"What?" Ava's heart pounded against her ribcage.

"You fix this man."

"I can't fix this man." She swallowed back the fear that bowled over her like a gusty west Texas wind.

The injured man moaned where he lay crumpled on the ground in a heap. She crouched down next to him and ran her fingers over the fresh scratches along his temple. His U.S. military uniform was faded and caked with red clay dirt.

"You fix." The older, surly guard raised his voice and nudged her shoulder. "You healer, you fix."

Ava's face burned with anger as she shot to her feet. "I don't know how to fix this man." Surprised at her own outburst, she clamped her mouth shut. She couldn't afford to make her captors angry, but she'd grown weary of being told what to do. Ava bit her lip to temper her burgeoning frustration.

The younger guard moved close to her and reached out his hand. Ava flinched and stepped back. She might have finally pushed the right button to make these hardened men want to end her life.

"You know physician?" The guard kept his voice low while he reached his hand out to her discolored jacket.

"What?" The question confused her. She'd told them she wasn't a doctor, but they believed she'd been at least trained as an assistant. On several occasions, she'd heard them whisper and call her the American nurse.

He leaned in and motioned toward the patch with the Swiss cross on her sleeve. "You fix this man."

Ava gripped the coat and pulled it snugly around her. The moments of the explosion galloped through her mind like runaway horses. Her head swayed. Taking in a few deep breaths, Ava fought to ignore the haunting image of Colby's face before he pushed her off the bed of the truck.

"I heard you last night. You asked a great physician to heal you." The man's stuttered English snapped her out of her troubled thoughts. "You wear his shirt."

Under Colby's name, the word *Physician* was embroidered in blue. Ava's heart sank. He'd heard her praying. Under certain circumstances, uttering a prayer might be more fatal than impersonating a doctor. She glanced down at the tattered lab coat, unsure what to say.

"I ... it wasn't ..." *What do I say? God, give me wisdom.* She couldn't deny she'd prayed, but they needed to understand she wasn't a medical professional. Ava looked back at the older guard. The skin on his face was weather-beaten and deeply scarred with old wounds. When he caught her staring, his eyes darkened with rage.

"You fix. He will bring a good price. Then, maybe we let you go."

Ava swallowed hard as a cool shudder worked its way down her spine. His expression and the tone of his words contradicted his promise to let her go. She understood this week could very well be her last if this soldier—half-dead on the floor—didn't miraculously get well. *God, please help me.*

The two men stomped out the door, and the familiar clang of the rusty iron bar slammed shut. She redirected her gaze back to the man lying at her feet and released a long breath.

Crouching again, she laid her hand on his chest. The soldier's rib cage moved up and down beneath her palm—a good sign —at least he was breathing, and they would spare her life for another day. Lowering herself beside her new roommate, she leaned against the grimy wall. Exhaustion and anxiety crashed over her like a bucket of ice water. "Why, God? Why did you put me in this situation?" Ava cried out in a whisper as her mind raced with petitions and prayers. It wasn't God who'd brought her here—but herself.

Two weeks ago, she'd been sitting in the sun on the back porch of her elegant home, drinking mint iced tea, and watching the leaves pinwheel to the ground across her yard. *I needed to leave. The memories were strangling me.*

She stared at the angled cut-out overhead. The sun's rays peeked out from dark clouds and danced across her skin. Did anyone back in Texas realize she'd gone missing? Had word even reached the United States about the tragedy that killed two of her friends?

The LORD bless you and keep you; the LORD make His face to shine upon you and be gracious to you; the LORD lift up His countenance toward you and give you peace. The Bible verse traced across her mind, and she forced a tired smile. Like the bright sun warming her cheeks, she believed the promise that God, even in this filthy room, still had His hand upon her.

It was my decision to come here. With little to no prayer or guidance, she agreed to join a mission trip with a few others from her church. Despite her rash decision, God had given her a sure way out—an easy way of excusing herself from the trip. No one would have blamed her if she had changed her mind. But she'd given in to her stubborn nature and tried to run from the tumult of emotions taking over her life instead of facing them with grace.

A quiet moan escaped the man's lips, and Ava pulled

herself back to the present. She leaned in his direction and put her hand on the battered soldier's shoulder. His name tape was dirty and torn, with the word *Maxwell* written in subdued green threads.

"Well, Maxwell, I sure hope you aren't as injured as you appear."

His eyelids fluttered, then shut.

Ava took a deep breath and prayed that God would intervene, and get her—and Maxwell—out of this mess.

Because now, until God separated them, they were in this mess together.

CHAPTER FOUR

As the sun reached its zenith, the prison door shot open, and a young guard walked in. Ava remembered him. The guard who'd questioned her about her praying. She jumped to her feet, clenched her hands into fists, ready—ready for what, she didn't know.

He moved close to her. A pair of raised patterned lines etched onto his otherwise smooth, dark cheeks caught her attention. She hadn't noticed them before. Did they have familial meaning? Or had they'd been put there as a punishment?

"Did you fix?"

Pulling her gaze away from his marked skin, she glanced down at the soldier, who'd fallen into a fitful sleep. His uniform was speckled with blood, but from her limited experience with minor injuries, the fact there wasn't a pool of blood on the floor by now seemed optimistic.

Determined to remain positive, she contemplated how she should approach the situation. Should she plead for her life and try to explain she wasn't a doctor? Or simply do her best to comply and hope the soldier had not been mortally wounded? *God, give me wisdom.*

Before she released any more silent prayers, the scruffy young man spoke up. "I fear for you. You need to fix."

Ava's heart dropped. She feared for her too. But, with nothing to lose at this point—except maybe her life—she straightened her spine and said, "I need some things."

The young man waited.

"I need clean water." Ava pointed to the bottle of water given to her yesterday. She'd conserved it, not knowing when she might have another. "I need many of these."

He nodded.

"I need bandages—cloth." She motioned to the soldier's head. "To clean."

He nodded again.

"I need boiling water, very hot."

The guard glanced nervously outside the prison door before he asked, "You need food?"

Ava's stomach rumbled at the mention of it. She hadn't eaten since last night, and that was a bowl of mushy grain. Of course, she needed food, but eating was the last thing on her mind. "Yes."

"I get you food."

Pointing to the soldier, she said, "He will need something. Soup?" She made a gesture with her hand like a spoon coming out of a bowl to her mouth. "Warm broth?" She had no idea how much English the guard spoke or what he understood.

"Yes, yes, I get."

"Sir?" The young man stopped before he shut the door. "Thank you." Ava hoped the sincerity in her voice sounded over the anxious tremble.

"You speak with the great physician. You need to fix."

He slammed the door before she could protest. Of course,

she knew the Great Physician, the healer of her soul, but she doubted the guard would understand her belief in God.

"Jesus." The whispered name crossed her parched lips, and the mention of it eased her spirit. She sighed. "I don't want to do this. I just don't have the energy anymore."

A pang of guilt shot through her. She shouldn't complain, but after everything that had happened in her life, she was worn out. She'd signed up for this trip on a whim, hoping a change in scenery would give her a reprieve from the see-saw of emotions she'd been clinging to. Now, her decision to journey to Uganda might be the most hazardous decision she'd ever made.

Ava backed up to the corner of the dirt cell and lowered herself to the floor again. Unwanted tears flowed down her warm cheeks, and her voice quivered. "I was only supposed to be here for two weeks. Then, I was going to go back and pick up the pieces of my life." Like a child, she wiped her face with her sleeve and sniffled.

Glancing down at the black, masculine watch on her wrist, she frowned. She was grateful the guards hadn't taken it when they shoved her into this room a week ago, but the silver numbers taunted her as the hands continued to greedily tick off each second of her day. *I miss you, Dylan.* The watch, a lavish expense, wasn't why she protectively concealed it with her long sleeve. It was her husband's, and he'd worn it the night he'd left her.

The prison door barreled open, and Ava sprang from the floor. The young guard strolled in with a case of water and a large metal pan with steam swirling from the top. She moved toward him as he laid the items down.

He shot her a lopsided, broken-tooth smile, then ducked back outside the room. He appeared again with a basket filled with bananas and a murky liquid sloshing around in what seemed to be a leaf rolled up like a bowl. A second basket held cut-up fruit, a few small potatoes, and a large cooked chicken wrapped in several moist leaves. The fragrant spices were intoxicating and unfamiliar as she swallowed back a kick of nausea. Her appetite craved chicken fried steak and brisket. Instead, the aromas reminded her of the street tacos at the state fair.

Once again, the man stepped out and brought in a bundle of ripped pieces of cloth and a bottle of whiskey. Ava raised her eyebrow at the sight of the amber bottle. She didn't drink liquor, but if circumstances persisted, she appreciated the gesture.

He held up the bottle. "Kill bugs."

Ava's voice cracked with fear. "Bugs?" Her heartbeat raced to life as she looked around the room. She'd already seen one spider the size of her hand, and she dreaded a repeat encounter.

The guards had laughed at her expense when she screamed for them. She could only imagine how foolish she appeared, smashing the ugly creature repeatedly with her shoe. She didn't care—she drew the line at sharing her space with arachnids. *What strange bugs do they have in Africa that die when exposed to whiskey?* She couldn't believe she'd agreed to travel to this desolate country.

The man lifted his arm and showed her a large scar, thick and pinkish with new skin. "It will kill things."

Infection. Of course. She'd always used rubbing alcohol and peroxide, but she appreciated what the young guard offered. Ava glanced at the battered soldier on the ground and crinkled her brow. *I wonder if he'd prefer to just drink the bottle.* Especially after he realized a mock physician was going to attempt to nurse him back to health.

The African guard shuffled on his feet, and she looked up. Ava forced a smile, unsure of what to say. "Thank you."

He nodded, then stood there, unmoving. Finally, he put a hand to his heart and said, "Andrew."

She stared at him for a second, trying to decipher if he'd told her his name. "Your name is Andrew?"

He nodded and flashed her a goofy grin. "Kileem."

"I don't ..."

"My name Kileem, but you call me Andrew."

She still didn't understand but guessed he'd attempted a form of friendly communication in spite of the not-so-friendly weapons fastened around his waist.

Ava lifted her hand toward herself. "Ava."

His voice deepened as he pointed at her. "Ava."

She nodded and opened her mouth to ask a question. Before she could, Andrew backed up, shut the door, locked it, and took off across the dirt road.

Shrugging off the odd encounter, Ava looked down and studied her new roommate. He lay quiet and motionless on the floor. "Where do I begin?" She wasn't a doctor, but she'd been a mom, and like riding a bike, her instincts kicked in.

Falling to her knees, Ava laid her ear on the man's chest. His heartbeat sounded strong, but his breathing appeared ragged and labored. Placing her hands on his forehead, she checked for a fever, then assessed the rest of his injuries. She checked for any apparent fractures or open wounds. In response to her hands running over his body, the soldier moved his head back and forth and murmured.

"Okay, Maxwell, let's see if I can roll you over." Her effort to move the man's body proved difficult as her weak arms strained under his weight. She frowned. Even when healthy and well-fed, she had little upper arm strength. "I should've gone to the gym more often." With a huff, she slipped her hands underneath his body and tried again. "One more push."

Ava concentrated all her energy and rolled the man onto his side. As she stared at his back, perspiration worked its way from the nape of her neck and twisted down her spine. *God, what happened to this man?* The back of the soldier's uniform was shredded, and the man's tanned skin glistened with streaks of blood beneath the mangled material. Startled, Ava let go.

The soldier rolled back and groaned in agony.

She gasped at the sight of her hands. Smears of sticky blood covered the pads of her fingers. Ava scrunched her eyelids shut and tried to swallow the sour lump in her throat. *I can't do this. I can't.*

Forcing her eyes open, she studied her previously manicured hands. She'd given up the glossy acrylic nails for the trip since she'd have no way to repair them in the middle of Africa. Instead, she opted for a neat French manicure. Now, the chipping white paint glared up at her from beneath the crimson stain of the soldier's blood.

"God, help me. I can't do this." With trembling hands, she attempted to wipe the blood onto the dirty fabric of the physician's coat, leaving streaks of crimson across the material. Leaning back on her heels, another wave of tears released like a flood. "God, why me? Why are you doing this to me?" The man stirred beside her, and she laid a hand on his shoulder. "I'm sorry. I'm sorry, I just can't do this. I'm not strong enough." As the tears flowed, she continued to beg God to intervene. God's answer—silence.

After taking in a few long breaths to steady the swaying in her gut, Ava did the one thing she knew how to do: make a list and execute a plan.

"Get yourself together." Straightening her spine, she said,

"First, clean the wounds." She felt like a fool talking to the air, but she hoped the illusion of formulating a plan would calm her fractured nerves. "Second, I'll cover the wounds and pray there's no infection. Third, I'll pray Maxwell wakes up." She swiped the back of her hand across her brow and blew out a breath. "Finally, if none of that works, I'll drink the rest of the whiskey." She forced a laugh because whatever was left of her sanity now dangled by a thread.

Taking off the man's uniform jacket, she folded it and laid it next to her. The fabric smelled like earth and blood and looked like it hadn't been washed in weeks. Frowning, she tugged at his worn, caramel-colored undershirt. Unable to lift his bulky arms out of their sleeves, she opted to rip the thin tatters of fabric and discard the shirt into the corner of the room. Now with him on his stomach, she studied the stripes on his back. Ava blinked back tears. The wounds were no longer bleeding but only swollen and wet. "What happened to you, Maxwell?" The question fell off her lips in a whisper as her heart twisted like a vine. Whatever he'd been through, she was grateful he'd made it out alive.

Scanning the small room, she eyed a metal bucket near the door. Blowing out the dust, she poured in some of the steaming hot water, dipped a cloth in part way, then waved the blazing hot fabric in the air before she wrung it out. Blinking back tears, she pressed the cloth onto the soldier's ripped skin. "I'm sorry, Maxwell. I hope this isn't too painful."

He flinched under her initial touch, his back muscles tensing and then releasing slowly. In a whisper, she prayed he wouldn't be too uncomfortable while she undertook the heartbreaking job of cleaning his wounds. Dipping the rag into the water, she repeated the process and begged God for the strength to continue. She'd only ever washed skinned knees and runny noses, not the beaten backs of grown men.

After several minutes, the soldier's breathing slowed under her hands, and Ava started to hum. Her lashes lowered, and her humming turned into the whispered words of *Amazing Grace*. She continued the refrain, along with her care of his wounds, being careful to keep her voice low and soothing. When her world was falling apart, it was the one song that gave her peace, and she hoped it would do the same for him.

Cleaning the soldier's cuts and abrasions took almost an hour. After she finished, Ava sorted through the pile of rags and picked up the cleanest cloth she could find. Laying the fabric across the man's back, she sang the final stanza of the song.

As the hours ticked by, she continued her ministrations over the rest of the soldier's body. Starting at his feet, she peeled off his wet, threadbare socks and draped them onto the iron bars of the window to dry. His arms were covered in bruises and dirt, but otherwise, the skin appeared unharmed. While she carefully wiped the grime off of his fingers, he curled his hands closed, then opened them—as if doing his own assessment of his injury. Cradling one of his hands in hers, she paused and studied his fingers. They were long and calloused, and the sinewy muscles and veins running on top of his hand looked strong and capable. After she held his hand in hers a few more seconds, she released it and stood to stretch her taut muscles.

Forcing herself to eat some of the food Andrew had provided, Ava watched as the sunrays moved their soft fingers along the gloomy, terra-cotta wall. The day was almost over. When would the cruel guards return? "Please, God, give Maxwell time to heal."

Andrew came for her nightly respite to relieve herself, then quickly ushered her back to the tiny mud structure at the back of the village. This time, he didn't smile but kept his face hardened and stoic. "How is he?" He murmured through clenched teeth.

Ava glanced over her shoulder, then answered, "I really don't know."

He looked past her at the soldier, and a flash of pain walked across his expression. "You don't have much time." Andrew directed his focus back to her. "They are gone a few days. But they will return."

She nodded as he turned and shuffled out the door. Exhausted, she slid down next to Maxwell and laid her head against the dusty wall. "What are we going to do?" She stared out the window, and the heavens, now heavy with clouds, transformed from a tangerine orange to a hazy purple. The animated colors warmed her, and she longed to return to her work with luxurious paints and fabrics. "Will I ever get to design again, God?" The question pierced an arrow through her chest. The one constant in her life had been the creativity she'd enjoyed through her interior design business. Ava glanced around at her dismal surroundings, and a sob escaped from her throat. "I want to go home."

She caught a glimpse of the soldier's boots, and guilt twisted in her belly. While she whined and complained about missing her livelihood, this man, who'd committed his life to serving his country, lay fighting for his life on a dirt floor. She blinked back a handful of tears and sniffled. The pale green fabric of his shoes was tatty and frayed, with red dirt clinging to the laces. *I can only imagine the story those boots could tell.*

Feeling as shabby as the worn-out boots, Ava laid her weary body down on her thin pallet and pleaded with God for a break. Next to her, the soldier stirred. When his eyes shot open, a vibrant hue of jade peeked through his dark lashes. Ava's heart jolted. *His eyes look like a set of precious jewels.* She blinked, shaking the startling thought away.

Alert but laden with fatigue, he tried to roll onto his back. Flinching, he released a gut-wrenching groan.

"I don't think you should move too much. Not until your back heals." She sat up and helped him move back into a more comfortable position on his side. Then, satisfied he was semi-comfortable, she laid back down and faced him until her eyes drifted closed.

He murmured something that sounded like a prayer as he took in deep, deliberate breaths. After a few minutes, the soldier's breathing evened out.

As her eyelids lowered, his hand slid over and grasped her fingers. His skin was rough and warm. Ava's lashes fluttered open. His intense gaze was again laser-focused in her direction.

"Thank you." The words fell off the soldier's parched lips, deep and ragged, while the fierce expression on his face conveyed his struggle to lie still.

Catching her breath, she nodded. "You're welcome."

He didn't let go, but instead, he gripped tighter. Ava could almost feel his pain transfer to her through their connection. Finally, their breathing joined a gentle cadence, and he closed his eyes.

Continuing to hold his hand, she prayed healing and peaceful sleep would come for them both.

CHAPTER FIVE

Blake's eyes sprung open from the dark dream of his capture. Blinking, he tried to acclimate to the pitch-black surrounding him as if he'd walked into the belly of a cave. *Where am I?* He slid his hand down his thigh to search for his knife—nothing. Gritting his teeth, he rolled deftly over onto his stomach. Then, as he squeezed his eyes shut to fend off the pain searing across his back, he tried to piece together what had happened to him. Like a movie with a skip, the distressed picture of the tiny African child swaying in a river flashed across his mind. *What happened to the little girl?* His gut coiled with irritation. *I couldn't save her.*

After the river, he'd woken in a room that reeked of decay and charred wood. The only furniture—a rusty metal chair his captors had strapped him to and a decades-old card table.

He opened his eyes and surveyed the room he was in now. The pungent smells of soil, blood, and sweat floated up to his nose. *I'm in another prison.* The clay earth rubbed against his stomach as his mind raced to connect the frayed edges of his thoughts. *Two men found me, threw me in the back of their truck, and carried me into a mud room.*

The full moon cast an eerie glow over the space, highlighting his boots and uniform shirt stacked next to the wall. Dirt clung to his feet, and burning pain clawed at the skin on his back like a red-hot flame. *What happened to my back?* As the question shot across his mind, the recollection of the brutal flogging they'd inflicted on him exploded through his memory.

Clenching his jaw, Blake forced himself to listen to the sounds around him. As he sensed the gentle breathing of another person, his body stilled. Then, positioning his arms in a bent push-up position, he readied his muscles to ignore the pain and leap upright in one stealthy move.

Before executing the maneuver, he considered the outline of the body next to him. *The woman who cleaned my wounds.* A lump formed in his throat, and he swallowed hard. The distress in her voice when she'd talked her way through dressing his injuries jumped to the forefront of his mind. *An American. How long has she been a prisoner here?* He recalled her sharp words when she spoke with her captors, and his lips curved into a slow grin. However long she'd been here, he was glad she'd not lost her will to survive.

Relaxing his arms, Blake lowered himself from the plank position, grateful he hadn't leaped to his feet and terrified the woman. He took several steady breaths to stabilize his thoughts. As he relaxed, his mind bounced back to the prison he'd been in before coming here.

His previous captors had injected him with a drug that did little to hold his mind together. Despite being blindfolded and beaten, he quickly deducted they weren't interested in killing him. Instead, their methods measured the limits of his pain and cognitive abilities. They asked questions about colors, seasons, and the capitals of countries—a crude and torturous version of a standardized test while under the influence of an unnamed narcotic.

They'd kept him in a dark, damp room with no windows, and he'd fought hard to keep his sanity. When he was lucid, he prayed Jacob escaped with as many children as possible. And the times when he thought he'd lost his mind, he begged God to end his suffering. Then, finally, his last memory, when they'd injected him with something that slowed his heart to a near crawl, he'd prayed his death would not be in vain and trusted his team could finish the mission without him.

The gentle stirring of the woman beside him pulled Blake from his dark reflections. *She must be exhausted from playing nursemaid to my wounds.* As he studied her silhouette, his heart tightened. He deeply regretted what the guards had forced her to do, but was grateful she'd kept him alive.

Relaxing, he returned to his side. He needed to rest and build up his strength for the coming days. As he drifted back to sleep, he sent up a simple appeal asking God to keep the woman protected and show him a way of escape.

Since providence had brought them together, he was now duty-bound to get her to safety.

Or die trying.

CHAPTER SIX

"So, how did you end up here?"

Ava looked up. The soldier had finished off a few bites of the meager meal the guard had thrown at him. After three days of broth and sleep, he had color in his face and was eating solid foods—all good signs of his recovery.

"Do you mean in this prison?"

"No, I mean in Uganda." He jumped from the floor with more get-up-and-go than she'd seen in him all week. "You're an American." He leveled his gaze in her direction. "You don't seem the type to have moved to Africa because you enjoy living in the wild."

"Really?" A challenge rose inside of her. "How do you deduce that?" She waved her hand around their dust-filled room. "This might be exactly my cup of tea."

"Well, first of all, since you said 'cup of tea,' I doubt it." His eyes flickered with a hint of mischief. "And, your nail tips have a remnant of white paint on them. They're manicured." Pausing he quirked an eyebrow. "You got those done recently."

He acts like I'm a pampered princess. "Any other observations?"

His lips twitched into a grin. "Your hands are soft."

When he looked down at her hands, she folded them into a ball in her lap. The room seemed smaller, and her cheeks blazed with heat—which was ridiculous because she was thirty-two years old, and she hadn't blushed in years.

He lifted up his hands and held them in her direction. They were covered in dirt and scratches. "I can tell you haven't been in this country long."

Ava glanced down at her lap and unfurled her fingers. Her gut twisted as she recalled his scarlet blood on her fingertips.

"Your accent, I'd say, is something Southern."

She lifted her chin to look at him.

"But no country bumpkin. You sound educated. Sophisticated."

Ava shifted on the floor, unsure about a stranger trying to size her up and make assumptions about her character. "There are a lot of educated people in Uganda." She pointed to her shirt. "Doctors, and even scientists."

"Yes, but *that* is not your shirt."

She froze as he continued his assessment.

"It's entirely too large for you, and it's a man's cut."

Leaning her head back, Ava blew out an exasperated breath. Since waking that morning, the soldier paced the room like a restless panther. She was grateful for his recovery, but she needed a reprieve from his interrogation.

"Your watch is a man's watch too—expensive, but not outlandish." He halted and crouched in front of her. "I'm a little surprised it's still on your wrist."

Ava pulled down her sleeve, shielding the watch from his line of sight.

He nodded to her left hand. "I see a tan line where your wedding ring would've been, and—"

"What is your point exactly?"

His face hovered a few inches from hers and even with a thick beard, his jaw appeared strong and angular. Did he always wear facial hair? Or was it only a byproduct of their circumstances? She shook her head at her distracted thoughts. *Why am I thinking about his beard?*

Faking a smile she said, "I'm not trying to be rude, but I really could use some quiet today." Folding her arms in front of her she held his stare. She deserved a nice long day of peace since the soldier she was ordered to care for no longer teetered on death's door.

Blake rubbed the back of his neck. "Understood." Standing, he winced as he straightened his back. His stripes were healing, but not as quickly as he hoped, she was sure. "I'm sorry, I'm just trying to get to know you." After stretching his neck muscles, he took a seat beside her along the wall. "It's my job to assess a situation. To do that, I need to know what I'm working with."

Ava frowned, annoyed he didn't get the hint she needed some space to breathe. His newfound energy might be an answer to prayer, but it exhausted her.

Feeling his gaze on her, she turned to meet it. In the shadows, the color of his irises morphed into a deep emerald green, reminding her of a cool Pacific Northwest forest. Blinking, she remembered what he'd just said. *I need to know what I'm working with.* Like she was an extra appendage or something. "Work with?"

"Yes." He cut a look at the door, then back at her. "You don't think I'm just going to sit here while those guards decide what to do with us, do you?"

Ava hadn't thought about it too long—leaving. If she let

her mind linger on the possibility of freedom, she'd sink further into melancholy. She'd been in this room for almost two weeks and prayed desperately every day that God would provide a way for her to escape. Whatever the outcome, she'd found peace with the possibility this might be where she took her last breath.

"I'm getting out of here, and I'm not leaving you behind." His lips slid into a self-assured smile. "I don't plan on dying in this hovel, and neither should you." Sparks of battle flashed in his eyes and a shiver worked its way down her spine. Despite the intensity, the soldier's stare made her feel more secure than she had in weeks.

Reluctantly she dragged her gaze from his as small tears gathered in her lashes. Then, trying to tamper the nausea in her gut, she leaned forward and grabbed a small piece of fruit from the basket on the ground.

"Ava, look at me." His voice was soft but demanding as he gently placed his hand on her chin and turned her face back in his direction. "I promise I will do everything in my power to get us both out of here—alive."

Refusing to respond, she shook out of his grip and took a bite of the banana. She wanted to believe him. He'd been trained for battle. But unfortunately, she had not.

The silence lingered for a few more seconds before he shifted beside her and nudged her playfully with his elbow. "I thought since we were roommates, I should tell you my name isn't Maxwell."

Ava cut her eyes back at him glad he'd changed the subject. "I know it isn't your first name." She pointed to the name tape on the jacket lying on the floor. "Isn't that your last name?"

"No." He picked up the tattered jacket and dusted it off. "Sometimes, my team and I wear uniforms with different names, depending on the mission."

"Oh."

"It's Martin."

"Your first name?"

"No, my last."

She didn't respond.

"Blake Martin. I'm from Atlanta." His expression turned serious. "I thought you should know, just in case *I* don't make it out of here alive."

Ava's stomach tensed. How could he go from 'I promise to get you out of here' to 'just in case I die' so quickly? "I like Maxwell better."

"What?"

"For your name. I like Maxwell better."

He laughed. "Well, okay, call me Maxwell." Turning, he looked at the small window above them.

She smiled, then followed his gaze to the crude cut-out porthole. "I said a lot of prayers for you, Maxwell."

"I know you did. I appreciate that."

She glanced in his direction, startled by his admission.

"I wasn't in a coma, Ava. Just badly hurt."

Her body tensed as she inhaled a quick breath. It was more comforting to think he'd been entirely out of it while she practiced unlicensed medical care on his injured body.

"I heard every tear and every prayer. The sound of your voice carried me through the past couple of days." A tenderness ribboned through Blake's voice, despite his strong, powerful presence.

She looked away and wiped away her tears with the back of her dirtied sleeve.

"So, do you want to tell me how long you've been here?"

"About two weeks." She looked down at the bulky watch on her wrist, thankful the calendar still worked. "I'd been here about a week before they brought you in."

"Are you well enough to travel on foot?"

She shifted, uncomfortable with his inquiry. Did he refer to her bouts of what appeared to be lingering food poisoning?

Blake didn't give her a chance to answer before he threw out another question. "Have the guards hurt you in any way?" With his second question, the muscles in his forearms contracted.

"No, they haven't hurt me." She understood what he asked. With her long sleeves and floor-length skirt, he couldn't know if she'd suffered any of the same mistreatment he had.

Blake stood and paced in front of her again. Realistically she could travel, but she was weak and wouldn't be an asset to whatever he planned. "I know what you are thinking."

"Oh, really. What?" He pivoted to face her.

"You're mulling over some plan on how to get *us* out of here."

"Of course, I am. I just told you I'm getting *us* out of here." His answer came off short and smug as he lowered himself beside her again.

"You need to get to safety, but you shouldn't take me with you."

"What?" Irritation dripped off his voice.

Since he was alert, she decided it was time for her to tell him what she knew. "The guards told me when they brought you in, they wanted to sell you."

"Is that so?" His mouth turned into a cocky smirk. "We'll see about that."

Ava took a deep breath to quell her frustration. She appreciated his can-do attitude, most likely a byproduct of his military training. Still, she couldn't believe how hubristic he acted after his encounter with torturous criminals.

"Is this funny to you?" She bounced to her feet. "Do you think it's funny they brought you in here one night and ordered me to tend to your wounds so they could sell you like a commodity?" Her heart pounded as she continued, "I could've been killed if you didn't make it through the first night." She wrung her fingers together and then lifted them in the air. "I have no idea what I am doing, but they want me to treat every person in the village."

BLAKE VAULTED to his feet and grasped her hands. They were trembling. "Shh. They could be listening to us."

A spark of fury ignited her violet-blue eyes.

"You're right. I'm sorry."

"No, I don't think you are," she murmured through clenched teeth. Ava jerked her hands away from his and turned to face the wall.

"Is that where they take you in the evenings?" He moved forward, reached a hand out to touch her shoulder, then resisted. "To treat sick people in the village?"

She nodded and sniffled.

He wanted to kick himself. He'd not taken time to contemplate what she'd gone through emotionally while being held against her will.

Her voice quivered. "My experience encompasses skinned knees and pink eye. But unfortunately, I don't know how to handle misaligned limbs and open sores."

His neck muscles coiled like a taut rope as he visualized what she'd encountered when the guards ushered her out each day. She was stronger than he'd anticipated—he was sure of that.

"Maybe if I tell them I'm a doctor, we could work together?" Blake edged closer to her and kept his voice low. "I've taken basic first aid and can field-dress wounds. I'm sure I could be of some help." Not only did he want to help, he wanted to protect her. The thought of her leaving on her own again did not sit well with him.

"That's not an option."

"Why?"

Kicking at the dirt, she glanced up. His heart nearly stood still. As tears pooled in her eyes, the color swirled into a liquid sapphire, reminding him of a dancing blue flame. He took in a quick breath. Forget the consequences. If he were a moth, he'd gladly allow her to pull him in. *Snap out of it, soldier.* Chiding himself, he quickly brushed off the unexpected jolt of attraction.

Her expression turned downcast. "I've tried to spread word that you have an infection, and you need more time to heal. I'm hoping to buy you a few more days."

Blake ran his fingers through his hair, contemplating his next move. His military training hadn't equipped him for this. Tactical operations and interrogation, he'd prepared for—not a beautiful stranger trying to keep him alive. He looked down at her feet and chuckled. His partners usually wore combat boots, not pink running shoes.

"Thanks." It was the only response he could push out.

When he glanced up, Ava was grinning. "Of course. Besides, I think the next thing I'll be asked to help with is a birth. I'm sure you don't want to assist with that."

He raised an eyebrow and stepped back a few inches. Her proximity suddenly felt uncomfortable. "You don't think I can handle it?"

"I'm sure you could, but I don't imagine you'd want to."

He shrugged, enjoying how she lightened the mood. "You're probably right."

The remainder of the day, they talked sporadically. She was weak and malnourished, so he was grateful when she napped during the heat of the day. He needed to get his head together and figure out a strategy to get them out of their prison—alive. Having a civilian with him would be tricky, but he'd find a way. He would not leave her behind.

A guard with a jagged scar across his top lip brought in their evening meal—a liquid broth and two pieces of fruit. If he didn't get some protein in his body, his muscles would begin to waste away. He needed meat or anything to give him the energy to finish his mission and get them to safety.

Blake glanced over at Ava. She slept soundly on the scrap of cloth they'd given her for a bed. The hours flew by quickly. His thoughts of escape went into overdrive. He positioned himself on his side with a clear view of her and the door. As he dozed off, the grinding of the iron bolt echoed in the room. Now wide awake, Blake stayed deathly still. The door sprang open, and two guards stood in the doorway. As they swept their flashlights around the room, elongated shadows danced against the walls.

"You're needed, healer. Time for you to come with us."

Blake scarcely resisted the urge to pummel the rotund guard as he swaggered into the room and pushed the end of his rifle into Ava's back. Instead, he coiled his hands into fists while the second guard, a skinny man who reeked of smoke and body odor, yanked Ava up to a standing position by her forearm.

"What is going on?" She blinked and then glared at the guards.

"You're needed." A cold look stole over the skinny guard's expression as he added, "My boss needs you."

Blake started to sit up. Ava shot him a stern, you're-supposed-to-be-injured look. He backed down to her demanding stare, but a fire sparked in him like a raging bull.

Blake gritted his teeth. Doing nothing while they jerked Ava around and shoved her out a door wasn't natural to him.

"Just do your job, and you won't get hurt." The portly guard slammed the door closed, and Blake slammed a fist on the ground and growled in frustration. The conflict inside of him intensified as he heard her yelp outside the door from their harsh treatment.

Lying there for a few agonizing hours, his body refused to relax. Ava's trips to the village might be the proverbial open door needed for their escape. But how long could he handle her being dragged away each night?

Maneuvering himself into a plank position, he cranked out a few dozen push-ups to release the tension twisting his insides into knots. While he fought his internal war, he compartmentalized every detail of the guards' faces for a later date.

He'd be back.

And they'd be the first two he'd visit when he returned.

CHAPTER SEVEN

The sun peaked over the horizon, splashing an array of pink and yellow watercolors across the morning sky. Andrew unbolted the door and flashed her a weary look. "Soldier is awake."

Ava glanced over at Blake. He appeared as if he'd stayed up the entire night. She looked back at the young man, his dark skin glistening with sweat. He nodded at the two water bottles lying on the floor with a basket of what appeared to be their morning meal. "I brought you more fruit."

She cringed. If she ate any more fruit, she'd scream—or throw up. Or both. She nodded and forced a smile. "Thank you."

Andrew's lips bent into a crooked grin as he backed out the door and secured the rusty lock.

Before she took another breath, Blake stood to his feet. "What happened? Are you okay?"

"Twins."

"Are they alive?"

She nodded but didn't have the strength to add to her

response. Instead, she closed her eyes and leaned against the dirty wall. After releasing a long, exasperated breath, she lowered herself to the ground and kneaded the tension from the sore muscles in her neck.

Blake knelt and laid his hand on her shoulder. "Try to get some sleep."

Exhaustion and sickness covered her body like a damp blanket. When her stomach clenched beneath her dirty shirt, she swallowed hard to chase back the spasm.

He lifted the back of his hand to her face and frowned. No longer able to hold back the sickness, she turned and reached for the bucket. She heaved, then finally, the minuscule bit of food she'd eaten the night before reared its ugly head. Tears rolled down her face as Blake stood, grabbed a scrap of his old shirt, and held it out to her. Embarrassment filled her cheeks with more heat. She took the cloth and swiped it across her lips. "I'm sorry, I just ..." Another spasm rocked her stomach, and she cringed. *Not again. Please, not again.*

"Shh. No need to be sorry." Blake knelt beside her again and held back her hair while she released the final contents of her stomach into the bucket.

She wanted to resist his kind, intimate gesture but was too tired and sick to move away. After a few seconds, relief washed over her, and her stomach slowed its churning.

Taking the bucket from her, Blake dumped the mess through the small hole in the wall for them to siphon out old food and dead bugs. The opening led to the outside, with a constant stream of water cleaning out the debris.

"We've got to get you out of here. Food poisoning is a nasty thing to deal with in this dump." Worry covered his expression as he took the soiled cloth from her and handed her another scrap of his shirt. "If you don't get more sustenance in your body, I'm afraid dehydration might be the least of your worries."

Ava cringed. At one time, she'd been so guarded and private, but there was no way to disguise what she was going through in these cramped quarters. "I don't think it's food poisoning." She groaned, then leaned back against the wall. Strands of her greasy hair clung to the muddy bricks. "I would love a warm bath. My skin feels disgusting."

Blake sat beside her, careful not to let his exposed back touch the wall. "The strange food in this country could do a number on anyone's system." Concern echoed in his voice as he handed her a bottle of water. "It happens to all of us at one time or another."

She took a drink and then wrinkled her brow. "The food is definitely different than what I'm used to." She forced a smile, imagining what it would be like to sit down at a clean table and eat a Caesar salad.

"I bet." Blake scowled. "At least we have bottled water for now. It won't be good if we have to resort to the local stuff."

Ava recoiled at the thought. He was right. "What's your plan?" She fought to hold her voice steady as she tilted her head to look at him. She wasn't cut out for this, and after the trial with the pregnant African woman, she'd risk anything to escape.

CHAPTER EIGHT

Blake ran a hand across his beard. His thoughts echoed her desire for a hot shower. "My plan? Well, I've got a few ideas. Do you have any hidden Houdini skills I should know about before I make the final preparations?"

"No, I'm afraid not."

"What do you do for a living?" Waiting for her answer, he took the liberty to analyze the bright, molten pools of cerulean in her eyes.

"For a living?"

He stifled a laugh. Was her heart beating as fast as his? Clearing his throat, he continued. "You'd be surprised at how much a person's profession can help in a situation like this." Holding her gaze, he watched as the morning sun sliced through the window and caused the colors to ebb and flow like the ocean at twilight. *What are you doing? Get your mind back on the mission.* Reluctantly he looked away and waved his hand around their gloomy surroundings. "What talents can you add to the mission, soldier?"

Ava leaned back against the wall and took another drink of

the bottled water. "Are you sure you want to know?" She smiled with a splash of playfulness.

He liked her spunk. He'd only known her a few days, but from what he'd deduced, she was fire and ice all wrapped into one. Smiling to himself, he recalled how she'd stared down the ugly guard with a Gurkha Kukri knife hanging on his belt like he'd been a disruptive teenager. Fearless. Another great attribute. Ava was intelligent and feisty and somehow maintained her sanity in the face of sickness and captivity. She would've been a good soldier—unless, as he'd recently observed, bugs were involved. The thought made him chuckle. "Well, I know you don't work with insects."

Ava rolled her eyes at his attempted joke. "I'm an interior designer."

Well, that wasn't what I expected.

"I own my own company in Dallas."

He pondered her answer. Unless someone in the village hired her to hang curtains, those skills wouldn't be needed. "Are you successful?"

"What?"

"Your business. Is it successful?"

"Yes, I guess it is." She shot him a confused look. "I doubt that will help us in any way."

He shrugged. "Maybe not, but it's good to know you're a good businesswoman should the need ever arise."

Pausing for a moment, she said, "I don't mean to brag, but last year I had a two-page article in a Southern decorator's magazine."

"Really?" He appreciated how she lightened a desperate situation with such a simple statement.

"Yes." Ava grinned like a kid at Christmas. "I did some makeovers in a few historic homes. My work earned me a feature on a local morning television show as well." She giggled. "Okay, admittedly, the morning host is one of my dear friends from college, but I welcomed the exposure for my business."

Warmth filled his chest. Her personality—a blend of humble peace and self-confidence—continued to break through the battle-hardened barriers of his heart. "Any hobbies?"

She hesitated a moment. "Do you mean, do I have mad kickboxing skills that'd be helpful in our situation?"

"Maybe." He arched an eyebrow waiting for her response.

"Nope, sorry. I avoid all exercise unless forced."

Laughter escaped his lips, then he sobered. "You look in shape to me."

As pink flooded her cheeks, he cringed. Ava folded her arms in front of her and pulled her knees up under her chin. *Well done, idiot. Well done.* He wasn't practiced in giving women compliments, and according to her body language, he'd just crashed and burned. Orders he could hand out. Compliments, not so much.

"Do you play sports?" He threw out the question in a rush. He wanted to stomp out his last statement about her physical appearance and move on.

"I love tennis." Her answer was hurried. "But, I haven't played in a while."

Blake sensed a sadness in her reply but didn't press. "So you can swing a racket?"

"Yes, I suppose I can."

"There are a lot of crude farming tools just beyond that door."

She shot him a questioning look.

"Just remember, you can use anything as a weapon."

"I guess you're right."

Pausing a second, he asked, "Can you shoot?"

"What?"

"Shoot. A gun."

She turned and batted her eyelashes. "Now, darlin', didn't I tell ya I'm from Texas?" Over-emphasizing a deeper Southern drawl, she sounded more like Dolly Parton than herself.

"So that's a *yes*?"

"Of course. A pistol, a shotgun—you name it, if it has a trigger, I *can* probably shoot it." She leaned forward and widened her grin. "I don't usually miss where I'm aim'n' neither."

Their laughter intertwined like old friends and filled the room. For the first time in years, the burden of feeling like an island, fated to walk through life alone, dissolved, and Blake's spirit lightened.

Could this woman, someone he'd been thrown together with, in Uganda, by no plan of his own, have the key to break through the guarded walls of his heart?

He shook his head.

Only God would have that kind of sense of humor.

CHAPTER NINE

Blake's deep baritone laughter fell over her like cool rain on parched soil. For a moment, her grief wasn't at the forefront of her mind. She smiled. How she missed casual, relaxed conversation between friends. How she missed connection.

"So you're a decent shot?" Blake's question pulled her out of her reflection.

"I am." It was true what she'd said. She'd been taught at a young age how to use a firearm. Her dad took her out to the range on her twelfth birthday and gave her a shiny new pink pistol with her initials monogrammed on one side. The gun, her dad's idea—the monogramming, her mom's. Ava laughed aloud at the memory.

"So, what about you?" She waved a hand in his direction, not wanting the conversation to stall. "Do *you* have any skills that might help us get out of here?"

Blake's smile widened, and Ava's heart fluttered to life.

"Let me think."

He has a beautiful smile. Ava jerked her chin down and

stared at her sneakers. *Where did that come from?* She traced the outline of the shoe's stitching with her finger, hoping to distract herself from his charming smile. *It must be the lack of clean air.* After a few seconds, she glanced up. He arched an eyebrow, and smoldering heat flooded her cheeks. "I mean," she tried to backpedal her question, "besides the obvious." His body indicated brawn and agility, and by the looks of him, his whole life revolved around intense physical activity.

Blake chuckled. The gleam in his eyes suggested he enjoyed watching her stammer. "The obvious?"

"Yes, you know," She kept her gaze level with his, compelling herself not to stare at his sculpted arms. "You obviously have the skills you learned in the military." Her mouth went dry. *Really, Ava? 'The skills you learned in the military?'* She bit back a groan. It seemed even with the passage of time from a teen to a thirty-something woman, she still acted awkward and tongue-tied around members of the opposite sex.

He folded his arms and shrugged. "I could have a desk job. How would you know?"

"I guess that's true. How could you know I didn't have mad kickboxing skills?"

"Exactly."

"You don't really have a desk job, do you?"

A wicked grin stretched across his face. "No, I don't."

As a quiver wrapped itself around her middle, she inhaled a short breath. "I didn't think so." Glancing away from his face and his arms, she toyed with her dirt-covered shoestrings. "These were the first new running shoes I'd bought in years."

"You mentioned you avoided exercise."

Ava wrinkled her nose at his quippy answer. "I don't like running at all." A string of memories from her clumsy high school years flashed across her mind, and she frowned.

Strength and agility were not her strong suits. She preferred the liquid boundaries of art and design. A well-decorated room didn't mind if you were a hot mess as long as the colors and fabrics didn't clash. She glanced back up and caught him looking at her.

"Nobody really likes to run." His brows lifted. "But sometimes you have to."

She smiled. *Sometimes you do. Sometimes you need to run from your memories.* "I had a rough couple of weeks when I bought these." Waving a hand toward her shoes, she said, "But, somehow, they just seemed like the right ones to buy." Staring at her feet again, a trickle of sadness occupied her mind. "I told myself these shoes would have a history to tell when I got back from hiking through the tranquil forests of Uganda."

She paused, but Blake remained silent.

"After I'd been in this room for about a week, I decided to burn them the minute I got home." Her voice caught in her throat. "Thinking like that gives me hope I *will* get home someday."

She looked up. Ava swallowed back the torrent of emotions carving through her like a sharpened blade. His expression conveyed hope, but she was terrified to trust in him—or anyone, for that matter. Turning away, she surveyed the sparse room. They had a basket full of bananas, a bucket, a couple of water bottles, and a spoon. The odds were stacked against them.

Blake followed her gaze. "I know what you are thinking."

"You do?"

"Yep. You're thinking there aren't any weapons in here, and the situation seems a little hopeless."

"Actually, I wondered how you were going to take down our guards with a banana."

Laughter fell off his lips as he said, "It's good to see this prison hasn't taken away your sense of humor."

I'm faking it. I don't see anything funny about being here. Her chest tightened, and she kept her thoughts to herself.

"We've only known each other for a short time, but I can tell you're a very strong-willed woman."

"Really?" Strong-willed wasn't the way she'd describe herself. Angry. Sad. Lonely. Afraid. Clumsy. Guarded. These were all much better descriptions.

"I've seen grown men trained for this stuff not do as well as you in these situations."

There were a few seconds of silence between them as she considered his statement. "It's my faith. Without God, I don't know how I could wake up each day."

He nodded. "I can understand that."

She was taken aback. No snide remark? No doubt in the divine? She thought maybe God dumped this man in her cell for her to tell him about what she believed in.

"What does *that* look mean?" Blake tilted his head.

Ava blinked, not realizing she'd given him a look.

"Are you shocked I agreed with you?"

"No, not really." *That's a lie, Ava, and you know it.* She hesitated before speaking again. "Well, yes. I thought since God left me in this hideous place, he wanted me to share my faith with someone before I died."

CHAPTER TEN

The calm in Ava's voice as she stoically mentioned her death jarred him.

"Do you really believe you're going to die here?" Blake blew out an exaggerated breath. "I already told you I'm going to get us out of here. Do you doubt me?" For some reason, it bothered him that she didn't believe in his ability to free them.

"I don't doubt you're going to try."

"For being a believer, you have a bit of a fatalistic attitude, don't you?" He stood and stretched his sore muscles. He didn't want to pick a fight, but her outlook frustrated him.

"Excuse me?"

"What happened to 'all things work together for good'?"

Ava drilled him with a hard stare. "I have a tendency to lean toward 'the LORD gave, and the LORD has taken away' these past few months."

Blake stalled. What had happened in this woman's life to make her feel this way? Now, with their shared faith, he wanted, even more, to encourage her to trust that, somehow, God would procure their escape.

She frowned. "I'm sorry. That was a negative thing for me to say. I know it won't be long until they"—she nodded toward the door—"know you're healthy enough to get rid of." Her voice caught. "It won't be long until somebody decides I've outlived my usefulness as well."

He walked over and crouched in front of her. "Ava, look at me." When she lifted her eyes, he wanted to dive into the pools of vibrant color and shake off the shackles of their situation. "We're going to get out of here. I just have to figure out how."

Her breath hitched. "You're running out of time." She nibbled on her bottom lip and blinked away a stray tear. "I heard them talking last night. They know you're getting better."

Internally, he fought to reign in his emotions. Her concern for him melted the barriers around his heart, but he didn't have the luxury to entertain those feelings—feelings, if she was indeed married, he wasn't at liberty to have.

"What are you going to do? Our captors want to sell you like you're a piece of property." She sniffled, and he wrestled with the urge to reach out to her. "Who does that? Who are these people holding us captive?"

Blake lowered himself to his knees in front of her. He understood the thought of him leaving scared her. She'd already shared her fears of being alone. He had to remember she wasn't a battle-hardened soldier. Instead, she was a woman with a tender spirit, unable to comprehend the type of people who held them captive—the type of people he dealt with every day.

"I don't know what their end game is." Pushing out a frustrated breath, he ran his hand over his shaggy beard. "But I'm not going to let them take me." He cracked a smile in an effort to lift her weary expression. "At least I won't go without a fight." He'd only seen a handful of guards around the village.

The place hadn't been set up to keep people in. If he'd been alone, he would have escaped days ago.

She lowered her chin. "Sometimes, we can't keep bad things from happening."

Her words burrowed deep. He knew *that* was a true statement, especially in his line of work. "You're right, but sometimes we have to trust that bad things *won't* happen."

When she glanced back up, the shadow over her eyes deepened their shade of blue. "I don't know if I have the strength to believe that anymore."

"What if you let me be your strength?" *God, help me be her strength.*

Ava blinked. A faint glimmer of relief passed over her expression, then, just as quickly, it vanished.

She didn't answer, but for now, the flicker of hope was enough to ease his mind.

CHAPTER ELEVEN

Andrew ambled into the room and nodded in her direction. "Ava, how are you?"

She forced a smile. "Good, a little tired."

"Of course, it is nighttime."

She wished she could somehow explain the numbness clinging onto her body wasn't just her need for a good night's rest.

As she lowered herself onto a wooden crate, she motioned for him to sit beside her. *Please let this be the right decision.* She'd wrestled for two days over her plan and prayed she wasn't making a fatal mistake. "Andrew, can I ask you something?"

He nodded, and his lips formed a cock-eyed grin.

She glanced back at the door. The guards had escorted Blake outside a few minutes ago, so she needed to get straight to the point.

"You said your name is Kileem, but you told me to call you Andrew. Why?"

"He's an apostle."

Lord, please give me wisdom. "Are you a believer, Andrew?"

He blinked but didn't answer. Had she crossed a line? She smoothed her sweaty palms across her skirt.

Andrew's countenance shifted, and he lifted his face to the ceiling. As he opened his mouth to speak, the prison door flew open and Blake fell through the doorway.

"Get your hands off me. I know where I need to go." Blake growled out the words and shot her a heated glare.

Ava opened her eyes wide and skittered off of the crate. The sinewy guard with pockmarks on his face shoved Blake a second time with the barrel of his weapon and spat on the ground. Her heart hammered as the four males in the room stared at each other like lions brandishing their claim over a fresh kill.

The muscled guard tore his seething gaze from Blake and scowled at Andrew. For a few seconds, silence hung heavy in the room. Then, breaking through the quiet, the hostile guard stepped toe-to-toe with Andrew and blurted out a couple of unrecognizable phrases. Several universal swear words jumped out of the guard's mouth as the conversation ignited into a scorching blaze. Finally, the guard turned from Andrew and hurled a scathing look in her direction.

Her heart dropped. What had the guard said about her? Andrew's expression altered, and the muscles along his jawline tightened and bounced. Straightening his posture, Andrew yelled a lengthy tirade back at the other guard. Blake moved closer to her, positioning his body like a wall between her and the guards. All four men were poised for a physical battle as the heated verbal exchange continued.

Afraid to move, Ava's heart thundered in her ears as she focused on the veins in Blake's arms. The deep blue lines beneath his skin swelled and pulsed as if they were connected to invisible electrical wires. *God, please help us.*

The hostile guard stopped shouting and shifted his gaze between Andrew and Blake. And, as a hush blanketed the balmy room, a sardonic smile slithered across the man's face. He held up two hands, backed out of the room, and yanked the door shut. When the knob rattled closed, she released a held breath.

Ava peered over at Andrew, confused by the surly guard's hasty exit, then she cut a look toward Blake. Blake scowled at Andrew. As he unfolded his arms, he stepped up to face Andrew in two strides.

"What did you say to the other guard, Andrew?" Ava's whispered question sliced through the tension.

Andrew didn't answer but instead kept his eyes narrowed on Blake.

"He told the guard he wants to spend time with you tonight. Alone." Blake's voice deepened, and if looks could kill, Andrew would already be dead.

"What?" Her voice broke across her lips in a hoarse whisper.

Blake nodded and motioned toward Andrew. "Ask him."

"You know how to speak their language?" She wasn't sure if she was more stunned by that or by what he claimed Andrew had said.

"I can understand some, and I clearly understood what he said."

Andrew lowered his gaze. "I did. But only to speak with you, alone."

She believed him. He'd never made any advances toward her before. For him to do so with Blake in the room appeared to be an unwise decision.

Andrew held his finger up to his mouth, then said, "Mukasa thinks the big soldier and I will fight for you." He glanced at the closed door. "He'll be listening for a while."

Ava's knees trembled, and she sat down. *God, what have I done? My plan is falling apart.*

"Well, we should give them something to listen to." Blake's voice snapped her out of her thoughts.

"Blake." Ava vaulted from the crate and gave his arm a shove. He didn't flinch. "Andrew obviously didn't mean it. He was just trying to get the guards to leave."

"Are you defending this creep?" His steely response sliced through her like a shard of glass.

She gawked at him, confused. Was he jealous of this lanky young African? Jealous over her? Or was he just being hot-headed and protective? She refused to buy into his macho intimidation. Instead, she plopped down on the crate and motioned for Andrew to join her. He hesitated and slid his gaze from her to Blake. She couldn't imagine he felt threatened by the unarmed American soldier when he held all the weapons.

Finally, Andrew sat down, leaned his head close, and whispered, "About your question, Ava, I am."

A shudder worked its way across her skin. *Is this our answer? God give me wisdom.* Without glancing behind her, she sensed Blake relax and lower himself to the floor. Andrew sighed, then picked up a broken stick. She watched as he pushed the dirt around in swirls and lines.

After he finished the graceful movements, she stared at the drawing. "It's beautiful, Andrew." She cut a glance in Blake's direction. He'd leaned against the wall, doing his best to ignore them.

"Thank you. It is what I do."

She chuckled. "What you do?"

"I share my beliefs this way." For a moment, neither of them spoke, then Andrew leaned in and said, "Ava, they come to purchase the American soldier in two days."

She'd already heard the rumors while in the village, but

hearing it from Andrew pushed the final button on their ticking clock. "Who's coming?"

"I cannot say. I do not know."

"I need your help."

"I know."

"He needs more time to heal. Is that possible?" She lowered her voice to a faint whisper.

"No more time, Ava. I cannot stop them coming."

"I understand." She pulled in her bottom lip while her thoughts crisscrossed in a tangled web of what-ifs.

"You will need to leave tomorrow night," Andrew spoke up, crinkling his brow into a scowl.

Tomorrow? So soon? She nodded unsure of how to respond.

"I will help you."

"Thank you." She looked up at him and asked, "Will you be okay?"

He nodded but a disheartening sadness crossed his expression. Ava's heart melted. One day, on the other side of this life, there would be no more sorrow, and she'd be reunited with this African brother in Christ.

"I'll never forget your kindness." She reached out her hand and laid it on his arm. "But, why do you stay here?"

"It was either my sister or me."

She stilled.

"If I go and be a soldier, she can stay."

"Is your sister okay? Do you know for sure?" She hoped her question would give him another opportunity to break free. People died all the time. There were wars, and sickness, and … ambushes. Her heart gripped as the memories of her friends floated across her mind. "Things can happen. Maybe you don't need to stay here anymore." She didn't wish his sister harm, but she hoped he wasn't living here as an indentured soldier in vain.

"She is well."

Ava waited and hoped he'd elaborate—or say anything to help her understand why he needed to stay shackled to this ruthless group of men.

"There is a small church, a secret one."

She nodded and waited for him to continue.

"They took her in. She is just a baby. They will help her."

"What's her name? So, I can pray for her."

"Amara." He looked toward the window as his sister's name hung in the air like a prayer. After a few seconds, he stood and walked over to Blake. "Soldier."

Blake acknowledged Andrew with a curt nod.

"May God be with you."

Blake nodded, then Andrew escaped out the door.

CHAPTER TWELVE

After the door slammed shut, his fury ignited like gasoline tossed on a roaring fire. "What were you thinking?" Blake jumped up from the floor and raked a hand through his hair. "I heard what you asked that guard." A tremble crawled down his spine, and he clenched his jaw like a vice. How could he protect her if she made decisions without him? He crouched in front of her and tried to tamper his frustration. "You could've gotten both of us killed."

Not waiting for Ava to respond, he bounced back to his feet, marched over to the window, and gripped the bars with both hands. As he glared out the trammels of their prison, the shadowy shapes of the village bowed and swayed in the moonlight. *What if I can't protect her? What if we don't get out of this prison alive?*

The slain bodies of the family along the river raced across his mind like a comet with a fiery tail. Chasing it, another image—a little girl, snatched from the muddy waters by evil incarnate, as he struggled, completely helpless to save her. With little time to compartmentalize his thoughts, he'd allowed them to smolder like an abandoned campfire threatening to devour the entire forest around it.

He released his grip on the rusty bars and turned toward Ava. Now he was left with this woman—kind and compassionate and oblivious to the evils all around them. He was trained to keep his emotions in check, but the thought of her dying in this hovel made him begin to question his tenacity.

Ava's brow furrowed as their eyes connected. Then, she jumped up from the crate and stomped over to him, eliminating the space between them in only a few quick strides.

Blake folded his arms, ready to spar. "You didn't think to run it by me? Your half-baked plan to ask the African guard to help us?"

A wounded look flickered across her expression, making him regret his scathing tone.

"Ava ..." When her eyes darkened, he stopped. Accustomed to leading soldiers who obeyed his commands, this head-strong civilian, without a clue for self-preservation, was liable to be the death of him.

She pointed a brazen finger his direction. "I don't know who you think you are, but I had an instinct, and I followed it." She lowered her hands and placed them on her hips, undaunted by his six-foot-two warrior's frame eclipsing her five-foot-five petite female body. "You are not my handler. Do I need to remind you that you'd be lying in a pool of your own blood if it weren't for me?"

He clenched his fists at his sides. She was right.

"I'm not a child, so don't treat me like one." Her glower brandished a challenge before she pivoted on her heels and walked to the other side of the room.

Blake scowled. He imagined if circumstances were

different, she'd stomp out of the room and gladly slam the door in his face.

"You didn't share any plan with me." She kept her back to him as she continued. "You must think I am some delicate imbecile incapable of understanding *your* great idea." She lowered her voice to a whisper. "For all I know, you planned to dig yourself out through the scrap hole in the corner of the room." She turned and waved in the direction of the opening in the wall. "There are two guards there day and night. I see them every time I'm out in the village." She paused and lifted her chin to meet his gaze. "By my menial calculations, you would've been dead as soon as you poked your head out the back of this shack." Folding her arms, she continued. "But if you go to the south side of the village, there is not one male— only females. It's where women cook, and the children play. In fact, there are exactly seven shelters, then a clearing of about one-hundred and fifty feet, followed by a copse of trees."

Blake stood there, stunned. *How long had she been gathering intel? When had she decided to enlist the young African guard to help them?* Her docile attitude led him to believe she'd all but given up.

He had been wrong.

"You do know Christians are killed every day on this continent for just admitting they are believers?" He threw the question out, impressed by her recon but still frustrated she'd not consulted him.

"Of course, I know that." She closed the distance between them and lifted her chin in marked defiance. "When I came here, I knew full well I could die for my faith, and if that happens, so be it."

He stilled. What happened in this Southern lady's life to make her so flippant about her own death?

"I have nothing to lose by dying but everything to gain by trying to survive."

"You have no one back home who'd prefer you not martyr yourself?" He asked the question cautiously, not wanting to step on any landmines.

"I don't." Ava turned and lowered herself back onto the crate.

Blake thought about what she'd said for a moment as he tilted his head from side to side to loosen his tense muscles. Then, he walked over and sat down next to her. As he examined Andrew's art, a wave of peace washed over him. It was just dirt—ordinary, raw African dirt—but Andrew had fashioned it into a detailed illustration of God's gift of salvation.

There were three crosses drawn on a hill. The one in the middle was more ornate and more prominent than the others. Next to the crosses was a cave with a large circular stone lying beside the opening. With finger indents, Andrew carved sun rays darting out around the cave. Next to the cave, a heart. The words *Andrew* appeared on the outside, and *Jeshua* was scribbled on the inside of the heart.

"So, he's a believer?"

"He is." Ava played with the stick by her feet.

His mind fought every instinct to adopt a plan involving busting down doors with guns a-blazing. The only problem, there were no guns, and the door they were behind was locked with an iron bar. "He's going to help?"

"Yes."

Blake looked back at the drawing and tried to gather his thoughts. Then, after admiring the art for a few more seconds, he picked up the stick and erased the sketch. "Do you think he understands he could be killed?" He didn't want Andrew's death on his conscience. He'd rather depend on himself.

"I think he does." Ava put her hand on his arm, and a pulse of electricity shot through his skin in response. "I think we all understand what is at stake here."

He held her gaze. She'd single-handedly bartered for their release—no blood, no brawn, no calculated attack—just a women's intuition and a love for Christ.

"Okay, then." He stood, feeling restless. "When do we leave?"

"Tomorrow night."

He halted. "So soon?"

"We have to. The guards plan on handing you over to the highest bidder in two days."

Her answer sent a chill down his spine.

Ava not only orchestrated a way out for them, but she also saved his life.

Again.

CHAPTER THIRTEEN

A va blew out a long breath to defuse some of the anxious tension in the sweltering room. The hours ticked by like an eternity. She moved her shoes around in the swirls of dirt at her feet and tried to make sense of the questions spinning like a gyroscope in her mind. Was this the open door for their escape? Or would they fail, and both of them lose their lives? Would Andrew be found out? If so, what would happen to him? He'd offered his help, but she didn't want to think about the consequences he might face when they were gone. Was there another way Blake and she could escape on their own?

Ava thought about her best friend, Caroline, and guilt rippled through her. She'd lied when she told Blake nobody would care if she died. She had scores of friends and clients in Texas who'd be beside themselves if she didn't return. A flutter blossomed in her stomach, and a second wave of guilt hit her. *I'm sorry, Lord, for running from my grief—and my responsibilities. Please forgive me.*

She cut a glance in Blake's direction. He'd resumed his place by the window, keeping watch—over what, she didn't know. As she studied him, a niggling feeling worked its way through her gut. No doubt, he'd not tried to escape yet because of her. *God, please don't let me slow him down.* Her body tensed, thinking about the day the guards dragged him into her room. The thought he could be handed over to another group of wicked torturers like a peddled bag of goods made her sick. *Protect us, please.* A sense of peace washed over her, and she was reminded of a Bible story. "Ever read the story of Joseph?"

Blake turned and smiled. "Yeah, I think I can remember most of it."

"His brothers sold him to a traveling caravan, and his family didn't see him for many years."

"I'm not sure my mother would approve of that."

"So the caged lion has a mother?"

"Don't we all?" He winked. The charming gesture made her smile.

"I guess we do." A trace of sadness washed over her like the brush of angel's wings. How she longed to see her mother again. When she got to heaven, it would be a great reunion.

"Mine fawns over me fervently when I go back home. It's rather embarrassing." Blake's lighthearted words broke through her sad thoughts.

"Somehow, it's hard for me to imagine you being fawned over."

He held up his hands in mock surrender. "It's true. A good soldier would never lie."

Ava stifled a giggle. "Okay, Joseph, it's time we change the story up a bit and get you out of this pit before the caravan arrives."

He paused for a moment, then his lips unfurled into a sly grin. "I wonder how much I'd go for?"

"What?" As he strutted around the room like a bodybuilder, the muscles in his shoulders arched and flexed, causing her heart to do the same. He stopped in front of her and struck an exaggerated pose. She doubled over with laughter. Finding out Blake had a playful side to him was like flipping a gold coin and being surprised by the ornate drawing on the other side.

"Maybe twenty dollars?" Blake flopped down on the crate next to her, and it creaked with his weight. "I'm the older model of a soldier. I feel like I'm sixty instead of thirty-three."

So now she knew his age, another peeled-back layer of her companion. Ava scooted next to him on the crate and nudged him with her elbow. "I think you're worth more than twenty dollars." Warmth traced across her middle as the words tumbled off her lips.

He laughed, and the joyous sound made her heart flip flop. "Really?" Throwing her a flirtatious look, he asked, "How much would a Southern girl pay for a broken soldier these days?"

She sucked in a breath. "I ... well ..." *You're priceless.* Like the glowing embers in a fireplace, her cheeks kindled with heat.

Blake held her gaze for a few long seconds. She couldn't help but notice how the aqueous green in his eyes mirrored the ocean's viridescent waves of color. *His eyes are beautiful.* Her creativity ignited as her mind flipped through paint colors and envisioned a masculine room decorated in various shades of illustrious jades. She blinked and released a sigh.

Like a microburst of energy, Blake shot up from the crate, leaned casually against the wall, folded his arms, and glanced down at her. Goosebumps traveled across Ava's forearm in the wake of his agile movement.

"Oh, I forgot." He grinned, looking amused that he'd rendered her speechless. "You designers have a thing for antiques."

A tingle swept from the back of her neck and traced down her spine. It was true. She did like antiques. But that wasn't what made her uncomfortable. Blake was flirting with her. Or was she flirting with him? No, she couldn't be. She was grieving. For a moment, Blake's muscle-bound antics had taken her mind off why she was here. Why she was a prisoner in Africa. Losing her husband had triggered something in her. A need to flee from her problems. A need to recalibrate her life. Ava shook off the thought. She had to focus on the task at hand. Andrew promised he'd help, but they were far from being out of danger.

A few moments of silence circled around them like a dense fog before the rusty creak of the iron bar cut through the room.

"I have some things." Andrew stepped over the threshold, then clicked the door shut behind him.

Ava scurried off the crate, and the three of them huddled in the middle of the room.

"You'll want this." Andrew pulled the baggy shirt over his head and handed it to Blake. "And here, Ava." He fished a palm-sized New Testament from his pocket and slipped it into her hands. "I found this. For your journey."

Ava's vision blurred. "Thank you." The text was in English, and dirt dusted the pages. It was just what she needed.

Voices from the road floated in through the window. Andrew glanced over his shoulder at the door. The room stilled. When only silence surrounded them, he turned back and said, "Tomorrow, at dark, you will leave."

She dared a glance at Blake. A solemn look blanketed his expression. With less than twenty-four hours until their escape, she could only guess how the wheels of his mind were turning.

"We'll need water." His brow furrowed. "And a knife. Or a small ax." Blake nodded to the weapon strapped around Andrew's shoulder. "I'd take one of those if you've got a spare."

Ava's tongue dried. Would they need the weapons for food or protection?

"I will see what I can find." Andrew turned to leave, then pivoted to face them. "More than anything, you need to pray."

With those final words, Andrew stepped out the door, leaving them both to contemplate tomorrow's journey.

And pray.

CHAPTER FOURTEEN

Ava stooped to examine the murky water swirling in front of her. She was thirsty, and the tiny rain droplets she'd caught on her tongue made her even more parched. Straightening, Ava stretched her toes in the confines of her sneakers and sighed. They'd walked for almost two days. Every joint and muscle ached with fatigue.

Blake leaned on a tree next to her. His hair and beard were soaked and dripping from the brief rainstorm they'd just walked through. He appeared as wild and unkempt as the rugged African terrain surrounding them.

"We aren't far now." Blake stared at the map Andrew had drawn, then looked toward the horizon at the setting sun. "We'll be at the church in a few hours. I want to approach in the dark. How are you holding up?" He glanced up and caught her watching him.

She hesitated to respond truthfully. Her clothes stuck to her with sweat, dirt, and now rain, but she was grateful to be out in the open air and away from their captors. "I'm good."

He nodded, then looked away.

Her thoughts turned to the night they'd left. After Andrew led them to the outskirts of the camp, he'd shoved a backpack and a map into Blake's hands. The rough sketch outlined directions to a small village church—a short detour to the north, where they could refresh their provisions.

Before they'd left, Blake's demeanor had transformed. He was all pent-up energy and seriousness, and she swore the muscles along his jaw had hardened into smooth marble.

Shortly before that nightfall, he asked, "Are you scared?"

Ava bristled at his question. Of course, she was afraid, but she wanted freedom more. "Not really." She jutted out her chin and tried to disguise the tremble in her voice.

"Good."

He hadn't followed up his answer with any unnecessary words or reassurances, but she didn't expect any. In the short time she'd spent with him, his moods ebbed and flowed between calm and fire. Most of the time, he looked ready for a fight. Swimming in her own insecurity, she was grateful to have him beside her as a fierce protector.

After they'd trekked several hours from the village, Blake admitted he was anxious about getting her safely beyond the Kenyan border and warned the journey would be long and grueling. She understood. But as she looked at him now, with his brow furrowed in deep concentration, she hoped she wasn't slowing him down.

A peculiar swooshing in the water near her feet brought her back to the present. She examined the hazy river but didn't see anything except a few green frogs balancing on a wet log. She inhaled a deep breath, then exhaled.

The memory of her time with Blake in their prison wandered through her mind. She'd grown to enjoy his company and his fiery demeanor, but she understood this might be the last few days they'd be together. *It's not like we could just hang out in Africa indefinitely. I mean, who would want to?* She frowned. She needed to get home and pick up the pieces of her life. Blake had already informed her he'd be heading back out to the field as soon as he knew she was safely on a plane bound for Texas. *Just like it should be. Right?*

Looking back at Blake, Ava thought about him returning to his job. How could he go through something like this and just push it off as a diversion from his original plans? *It's his job, Ava.*

She continued to study Blake as he rested against the gnarled tree trunk. He wore his military fatigue pants and the T-shirt Andrew had given him. For reasons she couldn't name, she requested they take his tattered jacket. Although beyond the point of serviceable, the idea of leaving anything behind with the name Maxwell on it made her sentimental heart want to break in two.

Recalling the dreadful weeks she'd just survived, Ava glanced down at her own clothes and grimaced. Her skirt was filthy, and her once-new pink running shoes were now crusted with dirt and fraying at the seams. She'd need to purchase a new pair if she made it out of this.

The cloudy water stirred below her again, and something slithered just below the surface. Crouching down, she squinted to get a better view.

"You probably should move back away from the edge of the river." Blake's voice broke through her perusal, and she froze. He'd warned her about the dangers of their trek and reminded her that while Uganda boasted a gorgeous landscape, the creatures roaming the land were to be respected and feared. If they got complacent and let down their guard, they'd most likely end up at the bottom of the food chain.

Straightening, she stood quickly—too quickly. Feeling

lightheaded, her stomach swayed, and she doubled over and vomited onto the muddy embankment.

Blake shoved the map in his pocket, stepped next to her, and held back her hair. Although he'd done it before, the act both warmed and humiliated her. She turned to face him, and he held the back of his hand across her cheek and then her forehead. Another round of sickness rose to the surface as he grabbed her wrist and checked her pulse.

"We need to get you medical care ASAP. I'm concerned you're having more than an adverse reaction to the local cuisine."

Reaching into her pocket, she pulled out the scrap piece of fabric she'd tied into a makeshift ponytail holder. As she tugged her hair back, she contemplated how to respond. She'd held on to her secret long enough. If she didn't confess the truth of her sickness, Blake would have her on a gurney, running tests for malaria or some other disease when they finally reached civilization.

"I don't have food poisoning." While he steadied her, Ava swallowed back her uncertainty and whispered, "I'm pregnant."

"What?" Blake's bottle-green eyes flashed with murderous rage. As if scorched by a branding iron, he dropped her arm and slammed an angry palm against the droopy tree next to the riverbank. After the outburst, his hand was scraped and bloody. "I'll go back and take out every male in that village."

Startled by his response, Ava wrung her hands together. She'd just confessed to being pregnant. She wasn't contagious. "What?" Her voice trembled. Did he regret helping her escape? "What are you talking about?"

He turned. Torment edged across his features. "How long were you in that village, Ava? You told me they didn't hurt you." He gripped her shoulders with his strong hands as his voice dipped into a low guttural tone. "How long had they *really* kept you there?"

His words and their implications connected in her brain, and warmth flooded her cheeks. "Oh, Blake, no! It's not what you think."

"Explain it to me, then."

"I was pregnant—when I came to Uganda."

Releasing his grip, he asked, "Why in the world did you travel to this place in your condition?" Accusation blanketed his tone as he glared at the gold band on her finger—the one Andrew had given back to her before sending them away. "And what kind of husband would let you travel here carrying his child?"

Ava stepped back. The stab of the insult directed toward Dylan fell over her like the scorching west wind. She didn't need his judgment. Her life had been in turmoil for years, and she needed a reprieve. Instead, she found herself filthy and sick in the middle of Uganda. Now, she traveled with a man who believed he earned the right to throw accusations at her because he commanded a group of armed soldiers into combat. Queasiness wrapped around her middle. She took in a quick breath, held his gaze, and considered how she wanted to answer him.

BLAKE KEPT his eyes locked on Ava's.

She didn't answer right away, which gave him time to reassess the thoughts pummeling through his mind like runaway boulders crashing down a ravine. When he'd thought she'd been harmed, there was no denying the lengths he might go to vindicate her honor. Now, he tried to digest that, she willfully decided to travel to this country—pregnant and alone. No, he couldn't. It was ludicrous. *She's married.* Blake raked his hand through his shaggy hair and tried again to unravel what she'd just admitted. *And you're falling for her. Idiot.*

The moment Andrew handed her the wedding ring, it was like Blake had stepped on a landmine. Even if she'd claimed she had no one to go back to, she was still married. His convictions forced him to honor that boundary no matter what his heart desired.

After a few torturous seconds, she turned away from him.

"Ava?" Before she could escape his reach, he grasped her arm. Every muscle in her body turned to stone. "Ava, please talk to me."

She jerked her arm out of his loose grip, turned, and drilled him with a look that could drop a platoon of soldiers to their knees. "What kind of husband?" She steeled her voice. "A dead one, that's what kind."

His heart lodged in his throat. She raked him with another angry look, then stalked away from him in slow, deliberate movements, lifting her legs high above the long grass. The way he'd taught her to keep snakes and other critters moving away from her.

Dead? Her husband's dead? He wasn't accustomed to being around women in her condition, but he knew the basic science and timeline. At first glance, no one would know she was expecting, which meant her husband had only been deceased a few weeks.

Blake exhaled a long breath. He needed to give her some space, but he didn't want to let her out of his sight.

She's pregnant. Why didn't she say something? The thought of her carrying her burden alone twisted his stomach into knots. *It's none of my business. If she wanted me to know, she would've told me.* He gritted his teeth and glanced out over the uninhabited terrain. The emotional connection he'd allowed to form with Ava frightened him more than any combat situation he'd ever been in. *Let it go. Your job is to get her home—in one piece.* White-hot fire shot through his veins as he shook off the burgeoning reality that now there were two he needed to keep safe. *We need to keep moving.*

Ava stopped just before the tree line and lowered herself onto a large rock jutting from the earth. She placed her hand on her abdomen, leaned back, and glanced up into the darkening sky.

When tears cascaded down her cheeks, tension wrapped around his neck and compressed. He'd been the reason for those tears. He slammed a fist against his thigh. *Why would she come to Uganda? Why did she willingly endanger herself and her unborn baby?*

Starting up the hill, he considered what he should say. Part of him—the part which led small hordes of soldiers into dangerous situations—wanted to berate her for agreeing to travel in her condition by herself. For his own sanity, he wished she had stayed in her safe little world back in the U.S., where he imagined she lived in a comfortable home and attended a good church. One who would've helped her through her time of loss and grief. She certainly would've had better nourishment and medical care.

However, the tender part of him—the part he kept locked away in a safe place so he could push through some of the worst parts of his job—crumbled at the thought of her suffering. With a heavy heart, he headed in her direction. When Blake reached her, he cleared his throat, then said, "I'm sorry. I shouldn't have said anything."

Ava didn't reply. She just looked up at him through tear-drenched lashes.

"I thought the guards hurt you." Turning away from her, he

paced in the long grass, not caring what slithering creature approached him in his mood. "I would have gone back if they'd hurt you."

It was quiet a moment, then she whispered, "Revenge isn't worth it."

She was right—vengeance belonged to the Lord—but he'd been given the task to take down some extremely heinous people in his job. For him, defending her honor would've been justified.

He pivoted toward her. "What about honor and protection?" Lowering his voice, he prayed she'd understand he wasn't a ruthless or vengeful person, but his job required him to make hard decisions—decisions he never took lightly. "I do believe in justice, Ava, and sometimes to attain justice, action needs to be taken."

Relief overtook him when a look of understanding traced across her expression.

Did she understand?

Did she understand what he was trying to explain—about his duty, about his mission, and, more importantly, about his heart?

CHAPTER FIFTEEN

*S*ometimes *to attain justice, action needs to be taken.* Ava straightened her shoulders as Blake's words sent a tremble tiptoeing down her spine. Whatever his job in the military, she imagined he could inflict pain on whomever he chose, but the tone of his voice startled her—reflective, questioning, maybe a bit pensive. *He's trying to explain. He's trying to let me in.*

Releasing a quick breath, her own words carved through her soul like a blade. *Revenge isn't worth it.* She'd come to Uganda with retribution in her heart—wanting justice for the death of her husband—but after her time alone with God in captivity, her heart had changed. More than anything, she wanted healing. To attain that, she needed to forgive.

She glanced over at Blake. He'd taken a few steps away, folded his arms, and leaned against a dead tree. While he never spoke openly about what he did for a living, she suspected there were things he kept hidden and buried deep. But the idea he'd been prepared to thunder back through the gates of Hades to defend her honor stirred a tingle through her entire body.

"Are you okay to go on?" Blake's voice jolted her out of her thoughts.

"Yes." She nodded and swiped a hand over her tear-stained cheeks.

His expression remained tender as he walked over, held out his hand, and pulled her to her feet. Expecting him to withdraw, she loosened her grip. Instead, he intertwined his fingers with hers and squeezed. Warmth radiated in her chest. She liked the way her palm fit snugly with his. Sighing, she quickly reminded herself that having Blake this close would only ever be temporary.

AS THEY TREKKED toward the church, his mind raced in a perpetual loop of uncertain outcomes. *Should I trust the directions to the hidden church? How much longer can Ava continue under these conditions? Worst case scenario, I'd need to leave her somewhere and come back for her. No, scratch that. I'm not leaving her anywhere—ever.* His mind stutter-stepped, and Blake cleared his throat, hoping Ava couldn't read his thoughts.

He hated the variables on this mission. The variables he couldn't control. They still had almost two hours until they reached the church under the cover of darkness. But it was two hours off course. If it was the haven Andrew promised, they'd rest and recover. Maybe even get some fresh clothes. Then, they could push through to the border.

If it wasn't—Blake shook off the thought. He only had so many options without his gear. *Stop! God will guide us.* The thought floated through his mind, and he cringed. When had he learned to rely only on himself and not God? If God wanted to get them to safety, no lack of weaponry would hinder that.

He glanced at Ava and wished he could read *her* thoughts.

He'd done his best to explain his need to protect her, but he wasn't always great at communication—well, communication in relationships. He smiled to himself. If he had to call in a drone strike or relay intel to his unit, his words would have come out much smoother.

I wish I could tell her more about me. There was so much about his life he couldn't share with anyone, which, if he was honest, isolated him. At times, he'd considered trying to find someone willing to share this journey with him. But military life was hard. Not many women would want to hold down the fort while he dropped into undisclosed locations with little to no info about when he'd return. Marriage was tough enough on its own. The unpredictability of his job thrown in the mix complicated it more. *Why am I even thinking about this right now?* He glanced down at their hands. The soft skin of her fingers intertwined with his question.

Pulling his gaze away from their hands, Blake surveyed the shadowy terrain. The desolate expanse mirrored his mood. *I need to focus.* Getting Ava and her unborn baby safely home struck him as more important than any mission he'd navigated before. As if sensing his thoughts, she looked up at him. Her blue-flamed eyes reflected the moonlight, and a shot of adrenaline ignited in his veins. *God, please help me get her to safety.* He'd never be able to forgive himself if anything happened to her—or her baby. *Like the little girl by the river.*

Shaking off his worry, he threw her a smile and squeezed her hand. "By my calculations, we have a few more hours until we reach the hidden church."

He'd considered sidestepping that stop on their journey since he didn't wholly trust the gangly guard who'd help them leave. However, their circumstances just changed. Even though he didn't have all the details, he understood Ava would need to rest more often. It wouldn't do either one of them any good if she physically gave up and he had to carry her across the border.

Ava returned his smile. "Sounds good."

As they walked along a river, he mentally formulated a plan for the next leg of their journey. They had fruit and a few more waters left to get them through the night and maybe one more day. He hoped the church could replenish supplies for the final leg to the Kenyan border. *And I hope we're not walking into a trap.*

Shoving away the negative thought, he glanced back at Ava. With her fingers still wrapped around his, he recalled the warmth of her touch while she'd tended to his wounds. Chiding himself, Blake cleared his throat. "After we leave the church, I have a plan that may help us shave some time off our trip."

She glanced up at him with a puzzled expression.

"Don't worry. No one will get hurt." He winked at her, then released her hand so he could concentrate. "We just need to get within twenty kilometers of the Kenyan border. After that, the rest should be smooth sailing."

CHAPTER SIXTEEN

Blake's heart pounded as he and Ava crept toward the small shack nestled in the clearing of trees. The air hummed with nature's night sounds, and the deep, ebony sky hovered above them like a thick, velvety blanket speckled with miniature lights. He still hesitated to trust their young captor's instructions to find the secluded church, but they needed rest. With no other options, he begged God to direct their steps.

Several meters ahead, he caught sight of the soft glow from a fire and the faint sound of singing. Lifting a fist in the air, he motioned for Ava to stop. Something seemed off. He closed his eyes and zeroed in on the noises floating through the tepid breeze.

A stick cracked, and behind him, a footfall squished in the mud. Ava screamed his name, and every muscle in his body coiled like a taut rubber band. Before he could react, someone shoved a blunt object between his shoulder blades. *God help us.* Reaching out, he grasped for her hand and whispered, "We'll get out of this. I promise."

Sweat slicked between their palms as hurried and angry

voices argued behind them. *How did I not hear them approaching?* Blake gritted his teeth. He'd let down his guard believing Andrew had given them directions to a safe location. Now, they both were about to pay the price for that decision.

Cutting a glance toward Ava, he tried to assess the situation. He didn't want to engage with these men, especially with her so near—but he would. He'd do anything to keep her safe. She whimpered his name again, this time as a question, and he weighed his options to react. *There are only two of them. This will be quick and easy.* A plan to extract the weapon from the man behind him sped through his mind. After that, he'd take out the other one.

What if more men are hiding in the trees? A hasty action could end at least one of their lives if he made the wrong move. *Breathe.* Blake sent up a silent plea to heaven, then went with plan B—diplomacy.

While he considered what to do, the men continued to argue between themselves, hurling accusations and pressing the weapon harder into the muscles of his back. They were angry, but the quake in their voices led him to believe they weren't seasoned killers. He'd use that as leverage, if only to distract them long enough to move Ava out of the way.

"We were given directions to this place." He kept his voice calm and steady. On his first attempt, he spoke in English. How they responded would determine his next move.

The two men yelled back at him in their language, and Blake sensed the tension escalate. *Okay, so that didn't work.*

"I have a map." This time he tried in their native tongue and motioned with his left hand to the cargo pocket on his thigh. A third man materialized from the darkness and pawed at his legs and hips, searching for weapons. *There are more of them. But how many?*

Blake constrained his mind to focus on Ava and the armed

men's movements. Every scenario racing through his thoughts was encumbered with his concern for her well-being. A sharp pang of anger shot through him like a stray bullet. *How could I let us get caught?* He ordered his heartbeat to slow as he planned his next move.

AVA SWALLOWED HARD when the barrel of a gun pushed against her back. Blake reached out to her and gripped her hand. She could only guess at his thoughts while they stood there, outmanned and out-weaponed in the shadowy copse of trees. *God, please help us.* Her frantic heartbeat flooded her ears as she attempted to listen to Blake converse with the men.

After a pause, Blake said something else but echoed their language. Her body gripped like a yanked rope as another man walked out of the trees. In her peripheral, she watched the man behind them say something and pat Blake down like a criminal. Slowly, Blake reached into his pocket and pulled out the wrinkled fabric Andrew had scribbled their map on. The armed man wrenched the scrap from Blake's hands and studied it. Blake cut a glance toward her and nodded. His in-charge look did little to quell the terror racing through her like a bolt of lightning.

After several long torturous seconds, one of the men clicked on a flashlight, and the high lumens formed a glowing circle around them.

"It's okay." Blake's calm whisper broke through her dread. "They're discussing the map Andrew sent with us."

She nodded and tried to steady her breathing.

"Andrew scribbled words on the back of the fabric. Hopefully, it will mean something to them."

She opened her mouth but didn't have a chance to whisper

a question. The rag-tag group of men dropped their weapons to their sides and whirled them both around to face them.

"Brother." One of the men curved his lips into a welcoming smile.

Confusion wrapped itself around her as the larger man pulled Blake in for a quick hug.

She looked at Blake, then at the burly man who wore thin linen pants and no shirt over his rotund belly. The man stepped back, shook Blake's hand, and pulled at his shirt sleeve. Then, with a broad smile, he aimed the beam of the flashlight at the cluster of inky twisted vines wrapped around Blake's bicep.

"Ink." The man pointed to the skin on the side of his torso. A three-inch tattoo of a cross with a crown of thorns was etched across his skin.

Blake nodded.

Releasing a pent-up breath, Ava shook her head. She'd almost died with a bullet in her back, and now these men were comparing tattoos? "What's going on?"

Blake winked at her. "I told you it was fine."

Lifting her brows, she pushed out a forced smile. "Right."

The fat-bellied man moved over in her direction and took her chin gently in his hands. As he skimmed the beam of light across her face, a deep, jolly laugh emanated from his lips, and his stomach jiggled in the shadows. "Violet."

She pointed to herself, already well versed in introductions with locals who barely spoke anything she could understand. "Ava."

The man flashed her a wide smile. "Yes, Ava. Violet."

She eyed Blake, confused.

"He's talking about your eyes." Blake leaned in close to her ear, and his breath brushed against her cheek. "They're the most striking color of violet I've ever seen."

Her cheeks warmed. She was thankful the guard moved the beam of light before anyone noticed her face turning crimson.

After a few more introductions, the three men motioned for them to follow through a blanket of low-hanging trees. She hesitated. Like a movie on fast-forward, her mind conjured images of insects crawling around her hair and skittering across her shoes.

Blake pulled her onward and flashed her an ornery look. "Don't worry, I've been trained to eliminate large insects if the need arises."

She sensed him laughing beside her, and she rolled her eyes. He mocked her like a schoolboy, but she didn't care. Instead, she focused on the security of his touch as he guided her through the thick vegetation.

When they reached a clearing, two women stood near a fire wearing dresses splashed in bright colors and geometric shapes.

"Who are these?" The taller woman's question came out in broken English, but the deep rhythm to her voice sounded soothing and inviting.

Ava listened as the three men tried to explain their visit as they pointed to Andrew's map. Finally, she picked out the words American soldier, ink, Ava, violet, and sleep. The last word sounded the most appealing. The woman smiled big and motioned for her to come near. Ava turned to Blake and waited to follow his lead. He nodded but stepped closer to her and threw out a few words in the woman's language. When he reached out and tenderly laid his hand on her abdomen, her cheeks burned even more.

Turning to face her, he said, "It's okay. We're safe now."

She nodded, then Blake turned back to the woman and said a few more words. The woman nodded, and her lips curved into a wide, pleasing grin. He pointed at Ava's shirt, said something with a chuckle, then winked.

The woman shot Blake a chiding look as she wrapped a comforting arm around Ava's waist. "You come with me, Violet. Your handsome man has a lot to say, doesn't he?"

"He isn't ..." Glancing back at Blake, she asked, "What did you say to her?"

For the first time in days, his expression mirrored a contented peace. "Just trust me, and go with the nice lady."

She stalled, but the woman prodded her along. Blake's voice floated on the breeze as he conversed with the group of men. When he laughed, she smiled. For a moment, it felt as if they both might be able to take a reviving breath.

The woman started to sing as she wrapped an arm around Ava and led her to a hut. Pressing in, Ava listened to the melodic sounds of the woman's voice. She didn't understand the words, but music had always soothed her. The calm melody floating across the woman's lips filled her with peace.

The lady pushed back a door of grass fibers, pointed to a cot with a thin blanket, and motioned for her to sit down. Continuing to sing, the woman gently tugged her fingers through Ava's tangled and dirty hair. Taking in a long breath, Ava sighed. The stress of the past few weeks fled her body at the woman's comforting touch, and all the anxiety she'd been holding onto began to dissolve. Her eyelids drooped shut. After a few seconds of finger combing, the woman stopped singing and asked a question.

"I'm sorry. I don't speak your language." Ava's eyes fluttered open, and the understanding expression on the woman's face wrapped her in comfort.

The woman nodded and spoke in melodious, accented English. "It's okay." She busied herself around the room as three younger ladies came in carrying large pitchers of boiling water, filling a deep basin in the back of the room.

A wave of exhaustion swept over her. *Colby and Sharron.* Out of nowhere, her friends' names popped into her mind. *My friends. What happened to my friends?* A wave of sorrow crashed over her as the thought of their bodies lying somewhere in the middle of this harsh country made her heart ache.

Not wanting to cry, she shook away the mournful thoughts. She needed to focus on getting to safety, and then, when she and Blake finally did, she'd allow herself time to grieve. Not only for Sharron and Colby but for Dylan too.

Steam filled the room as the ladies finished bringing in several pitchers of water. Finally, the tall woman came over and handed her a small oval piece of soap. Motioning to the wooden basin, she said, "You will feel better after a wash."

The kind gesture pushed Ava over the edge, and tears fell down her cheeks in a torrent. "Thank you." Sniffling, she tried to stand, but her knees buckled.

The girls rushed in, encircled her, and helped her out of the clothes she'd worn for nearly three weeks. Modesty was the furthest thing from her mind as they led her into the warm water. They helped wash her hair, then allowed her to soak as her tears mixed with the soapy pool of suds.

When the water cooled, the younger group helped her out and handed her a bright orange skirt and a deep grey T-shirt. Slipping into the clean clothes left Ava feeling pampered and reinvigorated.

"Your man said you are with child." The older lady handed her some flatbread and motioned toward her abdomen.

Ava sank onto the cot, stopped mid-chew, and let the words sink in. Blake told them she was pregnant and needed a bath. Warmth traced up her neck and coiled around to her ears. She didn't know if she should be embarrassed or burst out in a giggle. Glancing at the woman, she said, "Yes." Her hand slid to her belly as she finished chewing her bread. "Yes, I'm going to have a baby."

"Good." The woman smiled.

Ava cocked her head. What an odd answer. Especially after all she'd been through. She knew babies were a blessing from God, but she hardly believed her situation was good.

"Baby is good." The woman nodded with a toothy grin.

"Yes, the baby is good."

She offered her some meat, and Ava silently prayed it was something she could recognize.

"Man is good." Again, the woman waited for Ava to respond.

"Yes, he is good." She let the meat sit on her tongue as the aromatic and tasty spices filled her palate.

"Then today, all is good."

"Yes." She hesitated, then said, "I guess today, all *is* good." Thankful the woman had brought these truths to her attention, Ava smiled. Today *was* good. She'd been blessed in more ways these past two weeks than she'd realized. God provided a companion in prison, favor with a guard, and a bath in the wilderness. So yes, today, all was good.

"Man will be a good father."

Her jaw tensed as she tried to swallow. She wanted to correct the woman's remarks but refrained. Ava returned a weak smile as sorrow filled her. Was she sad because the *good man* was not hers? Or because her baby would grow up without a father?

The woman didn't say anymore. Instead, she gently squeezed her hand and motioned for Ava to lie down. As she did, the woman pulled a thin, colorful fabric over her and tucked her in. Then, while Ava nestled under the covers, the woman strode toward the grassy door. The young girls followed close behind, resembling a brood of baby ducklings following their mother.

She giggled and snuggled farther under the airy blanket. It had been years since her last tucking-in and weeks since she'd been so refreshed.

As she drifted off to sleep, she thanked God for the simple provisions she'd overlooked on her journey.

For the safety of their escape. For Andrew and his protection.

But more importantly, for the good man in the neighboring hut.

CHAPTER SEVENTEEN

Ava nestled into the dirt embankment as Blake approached the small group of African farmers. She examined her clothes and frowned. Her newly acquired outfit was already dusty and speckled with red dirt. *Well, that didn't last long.* Thinking about the two nights they'd spent at the hidden church and how handsome Blake looked after a wash and a couple hours of much-needed sleep made her smile. *He definitely cleans up well.*

A deep masculine yell pulled her back to the present. She scanned the field to find Blake. One of the farmers bellowed to another man and motioned for him to join them. Blake appeared confident and unaffected even though he was now outnumbered three to one.

Shifting the backpack to the ground, she glanced at the hunting knife in her right hand. While not her first choice in defense, acquiring it had been one of the perks of stopping at the hidden church—that and some local currency to use at the border.

As she wiped a bead of sweat from her forehead, Ava

continued to watch the men in the field. Sighing, she recalled how Blake flashed her a sly grin as he tried to reassure her all would be well today.

"I have a favor to call in." That's all he said to her before he handed her the knife and sauntered off to approach the trio of farmers.

She gripped the knife tighter, and her stomach clenched beneath her shirt. This had better be the plan where he promised nobody would get hurt. Shaking her head to release a sweaty piece of hair stuck to her cheek, she glanced out over the expanse of the open field. According to Blake, this was the final push in their journey. Soon, he promised, she'd finally be able to get off her aching feet.

Blake's voice carried in the wind. Ava squinted and tried to read his lips. He nodded, shook his head, then nodded again. Finally, after a quick back and forth and several gestures with his hands, Blake motioned for her to come out.

She crawled up from where she'd hidden and watched the confused looks on the farmers' faces. Unsure of what to do, she waved. Their eyes widened as they stared at her like she was an apparition swaying in the tall grass. Blake flashed her a grin, then took off a short distance down the dirt road and jumped into a battered truck. As he drove in her direction, the bone-shaking rumble of the engine sent a shot of terror coursing through her.

"I procured us some wheels." He pulled up beside her, flashed her a quick wink, and motioned for her to get in.

The dusty air swirling around her grew thicker as clammy sweat trickled down her forehead and cheeks. *No. No!* The truck was a muted green, and splotches of red soil clung to its rusty body. Fumes from the exhaust wafted up to Ava's nose and paralyzed her.

"Ava?"

Blake's voice evaporated as a thick fog tumbled over her thoughts. *No! I can't get in that truck.* Pin-pricks danced across her vision. She stood there, unable to move. Then, like a strike of lightning during a midnight storm, a scene flashed across her memory—Colby, Sharron, and the body of the charred, hollowed-out truck her missionary group had been riding in.

BLAKE MOTIONED AGAIN for her to move forward but stopped when her face turned ashen. "Ava?" He turned off the truck and, in one fluid motion, slid over and exited the passenger side. Terror blanketed her expression as she collapsed into his open arms.

One of the farmers yelled something in their direction. He held up his hand, motioning for them to keep their distance. Quickly he grabbed the knife out of her hands and placed it in the sheath tied to his waistband. Lowering himself to one knee, he helped her recline and cradled her in the crook of his arm.

"I just, I can't ..."

She murmured something as he ripped open the backpack. He grabbed a bottle of water and an extra shirt the ladies had given to her. He splashed some water on the shirt, then dabbed her forehead.

Ava's eyes fluttered, and she tried to speak again. "Blake, I ..."

"Wait, don't talk. First, take a couple of slow, deep breaths." He brought the bottle to her lips and waited for her to take a few sips.

Opening her eyes, she lifted her head.

"You don't have to get up right away." He checked her pulse, then asked, "What happened? Are you feeling okay?"

Pinching her eyes shut, she said, "I can't get in that truck."

Blake glanced at the truck, then back at her, trying to understand. He waited for her to take another sip of water before he carried her a few feet to a shaded patch of trees.

"Why can't you get in the truck?" He was confused. If she could drive in Dallas traffic, a short drive in a pick-up along deserted roads shouldn't be a problem. As he sat there with his arms wrapped around her, her body trembled.

"I can't—" Her eyes shot open, then she gulped several small breaths.

He held her closer. "It's okay. Breathe slowly in and out. Take all the time you need." He mimicked the rhythmic breathing beside her, hoping to calm her as he did.

"I can't, Blake." Tears burst from her eyes. "I can't."

"Okay, okay. Just relax."

One of the farmers walked in their direction. On high alert, Blake's body tensed as he tried to read the man's expression. A docile situation could flip to hostile like a flick of a match if the right fuel was added to the fire. Yelling, he commanded the man to stop and explained how the heat was making his traveling companion ill.

"Blake."

"Yes." He lowered his voice and relaxed, grateful the curious farmer had turned back to his field.

"It looks like the same truck." Her voice quaked, and she pulled her arms tighter around her middle.

"It's okay. I understand."

They sat there for a few moments while he held her and contemplated how to proceed. He had to get them to the border before nightfall, and the battered truck was their only option. Her feet were swelling with the heat, and her pulse, and most likely her blood pressure, had escalated. She needed more than just fruit to sustain the unborn life growing inside of her. She needed a doctor. "Ava, look at me." She turned to face him. "You need to get off your feet. I'm worried about your health and the health of your baby."

Concern etched across her face as she reached down and caressed her abdomen. "I know. I just don't know if I can do it."

Blake thought about his options. He wouldn't force her to do anything, but daylight was wearing thin. Taking her hand in his, he gave it a gentle squeeze. *God help me.* He looked out over the horizon. *We're so close.*

"Listen to me." He glanced back at her and helped her sit up. "You're stronger than any woman I've ever met. I know what you went through with your missionary team was extremely hard, and from my experience, you'll carry that memory for the rest of your life." He was not about to sugarcoat their situation. She'd already proven she was not a frail woman, and today, he'd treat her like one of his troops. Glancing down at her pink tennis shoes, he smiled. *I might need to get her a pair of boots when we get to the base.* Clearing his throat, he continued, "We need to get across the border before nightfall. I need you to push past your fear and get in the truck."

Ava blinked at him, and a spark of determination flashed in her eyes.

That's it. There's the fire I've seen before.

She glanced back at the truck, and Blake sensed she fought an internal battle.

"How do you do it?"

"Do what?"

She glanced back at him. "Put behind you what you've been through?"

His body tensed. He'd not shared much of his job, but he sensed she'd drawn her own conclusions. "It's never behind me." He glanced at the truck, and an uncomfortable pressure wrapped around his heart. "Every day, it's a battle. Sometimes I close my eyes, and I see things—things I can't change." The memory of the girl in the river came rushing into his mind like a dam that had just broken.

"It takes time. Time to heal." He turned and looked at her. Staring into the electric blue of her eyes, an urge to wipe away all her fears sparked inside of him. "Those memories will always be there, Ava. But as days go on, they'll become less pronounced."

The air stilled between them. He understood what she was going through, but most of his life, he'd just chosen to push those feelings down like packed wet sand in a bucket. Watching her struggle, the uneasy flashbacks of his job threatened to claw their way up from where he'd buried them.

He swallowed back an unwanted lump in his throat and tried to steady his voice. "I'll be here for you. Anytime you need a shoulder to lean on." Lifting his hand, he cradled her cheek. "But I need to get you in that truck, so I can get you and your baby to safety."

She nodded. "I want to try."

Getting to his feet, he slung the backpack over his shoulder and held out his hand to her. "I want you to keep your eyes on me and keep ahold of my hand."

She wrapped a death grip around his fingers as he pulled her up, and they walked toward the vehicle.

"Can you sing for me?"

"What?"

"I want you to sing like you did the night we first met." He flashed her a grin. He needed to think of a way to get her mind off of her fear. "You have a beautiful voice." Sweeping his arm out across the scope of the scenery, he said, "God created all of this, and we are walking through His landscape. I know what we are going through right now seems chaotic and fearful, but He *will* get us home safely."

Ava nodded. When she opened her lips, a melody encircled them like a spring breeze, and Blake's heart skipped a beat. From his peripheral, he noticed the farmers glance in their direction. "It seems even the locals know an angelic voice when they hear one."

Pink rose in her cheeks, but she kept her gaze level with his.

After they reached the truck, he turned and motioned to the passenger seat. She paused her song, wrapped her arms around his neck, and whispered a *thank you* that sent a tingle through his entire body. She held on to him for several seconds, and as her body relaxed, he reluctantly stepped out of her embrace. "Anytime."

After he helped her get in the truck, he flung the backpack onto the floor. She leaned against the headrest, shut her eyes, and returned to her song. Blake took another long second to study her before shutting the door. Then, rounding the truck, he jumped into the driver's seat.

Unable to resist, he glanced in her direction. *I could listen to her voice forever.* Ava opened her eyes and caught him staring. He cleared his throat and flashed her a smile. *Forever.*

Starting up the truck, her hand slid over and grasped his fingers. He wasn't sure what transpired between them in that brief moment, but if he could bottle it up and preserve it, he would. *Don't get too attached, Martin. She's heading back to her life in Dallas. Back to a life that's normal. Back to a life without you.*

Giving her hand a quick squeeze, he tugged out of her grasp, shifted the truck into drive, and drove as fast as he could toward the Kenyan border.

CHAPTER EIGHTEEN

Ava lifted a lazy eyelid as she tried to adjust to the sunlight slicing through the window. Her vision blurred, and she blinked several times to clear the haze. Then, closing her eyes again, she sighed as the crisp, clean sheets brushed against her skin. Ava grinned. *I'm so glad to be in a clean bed again.*

Fluttering her eyes open, she forced herself to acclimate to the light. The uninspiring tan walls wrapped around her, and she frowned. Fluorescent lighting, one window, and no pictures. This place could use some sprucing up.

Blake's smooth male voice pulled her out of her designer thoughts, and her heart quickened. She turned onto her side, careful not to snag the IV draping from the crook in her arm.

A whisper of cool air floated over her, and Ava reflexively tugged at the olive-green blanket wrapped around her body. Blake sat next to her bed, holding a newspaper in front of him with one hand and a cell phone to his ear with the other. She squinted and tried to read the scribbled lines on the thin grey paper.

"*Au revoir.*" His voice floated across her ears.

Ava rubbed her eyes, trying to wipe away the sleepy cobwebs from her mind. "Were you speaking French?"

He dropped the newspaper and smiled. "*Oui.*"

Staring at him, she blinked. *Well, he certainly looks ... different.* Now in a clean T-shirt and sporting a fresh haircut, Blake looked like he'd just stepped out of a recruiting commercial for the Navy Seals. Ava pinched her eyes shut, wondering what rabbit hole she'd just fallen into—or woke up in.

Blake chuckled, and her eyes popped open. Then, after he shoved the cell phone into his pocket, he flashed her a quick grin and snapped the newspaper back in front of his face. Lifting her head off the pillow, she tried to decipher the writing across the newspaper a second time. "Is that a French newspaper?"

He lowered the paper, folded it in his lap, and leaned forward, so his face hovered only inches from hers. "It is."

The fresh scent of masculine soap and shampoo tickled her nostrils, making her want to curl up in a ball and purr like a kitten. His lips twitched into a half smile, and she sighed. Reluctantly, she pulled her gaze from Blake's bright green eyes and glanced back down at his clothes. He wore boots, fatigue pants, and a black T-shirt with sleeves that clung to his arms like a second skin. Glancing up, Ava resisted running her fingers across his evenly trimmed beard.

"Do you speak the language?" He threw out the question in a husky whisper while she studied him.

"What? Do I speak French? No."

"Good. I'd hate to have to interrogate you before you left."

She chuckled, still weighted with sleepiness. "I'd like to see you try."

Sitting back in the chair, Blake threw her a boyish look.

"I'm not sure you would." He folded his hands in his lap and steepled his fingers. "In your weakened state, I'd find out all of your secrets, Ava Marie Stewart."

Her skin tingled beneath the cotton sheets. Hearing him say her full name sounded like a soft melody he'd composed just for her. Of course, her name probably wasn't all he'd uncovered—he most likely knew what street she lived on and what model of car sat in her garage.

Ava closed her eyes before speaking. It was easier to think when not staring at his handsome face. "Please tell me we're in Paris."

Blake's laughter bounced around the room. "I'm afraid not."

"Texas?" She opened one eye.

"Wrong again."

She groaned. "Am I still in Africa?"

"Yes, Kenya."

The thought of still being on the continent of her worst nightmare troubled her. However, the fact that Blake sat only a few inches away from her made her apprehension evaporate immediately.

"So, why French?"

He smiled but skirted the question. "Have you ever been to Paris?"

She released a long breath, thinking about her answer. "No, but I've always wanted to go." Her mind drifted to the beautiful architecture and design photos she'd seen of the city. The place was an interior designer's dream. Someday she planned to go there to expand her creative palette. Thinking about it now ushered a cloud of sadness over her thoughts. She quickly pushed it away. "Life, well, you know," she hesitated, then said, "Sometimes life has a way of disrupting your plans."

He nodded, and she recognized a hint of understanding in his eyes.

"How many languages do you speak?" Ava threw out the question hoping to change the path of her thoughts.

"Fluently?" His lips curled into a cat-that-ate-the-canary grin. "Five."

She blinked. "Really?"

"Yep."

What does this man do for a living?

"Do you know any?"

"Huh?" His question interrupted her thoughts.

"Languages?"

"No, I'm afraid not."

Blake muttered something under his breath, then folded his arms in satisfaction.

"Care to share?"

He shook his head and shot her an ornery look.

Ava rolled her eyes. It warmed her heart to be joking with him again. "Well, actually, I do speak Texan."

"What?"

"I speak Texan. So if you're ever in Dallas, look me up. I can be your interpreter."

"I'll remember that." He chuckled before he lifted the newspaper again.

Shifting her body, she tried to turn onto her back. Awkwardly, she lifted her blankets and stretched her legs all the way to her toes. A peek under the sheets confirmed she wore only a hospital gown and moss-green athletic socks. Heat crept up her neck as she glanced in Blake's direction.

"We have a wonderful medical team who took great care of you when we arrived." He kept the newspaper in front of his face as he talked.

Her cheeks burned even more. Along with understanding

several languages, he had the uncanny ability to read her mind. Giving a quick tug on the sheets, she tucked them under her chin, carefully leaving the one hand attached to the IV out in the open.

"They gave you fluids and vitamins." Blake peeked over the newspaper as he continued. "From what they tell me, you and the baby are doing quite well."

She flashed him a weak smile. *At least he had no part in getting me into this unflattering hospital gown.* Ava sighed. *Why does it matter? Who am I trying to impress? In a few days, I won't ever see him again.* The thought sat like a heavy stone on her chest, and she quickly cast it away.

"How long have we been here?" She sensed she'd been asleep for a long time, but the haze in her mind made her internal clock feel upside down.

"Fourteen hours." He folded the paper and set it on the nightstand.

"How long have you been sitting there?" The question popped out, embarrassment immediately following.

He shrugged. "A few hours."

"Oh." The thought he'd been watching her sleep sent another round of warm shivers through her body.

Blake stood and walked toward the sunlit window. He moved without flinching in pain, and she sent out a silent prayer of thanks for his healing.

"I was really concerned about you, Ava." He continued to gaze out the window. "Your heart rate dropped just before we got here, and ..."

She swallowed back a lump in her throat. Considering everything they'd been through together in such a short time, her heart swelled with gratitude. Even now, he looked like her fearless protector, standing guard at the foot of her bed. Ava didn't know what to say to him to make him understand how thankful she was for all he'd done for her during their confinement and escape.

"Blake, I ..." Her voice caught when he turned. Their hearts collided like a final crescendo of a symphony, and there was no need for words between them. Neither time nor distance would ever pull apart the connective thread woven through their life stories.

Blake raked his hand across his shorn hair and moved to the door. She recognized his discomfort since the same emotions made her insides a tangled mess too.

"I'm going to grab some coffee." He paused before he grabbed the door handle. "Can I get you anything? Some lunch, maybe?"

Her stomach growled in response. She groaned and wished she could disappear under the hospital bed.

"I guess that's a *yes*."

She nodded and resisted the urge to yank the covers over her head to conceal her flaming cheeks.

"I'll head over to the chow hall and see what I can grab for us."

For us? "Okay." The word squeaked out, and Ava cringed.

Blake turned the doorknob, glanced back at her over his shoulder, then bolted out the door.

CHAPTER NINETEEN

K nocking twice, Blake poked his head into her room. "Need anything before we call it a night?"

Ava looked up, and her blood heated. She'd thought about him ever since dinner. They'd been at the base for over a week, and knowing this was their last night together made her chest tighten with sadness. *If only I could make time stand still.* "Do you know anywhere I could get a hot cup of tea?"

His eyes brightened. "Sure, come with me."

She followed him out the door, across the dirt road, to a small temporary wood building. He pushed through the door and flipped on the light switch. The fluorescent bulbs hummed to life.

"Let me get some water heating for you." He motioned to the room and smiled. "Make yourself at home."

Ava glanced around the sizeable boxy room and took in the drab colors and textures. The center of the room was a U-shape configuration of couches with wooden arms and flat foam cushions. Blake shuffled through cupboards and drawers in the small kitchenette nestled in the far corner of the room. The compact space had a few coffee pots, a popcorn maker, and a midsize refrigerator. "Guess the military isn't a fan of art?" She motioned to the bare walls.

"No, but we do know what time it is—everywhere." He nodded at the triple row of black and white clocks. They displayed times from all over the world.

She muffled a giggle. Feeling more secure and rested than she had in weeks, her creative juices bubbled inside her as she imagined how she'd decorate the sparse space. Billowy curtains and matching throw pillows were probably the last things on the minds of the soldiers who frequented the room.

"I feel as if I've stepped back in time." She ran her hand over a 1970s veneer mid-century coffee table with canted peg legs. Pointing to the walls, she smiled. "And what is with this wall color?"

"You don't like this particular shade of tan?"

"I don't mind it, but it's everywhere." She walked over and studied the walls, a mixture of desert sand and apricot. "What do they even call this color?"

"You're asking the wrong guy." He flicked the switch on the coffee pot to heat the water. "From my understanding, there are several shades of this particular tan to choose from if you're interested. They sell it in bulk."

Ava lowered herself onto the couch. "I think I'll pass." Her arms brushed against the rough woven fabric on the dark maroon cushion, and she grimaced. "I might order a couple of these couches, though."

Blake's laughter, along with the clinking of mugs, filled the air.

Her olfactory sense sparked to life when the final hiss of the coffee dripped into the pot. "Hmmm, that smells wonderful." She'd given up caffeine for her pregnancy, and now it seemed her senses were throwing a protest against that decision.

"Would you rather have coffee?" He held up a glass pot of dark-colored liquid.

She frowned and pointed at her middle. "I'd love to, but ..."

"Ah, got it. Sorry." A slight tinge of red traveled across his cheeks and neck before he turned to put the pot back on the hot plate.

"It's okay. It does smell good, though."

"Well, I don't mean to brag, but I can make a marginally decent pot of coffee." He turned and grinned at her. "So, what kind of tea would you like? We have a wide assortment of Earl Grey and English breakfast." As he asked the question, he shuffled through a cardboard box of teabags.

"Ah, too bad, my favorite is Lady Grey."

"Well ..."

She heard more shuffling. "Blake, I'm joking. Just give me whatever you have that says decaf."

"English breakfast it is, then."

"That sounds perfect."

Blake handed her the steaming hot mug and sat down beside her. The cushion compressed with the two of them now sitting on the same couch. She took a long sip of the tea and savored the hot liquid as it traveled down her still-irritated throat. After a few sips, she put her mug on the end table and glanced over at him. He seemed to enjoy his steamy brew because, after a few measured drinks, he exhaled a long and satisfied sigh.

"Won't that keep you up all night?"

"Not really." He placed his mug next to hers and nestled his back into the corner of the couch. He'd been quiet most of the day, and the creases across his brow made her believe his thoughts were elsewhere.

"What are you thinking about? You look like you have a lot on your mind today."

"Nothing, really."

He hesitated, but she sensed he wanted to continue with his thoughts. She knew better than to pry, so she waited, hoping he'd open up.

"There is something I want to know."

"What's that?"

"Why did you do it? Why did you come to Africa?" His right eyebrow lifted as he threw out the questions.

"You mean, why did I make such a hasty decision after the death of my husband?"

"Maybe." His expression turned serious. "Mostly, I want to understand why you came knowing you were pregnant."

It was an intimate question, and the mention of her condition made Ava hold her hand protectively against her abdomen.

He shrugged and lowed his voice. "I mean, it's none of my business. I guess I was just curious."

Ava sighed. "People make dumb decisions after the death of a loved one." She brought her hands into her lap and folded them. "I wasn't thinking too clearly." She almost said her mission trip to Uganda was a big mistake. However, sitting next to him now and feeling the warmth of his presence so near to her, there was no question she'd make the same decision all over again. If only to have met him.

Blake glanced at her with his signature intense stare. Was he trying to read her thoughts? She took a quick breath, then fiddled with the seam on the couch. "Would you like the short version or the long version of what brought me to this place?"

He sighed, then stood and leaned against the wall across

112

from her. Folding his arms across his broad chest, he replaced his intense look with a pensive one. "Well, this is our last night together, so I'll take the long version."

Her heart sank when she caught a trace of disappointment in his voice. "Okay, then." She picked up her tea and took another sip. "I'll start from the beginning."

"Sounds good to me."

She released a deep breath to gather her strength. "I married my husband, Dylan, at a young age. We had an idyllic life." Ava crossed one of her legs under her and took another long drink. This was the first time she'd ever talked about her life with Dylan from the very beginning, and she prayed she'd have the strength to follow through.

"We went to the same church, moved in the same circle of friends, and supported each other in our dreams." She paused and swallowed the lump threatening to form in her throat. "About five years into our marriage, we found out we were expecting a baby girl." As she forced a smile, her eyes clouded with moisture. "Evelyn's heart was weak, and we went to several doctors to get the best help for her we could. Unfortunately, there was nothing anyone could do." She sniffled and sat her mug back down on the table. Blake grabbed a tissue box, handed it to her, then reclaimed his position against the wall.

"She was mine for four years." Sniffling again, she wiped her nose. "Her heart weakened significantly, and she needed to be admitted to the hospital. God was gracious, though. He took Evelyn home after only four weeks, and she didn't suffer."

Ava looked up, and Blake's eyes glistened with tears. Then, unfolding his arms, he slipped into the chair in front of her and took one of her hands in his. She studied their crisscrossed fingers, and a wave of warmth crept over her. He'd reacted the same way their first night together when he reached over and grasped her hand as they lay on the dirt floor.

"I'm so sorry, Ava." The husky tenor of his voice caused fresh tears to puddle in her lashes.

She picked out a clean tissue and dabbed her eyes.

"It's okay if you don't want to continue." He gave her hand another squeeze and continued to hold on to it. "I didn't mean for you to bring up so many sad memories."

"No, I want to. It's probably helpful if you understand why I ran from my life back in Dallas."

He gave her hand another squeeze before he released it and sat back in his chair. She picked up her mug of hot tea and wrapped her hands around the cup, hoping to replace the warmth of his touch.

"My mother was involved in a car accident a year after Evelyn passed, and the complications left her unresponsive and on life support." Blake kept his eyes laser-focused on hers as she took another deep breath and continued. "Two weeks after the accident, she passed away. I never got to say goodbye."

"What about your father?"

Ava shook her head. Her dad had abandoned her before she was a teen, but that wasn't a road she wanted to travel down today. "My mother was all I had, and when she died, I felt very alone."

"But you had your husband?"

"I did." She hesitated, recalling the long nights of silence between her and Dylan. It saddened her to think they were never able to recover from their loss. "Something happens in a marriage when you lose a child. Some couples never recover. We struggled a lot, but we worked hard to stay connected. Just like any couple, we had our ups and downs." Reaching out, she pulled another tissue from the box. "Dylan loved God, and he loved me, but sometimes I struggled to recapture my joy in our marriage after Evelyn died. We both did."

Ava's throat constricted, and she fought to swallow down another round of tears. "Dylan and I ... well, we never really reconnected." She paused and forced herself to complete her thought. "He was in a cycling accident and died instantly." She closed her eyes, still remembering the call she'd received from the police officer who arrived at the scene first. She opened her eyes and added, "In a few months, I'm due in court. I'll have to face the woman who—hit Dylan."

"I'm so sorry, Ava." This time, Blake pulled both of her hands into his. "I had no idea what you were dealing with. Will you please forgive me?"

"Forgive you?"

The muscles along his jawline contracted. "I acted like a jerk sometimes. I know I was a little intense to be around, and ..."

She held up her hand to stop him. "I was an emotional mess. Not to mention constantly sick." The memory of being ill so often in front of him made her cringe with embarrassment. Several more tears trickled down her cheeks. Finally, Blake released one of her hands and used his thumb to wipe them away.

"I didn't mind." His lips curved into a smile, and the two stayed anchored in each other's stare for a few more moments.

She sniffled as Blake released her other hand and passed her a few more tissues. Wiping her face, she inhaled a long, deep breath. It felt cathartic to talk with him and finally break loose from her pent-up sorrows. She smiled back at him, thankful he was willing to listen.

"Everyone handles traumatic events differently." His words broke through the silence as he shot a brief glance down at her midsection. "From what I've read, you handled things extremely well in your condition."

Ava chuckled through her tears. "From what you've read?"

He shrugged. "In my line of work, I'm not usually around pregnant women." Blake glanced down at his boots. For a quick second, his cheeks flamed crimson, then the color vanished. "I don't have any sisters, so I read some things."

The admittance made her heart melt. She imagined him sitting with his military buddies, reading a chapter of *What to Expect When You Are Expecting* between trying to plan his next mission.

"Besides, you slept for a long time. I had to find something to read."

"It was either that or French newspapers, right?"

"Yes." Pausing, he added, "I actually prefer crime novels or military strategy documents."

"Of course you do."

The heavy mood lifted for a moment, and Ava was grateful for the reprieve. Talking about her loss and her grief had been a hard path to wander down. "So, tell me, Blake Martin," she leaned back and moved her legs out in front of her to stretch out the kinks.

"Tell you what?"

Hesitating, she contemplated whether to ask the question rolling around in her mind. "Have you ever been married?" She looked down at his ring finger and motioned with her hand. "I doubt you could wear it a lot during your work hours," she smiled, remembering his observations of her, "but I don't see any tan lines."

Blake smiled. He seemed to understand her reference to their inside joke. "No, I've never been married."

She lifted her brows, goading him to go on with an explanation. "Interesting."

"What does that mean?"

"Nothing."

"Oh, no, you don't. Go ahead and say what you were going to say." He waved a hand, motioning for her to continue. "I've heard it all already." He tugged his mouth into a half-hearted grin. "I have a mom who likes to remind me she doesn't have any grandchildren."

"I mean, you are in your thirties." Ava giggled and threw out another question. "Have you ever thought of settling down?" After a lengthy pause, she added, "To finally give your mother some grandkids?"

"Oh. My. Goodness." He emphasized each word separately as he slapped his thigh.

"What?"

"It all makes sense now."

"What's that?"

"My mother must have orchestrated this whole event." He clapped his hands with a gleam in his eye. "She sent you to Africa to give me grief about grandchildren. Didn't she?"

Laughter shook her body. "Yes, that's exactly why I was waiting for you in that miserable place."

"I knew it." His smile widened, showing off his perfect gleaming white teeth. He quieted, then his tone turned serious. "To answer your question, yes, I do want to settle down."

She nodded and waited for him to continue.

"My job, well, it's not a very good conversation starter on first dates. 'So, what do you do for a living?' 'Well, I can't really divulge any of that information.'"

"I guess I could see how that would be a deal-breaker." For a second, she thought she detected a flash of disappointment edge across his face. She leaned back on the couch and brought her legs up beside her on the cushion again. "I hate to say it, but I wouldn't be a good reference for your dates."

Blake raised an eyebrow.

"Your job seems pretty dangerous to me." She frowned, remembering the night their captors dragged his body before her. "I'd tell your date to run and hold a sign above your head that said 'man prone to danger and injuries.'"

"Oh, thanks."

"Sure, anytime." She raised her mug in the air. "Us girls have to look out for each other."

He laughed. "Oh, I almost forgot." Bouncing out of his chair, he said, "I have a few of your things in my room. I'll be right back."

"Okay."

As he walked out the door, Ava wanted to burst into tears. The night was going too fast, and her soul begged for it to slow down. The heaviness of her days in Uganda wrapped around her like a shroud and she'd found it hard to sleep at night. Every time she closed her eyes, the nightmares of her captivity invaded her thoughts. The guards never abused her, but the isolation and uncertainty about her life during those days were complex emotions she needed to make sense of. She missed having Blake in the same room and hearing him breathe as he slept. Too many times, she awoke alone and afraid in the dark. Now, as she started to unpack all of the grief she'd been holding onto since the death of her little girl, Ava felt like she was underwater, gasping for air.

As she looked back at the door, her chest tightened. Blake's nearness represented security to her, and their time in Uganda would be etched onto her heart for the rest of her life. She blinked as her eyes filled with tears. The uncomfortable memory of him, injured and in desperate need of medical care, clawed across her mind. She'd never forget the hours it took to clean his wounds and the prayers she said for his health. Ava wiped her eyes with the back of her hand and sent out a silent prayer to God for her own emotional healing. If for nothing else but for the health of her unborn baby.

Feeling exhausted, Ava stretched her legs out on the couch, laid her head back, and closed her eyes. She wasn't sure what the future held, but she was confident Blake and Uganda had left a permanent mark on her heart that time or distance would never erase.

CHAPTER TWENTY

Blake walked back into the room and slowed. Ava rested, most likely uncomfortably, in the corner of the couch.

He laid her things down on the table. It felt good to finally relax, knowing she was safe from harm and receiving the medical attention she and her baby needed. But, as he looked over at the small pile of items—Colby's medical jacket, her husband's watch, a pair of pink tennis shoes that had seen better days, and a new basic issue duffle bag with the tags still on it—his heart stalled.

Tomorrow at dawn, she'd get on a plane and fly thousands of miles away from his reach and protection. He smiled. Not that she needed his protection. He'd seen a fiery spirit in her he'd only ever witnessed in the soldiers he served with. She'd be fine without him.

He lowered himself onto the couch next to her, and his pulse quickened. If only he could slow down time. Stop the sun from rising. Forcibly hold back the hands of the ticking clocks —anything to stop her from getting on the plane.

Ava stirred beside him. When she stretched out her legs,

her stockinged feet rested against his thigh. She looked peaceful, and her cheeks were rosy with healthy color. Memories of their time together in captivity skittered across his mind, and he knew she'd changed him, but he couldn't pinpoint how.

Along with their time in Uganda, their shared faith was another link binding them together. Her personal walk with God wasn't forced. It was genuine. The attraction of that connection pulled him in like a magnet.

Blake blew out a deep breath. A desire stirred in his soul, one he'd not entertained before. For the past week, he told himself he'd finished the mission, and his role in her life was over. She was safe, and now he needed to let her go. But like a stubborn child, his heart refused to comply.

Ava turned onto her back. Opening her eyes, she smiled up at him. "I'm sorry, I must have dozed off."

She sounded sleepy as she sat up and swung her legs to the ground. *She's beautiful.* The thought flew through his mind, and for a few seconds, his tongue stuck to the roof of his mouth.

"Ava, I ..." The words sounded breathless as he ordered his emotions to get back in line. He couldn't ask her to stay. That wasn't even an option. He knew he couldn't follow her. He had his other mission to complete—the official one. Blake looked up. She kept her gaze on him, waiting for him to finish his sentence. Warmth crept across his collar as he tried to unpack his emotions. *I don't want this to be the last time we ever see each other.*

The shadow of sadness still lingered in her expression, and he understood the depth of what she'd shared about her daughter's death remained fresh in her mind. *Not to mention, she's still grieving the loss of her husband.*

"I'm truly sorry about your husband—what happened to

him, I mean." The words came out in a jumbled mess as he tried to untangle his thoughts. "He sounded like a faithful man of God and … a good husband."

"Thank you." Her voice caught. "He was. He was a wonderful provider, and he was always there for me."

For a moment, they both stayed silent. Blake stared at the floor, uncertain of what to say next. He wanted to tell her he'd be there for her too, but with his job and her grief, the timing was wrong. He shook his head to recalibrate his thoughts.

"There are little things that happen after your spouse dies." Ava's voice broke through the silence and prompted him to look back in her direction.

"Like what?" He was grateful she'd picked up the conversation since his thoughts flailed around like a fish out of water.

"Well, for one thing, I packed away all of my bracelets."

He waited for her to explain.

She held out her bare wrist. "It's not easy to close a clasp by yourself." Pretending to have a bracelet draped over her wrist, she mimicked closing the clasp.

He nodded as she continued.

"I remember the first Sunday I decided to go to church. Alone. I wanted to wear the bracelet Dylan gave me for our anniversary. I tried every imaginable way to close it, and I couldn't get it to connect securely on my wrist." She let out an exasperated breath. "I'd always had Dylan around to help me work the clasp."

She paused, and Blake sensed her struggle to finish.

"Brushing his teeth, sitting at the computer," she chuckled softly. "Or one time, in the shower." Ava looked up at him, and through her sorrow, she smiled. "I would hold out my wrist, and Dylan would close it. Sometimes without even looking." Pausing, a shadow traced over her expression.

"That morning, after I'd wrestled with the bracelet, I sat down on the side of the tub in our master bath and cried for an hour."

Reflexively, he reached over and grasped her hand.

"After that, I gathered every bracelet, packed them away, and put them in the attic."

She intertwined her fingers with his, and a warm shiver traveled up his arm.

"A little crazy, huh?"

"Not really." His voice hitched, but he quickly recovered. "A pure and simple love like that just doesn't happen. It grows over time." He looked down at their hands, and his emotions warred inside of him. "And it probably grows even stronger through trials."

He glanced at the folded hospital uniform shirt next to her things. Someone had cleaned it, but a few blood stains still lingered on the sleeves. "What about the doctor?" The question flew off his lips before he could reign it in.

"Colby? You mean him and me?"

He nodded. His hand released hers as he pulled back his shoulders and straightened his spine.

"Oh, heavens, no! We were just good friends. We volunteered at church together." Ava fumbled with the drawstring in her navy-blue sweatpants. "He was five years my junior, and I taught his niece in Sunday school."

The war inside him tipped to one side, and guilt-ridden relief flooded his thoughts.

"Oh, no." Ava brought her hand up to her mouth. "His poor family." Her cheeks paled.

"It'll be okay." He reached for her hand again and tried to keep his voice steady. "We've notified your church about the situation, and I've sent a group to go find ..." Her hand trembled in his palm. He wished for an easier way to say what he needed to say. "There's a team going out to the scene of the accident as we speak."

"It's been so long, will they even ..." She didn't complete her question, but Blake understood precisely what she asked.

"In my experience, the family wants the body, no matter how long it's been." He tempered his words with deliberate tenderness and silently prayed for her comfort.

Ava looked up at him, anguish covering her expression.

"It will help with closure."

She nodded. "Thank you."

"Of course." His pulse quickened, and he studied their hands again, imagining what it might be like to have her hand in his every day for the rest of his life. Then, shaking off the thought, he released his grip and raked his fingers across his hair. "I don't understand the loss of a spouse"—he angled his body toward her on the couch—"but when my brother Benjamin passed away a few years ago, it devastated our entire family."

"What happened?"

"He'd been assigned to do door-to-door checks in a remote village in Afghanistan." Blake let his mind wander back to the day he received the news about Benjamin. The memory was difficult to uncrate, but he felt compelled to share this part of his life with her. "From what they told me, it was a homemade explosive strapped to an empty baby stroller."

Ava gasped. "I'm sorry. That's awful."

"A few members of his team lingered with the tank about a mile away while a detail kept watch on the rooftops. It all happened so fast." He shook his head, still in disbelief. "The thing that bothers me most—he was weeks from coming home. We'd talked earlier that morning." Blake released a breath as the layers of the memory snaked around his mind. "He told me he couldn't wait to get home on R & R." His breath hitched. "It's odd what we remember about those last hours we talk with someone before they ..."

Swallowing back the lump wedged in his throat, he continued, "We joked about coffee. I gave him a hard time because he liked the expensive stuff with way too much cream." Chuckling, Blake shook his head. "I like mine black. Just black." A heaviness filled his chest as he added, "Benjamin told me his first stop on his way home would be to a coffee shop. He wanted a hazelnut latte with two shots." Fighting back a wave of grief, Blake took a few seconds to recall Benjamin's voice over the phone. "That was our last conversation. He died instantly." *God, it's still so painful to think about.*

He hadn't talked about this with anyone other than his parents and his older brother. Blake trusted Ava, and it felt good to let her in.

"I'm so sorry, Blake." She reached out and touched his arm.

Her touch warmed his skin. He wanted so badly for her to understand he wasn't all tactical movements and strategy—he could relate to her broken heart.

"I would tease him and tell him to go home and get a normal job." He frowned. "Ben wouldn't listen. Instead, he said he was born to crawl in the sand, and he loved the smell of jet fuel."

"He had a steady girlfriend back home. Chloe. They were young and madly in love. She was a military brat, so the lengthy times away didn't sway her."

"How old was he?"

"Twenty-four." Blake hung his head for a few seconds trying to unpack his thoughts and simultaneously govern his emotions. "My brother Brent and I went home for the funeral, and it was brutal. The sorrow in Chloe's eyes during the service nearly crushed me." He lifted his face and locked on to Ava's gaze. "I guess, after that, I didn't consider trying to pursue a long-term relationship while attached to my team. I knew I never wanted to break anyone's heart like that."

She nodded but didn't comment.

I don't want to break your heart like that. Blake cleared his throat and pushed away the thought.

"Brent and I, we put on this tough masculine façade, holding in all of our emotions, at least until we got behind closed doors. But, Chloe's grief," he paused, "well, that was raw, unbridled emotion, and it nearly broke the both of us."

AVA'S VISION clouded while Blake continued to talk. She understood Chloe's pain. The memory of her own husband's funeral was still so fresh in her mind.

"The way she cried over his coffin," Blake's voice caught as he picked up his story.

Sensing his struggle, Ava let her fingers slide down his arm and rejoined her hand to his.

A weary look filtered across his expression as he continued. "I could tell the grief shattered her soul. It was heartbreaking to watch."

Ava sniffled, feeling the weight of his sorrow descend upon her.

"I had no way to comfort my mom. She was so distraught." He took in a short breath. "I'm sure it didn't help that her two remaining sons had hazardous jobs to return to." Turning to face her, he said, "My brother, Brent—well, let's just say he doesn't have a cushy desk job."

Why did the Martin men choose to live with such risk?

"And, as you've already guessed, I don't either."

Smiling, she recalled their previous conversation. "I think I've figured that out."

"However, it's actually Brent my mom should be more concerned about."

"Why's that?"

He didn't answer right away, but she sensed the walls he'd lowered for the few minutes to talk about his grief shifted back into position. "If I told you, I'd have to keep you here as my prisoner. Indefinitely." Blake's eyes sparked to life as he flashed her a wicked grin.

Ava caught her breath. His expression suggested he wasn't joking. Heat rose in her cheeks as she struggled to form a clever comeback. "Well, you did say you have a highly trained medical team here. I guess I'd be in good hands."

He ran his fingers over his beard, a nervous habit she'd come to adore since they met. "That's true, but I'm not sure my team and I are equipped to handle an infant at this facility."

Ava smiled. She enjoyed their back-and-forth and didn't want it to be her last night for them to do so. "That could be a problem since you said I'd be your prisoner *indefinitely*." The statement lingered in the air and stirred an unexpected yearning in her heart.

Blake bolted out of his seat, ripping their hands apart. "I guess you should get some shut-eye before your big day tomorrow." He picked up the mugs and placed them in the sink.

"*My* big day?"

"Yes, *you* get to go back to Texas." He attempted to make the statement sound enthusiastic, but a vibration in his voice told her he was anything but. Blake walked over to the table, placed her things in the duffle bag, and jerked the zipper closed. Looking up, he said, "You'll be home before the holidays."

She stood and moved toward him. The mood in the room shifted, and Ava's heart screamed at her to stop the night from ending. Before she could think it through, she blurted out her thoughts. "Aren't you going with me?" What a ridiculous question. Of course, he wouldn't be going with her. What business did he have in Texas?

Blake's brow furrowed, but he didn't answer. Instead, he pivoted on his heel and turned toward the door.

She walked close behind him, ready to follow him out of the room. "I mean ..." Ava struggled, hoping to fix her blunder. "Aren't you going back to the States? What about your mom? As you said, it's almost the holidays."

He halted and did an about-face, which brought him within arm's length of her body. "My mom knows I'm alive, and I have an assignment to prep for." The timbre of his voice lowered as he glanced down at her lips, then yanked his gaze back to her eyes.

She stood there transfixed. Genuine regret lined his answer, but she didn't understand why. Did he miss his family? Would he miss her?

"Where's your assignment?" It was the only thing she could think to ask. She kept her gaze level with his, but from beneath her lashes, she noticed his upper body rise and fall with each breath he took.

He took a step forward, closing the gap between them. The muscles in his jaw flexed. "That's not information I can tell you. Remember?"

"Oh, that's right." A rhythmic thudding of her heart echoed in her ears. Part of her wanted to retreat. The other part of her wanted to move in, closer, and let him wrap her up in the security of his strong arms.

For a moment, neither one of them said anything, then without warning, Blake leaned in and placed a gentle kiss on her lips. Ava closed her eyes as every limb of her body hummed with energy. Afraid to alter the atmosphere, she fought the urge to rest her hands on his chest. *Hold me.* Before another thought could enter her mind, he pulled away.

Reluctantly her eyelids fluttered open. But instead of staring up into his fierce, evergreen eyes, she was greeted with an open door and a whoosh of tepid air brushing across her heated cheeks.

Confused, Ava stepped outside in time to see Blake's retreat. Without even a glance back in her direction, his silhouette disappeared into the inky darkness.

CHAPTER TWENTY-ONE

Ava slid onto the sturdy wooden bench, a little out of breath, and scanned the courtroom. *This will finally be over.* She laid her hand on her burgeoning belly as relief washed over her.

Surviving the holidays without Dylan nearly crushed her. Now it was January—cold and dreary. The turn of the calendar promised a fresh beginning, but with grief holding her heart captive, she struggled to be excited about the new year. *In a few months, I'll be a single mother.* She blinked away the moisture in her eyes. *But you're safe now.*

A bustle of conversation floated around the room, and her lawyer, whom she was confident she no longer needed, sat beside her on the bench. Randall was a family friend, and even if she had released him from his duties, he still would've sat with her today.

A gentle stirring in her middle caused Ava to cradle her abdomen. After today, she'd focus on her future and the arrival of her baby boy. *Just a bit longer, little one.* The sorrow over her husband's accident lingered, but the gnawing demand for vengeance—forgotten. Although the seventeen-year-old woman was at fault, hitting her husband had been an accident. Ava didn't wish for her to be left with a ruined life because of a miscalculation on a rainy night. Dylan would've agreed. Ava's time in Africa had brought her life into focus, and it was time for her to pick up the pieces and move on.

Thinking about Uganda, Blake's jade eyes flashed across her memory. *That kiss.* As she recalled his lips brushing against hers, a quiver traced its way across her skin.

The next morning, as she prepared to leave, he stood outside her room, appearing as uncomfortable as she felt.

"All packed?"

She stifled a laugh. She didn't have much more than the clothes on her back. "Yeah." Glancing up at him, her heart pleaded with him to look at her. "Blake, I ..."

"The Freedom Bird leaves at oh-eight-hundred, so we better get moving." He cut her off as he motioned for her to follow him.

With a curt nod, he slipped on his sunglasses and took off down the road at a clipped pace. Her chest tightened. His crisp military fatigues and his boots clopping across the rocks suggested he was all business and fixated on his next mission —sending her back to Texas.

She followed him onto a massive plane bustling with supercharged energy. Several soldiers scooted into seats in front of her, all with happy expressions on their faces. No doubt they were excited to be going home on R & R. Blake tucked his sunglasses into the V of his uniform, his expression unreadable.

"You can sit there." He motioned to a seat near the window and then turned to speak with one of the men sitting across from her.

Ava nestled into her seat, confused and bewildered by his

standoffish attitude. Even now, watching him load her luggage into the area above her head, her heart skipped a beat. How could he let her leave and not mention anything about their kiss?

Blake turned to her. "It's been quite a journey, hasn't it?"

A flash of sorrow shadowed his expression, and a lump formed in her throat. His gaze lingered on her eyes for another brief second, then dropped to her mouth. Goosebumps traveled across her arms while she guessed at his thoughts. When the muscle in his jaw twitched, he appeared to reprimand himself and took a quick step away from her seat.

"Blake ..." Her words melted in the air, and she struggled to continue. "Thank you for everything."

"No need to thank me. We made a great team." The semi-courteous tone of his words split her heart in two.

"I hope you have a good flight, Ms. Stewart." One of the doctors approached her, breaking the uncomfortable tension between them.

Ava stood, leaned across the seat, and shook his outstretched hand. "Thank you so much for all you've done for me." She looked back at Blake. "I'll never forget it."

"Of course. It's not every day Martin brings such a pleasant guest back from a mission."

She turned back to the doctor and forced a smile. Still feeling the strain of Blake's gaze, a shiver worked its way down her spine.

"I wish it could have been under better circumstances." The doctor frowned.

"Me too."

"I can imagine you're anxious to get back to the great state of Texas. I've been there a few times myself—nice place."

"Uh, yes." She shifted on one foot and cut a glance back to

Blake. His hands clenched at his side. "It's not like I could've stayed in Africa forever. Right?"

"Isn't that the truth?" The doctor bit back a chuckle. "Well, have a good flight, Ms. Stewart." He patted Blake on the shoulder, then departed the plane.

Blake pivoted in her direction before she lowered herself into her seat. Ava opened her mouth to say something. Before she could, he replaced his sunglasses, gave her a curt nod, and, without another word, exited the plane.

"This should be over in a few minutes." Her lawyer squeezed her hand and pulled her attention back to the present.

Ava nodded and released a quick breath. After arriving back in Dallas, she'd written a letter to the judge asking for leniency in the sentencing of the young woman who'd hit and killed her husband. She also asked to be able to limit her appearances in court. After continuous media coverage of her friends' deaths and her kidnapping, the trial became a prime target for the five o'clock news.

Newspapers and local television stations salivated over the story of the local widow and interior designer-turned-kidnapping-victim. If the press had their way, they'd pin all of Ava's misfortunes on the young lady standing before the judge today. She understood, according to the law, the woman would be charged with a crime. However, she prayed the girl would have some semblance of a life when this all blew over. She'd left Dallas a grief-stricken and bitter woman but returned thankful for God's grace.

Attempting to listen as the judge read through several documents, her thoughts continued to return to Uganda. *I wonder how Andrew is doing. And what about the woman from the hidden church?* A calm filled her as she recalled her time in the secluded village. *Today is good.* The words of the kind African woman echoed in her mind. Ava scanned the courtroom. She needed to remember there was always something to find in the day that was good.

Is the man good? The question floated through her mind, and a wave of sadness washed over her. She missed Blake. Sure, he was headstrong and, at times, a tad arrogant, but he'd motivated her to have courage in the face of danger. He'd listened to her when she unpacked her grief. He'd helped keep her safe. He'd kissed her.

Reflexively she traced a finger over her lips. *Where are you, Blake? Are you safe?* Her lawyer shifted next to her, and she reluctantly pulled her thoughts away from the handsome soldier.

The judge cleared his throat as he lowered the documents he'd been reading and motioned for the woman to stand. Ava's heart thumped like a drum in her ears as she listened to the sentencing. *Please, Lord, bring good out of this.*

The judge stood, and everyone in the courtroom rose to their feet. When the door closed to the judge's chambers, she exhaled a long breath, grateful she could finally go home.

"It's over." Randall wrapped an arm around her shoulders and gave her a quick hug.

"It is."

"Are you expecting a visitor?" When Randall turned, he looked past her to the back of the room.

"No. Why?" Ava shifted following his gaze and zeroed in on a tall, handsome man standing near the back of the room. "Blake?" As she said his name, her vision swayed, and she reached out for the bench to steady herself.

CHAPTER TWENTY-TWO

B lake swooped in and slipped his arms around her waist. Scents of woodsy aftershave and black coffee wafted up to her nose as gooseflesh sprang to life across her skin.

"Ava." Concern filled his voice as he held on to her. "Are you okay?"

She stood ensconced in his arms, staring up at him. "Yes. You're here." Trembling, she stepped out of his embrace and lowered herself back onto the bench.

When she caught Randall's surprised expression, her cheeks heated. "Randall, this is Blake Martin." She motioned toward Blake, attempting to wrap her mind around seeing him in the flesh. "He's the one who helped me get to safety in Africa."

Randall nodded. "Nice to meet you, Mr. Martin. Ava speaks highly of her rescuer. I know many people appreciated you keeping her safe." Randall threw Ava a quick wink as he extended a handshake toward Blake.

"I hope she told you about her part in getting us out as well." Blake looked from the older gentleman, then back to her.

Randall peered over his glasses at her as they sat low on the bridge of his nose. The motion gave him the air of a kindly grandfather. "Well, no, she hasn't."

She opened her mouth to say something, then closed it.

As if perceiving her discomfort, Randall laid a gentle hand on her shoulder. "Perhaps a story for another day."

She swallowed and prayed the sway in her gut would cease. "Yes, yes, of course."

Randall pushed his glasses back up on his nose. "I'm glad the judge considered your request today. The whole ordeal was truly just a tragic accident."

Blake sat down on the bench, and the heat from his presence wrapped around her like a summer day.

Randall flashed her a smile, then continued. "It wouldn't have benefited anyone for her to serve time. After a few months, she'll complete her community service, but this accident will be on her mind for the rest of her life."

Ava nodded. On hers too.

Randall picked up his worn leather day timer. A creature of habit, he'd yet to switch his lengthy calendar of family law appointments to a more streamlined digital form. Tucking it under his arm, he said, "I'll see you at church Ava, and again, it was nice to meet you, young man."

"Thank you, Randall."

"Anytime." His voice returned to a paternal lilt. "Go home and get some rest." He glanced down at her protruding belly, then pivoted on his heels and walked away.

A rush of mixed emotions surged through her as she turned toward Blake. "Blake." His name came out in almost a whisper. "What are you doing here?"

"I had some intel your court date was today." He grinned, and her heart melted.

He remembered.

"How did you ... when did you ..." With him so close, she couldn't link her questions together in a coherent order.

He laid a finger on her lips. The warmth of his touch silenced her. "I'm sorry, Ava." After a heartbeat, he dropped his hand.

"What?"

"I said I'm sorry." A solemn tenderness blanketed his voice. "I wanted those to be the first words I said to you today."

She remained silent, hoping he'd elaborate.

"I acted like a jerk the day you boarded the plane. Can you ever forgive me?" He lifted her chin with his forefinger. "I shouldn't have let you leave without saying ... something."

"As I recall, you did." She bit back a chuckle. "You said we made a great team, and something about it being quite a journey."

He groaned as he dropped his hand and looked past her at the caramel-colored wood wainscoting. "I'm an idiot." Raking a hand through his hair, he added, "I tried to tell myself we'd just come through a very complex several weeks, and I shouldn't make it more complicated by—"

"By kissing me?" Ava cut in, unwilling to let him off the hook.

The lines around his eyes crinkled. "Exactly."

Ava turned on the bench and faced forward. It was lunchtime, and the courtroom would be quiet for at least another thirty minutes. "Thank you for coming today. I never expected you to be here or even remember I mentioned it."

"I couldn't let you go through this alone." He motioned in the direction where the defendant had stood just minutes before. "The woman. She's so young. It's very tragic."

Ava's gaze rested on the empty wooden chair. "Her life will never be the same. I know she didn't get in her car that night intending to kill my husband."

Blake nodded.

"I've learned a lot about life and loss over the past few months. I need to believe God is authoring my steps, even in tragedy."

"That's so true."

"She'd left her house in a hurry." Ava grabbed a tissue out of her purse and dabbed away her tears. "Her grandmother had just suffered a heart attack. It was raining and dark, and despite Dylan having all the required lights and reflectors, she never saw him." Her thoughts lingered a few more moments on the vacant chair. "Dylan wasn't supposed to be cycling that night."

Blake squeezed her hand when she hesitated.

"Cycling was his outlet. It was a nice day, but the rain," pausing, she sucked in a quick breath. "The rain came out of nowhere. Typical of Texas. The summer storm blew in with a torrent of water."

Attempting to steady her voice, she continued. "The road was easy for any avid cyclist. But for him, that night, the trek ended his life." She turned back to Blake. "Before I left for Uganda, I was so angry. I wanted revenge."

Understanding flashed in his eyes.

"I wanted to wrap myself in a blanket of my own misery and never break free. God wouldn't let me. I held so much resentment toward the woman. I convinced myself she'd destroyed any bit of happiness I might ever have again." Blowing out a pent-up breath, Ava continued. "I wanted *her* to pay for being on the road that night and ultimately ending his life. But, in the end, I knew who I was angry at—God. I was convinced He'd let Dylan and me down."

She paused as another layer of her burden lifted. "Before you showed up in that prison, I told God exactly what I thought about Him." Smiling, she said, "God used my isolation to come clean about my anger and bitterness. He already knew how I felt, but because I had nowhere else to run, He forced me to admit it to myself. I got real with God, in the middle of a dirt floor with the ugliest insects I'd ever seen."

Blake tipped his head back and laughed.

"I thought the insects were big in Texas. They've got nothing on that continent."

He suppressed another chuckle as a few people streamed into the courtroom. Leaning toward her, he said, "Looks like we need to move to a new location."

She stood, her legs still unsteady.

Blake stretched out his arm and wrapped it around the small of her back. "Is everything okay?" He glanced down at her baby bump, concern etched across his face. "With you and the baby?"

"Oh, yes. I just get tired. A lot." She reached into her purse, pulled out a granola bar, and waggled it in the air. "And I probably need some lunch."

Relief washed over his features as they walked out of the courtroom and made their way to a small, secluded seating area at the end of the hall. Ava unwrapped the bar and took a small bite.

"Do you know anywhere good around here to eat?" He grinned. "I took a taxi, so I'm at your mercy for transportation."

She finished off the snack and grabbed a water bottle out of her purse to wash it down. The quick shot of sugar and protein already stabilized her. "There's a great BBQ place down the street." Glancing around the crowded hall, she added, "We can head over there in a few minutes if you'd like."

"I'm up for anything."

After he answered, she took a second to study him. Though still lean, he was less gaunt. His rich, ebony hair was shorn neatly around his neckline, and his beard had filled in thick across his jaw. Her gaze lowered to his attire. He wore a body-hugging dark navy T-shirt and chinos. *He's just as handsome as I remembered.* Ava swallowed and glanced back up at his face, hoping he'd not read her mind.

Flashing her a playful smile, he looked down at his clothes. "Is there something wrong?"

Realizing he'd caught her sizing him up, prickly heat raced across her cheeks. For so many weeks, she imagined what it would be like to see him again. Now he was here, in the flesh, sitting in front of her. She wanted to pinch herself to make sure it wasn't a dream. "I, uh ..." Stumbling over her embarrassment, she said, "I'm just so glad to see you."

"I am more than glad to see you." His voice deepened. The way it did when he said less than he was thinking.

She twitched her lips into a smile. "You asked me in the courtroom if I could ever forgive you."

"Yes, I guess I did." Blake rubbed the back of his neck.

"Well, I've been thinking about it."

"You have? For the past thirty minutes? Should I be worried?"

Ava's insides warmed. How she'd missed their back-and-forth. "I guess it depends." She let the words linger in the air as she internally weighed her response. She'd lived a lifetime these past few months, and as weak-kneed as she felt right now, she had to say something.

"Depends on what?"

"Are you going to kiss me again?" Blurting out the question, her heart lodged in her throat.

Blake's eyes widened. "I, well ..."

"And if you do, are you going to leave me, with my eyes shut, and just walk away?"

He blew out a long breath as pleasure replaced his shocked

expression. "You've been waiting a while to ask that, haven't you?"

She nodded.

"What if I say I *am* going to kiss you again? Only this time, I'll make sure your eyes are open."

Her pulse quickened as warmth blossomed from her cheeks and traveled to the tips of her toes. "I would say that sounds nice."

For a moment, silence lingered between them. Then, Blake rubbed his hand along his chin and said, "I have to leave early in the morning. I was only able to coerce a few days out of my group for leave."

Her heart sank. *What am I doing? He's only here for the day.* Africa had changed her, but she was halfway through her pregnancy and needed to prepare herself to become a single mother. She didn't have the luxury to entertain uncertainty. Or romance.

Ava tore her gaze away from his as a thousand questions exploded in her mind. When would she see him again? Would he be safe? Where was his next mission?

Blake seemed to interpret her concern as he reached out and wrapped his fingers around hers. "I want to see you again." His words pulled her away from her internal questions, and she looked back at him. "I'd like to be with you when the baby is born." His expression turned pensive. "But only if you want me to be."

She hesitated. What was he asking? Was he asking to be a part of her life? Or did he only want to support her during her time of need? After a second, she nodded. She didn't care. "I want you here."

Blake's expression lightened. "I'll do my best to be back in Dallas when the baby is due. I promise."

Her heart begged for more reassurance, but she wasn't sure what he could give. "Can you tell me where you're going?"

He shook his head and sighed. "I can't."

A lump formed in her throat as the conflict between their two worlds took up their weapons and chose sides.

"I'm going overseas." As he whispered the words, his viridescent eyes darkened like an approaching storm. "That's all the info the married men in my unit give their wives when they leave."

Ava's breath left her body. *Wives?* A startling sense of awareness washed over her as she stared down at their intertwined fingers.

Blake had just shifted the relationship, and there was no way of predicting where this path would lead.

CHAPTER TWENTY-THREE

Ava walked through the restaurant, scanning the tables for Blake. After landing at DFW today, he'd asked if she could meet him for lunch. The months had flown by, but the idea of seeing him again sparked a fire in her belly.

Inhaling a quick breath, Ava rested her hand on her middle. Her baby boy, who'd almost outgrown his living space, shifted, then placed a soft kick against her ribs. *Any day now, little one.* Two days from her due date, she was more than ready to shed some weight in this summer heat.

With cumbersome steps, she weaved through the tables of the busy restaurant. Seated next to the window, Blake eyed her as he stood and waited for her to reach the table.

When she approached, he took her hand. "You look"—Blake glanced at her protruding belly—"radiant."

"Thank you." After he released her hand, she slid into a chair, a little out of breath, "I'm sorry for being a few minutes late. My client meeting went a little longer than expected."

"Not a problem. I'm on leave." He took his seat next to her

and flashed her a warm smile. "For a few days at least, I don't have a schedule."

Patting her baby bump, she said, "I'm looking forward to some time off. I'm hoping to finalize the sketches for this job before I take *my* leave."

Blake chuckled. "Are your clients going to make it without you?"

"I'm not sure. While I was in Uganda, one of my regulars wallpapered her office."

"Tried their hand at a little DIY?"

"She put the pattern up horizontally." Ava smiled. "The design called for vertical."

"Ouch. That's not good."

"It wasn't. I hired someone to remove it, and now we're back to square one. The pattern's still on back order." Ava hung her laptop bag on the back of her seat. "Thankfully, Mr. Kentwood, with whom I met today, won't have his downtown office space ready for me to decorate for three months." She smoothed the creases on her billowy button-down shirt. "It will take longer than that to commission the Amish furniture pieces he wants to use."

"I can imagine."

"You wouldn't believe what people will pay for handmade furniture these days."

The waitress sidled up to the table, set down their glasses of water, then took their order. Before she left, Blake said, "We might have another join us for lunch. He's running a little behind."

The waitress nodded. "No problem, sir. I'll put in your drink orders and check back with you."

Blake glanced back at her after the waitress walked away. "I invited Brent to lunch with us. I hope that's okay."

She'd lifted her glass to her lips, but as his words hit her, her arm stopped mid-motion. "Um, sure."

"Brent's been asking to meet you, and he has a layover in Dallas today." Blake shrugged. "I thought this would be a great time."

"Are you sure this is a good time?" She set her drink down and motioned toward her massive belly. "I feel like we'll have a lot to explain."

"Oh, no, don't blame your condition on me." He leaned in, his eyes full of humor. "Brent is very moral. He'd probably punch me in the middle of this restaurant."

She slapped him playfully on the forearm. "I mean, he's going to show up and meet your *friend*," Ava held finger quotes in the air to emphasize the word friend. "Who happens to be nine months pregnant."

"To calm your fears a bit, Brent knows I flew in to be with you." He reached out and took her hand. "And the baby."

"He does?" It surprised her to be a topic of conversation between him and his brother.

"Yes, he does."

She pursed her lips, unsure how to respond. Then, while she mulled it over, a tall, confident-looking man strolled through the restaurant and sauntered up to their table.

Blake released her hand and darted out of his chair. "Hey Brent, how have you been?" The two of them came together in a quick bear hug.

"Life's well!"

"This is my older brother Brent." Blake grinned from ear to ear as he introduced his sibling. "And this is Ava."

"Hello, Ava. It's nice to finally meet you." Brent smiled and offered her his hand.

When he stepped back, she noticed the family resemblance. The brothers shared the same emerald green eyes and straight nose. However, Brent's jaw was clean-shaven, and he stood an inch or so taller with a leaner build.

"I'm the better-looking one." Brent flashed her a mischievous grin.

Another Martin trait—humor. She chuckled. In her heart, she silently disagreed.

"So, tell me, how did this all begin?" Brent motioned between Blake and her as the two brothers sat down.

A quick shiver ran through her. Brent's question cut straight to the point. She looked to Blake, curious how he'd answer since they'd never clearly defined what *was* going on between them.

Blake bit back a chuckle as he took a sip of his drink. "Well, it all started in a village in Africa."

Brent slapped Blake on the shoulder. "Doesn't it always?"

Ava relaxed in her seat, enjoying the banter between the two.

"Catch me up. It's been a long time." Brent cut a brief glimpse at her midsection. "I've been off the grid for a few weeks. So, I may have missed some things."

Blake motioned for the waitress to come and take Brent's order. "Yes, you have."

Brent ordered quickly, then he glanced back at the two of them, waiting for one of them to fill him in.

"I told Brent how we met, but not all the exciting details." The glint in Blake's eyes told her he wasn't caught off guard by the probing inquiry.

"You mean like the giant spiders who wanted to eat us for dinner?" She cocked an eyebrow, then threw a look at Brent.

Brent bent his head back and laughed.

"She has a thing about bugs." Blake chimed in. "Even the little ones."

"Don't worry, Ava. I totally get it. I'm not a fan of them either."

"Thank you, Brent." She glanced back at Blake and smirked.

"So, back to our story ..." Blake put his fork down after he took a quick bite of his salad.

Ava's heart melted. *Our story.* As if sensing her thoughts, he reached out and held her hand across the table. Brent cut his gaze at their hands, then shot Blake a knowing look. Ava's insides warmed like a blacktop on a summer day. Instead of releasing her, Blake gave her hand a reassuring squeeze. He winked at her and continued to rattle on about their adventures in Africa.

"Ava saved my life. Would you believe she has great nursing skills?"

Brent waggled his eyebrows at Blake. "Is that so?"

"True story." Blake squeezed her hand a second time, then released it.

The blazing heat inside her walked around her neck and crawled up her cheeks. Ava reached for her water and took a drink.

"Sounds like a regular Florence Nightingale." Brent folded his arms and leaned back in his chair.

She shook her head as she hovered on the outskirts of the conversation. After a few more details about their captivity, Blake finished the retelling of their time in Uganda and ended with the escape that brought them to a military base in Kenya.

"Wow. What a way to start a relationship." Brent took a sip of his water as the table quieted.

A relationship? Ava lowered her gaze, afraid to catch the look of either brother.

Blake cleared his throat. "So, what's occupying your life this week, Brent?

Brent paused, then accepted the redirect. "Work."

Both of the brothers erupted into laughter.

As they continued their lunch, Brent and Blake caught up on each other's lives, discussing everything from politics to the most reliable truck to haul Brent's new boat. She enjoyed watching Blake with his brother—his demeanor relaxed and peaceful. What would it have been like to meet their younger brother Benjamin in the same capacity?

The three talked for over an hour, and Brent made Ava feel like they'd been friends for years. She appreciated how Brent didn't push for more information about her and Blake. It made it easier to relax and finish her meal. Still, the few knowing glances between them led her to believe Blake shared more about her over private conversations than he'd let on.

"I hate to break up our lunch, but it's time for me to go." Brent checked his watch. "My flight leaves in three hours, and you know the drive to the airport can make a man want to cry."

Blake nodded. "I hear you."

"Looks like you'll be flying into Dallas more often?" Brent glanced at her, then cocked his head toward Blake.

"I certainly hope so."

Her heart cartwheeled to life. *Me too.*

Brent and Blake said their goodbyes, and silence hung in the air for a few moments after Brent left the table. Ava pushed around the last bites of key lime pie on her plate while her thoughts overflowed with questions.

"Ava." Blake leaned toward her and reached for her unoccupied hand under the table. "I hope you know you're more than just a friend to me."

He swallowed hard, then opened his mouth to say something else, hesitating as if second-guessing his next statement. Releasing her hand, he took a long drink of his water, draining the contents in one gulp.

She shifted in her seat. She didn't know what to think. *What about his job? It's dangerous, and I don't even know what he does when he leaves. Can I handle not knowing where he's going or what he's facing?*

Blake turned back to her, and she responded with a weak smile. Then, feeling unsure of what to say, her attention shifted to the window, where she watched families play at a park across the street. Smiles covered the children's faces. Dogs chased frisbees. Jubilant families appeared happy and content as little boys and girls laughed while being pushed on swings.

The sweet family snapshots sent a tingle through her as she imagined what it would be like to bring her own child to this park and play. *Will I be alone or*—She swallowed before she finished the thought. *Will Blake be a part of our family portrait?*

BLAKE FOLLOWED HER GAZE, wishing he had the right words to make her understand how he felt about her. Watching the happy families across the street aimed a spotlight on the longing in his heart. He wanted a family someday. A couple of kids. Maybe a dog. How could he ask Ava to consider a life alongside him? She'd already expressed her caution and fear about his job. Did he genuinely believe she would consider a serious relationship with him? Knowing he'd be gone—a lot—with no explanation about his destination?

A deep connection stretched between the two of them, born out of hours of conversation and learning to trust one another. More than a need to protect her, he wanted to walk through life with her. Forever. *God, help me say the right words.* Drumming his fingers on the table, he weighed his next move. If only Ava could read his heart to fill in the gaps where his words failed to make sense.

He smiled, thinking about the lunch with Brent. He'd already shared his feelings with his brother. Most of them, anyway. Brent's advice? If Blake loved her, he should let her know and not wait too long. Then, as brothers did, Brent taunted him about not getting any younger.

Ava glanced back at him. The wistful look in her eyes made his heart melt. He needed to be sure of what he wanted before he risked her heart—and his.

"Nightingale syndrome." The words floated off her lips and snapped him out of his tangled thoughts.

"What?"

"I nursed you back to health, and now you're falling in love with me."

He sat back in his chair and looked past her out at the park. *So, she thinks I am falling in love with her?* Did she know how close to the mark she was?

Shifting his eyes back to hers, he replayed what she'd just said to him. She had the concept backward. He chuckled. "I think it's the opposite."

"What do you mean?"

"Nightingale syndrome." Blake locked his gaze onto hers like he'd been trained to do in the midst of an interrogation. "The nurse falls in love with the patient."

Ava blanched, and he couldn't help but grin. She opened her mouth, then closed it. Just as quickly, her cheeks pinked.

After pausing to let his statement sink in, he threw out a question he'd been wrestling with for a while. "You don't believe we're only connected because of Uganda, do you?" Keeping his gaze pinpointed on hers, he added, "I think we'd have the same connection if we'd met at the—"

"At the grocery store?" She cut in and flashed him a flirtatious smile.

"Um, well, okay, the grocery store."

She laughed, and Blake's heart skipped ahead as she lightened the mood with her teasing. He tried to imagine them bumping into each other in the produce section. The idea made him smile.

Her expression turned serious. She set down her fork and released a long breath. "Blake."

At his name, his body tensed.

"Sometimes, when it comes to you and me, I don't know what to think." Her expression implored him to come clean with his feelings, and his mouth grew parched.

"Ava, I ..." The words stutter-stepped on his tongue while he considered her beautiful, pregnant belly.

Until this point, his life balanced between order and chaos —and the thrill of the next mission. However, being here, with her, made him consider a deviation from his usual plans.

She blinked, then let him off the hook by averting her gaze back to the children at the playground.

Jerking his fingers through his hair, he stifled a groan. His next mission was undercover. He'd be gone for months. Feeling the pull between two worlds, his heart ached.

Part of him wanted to finish his mission, but another part of him wondered if it was even worth it to continue. *Is what I'm doing in the field even going to matter? Or is it time for me to step away and let someone else finish the job?*

Blake pushed away the questions and straightened his posture. He'd sunk years into his career, and he didn't want to walk away now. *Not now, when I am so close to completing the mission.* He swallowed hard and studied Ava's profile. He knew what his heart wanted. But was it possible to have both?

CHAPTER TWENTY-FOUR

Blake slowed his pace to a jog as he wrapped up his run through the neighborhood. The June morning carried a warmer-than-normal breeze. Good thing he'd started his run early. As he reduced his pace to a walk, Blake checked his phone. No messages. In Dallas already for a week, he was still on what Ava's friend Caroline called *baby watch*. It was like being in a holding pattern. Lots of flying in circles, but no landing.

He rounded the corner to Caroline and Craig's house, slowing to a walk. He was grateful they'd offered the garage apartment for his stay. When he reached the edge of the yard, a round of giggles and laughter carried on the breeze.

"Good morning Blake." Caroline threw him a smile as she slid the door to her minivan shut. "Did you enjoy your run?"

"I did."

Craig walked through the garage carrying a thermos and his briefcase. "You're making me look bad, Blake." Glancing at Caroline, he said, "Remember when we used to exercise?"

She picked a backpack off the ground and laid it in the back of her van next to a mountain of sports equipment. "Yeah. That was like three kids ago."

Blake laughed at their banter. "Have you heard anything from Ava this morning?"

"No." Caroline grinned. "She's probably still asleep. Being nine months pregnant is tough work."

Before Craig slipped into his sedan, he shot Caroline a sly look. "So I was thinking, maybe we should have another one."

Caroline shook her head, then nodded toward the van. "We're almost out of seats."

Craig shrugged as he winked at her. "Just thought I'd ask."

Blake waved at Caroline and Craig as they backed out of the driveway, then took the stairs two at a time up to the garage apartment. He'd take a quick shower before heading out to Craig's workshop while he waited for Ava to call. Craig had given him a jumpstart on his project by pre-cutting all the wood before he arrived. With only a few weeks' leave, finishing the nursery gift for Ava would be a rushed job.

He jumped in the shower and thought about the small wooden seat with a wraparound bookcase. The little guy wouldn't use it for a while, but when he started to toddle, he'd have a pint-size seat to read his books in.

Blake stepped out of the shower, and as he wrapped the towel around his waist, his phone buzzed on the dresser. He smiled. Ava must have woken up early today.

He picked up the phone, and his heart lodged in his throat. "Hey, Caroline. Everything okay?"

She squealed, then said, "It's time!"

"Really? Now?" He looked down at his bare torso. Blake gripped the phone harder, and his pulse skipped to life. Then, racing around the room, he yanked a forest green T-shirt and a pair of jeans out of the chest of drawers. He picked up a pair of chinos and glanced at his polo shirts hanging in the closet. What's the dress code for the birth of a baby?

"Yes, now." Caroline's giggles broke through his thoughts. "Well, not now. Soon."

Blake flipped the phone to speaker and shrugged on his jeans.

"Hey, Blake." Ava's sweet voice floated around the room, warming his skin.

"Hey, sweetheart. Are you doing okay?" He pulled his shirt over his head. "I just have to throw on my shoes, then I'm on my way."

She blew out a long breath. "Promise?"

He grabbed the phone, clicked off of speaker, and held it up to his lips. "I promise."

There were a couple seconds of silence before Ava said, "I'll see you soon."

Blake ended the call, tied up his running shoes, took off down the stairs, and jumped in the car. When he finally pulled his rental car into the hospital parking lot, his heart drummed against his ribs like he'd pulled an all-nighter at the gym. *It's only a baby. How hard can this be?* Blake chuckled as he jumped out of the vehicle, jogged across the parking lot, and stepped through the double doors of the hospital.

Bounding up the stairs to labor and delivery, he spotted Caroline sitting in the waiting room. "Is everything okay?"

"Yeah, she's good." Caroline flashed him a worried look. "Are you okay?"

He nodded. Everything was great. Except for the adrenaline tearing through his body like a trail of fire.

Caroline replaced her worried expression with a smile. "They're prepping her. It shouldn't be long." She motioned to the chair next to her. "Take a seat, Blake."

He shook his head. He'd rather pace like a caged tiger.

Minutes later, a petite nurse approached them, carrying an electronic clipboard and wearing a harried expression on her face. "Ms. Stewart's contractions are light. We're going to continue to watch her." The woman shifted her eyes to Blake. "Are you Mr. Martin?"

"Yes." His palms glazed with sweat.

"Ms. Stewart listed you as her labor coach. Is that correct?"

"Uh ... yes, that's correct."

"Okay, very good." The woman pointed to the room across the hall. "There's a pair of scrubs for you in the room." Turning to acknowledge Caroline, she said, "Ms. Stewart's ready for you both to go in."

When they entered the room, Ava sat upright in the bed, her cheeks pink with a delicate flush.

"How are you feeling?" Caroline leaned in and gave Ava's hand a quick squeeze.

"Good. Tired." She looked past Caroline and smiled at him. "I'm glad you're here."

"I wouldn't miss it." Blake picked up the scrubs and escaped into the bathroom. His hands shook as his pulse thundered in his ears. "Get a grip, Martin. You aren't dropping in behind enemy lines."

Rolling up his jeans and shirt, he shoved them under his arm, released a quick breath, then stepped back into the room.

Caroline turned. "Nice scrubs, Blake."

He threw his clothes on the vinyl settee and smiled. "Thanks. Can't say I've ever worn a pair before."

"You look good." Ava flashed him a smile, sending a cool shiver down his neck.

"I'm not sure this green is my color. I prefer something a little darker."

Ava bit back a laugh as a nurse walked into the room and

studied some readings on the monitors whirring and humming with sounds and beeps.

"Everything looks good, Ms. Stewart." The nurse smiled at the three of them and made a few more notes on the chart.

Caroline glanced down at her watch. "I'm scheduled to volunteer at Johnathan's preschool." She leaned in and gave Ava a gentle hug. "After I'm done, I'll drop him off at his grandma's, then head back over."

"Sounds good." Ava closed her eyes and took in a few quick breaths. The beeping on the monitors showed another light contraction.

Caroline's face brightened. "It shouldn't be long." As she walked toward the door, Caroline reached out and gave his arm a quick squeeze. "You'll do fine."

Blake nodded and slipped into the chair next to Ava's hospital bed.

She looked over at him. "Are you ready for this?"

His tongue dried.

"Blake, are you sure you want to go through with this?"

"Yes." He stood and kissed her forehead. "I'm sorry. I'm trying to wrap my head around what's going on." As he studied her, fire ignited in his veins. "You look so beautiful today."

She looked down at her pale pink hospital gown. "I've looked better."

Reclaiming his place in the chair, Blake reached out for her hand.

The nurses scurried around the room, rolling in carts and prepping for the delivery. Soft beeps continued to emanate from the screen next to him.

One of the male nurses pointed to the blip on the screen. "That's the baby's heartbeat."

Blake nodded, then glanced back at Ava. "How are you feeling?"

"Large and ready to get this baby out."

He smiled, and some of his nervous jitters fell away with her answer. "You don't look like you're nervous at all."

"You do." She chuckled.

"This is all new to me."

"The military didn't train you for this?"

Blake smiled as he recalled their past exchange. "Hardly."

An older nurse patted Ava's arm before she walked out. "Let us know if you need anything, sweetheart. We'll leave you two alone until the contractions get closer together."

The afternoon breezed by with light conversation and the occasional nurse popping in to check the monitors. Blake shared with her a few stories from his childhood, and she reminisced about her mother. He'd even made her giggle after he folded several paper airplanes out of napkins, then pumped out a few nervous push-ups on the floor near the window.

"You might want to save your strength."

Blowing out a quick breath, he jumped up from the floor. "I feel like I should do something."

"I do too." Patting her belly, she added, "I'm just waiting for this baby to tell me when it's time."

"Amazing."

"It is, isn't it?"

"It's hard to believe a tiny human can make such a big decision."

Ava laughed.

As the day wore on, Blake noticed a change in Ava's demeanor. It reminded him of when he and Jacob left on a mission. She grew silent and focused.

Finally, when the contractions increased in intensity and frequency, the medical team moved in and did a final prep for the baby's arrival.

Sweat dappled his brow. *It's almost time. Wait. It's time!* He cleared his throat. *Breathe.* Biting back a chuckle, he moved in next to Ava. *You're supposed to tell her that.* "Breathe, sweetheart. Remember to breathe." As he mimicked the quick breaths for her to take, Blake held Ava's hand through each contraction. "I wish I could do more to help." He'd read about the role of labor coach, but standing here instructing her how to breathe didn't feel adequate for the work her body was doing.

She took a few more strenuous breaths and looked up at him. "Just having you here helps. I didn't want to go through this alone."

Sorrow pierced his heart. She missed Dylan. *Am I an adequate replacement? God, help me be what she needs today.* Blake wiped her forehead with a cool cloth and watched as the monitors registered her progress. He reached out and took her hand again. "You're doing great, Ava. Your baby boy will be here soon." Pride welled in his chest each time she wrapped her fingers around his in a vice grip and breathed through the contractions pulsating through her body. Her strength amazed him.

Ava sustained labor for nearly eight hours before her little boy made his debut. After her final push, the nurse wiped the baby's wrinkled face, then lifted him into Ava's open arms. Cradling him close to her skin, tears streamed down her face.

Blake leaned in and placed a kiss on Ava's sweat-covered brow. "You did amazing." As he gently brushed his fingers against the soft fuzz on the baby's scalp, his vision blurred. "He's so beautiful, Ava."

"What's his name?" The older nurse jotted down the baby's vitals as she asked the question.

"Dylan Maxwell."

They both said the name in unison, and the nurse laughed. "It sounds like you two have known that for a while."

Ava's face radiated happiness as she explained, "I named him after his father and ..." She glanced up at him, and Blake's world stood still for a moment. "And the man who made sure he got here safely."

Warmth expanded in his chest. *I love you, Ava.* Blake blinked at the unexpected thought. *Where did that come from?*

"Thank you for staying with me today." Ava's wistful voice yanked him out of his thoughts.

He pushed back a lock of hair from her forehead and attempted to steady his pulse. "Thank you for asking me to be here."

As he studied the tiny bundle in Ava's arms, Blake's throat tightened. He had one more week left of leave. Then, he'd be gone. For months. A cord wrapped around his heart and twisted. He didn't want to leave.

While the nurses finished their checks on Ava and Dylan, Blake walked over to the window. *God, I think I'm in love with Ava.* Running a hand across his chin, he smiled. *I'm in love with Ava.* Blood pounding in his veins, Blake pulled back the gate to his heart. *What am I going to do?*

He pivoted to look at her. When their gazes met, his breath caught. Did she feel the same way about him?

Warmth traced around his collar as he released a held breath.

If she did feel the same way, could he be the man she needed him to be? Could he step in and be a father to little Dylan?

CHAPTER TWENTY-FIVE

13:33 Paris, France
Four Months Later

A murky haze blanketed the dining room as Blake fought to push past the drumbeats banging against his skull. His eyes burned. He forced them to stay open while he tried to reorient himself to his surroundings. The blast came out of nowhere, and now he sat drowning under a cloud of dust and ashes.

"Ava," Blake whispered her name as he pinched his eyes closed to combat the sharp ache pulsing behind his eyelids. A moment of eerie silence floated around the room.

Seconds later, a loud crash made Blake jerk his head to the side. He blinked and gritted his teeth when the quick motion wrenched his shoulder muscles in pain. *What was that?* His pupils stung, and a smog mixed with the bright light of the sun floated across his vision.

In the distance, sirens wailed, and the thundering in his skull grew worse. The acrid tang of smoke coated his mouth as he tried to moisten his lips with his tongue. *My throat feels like it's on fire.* When he coughed, the tender skin in his mouth waxed with pain. *Where did that explosion come from?* Leaning forward, he spat on the ground and groaned as a sharp pain exploded across his ribs.

The rhythmic sound of emergency vehicles grew louder and ricocheted off every inch of his skull. Blake squeezed his eyes shut in a long blink and prayed for the commotion to subside.

A snapping sound broke through the air, and his eyes zeroed in on the loose beam in the doorway. The wood appeared splintered and bowed under the weight of the shifting ceiling. *I need to get out of here!* He stood, but he'd done so too quickly, and the room teetered.

Like someone turning up the knob on the radio, a cacophony of shouting and alarms pressed hard against his ears. Then, lightheaded, he sank onto a chair to catch his breath.

As he leaned his head against the wall, something sticky trickled down his cheek. Frustration wrapped around him as he ran his fingers across his brow and then studied the blood on his hand. *I'm injured. That's going to leave a mark.*

Closing his eyes, he took inventory of his appendages—arms, legs, fingers, toes—all moved as usual. He lifted his hand back to his forehead. An open slash of skin tracked along his brow, but nothing deep enough to require anything more than a handful of stitches. Releasing an irritated sigh, his ears continued to pulsate and ring simultaneously, making his brain throb at a tempo he couldn't control.

Pushing past another wave of torturous pain along his ribcage, he struggled to take in a deep breath. His senses were on high alert as a blend of smells wafted up through his nostrils—burning metal, rubber, and flesh.

He made a second attempt to stand, thanking God his spine was still in working order. He winced. Unsteady on his feet, he lowered himself back into the chair a second time. *You've got to be smart about this.* He didn't want to lose his footing in the debris and risk further injury.

Taking a deep breath, Blake cautiously moved his head to assess the damage to the apartment. The vintage metal dining table he'd been sitting at lay on its side in a twisted heap several feet away. Next to where the front window used to be, ripped curtains hung haphazardly, and his line of sight went straight through to the street. The gaping hole in the ceiling near the front door caused his heart to drop. Blake glanced down. Sprawled out in the rubble, a lifeless body was covered in dust and blood.

Sorrow wrapped around him as the sweet picture of Ava holding her newborn baby shot across his mind. *I told her I'd be safe.* Exasperated, Blake clenched his eyes shut and tried to piece together why a bomb had just gone off next to his apartment in downtown Paris.

CHAPTER TWENTY-SIX

13:39 Paris, France

A distant voice hollered his name, and Blake's eyes darted open. The memory of Ava and the newborn baby dissolved into a cloud of smoke.

"In here." His throat still burned from the vapors swirling around the room, making the sound tumbling past his lips barely audible. "I'm in here." He tried a second attempt, this time a decibel louder. Jacob had already crawled through the rubble and found him. "What happened?"

"Car bomb." Jacob moved his hands over Blake's body, his medical training taking over as he spoke.

"In downtown Paris?"

"Yeah, can you believe it?" Jacob looked satisfied there were no life-threatening injuries and slowly pulled him to his feet.

Blake winced. "Heard any chatter?" He hoped the question would take his mind off the pain.

"I don't think it had anything to do with Rideau."

Jacques Rideau, a Canadian-born scientist, had risen to the

top of America's terror list and cemented himself as the leading engineer for weaponized drugs. When they'd finally tracked Rideau to Paris, Blake believed the mission had neared its end.

Blake pinched his brows together. "You're kidding."

They walked a few paces before Blake stalled and peered down at the body on the floor. The lifeless young woman who lived in the apartment above them looked barely twenty. Jacob released him for a brief second and checked for a pulse.

"Nothing. She's gone."

His heart dipped as his mind flashed back to the courtroom when he'd watched a woman, about the same age, sentenced for the accidental death of Ava's husband. Sorrow flooded his thoughts. A young life should be lived carefree and joyful, not interrupted by tragedy.

His partner glanced at the gash above his eyebrow. "That's going to leave a nasty scar, my friend."

Blake moved his head from side to side in an attempt to shake off the muffled static still pervading his ears. He was grateful to be alive. He'd worry about the wound later. "Think Ava will notice?" He pointed to his forehead and flashed his partner an amused grin.

Jacob rolled his eyes. "A car bomb just obliterated our apartment, and all you can think about is your woman in Texas?" His partner paused and looked him over again. "Your head injury must be worse than it looks."

Medical teams and police closed in around them, shouting orders and moving debris. Jacob called out and pointed to the woman with no pulse lying just a few paces ahead. The medic narrowed his eyes at Blake, zeroing in on his bloody forehead.

Blake waved him off. "*Je vais bien.* I'm fine." The man paused, then threw him a quick nod as he continued past.

"Are you hurting anywhere else?" Jacob put his arm around him, positioning his body like a human crutch.

"My ribs."

The two of them skirted the threshold of their apartment's shattered wall. Jacob pulled him a few feet from the chaos, and Blake grimaced. Using his fingers, his partner traced his ribcage and flashed him a concerned look. "I think you may have a few broken or bruised ribs."

"Most likely." Blake took in another short breath. "It felt the same way last time."

"Okay, old man, let's get you out of here."

Blake scanned the rubble on the street. The twisted metal of the decimated SUV lay flattened like a pancake in front of where their door had been. "We need to take some pictures and get the make and model."

"Already did before I came in to look for you."

He wanted to laugh, but it would hurt too much. "Thanks."

"Of course." Jacob helped him walk to the corner of the street. The local police had placed barriers along the road to keep the general population out of the blast zone.

He glanced back at the apartment. "Judging by the angle of the blast, it looks like a low-order explosive."

The apartment's front was decimated, but the back looked untouched. The complex stood three levels tall, and by God's grace, the only flat available to them when they'd arrived in Paris was the lower level. He thought of the woman lying on the ground. Had they been on either of the upper levels, he might not have made it out alive. *Thank You, God, for Your protection. Again.*

"Most likely, the ordinance was homemade and compact." Blake nodded in the direction of the charred SUV.

"True." Jacob scanned the street, then looked back at him. "You're lucky you were back in the dining room when this happened." His partner pointed at the cars across the street, most of their windows blown out, shards of glass scattered everywhere. "It looks like a warzone out here."

Blake cringed. It did.

A small wave of confused people mulled around the street, many of them stepping out of their homes to survey the damage. The police spread out and started door-to-door evacuations.

"These hospitals are going to be a madhouse." Frowning, he watched as the medics pulled an injured young man from his car. He hated being incapacitated. The rescue teams needed more hands, but there was no way he'd be any use to them.

"Probably, but we should still get you looked at." Jacob pointed toward the opposite end of the street, where the medics had set up a makeshift triage unit.

"I guess you're right." More emergency response vehicles rounded the corner as several onlookers lined the avenue. "Do you still have our laptops and equipment?" Blake's mind raced ahead, thinking about the mission.

"Yeah. Glad we didn't have much with us this time."

He sighed in relief. "Thank God you were out getting lunch." He thought of the car with their surveillance equipment and rucksacks secure in the trunk. "We would've been parked near that vehicle today."

Jacob helped Blake move slowly through the growing crowd. "Yeah, I guess I got lucky this time."

Blake cut his eyes in his partner's direction. Jacob didn't believe in God, but Blake doubted luck had anything to do with today. For him to have been able to stand up and walk out of that building was a miracle. He frowned. They constantly sparred about his faith in God or Jacob's lack thereof, but both agreed to respect each other's beliefs. However, Blake couldn't push aside the nagging feeling that maybe an event like this opened the door for a more meaningful discussion.

"Maybe you weren't there because God thought you needed more time."

Jacob stopped walking. Blake grinned, expecting a sarcastic comment but silently hoping the statement would plant a seed.

"Are you going to go there?" Jacob shot him a fiery look. "Do not make me break the rest of your ribs, brother."

He snorted a chuckle, then cringed. "Ugh, don't make me laugh."

Jacob nodded toward the ambulance. "There's a medic over there. Let's have him do a quick examination and check in with the police."

Checking in with the National Police was necessary to keep up their cover. They'd give their names, albeit fake, but the performance was vital to avoid drawing any attention to themselves. If they tried to escape down the road unnoticed, they could risk the scrutiny of looking like one of the perpetrators.

Their backstories were simple. They worked for a high-end Stateside real estate agency and looked for properties for the American elite. Via the web, they interacted with American congressmen, professional athletes, and celebrities as a front. While in Paris, they lived in a well-established affluent neighborhood and meandered through upscale properties at their leisure. It gave them easy access to Rideau, who lived directly across the street.

With his fluid French and medical expertise, Jacob did most of the talking to the medic. As he pointed to their apartment, he shared their aliases and explained that their friends, who lived a few streets over, would take them to the local hospital. The medic nodded and assessed Blake. He could tell by the weary look on the man's face he was overwhelmed and distracted.

"*Merci.*" Blake nodded his appreciation and said a silent prayer for all the first responders milling about the street. The road was a mess, and people were hurt and confused. No doubt they'd be dealing with a string of injuries and investigation long into the night.

CHAPTER TWENTY-SEVEN

13:58 Paris, France

The medic cleaned Blake's wound and placed several butterfly strips across his skin. The pain continued to claw at his torso as he gingerly took each step across the street.

"Any news on Rideau?" Blake winced as they turned and made their way through an alley.

"No. He left for the day, but I doubt he'll be back to his apartment after this hits the news."

"Great, all that work for nothing." Once Rideau got spooked, he went into hiding for months. "It's still hard to believe this was a random car bomb."

Jacob halted and flashed him a frustrated look. "Do you think someone had a read on us?"

"I'm not sure."

Two men pushed past them in the congested alley, and a searing pain racked his achy bones. He flinched as Jacob yelled out a few colorful French expletives in the men's direction.

"Come on, leave it." He nudged his partner's shoulder. "It's not worth it."

Jacob fumed under his breath.

Blake grinned. "Besides, I'm not in a condition to have your back this time."

Jacob grunted, and a flash of anger sparked in his eyes. Between the two of them, Jacob was more prone to incite a fight.

"Can you believe these people running toward ground zero? How do they know there isn't a second one?" Jacob huffed, then continued with him down the alleyway.

"Curiosity, I guess."

They walked out onto the next street and took a right. Jacob pointed, then said, "Our car is about two blocks over. I left it near the café after I heard the explosion."

Blake nodded. The jostling of his ribcage had become increasingly unpleasant, and he'd be grateful when they could stop moving.

"You might have earned yourself some extended R & R with this little number." Jacob threw him a devilish look. "Going back to the States again?"

He smiled and nodded.

"Oh man, you got it bad."

"I think I've earned a couple of weeks at least."

Jacob snickered. "This coming from the guy who would come in wounded and beg our unit leader to release you back out on a mission in forty-eight hours."

"I think it may take a little longer for me to heal this time around. I'm getting older, you know."

Jacob maneuvered him toward the parking area. "You are old, aren't you?"

"I can still keep up with you, can't I?"

"Okay, I'll give you that."

Jacob was six years Blake's junior, but you would never know it to look at them. He stood a few inches above his partner and still outlifted him in the gym. What Jacob lacked in brawn, he filled in with wit, speed, and medical knowledge. What one lacked, the other contributed. His analytical ingenuity and Jacob's camaraderie with the locals were both equally helpful in getting them out of more than a few scrapes in the past.

Jacob unlocked the car, and Blake lowered himself into the seat.

"Are you feeling dizzy at all?"

He gritted his teeth. "No, but my ribs hurt like I've been run over by a tank."

Jacob furrowed his brow as he popped the trunk and dug through their bags. "Here are some pain meds." He chucked a bottle at him and then slammed the trunk closed. "I left our lunch on the counter when I took off. Let me run into this grocer and see if I can grab us some grub before we head to the drop point."

"Sounds good."

Jacob took off like a shot into the small grocery store and returned in less than five minutes.

"What did you do, loot the place?" Blake looked around. The street sat almost empty since most of the Parisians escaped to the safety of their apartments.

Jacob grinned. "There's this sweet French girl who works there, and she's been making me the same sandwich every week since we've been here."

"Oh, brother." He rolled his eyes.

"What can I say? She likes the accent."

"Which one?"

Jacob threw the paper sack in Blake's lap and stuck two bottles of water into the center console. "She swooned when I told her in perfect west-coast English I needed *deux* sandwiches this time." His partner held up two fingers in front of his face. "By the way, how many fingers do you see?"

Blake shoved his hand away. "Two."

With his fresh-faced California looks, Jacob's cover was always a lovesick, single American tourist. And he played it quite well.

"I'm really going to miss that grocery store."

Blake wanted to laugh but remembered the excruciating discomfort it would cause. Instead, he took a giant bite of the warm baguette stuffed with ham and cheese. "This sandwich is great."

His partner gave him a sideways glance. "It was made with love."

He shook his head and finished the rest of the sandwich before he opened his phone. "Last intel I got, the check-in is in Nanterre."

"That's about thirty minutes from here."

"The exchange will be at a church." Blake ran through the notes on his phone. "Just off the A14."

"Well, you'll feel right at home, won't you?"

He let the remark slide. He didn't have the energy to spar with his friend. "Let me get the address loaded into the GPS."

Jacob flashed him a quick look. "What? No quippy evangelical retort?"

"I guess not." Blake took another slow breath. "Must be the blow to the head."

"Bummer. I like the Bible-thumping Blake better."

"Is that really what you think of me?" Even though his partner was doing his best to keep him alert during the short drive to Nanterre, the comment hit a nerve.

"No, I don't." Jacob drummed the steering wheel with his fingers. "You have to admit some of your buddies are, though."

"My buddies?" He found the remark amusing since he couldn't remember the last time he'd been out with friends socially or been buddies with anyone outside of their unit.

"Yeah, other Christians."

Blake leaned back, closed his eyes, and tried to ignore his partner. He couldn't wait to have a little rest and recovery from this mission, and he couldn't think of any place better to recover than the great state of Texas.

Cracking his eyelids, he glanced over at Jacob. He prayed silently one day he'd be receptive to the saving grace of Jesus Christ. Also, Blake silently thanked God for keeping him safe during the explosion.

"Don't fall asleep on me. Got it?" Jacob punched his shoulder and then swiped a bottle of water from the center console.

"I won't. My eyes feel like they're on fire. I'm just going to shut them for a second." Blake pulled his eyes closed and started to pray. God had been his refuge in more ways than he'd dared to count during his life devoted to military service. Every time he escaped from disaster, he'd ask God to guide him to know when he should retire. So far, God had remained silent.

Before he could step away, he needed reassurance he'd done all he could do to help justice win, albeit sparsely throughout the world. The silence lingered. For now, he'd continue the mission to catch Rideau and believe God would keep him alive long enough to share a few of his years with someone and maybe start a family. *Someone like Ava.* Casting off the thought, Blake smiled as a bit of mischief rose inside of him. "You know, Jacob ..."

"Yes?"

"You've been asking a lot of questions about my faith

lately. Are you sure you aren't searching for the truth?" Blake smirked, feeling his partner's eyes cut in his direction.

"You're playing with fire, old man," Jacob grunted. "You keep it up, and I might just drive us off this road."

He opened his eyes and turned toward Jacob. "I know where I'm going when I die. Do you?"

"On second thought, why don't you take a nap?"

Blake laughed.

"Or, at the very least, stop talking while I drive."

"Fine with me."

"Don't go to sleep."

"Aye, aye, Captain." Blake shot up his hand in a mock salute as he leaned against the headrest of the small sedan.

CHAPTER TWENTY-EIGHT

14:32 Just Outside of Paris, France

They'd been driving for fifteen minutes, and the swaying of the vehicle threatened to lull him to sleep. Thankfully it wouldn't be long before they arrived at the exchange. After that, the two of them would transfer to another vehicle and drive thirty minutes to a nondescript farm nestled in the center of several acres of land. The agrarian landscape would make an idyllic backdrop for their debrief with their team leader Mike Adams.

"You still awake?" Jacob threw out the question as he nudged him. "No sleeping until you get a full physical back at the farm."

"I'm awake." Trying to stay alert, Blake redirected his thoughts back to Ava and little Dylan. He still couldn't believe he'd been there to see Dylan come into the world. Blake smiled as a happy recollection of that day overtook the horrific events of the carnage he'd just survived. *I miss her. And Dylan.*

A car horn snapped Blake back to the present. Reluctantly,

he opened his eyes and stretched his legs in the tiny car. The vanishing memory trailed with a thought about the gift he'd made Ava before he'd left—a custom bookshelf for Dylan's nursery. After he met Craig and Caroline and shared his love for woodworking, Craig offered him the use of his shop. Working with wood was therapeutic for him, and Craig's shop was the perfect place to work a few hours a day and keep the bookcase a surprise from Ava.

When he presented it to her, she was shocked. Ava hadn't known about his love for carpentry, and it felt good to do something meaningful and creative with his hands again. Blake angled his eyes down at his calloused palms. The last time he used woodworking tools in any capacity was before he'd been stationed in Africa.

"Hey man, you still awake?" Jacob's voice yanked him out of his memories.

"Yep. Still here." His mind was hazy, but the ringing in his ears had lowered to a soft hum.

"Our exit is just ahead. Looks like we'll be out of Paris a week early."

"True. We won't hear anything new from Rideau for a while."

"No, doubt." Jacob glanced in his direction. "It will be interesting to see who takes responsibility and how the press spins it."

He nodded but didn't respond. It always amazed him how the headlines splashed across the nightly news were so distorted from the actual story.

"I think we better focus our efforts on Africa before we lose any more leads," Jacob smirked. "The little vacay you took in Uganda with your Texas girl halted some of our progress."

Blake's head throbbed a little more at the thought of returning to their unit base in Kenya. He'd grown tired of the long hot days and even more exhausted over the dead-end information they'd dug up.

Rideau was looking for the highest bidder for his latest lethal concoction. It promised a quick death while being untraceable. If it fell into the wrong hands, it could leave a tidal wave of upheaval, and the ripple effects would be felt across the world. Everything they'd uncovered pointed to a buyer in Uganda. Blake scowled and pinched his eyes shut. And a child trafficking ring that footed the bill. *God help me find that little girl.* His gut twisted as a flash of the little girl's face from the river clawed across his mind.

He released a long-exasperated breath as he shifted in his seat. He wanted to wrap up things with Rideau and the traffickers in Uganda as soon as possible. Then, hopefully, he could put a nice little period on the end of a very long sentence of military service.

"We're here."

Blake opened his eyes as Jacob turned into the cathedral's parking lot. They transferred their things into the small black van waiting for them as a man in a navy-blue jogging suit jumped out of the vehicle and slipped into their car.

"So, where are you going this time for R & R?" As Blake asked the question, he sat back in the tweed-covered van seats, grateful to have more room for his long legs.

"I'm going to head to the Bay to see my mom and sister."

"Sounds good."

"What about you?" Jacob nudged him. "Did you decide on Dallas?"

"Yes. I think I'll surprise Ava."

"Is that a good idea?"

"Why?" Triggered by the tone in his partner's voice, Blake questioned if maybe it was a bad idea.

Jacob looked him up and down. "You look like you've been hit by a bus."

He took in a quick breath. He hadn't had a chance to look at himself in a mirror, but he imagined, based on his partner's observation, the picture wasn't pretty. Heat stretched around Blake's collar as his memory flashed to the first night he'd met Ava when she so tenderly cared for him. "Maybe so, but there's nowhere I'd rather be recovering than with her."

"Why don't you just do it?"

"Do what?"

"Ask her to marry you?"

"What?" Blake couldn't believe his anti-marriage partner's suggestion.

"You heard me."

Pursing his lips together, Blake mulled over his answer.

"Have you thought about it, at least?"

He shifted in the seat, knowing full well he'd done more than think about it. A ring sat at his parent's house, hidden beneath his old college hoodies in a drawer.

"I know that look."

"What look?"

"You have thought about it!"

Clenching his jaw, Blake remained motionless.

"Did you buy a ring?"

He sighed.

"Oh, man." Jacob pushed out a low whistle while he shook his head. "I know what you're doing. You're thinking of every scenario that could go wrong if you do ask her. Aren't you?" His partner paused a moment before he continued. "Buddy, that's okay to do out on a mission, but something like this, you may just have to jump." Jacob flashed him a teasing grin. "Even if it is without a chute."

Blake raked a hand over his hair, and a few crumbling

particles of debris—souvenirs of their destroyed apartment—fell onto his collar. "Come on, Jacob, look at me." He turned to look at his partner. "My job doesn't really scream husband material."

Jacob dusted particles of grit off Blake's shirt. "That's true."

"I can't even tell her where I'm going when I get on a plane, let alone what I'll be doing when I reach my destination."

"Or how you got that nasty gash above your eyebrow."

"Or the injured ribs." He breathed out slowly, thankful the van was a smoother ride than the car.

"What *are* you going to tell her about the injuries?"

"Maybe she won't notice." Blake ran his hand along the fresh stubble on his chin. For the most part, he'd been clean-shaven while in Paris. Would Ava notice that too? Would she like it, or did she prefer a beard?

Jacob gave him a sideways glance. "Take it from me—women see everything."

He winced. If anyone kept track of details, Ava did.

Silence lingered between them for a few seconds before Jacob spoke up. "Make sure you invite me to the wedding if you pop the question on R & R."

"Are you sure? The wedding will be in a church." He paused for effect. "A big one."

Jacob pinched his brows together. "I guess for you, I'd deal with it."

"Thanks." Warmth trickled through him as he thought about Ava. "I'll let you know."

CHAPTER TWENTY-NINE

Ava picked up the colored pencils and added a few quick strokes over the design sketch in front of her. "Just a few more pops of yellow."

Her lips curled into a smile as she studied her drawing—a child's bedroom arrayed in an ombre of rustic orange and yellows accented with natural wood furnishings. The bedding was an understated nod to the geometric shapes she'd seen splashed across the ladies' dresses in Uganda. But, instead of vibrant colors, the patterns were drawn in subdued greys and pale greens.

Satisfied with the blend of rustic colors, Ava set the sketchbook aside and glanced around her living room. She still lived in the house she and Dylan built years ago, but it felt different now. Hopeful energy and new life looped through every corner like yarn woven through a loom. Her home, which usually resembled a backdrop to a museum, she'd converted into something more relaxed—homier.

The open-concept living area was dappled with infant toys, a cherry wood highchair, and several colorful quilts, while the sweet smell of baby shampoo permeated the air. Ava released a contented sigh as she took in the space. Four months had passed since she'd given birth to Dylan Maxwell, and autumn would soon slip into another holiday season. She'd come to enjoy the comfortable rhythm of her life, which revolved around late-night feedings followed by early-morning naps. Her wounded heart was healing. Her creativity had begun to flourish again.

Ava studied her drawing. During her quiet moments, she'd envisioned the new direction she wanted to take her design business. A desire to incorporate more eco-friendly materials and infuse natural elements into the furnishings began to take shape. Her time in Uganda, while unsettling, opened the door to a reenergized, unique personal style.

Scanning the room once more, her gaze landed on the antique bike frame hovering on the far wall. It was a gift to her late husband years ago and a tribute to his hobby.

"Oh, Dylan, I miss you." Her heart sank. She missed Dylan's company and craved the familiarity of being a wife. It grieved her to know he'd never get to meet their baby in this life, but she was grateful he'd left a part of himself behind for her to hold on to.

As Ava continued to study the antiquated bicycle, she recalled the day she found the hidden gem at a flea market. Hanging on her wall now, it was painted and polished, nothing like when she found it behind a pile of old pallets.

The 1950s Hawthorne sat coated in rust, and the white-walled balloon tires were bald and flat. However, something about the bike drew her in. Maybe it was her creative bent, but she believed there was something to salvage underneath all the wear and tear. She smiled, remembering the moment she'd wheeled the bicycle up to Dylan after negotiating a great price.

"What in the world?" He flashed her a 'you're-a-designer-so-I-won't-ask' look.

"It reminded me of you." She'd nudged him in the ribs.

"Of me?" Her husband bent over and planted a quick kiss on her nose. "Rusty and old?"

"No, silly, a rare find."

Dylan smiled and brought her in for a quick kiss on the lips, then took her treasure back to the van.

Like a butterfly trying to push out of its cocoon, a glimmer of something unexpected formed from the memory. She tried to run from her grief in Uganda, but maybe like a caterpillar, her sad memories didn't need to be pushed aside—they needed to be transformed.

She picked up her sketchbook, turned the page, and glanced back up at the bicycle. On a fresh piece of parchment, she drew out a quick sketch of the bike, then made separate smaller illustrations of the wheel's spokes and the curved shape of the fenders. After she finished, she stood to stretch. Walking over to the Hawthorne, she ran her hands along the glossy metal. *How can I incorporate this design into a room?* The idea struck her as a fitting way to memorialize little Dylan's father.

A soft knock at the door drew her from her artistic musings. Ava snuck a quick peek at little Dylan, who was sound asleep in his pack-and-play. Another knock echoed down the hall as she hastily tiptoed toward the door, hoping whoever was on her front porch would not get antsy and use the doorbell.

Ava opened the door, and a massive bouquet of sunflowers filled the doorway. "Oh, my!" She covered her mouth and stifled a giggle as she studied them. Blake had sent small bouquets of sunflowers to her ever since he'd left, but these flowers were as large as dinner plates. The delivery person shifted on his feet while she admired the giant cluster of burnt orange and yellow.

"Those are beautiful." She reached out her hand to accept them.

As the man handed her the bouquet, he let his fingers brush against her skin and intertwined his fingers with hers. Startled, Ava peered through the flowers. Blake smiled behind the massive honey-colored blooms. Without a second thought, she dropped the bouquet and propelled herself into his arms.

"Blake!" Happy tears flowed down her cheeks as she nuzzled herself into his neck and breathed in the warm, spicy scent of his cologne.

"Ava." He said her name in a breathless whisper as he held her firmly against his body.

When he flinched from the impact of her enthusiastic embrace, she pulled back. "I'm sorry. Are you okay?" Glancing up at the row of butterfly bandages stretched taut above his eyebrow, she frowned.

Waving his hand over the injury, he said, "Oh, this? It's nothing."

She looked away from the dressing and down at the ground where the bouquet lay in a heap. "I nearly trampled the flowers."

Simultaneously they bent over to pick them up, but Blake paused midway down. Then, as their gazes locked, he grimaced.

"Blake, you're hurt." She grasped the bouquet, and her heart sank as she reached out to him.

"I'm okay." He lifted her chin with his forefinger and smiled. "The discomfort was worth it for that kind of reception."

She blushed, suddenly shy about her clumsy jump into his

arms. "What are you … how did you …" She didn't know what to ask—she only knew she was thrilled to see him.

"I'm in between assignments, and I have two weeks R & R." He wrapped his strong arms around her and brought her in for a slow embrace.

She tilted her head to look up at him. "What happened?"

"Just a couple of bruised ribs. It's not as bad as it looks."

She didn't know what to say, so she just let him hold onto her. Then, Ava's ears perked at the sound of gentle cooing noises coming from down the hall.

Blake looked beyond her into the house. "Is that Dylan?"

Grabbing his hand, she eagerly pulled him through the front door. *I can't believe he's here.* Her heart pounded as they made their way down the long hallway and into the open living room.

Blake approached the infant and beamed. "Can I hold him?" Dylan kicked his little legs in the air and opened his eyes.

She nodded, still in awe that he stood in her living room, so close she could smell the rugged scent of his after-shave. "Is it easier for you to sit down?"

"Yes, probably."

As he lowered himself onto the couch, she reached into the bassinet, picked up Dylan, and handed him to Blake.

"He's getting so big."

"He is." Ava sat next to him and watched as he held her baby in his protective, muscular arms.

"How have you been?" She threw out the question, hoping he'd shed some light on how he'd been injured.

"I've been good." His lips lifted into a grin as he raised his hand toward the bandage. "This was an unexpected hiccup in my deployment, but it allowed me to get some time off."

She frowned. *Is this what it's like to be in a relationship with a man in a covert branch of the military? Will he be injured every time he comes home?* While the questions weighed heavy on her mind, she didn't want to ask them.

Angling her body toward him, she tried to make sense of seeing him again. *I have no experience with this, God. Please help me.* It was still hard for her to wrap her mind around what he did for a living—flying off to secret locations worldwide and propelling himself into danger as if it were normal.

Ava's heart tightened. "I prefer you not stand in front of a moving train for a few days off."

Blake stifled a laugh, and her pulse drummed in her ears. She wanted to tell him how much she missed him, but she also wanted to guard her heart. His job demanded he answer only to the government, and she didn't know how he'd feel about her concern. *Was acquiring an instant family something he'd even considered?* Her throat dried. *I need you in my life, Blake, but I want you to promise you'll come home safe.* She wanted him to promise something he had no control over.

"How have *you* been, Ava?" His tender tone interrupted her anxious thoughts.

"I've been good." She let her eyes roam the chiseled lines of his face. It was the first time she'd seen him without a beard. She didn't fight the urge to bring her hand up to his jawline and let her fingers glide along the smooth skin. "You shaved."

"I did." A trickle of amusement blanketed his voice. "Our mission required me to look more ..." He paused. "Refined."

Ava's arm dropped. She was aware she'd let her hand linger on his face for a few seconds longer than she'd planned. "I like it." *A lot.* Her breath hitched as a shiver worked from her fingers to the tips of her toes.

CHAPTER THIRTY

I f Blake's arms weren't occupied with a recumbent baby, he would've reached out and pulled her hand back to his bare skin. Instead, he tried to relax his beating heart and enjoy the delicate pink flush stealing across Ava's cheeks.

"I'm glad you like it." He smiled while he held her gaze. "I wasn't sure if you'd notice." *Women see everything.*

"I noticed." She said the words barely above a whisper and looked up at him through her long lashes. Hearing the breathlessness in her voice sent an uncontrollable shudder through him. He shifted the tiny bundle in his arms, barely feeling the insubstantial weight of little Dylan. For the first time in weeks, his soul overflowed with contentment.

Blake glanced around the room, noticing how baby paraphernalia now decorated Ava's usually pristine living room. His heart surged with a longing to never leave the peaceful scene as he took in all the sights and smells of her home. He moved his gaze back to Ava for a moment, then down to the baby. "He has your eyes."

Ava moved closer. The warmth of her bare arm brushed against his skin. "Yes, he does."

Studying the infant's tiny features, Blake marveled at how beautiful and perfect he was. His own body ached with the discomfort of his injuries, but knowing he'd missed so much time with Ava pained him even more. Each time he visited, the conflict never to leave intensified.

Ava laid her head on his shoulder while her hands played with Dylan's tiny feet. Those same hands that had washed his wounds now tenderly caressed Dylan's unblemished skin.

Her hands traveled from Dylan's feet to Blake's fingers. When she intertwined her fingers with his, a second wave of sentiment hit him. *I want to be with her. Forever.* Dylan opened his mouth, and a small coo escaped over his lips as if answering the silent plea building in Blake's chest.

"I wasn't sure when I'd see you again." She lifted off his shoulder and glanced at the bandage stretched across his eyebrow. "It looks like wherever you were, it was pretty dangerous."

He threw her a playful smile, trying to lighten the mood. "It wasn't supposed to be."

Her brow furrowed as she stood. "You're not going to tell me anything else, are you?" When she glanced back at him, the heat in her violet eyes cut through him like a searing cerulean flame.

Blake sighed. *This relationship is tricky ground to traverse.*

After a few seconds, Ava reached out and took Dylan from his arms and placed him gently on the crisp cotton sheet in the pack-and-play. Blake followed her every move. Observing her as a new mother sent a peaceful shiver down his spine. He guessed her mind raced with a million questions, but he also believed she'd refrain from asking most of them.

She turned back toward him, folded her arms, and drew a long gaze over his body.

It's like she's trying to decipher my body language. Blake's insides heated. If he didn't know any better, he'd assumed she'd trained with some of the most proficient interrogators in the field.

"I've seen some things on the news."

Clenching his jaw, he flashed her a look to let her know she was treading forbidden water.

"I won't ask because I know you can't tell me." Her eyes traveled up and down his frame a second time. Blake found it comical how his body responded to her examination. Normally unshaken, he suddenly felt uneasy under her scrutiny.

"It's probably wise if you don't make assumptions based on the news."

She raised an eyebrow. He suspected an internal conflict warring inside of her.

Blake gripped the armrest of the couch and braced himself for the pain as he stood. *How can I make her understand what I do?*

"I'm trying to make sense of this." Ava held his gaze as one of her hands motioned down the length of his body. "Is this what you signed up for?"

He took a step toward her and closed the distance between them. "Yes. This is what I signed up for."

A few tears pooled in her eyes as he opened his arms to her. She gently moved in and dissolved into his embrace. Blake pulled her closer and held her snugly against his body as he tried to explain. "I committed my life to this job, Ava. I knew what I was getting into when I signed the contract."

She leaned back and tilted her face to look up at him as he continued.

"What I didn't expect," he reached out and held her cheek

in his palm. "Was for you to be thrown into my life and force everything off-kilter."

A few tears trickled down her cheek, and Blake lifted his thumb to brush them away.

"I didn't either." She threw him a wistful smile before she pressed into him again. "Where do we go from here?"

The soothing smells of lavender and vanilla wafted up from her hair as he rested his chin on her head. "I don't know." The words caught in his throat as he repeated them. "I don't know."

CHAPTER THIRTY-ONE

"**D**o you love him?"

"What?" Startled, Ava glanced up.

"You heard me." Caroline, her best friend since college, sat across from her at the table.

"That's an unfair question to ask me."

"Why?"

"Well, for one thing ..."

"I'm listening."

"For one thing, Dylan has been gone just over a year." A lump wedged in her throat. At times she still couldn't process that Dylan had left her the way he did—alone and caring for their child. *The Lord gave, and the Lord has taken away.* Ava sighed. The words from Job skipped across her mind but didn't bring any comfort.

"I know." Caroline leaned forward. "But have you ever thought of allowing someone into your heart again?"

"How can you ask me that?" She bit down on her lip. She loved her friend, but Caroline had no idea what she was going through. Yes, her heart stirred when Blake was around, but the guilt of betraying Dylan made her feel like a traitor.

"Ava, it's not like you're getting divorced. You loved Dylan. There is no doubt in my mind about that." Caroline moved a stray hair out of her face as she continued. "I don't want you to be alone for the rest of your life. You're only in your thirties."

Ava considered Caroline's words. She didn't want to be alone either.

"It was tragic losing Dylan, but what kind of friend would I be if I begrudged you the possibility of having love in your life again?" Her friend leaned across the table and smiled. "Blake adores you and little Dylan."

"Is that your professional opinion?"

Caroline rolled her eyes and slumped back in her chair.

Ava smirked. She loved to jab her friend about being a marriage counselor, but it was all done in fun. Caroline had always been the first one she turned to for godly marital advice when she needed it.

"So?" Caroline thrummed her fingers on the table.

"So, what?"

"Do you have feelings for him?"

"It's not going to happen."

"Why not? He's handsome, he's a believer, he has a job, and—"

Ava lifted her hand to cut her off. "Exactly."

"What?"

"I can't think about entertaining a relationship with someone who willingly puts himself in danger." She shook her head and added, "I don't want to be a widow twice."

"Really, Ava. Is that your best defense? You're afraid Blake is going to die?"

"You don't understand what I witnessed when we were

thrown together in Uganda. Whatever he was doing there almost got him killed." Fear wrapped itself around her heart and constricted. She couldn't bear to think of losing someone else.

Caroline didn't respond, so she continued. "When he was brought to me, it looked like someone had shredded his skin." Ava grabbed a napkin and dabbed her eyes. "When he slept, he fought with hallucinations. He told me later his captors kept pumping different kinds of drugs into his body while in captivity."

Caroline winced.

"He could barely speak and there was blood everywhere. I'll never forget how he looked the first day I saw him."

"Yes, and you nursed him back to health."

Ava didn't respond.

"I'm not saying you need to run off and get married. I just think you should keep your heart open to the possibility this man may be in love with you."

Shifting the weight of Dylan in her arms, she sat back. "I don't need his chaos in my life right now." She looked down at her baby, sleeping peacefully in her arms. "I'm trying to revamp my design business and provide a comfortable, stable life for Dylan." *And pick up the pieces of my broken heart.*

"Well, you have to admit, the story of you two is rather romantic."

"I hardly think it's romantic that a man chooses to risk his life on purpose."

"He's serving his country, Ava." Caroline reached out her hand and laid it on hers. "There's something to be said about a man who holds duty and honor in high regard."

She pursed her lips, recalling when Blake almost stormed back into a village to defend her honor.

"Well, look at Dylan. He was a bank investor, and he still died."

"Seriously? How can you be so callous, Caroline?"

"I'm not. I'm just saying you can't keep everyone from dying. It's a fact of life."

Caroline was blunt, which made her a good counselor, but today those words cut to the marrow of Ava's soul. Memories of Evelyn flashed across her mind, and she swallowed back the urge to sob. No, she couldn't keep everyone from leaving her, but she didn't think it was wise to grow close to someone like Blake, who had a higher risk factor of not coming home.

"Oh, Ava, I'm so sorry." Caroline frowned. Most likely regretting the words as soon as she said them. "You know I can be a fool sometimes. I just spit out whatever pops into my brain. I'm truly sorry."

"No, no, it's okay." Ava took a napkin and blew her nose. "I couldn't save Evelyn, either. I know that." Her stomach knotted under her shirt. *It's been years, Lord. Will I always feel this sad when I think about my little girl?*

"What about Dylan? Before you two married, he'd trek around the country with his cycling club, searching for the next impassable trail. He loved it. I remember when you started dating in college, he'd call you, out of breath and excited, explaining how he'd made it up another mountain or through another canyon."

Ava smiled, remembering Dylan's daring nature. It was one of the traits that had drawn her to him. Her heart sank. She'd never considered how similar Dylan and Blake's personalities were. *Oh, Dylan, you loved the risk. Didn't you?* Her husband might have worn a suit every day to work, but he was all adrenaline rush and adventure on the weekend.

A cloud of sadness passed over her and pressed down. After they'd lost Evelyn, Dylan rode less, even stepping away from his cycling group. *Had he considered her too fragile emotionally for him to venture far away from home?*

Ava shifted in her seat. That was one reason she'd decided to run to Africa, to prove to herself she wasn't afraid to truly live again. *But am I really living now? Or am I still scared to step out in faith?*

"I'm sorry, Ava." Caroline's soft voice snapped her out of her inner query. "I'm not trying to be flippant. I hope you don't think I'm being heartless about losing Dylan." Caroline leaned in and gave Ava's hand another squeeze. "Maybe it's because you have been through so much that I want you to have someone you can share your life with again. From what I've seen, Blake has been genuinely kind and supportive."

A small tear slid down her cheek, and she nodded. "He has."

"What happened to Dylan was an accident, but his hobby could've taken his life many times. I mean, that man would have mountain biked just about any kind of terrain. To take that away from him, he would've lost a piece of his soul."

A cool shiver trickled down her spine and she glanced up. "Are you telling me if Blake didn't have his job, he'd lose a part of himself?"

"Well, for one thing, if he hadn't decided to go back to his job after the death of his brother," Caroline stood when the tea kettle whistled. "You two would've never met. Who knows? You might've died in Uganda."

Ava hadn't thought of that. She watched as Caroline made herself at home in her kitchen, grateful she didn't have to play hostess with Dylan sleeping soundly in her arms.

"Yes, he has a dangerous job, and we have no idea why he chose that path, but for some reason, God saw fit to bring you two together."

Caroline slid into her chair with her instant coffee and handed Ava a steaming cup of decaf Lady Grey. "There's a bond there. I can tell when you talk about him." Caroline tossed her a knowing look. "I can also tell when he looks at you."

"How do I know it's not just a survivor's bond? You know when people go through a traumatic event together, they're connected forever."

"Well, first of all," Caroline's voice shifted into a professional tone. "His job puts him in situations like that all the time. I doubt he allows himself to intimately connect with everyone he rescues or goes on a mission with."

Ava rolled her eyes, but she could see Caroline's point.

"Ava," Caroline's voice lowered, "he came back to be with you for the birth of little Dylan. He wasn't sitting in the waiting room with the rest of us—he was right next to you, wiping sweat off your brow after each contraction."

She resumed gently patting Dylan on his back and studied the vase on the counter. She hadn't missed Blake's attentions, but was she prepared for what they might lead to?

CHAPTER THIRTY-TWO

Caroline followed Ava's gaze. "Did he bring you those?"

Ava nodded and warmth wrapped around her. She had been so excited when she realized Blake was the one holding the large bouquet.

"This hardly looks like a survivor's bond to me. He comes to visit whenever he can."

She took a deep breath and released it. "He's injured, Caroline."

"He did look a little beat-up when he picked up the apartment key last night." Caroline had offered the use of her garage apartment to Blake anytime he was in town.

"I hugged him, and he flinched." She exhaled. "He told me he has a few bruised ribs, but there are other scrapes and abrasions all up and down his arms."

"What happened?"

"I don't know."

"Did you ask?"

"No. I know he can't tell me anything." Ava let out a long, frustrated breath. "I wanted to ask if his injuries had anything to do with the recent disasters on the news. His body language told me not to even attempt to figure it out."

"That's tough."

"When he flew in for Dylan's birth, his bicep was wrapped in gauze. He never mentioned anything about it. I only caught it because his sleeve moved up while we had lunch."

"Maybe he's accident-prone? I mean, boys will be boys. Maybe it was a fight?" Caroline threw her a wink. "You said sometimes he gets a little hot-headed."

"No, his job is dangerous, and he keeps going back."

Caroline sipped a long drink of her coffee.

"It's like he wants to get close to me, but he has this other part of him he needs to keep locked away. I'm not sure if that's a good way to enter into a relationship. What do you think?" Ava waited for Caroline to say something—anything to help her make sense of how she was feeling.

"Just don't give a hasty answer when he asks you to marry him."

"Marry him?" Her voice quavered. "You're not giving very sage advice right now."

"I think you should take it slow and just hear what he has to say."

Ava rolled her eyes. "I don't think he's going to pop the question any time soon."

"He flies in from who-knows-where every time he's on leave to see you."

Her heart beat faster. *She's right.* Ava shook her head to harness her runaway thoughts. "I think my nursing skills have blinded him."

"I hardly think it's that. There aren't many people you'd impress with your nursing skills."

"Thanks."

For the moment, the serious mood lifted, but Ava's mind

quickly went back to Blake. *What if he does want a more permanent relationship? Could I support him in his risky job? Would I always worry he might not make it home?* She shuddered as anxiety bubbled inside of her.

"I've lost too many people, Caroline. I just don't think I can put my heart out there and risk losing him too."

Caroline didn't respond. Instead, she just stirred the cream she poured into her second cup of coffee.

"Caroline?"

"Yes."

"Why aren't you saying something?"

"Humm ..."

"Seriously?"

"I'm just saying you need to prepare yourself for that man falling hopelessly in love with you. In all my years as a marriage counselor, I've never seen any woman pursued as much as you."

Ava's cheeks burned as her friend continued.

"He sends you a bouquet of sunflowers for every week he isn't with you."

"That is really sweet, isn't it?"

"If he doesn't make his feelings known soon, he's either going to run out of sunflowers or money."

"That's true."

Caroline glanced back at the flowers. "What's the story behind the sunflowers, anyhow?"

"It's a long story."

"Well, little Dylan just settled down for a snooze." Caroline motioned to Dylan, asleep in her arms. "I think we have some time."

"Once upon a time ..." Ava started with a dramatic voice for the benefit of her friend.

"There was a handsome soldier who had a thing for sunflowers." Caroline finished her sentence with a sigh.

"Okay, okay, I'll tell you about the sunflowers."

Caroline waved her on as she took another sip of her coffee and settled back into her seat.

"Blake and I were walking in—"

"Africa."

"Yes, Africa."

"It sounds so exotic. Usually, people meet in the grocery store."

Ava chuckled, remembering the conversation between Blake and her.

"What?"

"Nothing, never mind. Are you going to let me finish?"

"Yes, yes, sorry." Caroline waved her on.

"We stopped at this hidden church in the middle of—"

"Africa."

"Yes, Caroline, Africa."

"I'm sorry, I won't interrupt again." Caroline muffled a giggle.

"We stayed at this small village for two nights." Ava stopped for a second. Their time in Africa came back in a rush of memories. She cleared her throat to temper the intense emotions. "I woke up early the first morning we were there. I was feeling sick—my morning sickness. I went on a walk to get some fresh air. I trekked past a few rows of clothes drying on frayed ropes. Then, after I pushed through a makeshift wooden fence, I stumbled upon the most magnificent sight I'd ever seen: miles and miles of sunflowers waving in the warm breeze."

"It sounds magical."

She nodded. "It was."

"Was that the night you finally got a shower?" Her friend chuckled as she asked the question.

"A bath."

"Ah, yes, Blake found you a bath and clean clothes in the middle of the grasslands of Africa. A true gentleman."

Ava looked sideways at Caroline. "So, back to the sunflowers. As I glanced out over the array of orange and yellows, my stomach swayed with nausea. Before I had time to take in another breath of the fresh air, I sensed Blake's presence behind me."

"Hmmm." Caroline sighed.

"He leaned in and whispered in my ear, 'Are you okay?' I remember thinking about how deep and soothing his voice sounded."

"I bet."

"Oh, Caroline, those romance novels you read have turned your mind to mush."

Caroline stuck out her tongue.

"I didn't turn toward him. I just stared out at the sunflowers while they waved in the warm breeze. For a few seconds, he didn't say anything either. He just stood there, making me feel secure and protected."

Caroline leaned in as Ava finished her story.

"Despite the beautiful landscape, I felt queasy."

"Well, that's romantic."

"At this point in the trip, he'd seen me get sick more often than I cared to count. I wasn't thinking about romance, I was thinking about survival."

"I can see that."

"When I swayed, Blake grabbed onto my elbow. I was still so weak from the lack of nourishment." She paused a moment then continued. "I sank to my knees, and Blake knelt beside me." Her cheeks warmed, recalling his nearness. "I was overcome with fatigue, and thoughts of what we'd just escaped filled me with anger." Her voice caught in her throat. "I dug my fingers into the earth as the tears came in uncontrollable waves."

"Oh, Ava." Caroline reached out and patted her hand.

"The tears just kept coming. I felt like I was drowning."

"What did Blake do?"

"He wrapped an arm around me, then whispered, 'It's okay. I'm here.'"

"How sweet."

"After I finished crying, he helped me to my feet and gently wiped the tears off my cheeks. He tried to reassure me it was a perfectly normal response to our situation."

Caroline took another sip of her coffee and smiled wistfully.

"My first thought—there's nothing normal about having an emotional breakdown in the middle of a sunflower field in Uganda."

Caroline frowned. "Here you are, having this tender moment with an attractive soldier, and that's what you're thinking?"

"It was anything but romantic from my point of view. I'd just finished wearing the same clothes for weeks."

Caroline nodded. "Okay, well, there is that."

"Yes, there is that."

"He did, however, find you a mini spa in the middle of nowhere."

Ava smiled. "True."

"So, back to the sunflowers."

"Yes back to the sunflowers. When I turned into him, he pulled me close. We stood there for several minutes—"

"—in a lengthy embrace ..."

Ava held up her hand to stop Caroline. "Does Craig know about your obsession with romance novels?"

"What? I'm a marriage counselor. I try to see the romance in everything."

She considered Caroline's words. Was their story turning into a romance? Ava shook off the thought. "I stepped out of Blake's arms and glanced back out over the field." She paused as the memories came back to her like a flood. "And finally, after years of grieving Evelyn's loss, peace wrapped around me like a warm blanket."

Ava glanced at Caroline. Moisture pooled in her friend's lashes. Without a need for words, an understanding passed between them—when God gives His peace, it's restorative and complete, not lacking in anything.

She took a sip of her tea, then continued. "I knew we were far from being out of danger, but it was as if God had planted those sunflowers just for me. After weeks of only seeing terror in the landscape of Uganda, I was able to find the beauty again." She waved a hand in the direction of the vase of sunflowers. "I looked out over the horizon and simply said, 'they are so beautiful.'" Dylan squirmed, and she patted his bottom while moving him in a gentle rocking motion.

"Is that it?"

Ava sighed and stirred her tea. Then, looking past Caroline, she stared at the large bouquet on her counter. That day with Blake in the sunflower field traced across her mind in vivid color.

"Hello, Ava?" Caroline waved her hand in the air in front of her.

"Hmm?"

"Is that it? You said they were beautiful, and that induced him into a life of servitude to provide you with endless deliveries of sunflowers?"

Ava's cheeks warmed as she looked back at her friend.

"Oh, there *is* more." Caroline grinned.

"Blake wrapped his arms around me and whispered a few words in my ear." Her cheeks heated, recalling how his breath caressed the skin on her neck.

"What did he say?"

"Well, at the time, I had no idea what he said."

Caroline shot her a confused look.

"He spoke in Swahili."

"You're kidding?"

"No, he speaks several languages."

"Of course he does."

"I didn't ask for him to interpret." Pausing, Ava recalled what her heart was thinking. "All I could think about was him holding me."

"Aww, Ava, that's so—"

"Romantic?"

"I don't think you are grasping the tenderness of this whole story." Caroline made a pouty face, and Ava laughed.

"Remember, my swooning was induced by morning sickness."

"Okay, I see your point."

Ava threw her friend a stern look. "Oh, and don't forget we were running for our lives."

Caroline chuckled, then leaned in. "Did you ever find out what he said?"

She nodded but didn't elaborate.

Caroline clasped her hands together like an excited child. "Oh, Ava, you know I'm dying here."

Ava's body flooded with warmth. "I can still hear the words and how he said them."

"How did you find out what he'd said?"

"Later that night, before we left, I asked one of the ladies who spoke a little more English than the others."

"And?"

"She told me the words were, '*You* are the one that is beautiful.'"

"You're kidding."

"No." Ava's voice lowered into a whisper.

"Do you know what, my dear friend?"

"What?"

"I hope you're prepared."

Shooting her friend a look, she asked, "Prepared for what?"

"That man has already fallen in love with you."

CHAPTER THIRTY-THREE

Blake ran his hands along the sides of the smooth wood. Not one splinter. He stood back, admiring his handiwork.

Grabbing a rag from the table, he wiped off the excess dust. "Not too bad for a quick project."

A few days ago, he'd applied the dark ebony stain to the rustic cookbook stand—the perfect color to highlight Ava's farmhouse kitchen.

He smiled to himself. He was looking forward to dinner tomorrow night. *But do I have the guts to go through with my plan?* A tremor of trepidation snaked through him. *Sometimes, you need to jump. Even if it is without a chute.*

Jacob's remembered advice sparked a laugh. "Right. That's what I feel like I'm doing—jumping without a chute." His feelings for Ava were no longer something he could push aside, and life was too short to ignore them anyway. Wasn't it?

Glancing around the large metal building, thoughts of the future traveled across his mind. Someday he'd love to have a shop like this—with a planer, a lathe, and a workbench with a built-in vacuum. It was a woodworker's dream. Blake grabbed the soft-bristled brush and popped open the can of polyurethane. As he glided the brush up and down in long swipes across the wood, his mind turned to the recipient. *I hope she likes it.*

He pushed the lid back on the poly and stuck the paintbrush into the thinner for a quick soak. As he did a final clean-up around the workbench, his mind reverted to a few nights ago when he'd formulated his plan.

He and Ava had decided to cook dinner together—steaks on the grill, his specialty. While he wasn't a gourmet cook, give him a flame and an iron grate and he could cook just about anything.

While the steaks sat on the counter, dusted in a rub he'd found at the local supermarket, Ava volunteered to make biscuits. He'd expected her to grab something out of the freezer or a can from the fridge, but instead, she pulled out a bulky red-and-white-checkered cookbook and slapped it on the counter.

Flipping through the well-worn pages to the recipe she searched for, she tipped the book against a wicker basket to see the words easier. Then, she busied herself in the pantry, grabbing ingredients and a large glass bowl. No sooner did she pick up a wooden spoon than the book slid and landed with a thud on the granite countertop.

Blake smiled, recalling how her brow furrowed each time she picked it up and tried to place it at the right angle to read. Watching her made him chuckle, but then the craftsman part of his brain clicked to life. He glanced down at his finished product, happy with how the stain darkened in the woodgrain. *Perfect.*

He reached around, flipped off the switches on the

workbench, and slid the stool back under the front of the table. It felt good to work with his hands again.

Stepping out of the shop, he pulled the door closed behind him and looked up at the darkening evening sky. His thoughts turned to tomorrow, and mixed emotions swirled inside of him. Tomorrow would be his last night Stateside for another long length of time, but he wasn't leaving without telling Ava how he felt about her.

Blake's breath hitched. If he was this anxious now, how would he feel tomorrow? When he was face-to-face with Ava? *Remember, don't overthink it.*

He released a held breath and sent a quick prayer asking God to give him strength. He needed to know how she felt about him. He just prayed he had the courage to accept her response.

CHAPTER THIRTY-FOUR

B lake walked up to the front door holding a brown gift bag in one hand and a bouquet of sunflowers in the other. He needed to tell her. Tonight. Shifting on his feet before he knocked, he released a quick breath. A piece of cake. An easy mission. Slipping the bouquet under his arm, he patted his right jeans pocket. Cargo secured. He bit back a chuckle. This was ridiculous. It was just dinner.

Ringing the doorbell, he pulled the flowers from under his arm and angled the oversized buds in front of his face.

When the door opened, Ava's soft laugh floated around him. "Sunflowers. My favorite."

Blake moved the bouquet to the side and grinned. "I took a wild guess."

Ava shook her head and motioned him inside. She glanced at the bag, then turned away. His smile widened. Ava loved gifts. Following her down the hall, he said, "Dinner smells amazing."

"Thanks. I broke out some old recipes from my mom's cookbook."

Blake's stomach growled with anticipation. When he entered the great room, he glanced around. "Where's Dylan?"

Ava's cheeks pinked as she turned and withdrew the flowers out of his hand. "Caroline just picked him up." Her eyes glistened as she added, "Since you're leaving so early tomorrow, I ..." her words halted.

Blake placed the bag on the table and opened his arms. She sucked in a quick breath, then set the flowers down and leaned into him. A muffled sniffle hung between their embrace.

"Oh, sweetheart. I know this is hard." An uncomfortable ache crawled from Blake's chest to his throat. How could he soothe her fears? How could he take away her sadness? Leaving had always been easy for him. Until now.

After a few moments, she stepped back. "My heart hurts."

Her words pulled on the strings of his own heart and twisted. "I know. I wish there was something I could say to make it easier."

She nibbled on her bottom lip as if trying to keep herself from saying anything else.

Blake slid his thumb along her chin, and she pushed out her lip into a pout. He smiled. She was adorable.

"Can you give me a hint of where you're going?"

He leaned in and placed a gentle kiss on her lips. When they parted, he said, "I'll be safe. I promise."

"I guess I'll have to accept that."

"Let's enjoy dinner tonight." He turned and picked up the bag. Holding it out like a peace offering, he said, "I made you something."

Ava's expression lightened as she took the bag out of his hands. Reaching in, she pulled out a camo-green stuffed helicopter. She giggled. "I didn't know you could sew, soldier."

Blake swiped the helicopter from her grip. "That's for the

tiny troop." He cocked an eyebrow. "I guess you'll have to give it to him since you transported him to another location."

"He'll be back at"—Ava glanced at the clock and pinched her brows together—"twenty-one hundred hours." She took the helicopter back and placed it on the table.

He laughed and watched as she peeked into the bag, then pulled out the tissue-wrapped bundle. His anticipation grew while she carefully unwrapped her gift.

"Oh, Blake." Running her hands along the smooth wood, she sighed. "A cookbook stand. It's beautiful."

"I noticed your cookbook kept slipping on the counter the other night." He shrugged. "I wanted to make you something useful."

"I love it." Turning it over, she traced her fingers along the carved heart encircling their initials. Sadness crept across her face before she added. "It will go perfectly in my kitchen."

A timer dinged. Ava reached out, tugged on his arm, and guided him to the kitchen. "The bread's done. Let's go eat."

The two said grace, then Blake cut into his chicken-fried steak and took a bite. "This tastes amazing. You mentioned this was your mom's recipe, right?"

Ava nodded. "She was an amazing cook. Southern through and through." After a moment, she asked, "What about your mom? Does she like to cook?"

"She's a great cook, but her specialty is baking. Cookies, cakes, anything like that. Every Christmas, she makes the best cookies and sends boxes of them to the neighbors." He laid his fork down and took a drink of his water before adding, "She sends a box out to me if I'm downrange during the holidays."

"Downrange?"

Blake fiddled with his napkin. "Sorry, that's a pretty generic term. Deployed."

A few seconds of silence lingered before she asked, "Are you deployed a lot over the holidays?"

He shrugged. "I haven't really kept track."

As a shadow blanketed Ava's expression, tension coiled in his gut. *God help me explain my life to her. Give me a way to bring her in.* Blake picked up his fork and scooped a portion of his green beans.

"I feel like you know what I do, but I'm a little confused as to what you do for a living." Ava dabbed her lips with her napkin, then laid it next to her plate. Shooting him a playful smile, she added, "Besides commandeering trucks in the wilderness from unsuspecting farmers." She leaned back in her seat and folded her hands in her lap. "I suspect if you tried that around here, it wouldn't end well."

"No doubt." Plunking the last portion of his dinner roll in his mouth, he contemplated his job and what he could share. After he finished chewing, he leaned back in his chair and folded his arms. "So, my job ..."

Ava nodded.

"It's not terribly interesting."

The melodic sound of her laughter circled around the dining room. "A regular nine-to-fiver, huh?"

Blake snorted a chuckle, then he held both palms up, offering his surrender. "Okay, okay. It's exciting. Actually, it's my dream job."

"Really?"

He nodded. "Ever since I was a little boy, I wanted to be in the military." Grinning, he said, "I wanted to see the world and defend my country. My recruiter told me to be ready to dress like a tree and eat dirt."

Ava's eyes widened. "That drew you in?"

Blake waved a hand around her decorator's dream interior

and said, "About as much as choosing a paint color gets your blood pumping."

She nudged him in the arm. "Very funny."

"Am I wrong?"

"No. You're not wrong." Without skipping a beat, she asked, "Was your dad in the military?"

"No, but he supported all three of his sons when we told him we were signing up to serve." A weighty silence hovered over the room as thoughts of Benjamin traced through his mind.

As if reading his thoughts, Ava reached out her hand and laid it on his arm.

His vision blurred. "Benjamin was a great guy. I wish you could've met him."

"Me too." Pausing a few moments, she asked, "What's a typical day look like for you?"

Blake blew out a breath, thankful for the redirect. "Every day is different. It's a cycle of missions, reports, breaks, then the cycle begins again. I usually go home on leave. If Brent's around, we go camping or fishing."

Ava's cheeks pinked as she withdrew her hand. "I, uh … you're missing time with your family." She glanced down.

Warmth wrapped around his collar. He wanted nothing more than to be here with her. "Trust me. They understand."

She lifted her chin. Delight covered her expression.

Even though he suspected questions still lingered, sharing the little he could about his job had lifted a weight from his shoulders.

"I made dessert. Would you like some?"

Leaning back in his seat, Blake patted his stomach. "If you keep feeding me like this, I'll need to buy new uniforms."

"It's caramel apple pie." The corners of her lips twitched up. "Extra caramel."

"I'm in." He picked up their plates and took them to the sink.

Ava returned from the mudroom with a bucket of vanilla ice cream. "Can you scoop? It's always frozen solid when it comes out of the deep freezer."

Blake flexed his arms. "Challenge accepted."

"Good, because I have no forearm strength."

He laughed as he opened drawers, searching for the metal scoop. "You need to do more push-ups."

"Did you forget? I avoid exercise." Ava sliced two hearty portions of pie, then slid the bowls over to him.

Mid-scoop, he turned to face her. "Except for hiking. You like hiking." Blake resumed scooping. "Long distances. With lots of bugs."

She elbowed him, then snapped the lid back on the ice cream. "Never again. You hear me? If I never see that continent again, it will be too soon." Her laugher drifted behind her as she walked back into the mudroom. When she returned, a smile brightened her face. "There was one activity I'm sorry I missed out on."

"What's that?"

"Feeding the elephants."

"Really?" Blake leaned back against the counter, interested in discovering another layer of her personality.

Ava nodded. "Our group was going to stop at a wildlife reserve before our flight out. Colby had really—" She paused a moment, exhaling a long breath.

Understanding her hesitation, Blake reached for her hand and drew lazy circles on her skin with his thumb. He hoped the repetitive motion soothed her.

Ava blinked and waved her other hand around as if swatting at a fly. "Sorry about that. Sometimes the memories creep in, and ..."

"It's understandable."

She took a steadying breath. "Anyway, I was looking forward to feeding the elephants. They're such amazing animals."

"They are. Definitely one of God's more unique creatures." Picking up their bowls, Blake waited for Ava to take the lead, then he followed her to the couch. After he took a bite of the pie, he sighed. "This is delicious."

She watched him take another bite, then said, "I added a secret ingredient."

"Care to share?"

"I can't divulge any secrets, Martin. If I did, I'd have to keep you here indefinitely."

Her words laced a ribbon of warmth around his soul. They were the same words he'd said to her. If only they rang true. If staying were an option, he'd plead with her to share all her secrets and agree to never leave.

As he finished his dessert, Blake's mind raced in circles like a dog chasing its tail. Was tonight the right time? How would she respond? Did she feel the same way?

He glanced at the ticking clock. It was eight. He bit back a smile. Or twenty hundred hours. He had an hour before Caroline dropped off Dylan. If he didn't speak now, he'd have to wait months to tell her.

Ava placed her empty bowl on the table, pulled her legs up under her, and snuggled into the corner of the couch. "Something on your mind?"

At her question, he lifted his gaze. His tongue felt like he'd swallowed sand.

"You seem a little far away right now." She pulled a pillow on to her lap and fiddled with the tassels.

It's now or never. He put his bowl next to hers and scooted closer to her. "There's something I need to tell you."

"Okay?" Apprehension flooded her expression.

He shifted in his seat and prayed. This was harder than his first night at basic training.

"We've been through a lot together. I wanted to give you something before I left." Blake withdrew the velvet bag from his jeans pocket. Handing it to her, he motioned for her to open it.

Ava pulled out the diamond tennis bracelet and released a blissful sigh. As she examined it, a gold charm in the shape of Africa dangled from the clasp. She flipped the charm over and read the inscription. "Little things."

Blake lifted her chin with the crook of his finger and tried to read her expression. "I want to be there for the little things. I want to be someone you can lean on. Always." He pulled back his hand and tugged at his collar. He'd stepped into uncharted territory. "I've fallen in love with you, Ava. From the first day we met, I felt drawn to you. I've tried to fight it, but I can't. I know we come from two different worlds, but I wanted to tell you how I felt before I left."

Silence wrapped around them like a cool breeze as Blake fought to tamper the uncertainty clawing at his emotions. *Say something, Ava.* He searched her expression but failed to see the response he was hoping for.

Her eyes welled with tears. She lowered her gaze back to the bracelet. A single tear fell through her lashes and tumbled down her cheek. With shaky hands, Ava slipped the delicate chain back into the bag, stood, and placed it in her back pocket. Without saying anything, she picked up their bowls and scurried to the kitchen.

Blake's gut twisted. Had he read their situation wrong? Had he moved too fast?

The faucet turned on. Glasses clanked together as Ava loaded the dishwasher. He rubbed his hands across his thighs and released a long breath. *God, tell me what to do. Please.*

Standing, he took his time walking into the kitchen, each heavy step mingled with more pleas for direction. Ava walked to the stove and scooped the leftover vegetables into a square glass dish.

He frowned. She was avoiding the elephant *he'd* dragged into the room with busy work. What a mess. *I can't pretend I said nothing. We need to talk about this.*

She pressed the lid on the container, picked it up, and turned toward the refrigerator. Blake stood in her way, removed the dish from her hands, and placed it on the counter.

"Ava." He gripped the back of his neck while he weighed his words. "Did I say something to upset you?"

She inhaled a long breath, then released it. "No." Her answer was short, but not unkind.

"Sweetheart." Reaching out, he pulled her into his arms. Resting his chin on the top of her head, he asked, "What's wrong?"

She sniffled but didn't answer.

After a few seconds, he pulled back and cupped her face with his hands. Moisture from her tears pooled on his thumbs. "Please, don't cry. Whatever it is, we can talk about it. Just tell me what you're thinking." *I need to know if you feel the same way.*

She stepped out of his embrace. After she swiped her cheeks with the back of her hand, she withdrew the velvet bag out of her pocket. Tugging the bracelet free from the pouch, she handed it to him, smiled through her tears, and lifted her left wrist. "Will you help me put it on?"

"Are you sure? I won't be upset if—"

She laid a finger on his lips and silenced him. "I love the bracelet. It's beautiful. It's just ..." She sucked in a quick breath and tossed him a shy look. "I'm trying to process everything. My pulse feels like I've just run across Uganda. Again."

Warmth flooded his body. "Mine too." Lifting her hand, Blake draped the bracelet around her wrist. As his fingers glided across her soft skin, sparks of energy arced in his veins. After he attached the clasp, he pressed a gentle kiss over the pulse point atop the blue vein trailing beneath her skin.

Ava didn't pull away. "That's not helping my heart rate."

"Mine either." Tugging her arm closer, he landed a trail of kisses from the bracelet to the inside of her elbow. She murmured a sigh and wrapped her arms around his neck. He leaned in and brushed her lips with a kiss.

When they parted, she said, "Thank you for the bracelet. It's perfect." Pinching her brows together, she added, "I'm sorry about ... you just caught me off guard, and with you leaving tomorrow ..."

Pulling her in again, he relished the warmth of her body against his. He hoped she'd mention his declaration, but she danced around the topic. "Ava, I—" A knock at the door interrupted his uneasy thoughts. She pulled away and another coil of knots kinked in his gut. *Does she feel the same way?*

"We're back." Caroline's voice carried down the hallway as she walked in the door.

Heat traced around Blake's neck. He took a step back. Their kiss, intermingled with her lack of response to his confession, sent his emotions into a tailspin. *How am I going to bring the subject back up?*

Ava threw him a weak smile and mouthed 'I'm sorry' as Caroline walked around the corner holding Dylan's car seat.

He shrugged and whispered, "It's okay." It wasn't. But what could he say with her best friend in the room? *Hey, could you give us a minute, Caroline? I'd like to see why Ava went silent when I told her I loved her.* He kept his eyes on Ava, but she avoided his gaze.

Dylan kicked and cooed in his car seat. Ava smiled. She unclasped the seat straps and wrapped him in her arms. "Hey, sweet boy. Did you have fun with Aunt Caroline?" Ava nuzzled Dylan's neck and he laughed.

"Hey Blake." Caroline glanced at him, then back at Ava. "How was dinner?"

"Good." They both answered in unison.

"Was it?" Caroline surveyed the kitchen like a detective searching for evidence.

Blake shifted on his feet, shoved his hands in his pockets and leaned against the counter.

"I made chicken fried steak. My mom's recipe." Ava pointed to the cast-iron skillet on the stove. "I even brought old faithful out to cook with."

While Ava rattled on about the meal, static filled Blake's ears. *I need to pack. More than that, I need a couple more hours to talk to Ava. Alone.*

"Blake?" Caroline's voice cut through his murky thoughts.

He blinked. "Hmm? Sorry, I zoned out a little."

Caroline smiled, then asked, "What time do you leave in the morning?"

"Five."

"Wow. That early?" Caroline peered at the clock above the stove. "Are you even going to sleep?"

He pressed his lips into a thin line, then shrugged. "I'll sleep on the plane."

She nodded and glanced back at Ava. The look they shared made him feel like an outsider.

Blake cleared his throat. "What can I do to clean up?" He picked up the dish of vegetables and placed it in the fridge. When he turned, both ladies were staring at him.

Caroline spoke up first. "Hey, why don't I pack up the leftovers and you three can go into the living room?" Her tone switched to counselor mode. "So Blake can say his goodbyes to Dylan."

Tension pulled at his shoulders. *Is this what it's like to leave a family behind?* He blew out a long breath, then forced a smile. "Sounds good. I've got a gift for the little man."

"That's right." Ava met his gaze and nodded toward the living room. "Let's go give it to him. I'll need to get him in his jammies soon."

Blake followed Ava to the couch while Caroline finished up in the kitchen. As she sat down next to him, she cradled Dylan in her lap. Picking up the helicopter, he handed it to Dylan. "Here you go, buddy. I thought you could practice your flying." His chest tightened. *I can't do this.* When he glanced up, Ava's eyes welled with tears.

Dylan's expression lightened, and he grabbed for the helicopter.

Smiling through watery eyes, Ava said, "He'll carry that helicopter everywhere."

Blake leaned back in his seat and smoothed imaginary creases out of his shirt. Ava scooted next to him. Wrapping his arm around her shoulders, he pulled her closer and placed a kiss on the top of her head. "I'm going to miss you both."

She nodded but didn't respond.

He held her for a few moments before Dylan let go of the helicopter and it tumbled to the floor. Blake released his hold on Ava and leaned forward to pick it up. When he turned back, Dylan sniffled and fat crocodile tears rolled down his cheeks. Blake's heart tore in two. "Here you go, buddy." Holding out the toy, Blake forced a smile. *He'll be almost a year when I get back. How much will he change?*

Dylan took the helicopter and shoved a thumb in his mouth.

Ava stood, patting Dylan on the back. "I better get him ready for bed. It's past his bedtime."

"I better go pack." Standing, he followed her down the hall. *I should say something. But what?* A gaping hole opened in the pit of his stomach. After she opened the door, Ava turned to face him. Her fiery blue eyes carried a mixture of pain and regret.

"Ava, I ..." The doorway was no place to have a conversation.

She lifted on her toes and placed a kiss on his cheek. "Be safe, Blake."

He nodded, stepped out the door, and said, "I promise."

As the door clicked shut, the darkness wrapped around him like a shroud. Could he truly promise he'd be safe? Or was it just an empty saying he'd learned to repeat?

Glancing over his shoulder, he watched as the light in Dylan's room turned on, and two shadows drifted in front of the curtains. Tonight's mission was a disaster.

I've fallen in love with you, Ava. As he replayed his words, he cringed. *I feel like an idiot.*

He'd have to wait months to talk to her in person. Months. How could he wait that long to find out how she really felt about him?

CHAPTER THIRTY-FIVE

B lake shoved a pair of jeans into his duffle bag. "Well, that went well." After he checked his phone for his flight reservation he stomped into the bathroom and stashed his toiletries into his travel bag. "You come back injured and profess your love. Real smooth."

A light knock at the door interrupted his rant. He checked his watch. Four-thirty—a little early for visitors.

Dropping the bag on the counter, he shuffled across the room and swung open the door. Ava stood at the threshold wearing jeans and a faded burnt orange hoodie. She looked like she hadn't slept since he'd left after dinner.

"I can't do this, Blake."

"What?" He looked at her and then out on the landing. "Where's Dylan?"

"Caroline's watching him." She walked past him into the room. "I couldn't sleep after you left."

He closed the door behind her and walked back over to his bag. She'd only moved a few feet into the room and folded her arms protectively around her middle.

"I can't do—" Her voice cracked, and she nodded toward his luggage. "This."

He assumed when he'd left she was at least open to the idea of having him in her life. But, from her tear-stained cheeks, he was wrong.

"I know you care about me, Ava." He'd shared more about his career in the military with her last night than he'd done with anyone—ever. His work was precarious, and there was no way to skirt around the issue of his safety.

"You know I do."

"Then what's there to question?" He immediately regretted his arrogant tone, but he hadn't slept a wink either. The pull between their two worlds—staying with her and completing his mission—had made him anxious all evening.

Tonight had been a mistake. Did he really expect her to sit and wait for him to roam back into town when his missions allowed? She had questions he couldn't answer and reassurances he wasn't at liberty to give. Her expression radiated worry as she glanced back at his duffel.

"Okay, let's just put it out there." Her voice sharpened, and she brought her gaze up to his. "You want me to just wait here for you? Until your mission is over?"

The questions made him cringe.

"Then what will happen? Will you just fly in unannounced? Back into town and back into mine and Dylan's life?"

He didn't respond. She was right, and until now, he'd ignored the logistics of what he might be expecting.

"Is that okay with you?" Ava flashed him a steely look. She was the only person in the world who could make him think twice about how he wanted to respond. For now, he chose to keep silent.

"Can you tell me where you're going this time? Give me

something to hold on to while I wait for you?" Her voice quivered. "You showed up this time with bruised ribs, stitches across your forehead, and other injuries. It looks like you were in a war zone. What's next?"

His whole body tensed as she verbally assailed him. Finally, he took two steps and closed the space between them.

"You know I can't tell you." He reached for both of her hands, and they trembled.

"I know, Blake." She said his name with a coolness he'd not heard before. "That's part of the problem."

"Is it because I can't tell you where I'm going that you don't want to pursue this?"

"No."

"Then what is it?"

"It's because you can't promise me—" her voice hitched. "You can't promise me you'll come back."

"Do you want me to retire?" The words flew off his lips before he could retrieve them.

"What?"

"Retire?" He repeated the idea, but this time his tongue dried when he asked it. *Am I ready to retire? To give up a job that I've invested so much in?*

"No, Blake, I don't want you to retire."

"Why not? If you want to make a go of this, I'll quit my job if you ask me to." He held her gaze for several seconds. The mournful look in her eye told him she'd never ask him to leave his job.

Blake glanced down at his watch. He had a plane to catch but didn't want to leave the discussion unfinished. "Can we talk when I get back?" The question was a long shot, but he asked it anyway.

"Can you honestly promise me you *will* be back?"

He hesitated before he answered. "You know I can't, Ava."

As he said her name, she withdrew her hands from his.

"There's always a risk I won't come back from a mission. It's something I've found peace with."

By the anguished expression on her lovely face, the same couldn't be said for her.

CHAPTER THIRTY-SIX

va stepped away from him, trying to process his words. *He's found peace with it? With not coming back?* He'd been honest about his feelings tonight, but she'd kept hers tucked safely away. She loved him too, but she didn't want him to leave.

"Are any of us promised tomorrow?" His question jolted her from her inner turmoil. He reached toward her, but she clutched her hands in front of her.

A look of disappointment traveled across his face as his hand dropped back to his side. "Don't you think I worry about you and little Dylan? Dallas isn't a small midwestern town anymore. It's a big, and at times dangerous, city. We can't protect each other from everything."

What he said was true, but the thought of him leaving again made her heart ignite with fear. "How long will you be gone? Can you tell me anything?"

Blake ran his fingers along his jawline. "Most likely," there was hesitation in his voice, "six months, maybe longer."

"What?" Her voice cracked with anger and exasperation.

She did an impromptu mental calculation. Dylan would be almost a year old before he got back. She wanted to throw something or scream—or both. "I was under the impression you were a go-in-and-get-the-job-done kind of guy."

"It depends on the mission."

She wasn't ready to have this conversation with him, but for the sake of her heart, she had to. "How long were you in Uganda?"

"What?" He looked caught off guard by her question. "I was stationed in Kenya."

"That is not what I asked, Blake. How long were you in Uganda?"

He didn't respond.

"How long?"

"A few weeks." He kept his voice tight, like someone who'd been well trained at veiling his answers.

"Before you were captured?"

"Yes."

"If you hadn't been captured, how long would you have been there?"

He turned, walked toward his luggage, rolled up his shirts, and threw them in his bag. "I can't tell you."

"You can't, or you won't?"

The muscles in his jaw twitched. Then, finally, he turned and took a step toward her. She backed closer to the door.

"I can't give you any of the details, and you know that. First of all, because I don't know how long I would've been in Uganda." He paused. A storm gathered in his eyes. "I would've been there until the mission was finished." He shoved his hands into his pockets and blew out a breath. "Secondly, I can't disclose anything about what I was doing there."

Ava opened her mouth to respond, then closed it.

"I meant what I said." In one fluid motion, he reached out

and took her left hand. Turning it over, he looked at the dainty diamond tennis bracelet he'd slid on her wrist hours ago. "I want to be there for the little things. I'm asking you to give me a chance to figure this out." His jewel-toned eyes flamed with passion. "Ava, I love—"

"Don't, Blake." She jerked her hand away. Her heart was breaking, and she couldn't think with him touching her.

"Don't what?" His posture stiffened. "Haven't I shown you I want to be a part of your life?"

Ava took a deep breath to push back against her rising anxiety. *He said he loved me, but how can I keep from thinking about what he might be going back to? Africa almost killed him.*

"Other couples make it work. There are men in my unit who have wives. I think you're being unreasonable."

"I guess I'm not cut from the same cloth they are." Her pulse quickened as fire shot through her veins. "You've been injured the past two times you came back to Dallas, and we can't even talk about it." Every time she thought about him getting hurt again, the images of him lying in a heap on a dirt floor rushed across her mind like a comet.

There was no way she could let him in further. Losing Evelyn sparked a fear she'd never learned how to snuff out. After Dylan's death and her kidnapping, the stress of trying to hold all the pieces of her life together became an unbearable burden she couldn't release. There was no way she'd risk losing her heart to someone whose job required him to live balancing along the razor's edge of danger.

A shiver tip-toed down her spine. "I'm not strong like your partner's wives. I need stability."

"No. What you need is control." His expression screamed frustration. "You escaped that prison in Uganda, but Ava," he paused, "you're still chained to your fear. Neither one of us can see the future, and I can't guarantee I won't get injured doing my job."

"Maybe you're right." Ava sniffed back her tears. "But I know I can't have someone in my life who willingly throws himself into harm's way."

Blake looked down at the delicate bracelet on her wrist. "You're going to need someone to help you with that."

He folded his arms and leaned back on his heels. She'd seen his anchored stance before, along with his guarded expression.

"I can manage." She covered her wrist and turned toward the door. *I will not let him see me cry.*

"Ava, wait."

She ignored him and swung open the door. Stepping out onto the landing, her eyes burned. *Once he's gone, you'll be free —free from the worry of the unknown.* The fear and loss she'd nursed for years coiled around her heart. *This doesn't feel like freedom. It feels like drowning.*

Glancing over her shoulder, she ignored the niggling undercurrent of second guesses. "Please don't contact me anymore. I can't have you dropping into my life on a whim while I try to make a stable home for Dylan and me." The words left an acrid taste on her tongue and didn't bring any relief from her sorrow.

Despair shadowed his expression.

It didn't matter. She needed security. All he could give her was secrecy. Letting him go was her only option.

Lonelier than she'd ever felt before, Ava took off down the stairs and didn't look back.

CHAPTER THIRTY-SEVEN

18:00 US Air Base, Kenya

B lake bundled another caramel color T-shirt and shoved it into his rucksack. *I haven't talked to Ava in over seven months.* "Dylan's birthday." A mental picture of Dylan blowing out a candle skipped across his mind. His throat constricted. "Don't even go there."

The heartbreak hung on like a drowning victim dangling from a life preserver. He'd done his best to respect her wishes and not contacted her, but it killed him. Thinking about the last morning they'd seen each other brought another fresh wave of regret. *You're going to need someone to help you with that.* Blake shook off the replay. Recalling the flippant words he'd said to her burned worse than a hot branding iron thrust onto his flesh.

"You ready? Wheels up in twenty." Jacob pounded on the door frame as he poked his head into the room.

Blake turned. "Yeah, I'll be there in a minute."

"You sound grumpier than usual. Everything okay?" Jacob folded his arms and shot him a look.

"I'm fine." Glancing down at his watch, Blake attempted to redirect. "I didn't get much sleep last night."

"Uh, uh. Not buying it."

His partner could read him better than an open book, but this time he hoped he'd let it pass.

"Your mood have anything to do with a pair of fiery blue eyes?"

Blake folded his arms. He tried to steady his tumultuous thoughts at the mention of Ava's unforgettable eyes.

"Ah, so it does."

"Just leave it." He threw out the statement in a huff. "I'll be out in a minute."

"Okay, whatever you say." Jacob held up his hands and backed out the door.

His partner's boots escaped down the hall, and Blake let his mind return to that morning. *There's always a risk that I won't come back from a mission. It's something that I have found peace with.*

Those words still haunted him. *Had* he found peace with it? Since he'd met Ava, he questioned what he did for a living. Had he really come to grips with the realization he might not return to her?

Slamming an angry fist against the half-packed rucksack, he let out an exasperated breath. There was an unopened box sitting at his parent's house with a ring inside intended for Ava. And now, he doubted it would ever see the light of day. *What was I thinking? Was I really going to ask her to marry me? Then what? Leave again?*

"God, please tell me what to do."

Silence from the drab-colored walls answered his plea.

In a fog, he threw the rest of his uniform into his bag and

packed his toiletries. Ava had asked him not to contact her again, and he'd honored her request. But, while their last conversation replayed in his mind, he wondered if it was a directive he should've ignored.

He picked up his wallet and shoved his laptop into his bag. He loved her. And life was too short not to do something about it. *But I told her I loved her, and she pushed me away.* He scanned the bare room one more time. Maybe this was the nudge he needed to finally hang up his combat boots and retire. He didn't want to be alone for the rest of his life. His throat tightened. *If we could just wrap up things with Rideau, I'd feel okay with stepping away.*

He flipped off the light and marched out the door. In less than ten hours, he'd be in Baghdad on his next assignment.

When he returned, he'd call her. One last time. For now, he needed to push thoughts of Ava out of his mind and complete his next mission.

CHAPTER THIRTY-EIGHT

A va stuck the last of the breakfast dishes into the dishwasher and glanced over at Dylan. His fingers curled around the rail of the play-yard as he bounced on chubby legs. He was getting so big. Where had the time gone?

Pushing open the curtains above the sink, the summer sun's rays warmed her cheeks and cast a cheery glow over the kitchen. It was beautiful outside. No storms on the horizon. She needed to take advantage of the mild morning before the afternoon brought in the sweltering heat.

Ava looked down at her clothes. Both she and Dylan woke up late, so she'd stayed in her robe and lounge pants through breakfast. "Let's say Mommy gets dressed, and then we go outside for a walk."

She walked over to the play-yard. Dylan looked up at her and smiled. Then, after he catapulted one of his toys out of the pack-and-play, he relaxed back on his bottom and giggled.

"I guess that's a *yes*, little man."

Dylan laughed again and nibbled on a toy ring.

She picked him up and breathed in his fresh baby scent.

"Come on, handsome, let's go get your clothes changed." A knock at the door halted her momentum and she turned to check the doorbell camera on the security screen. "Who could that be?" Her heart skipped. In the screen stood a delivery man holding a bouquet and a clipboard.

Plopping Dylan back in the pack-and-play and giving her robe a quick tug around her waist, she shuffled to the front door. *Who would've sent me flowers?* One name waved itself across her thoughts like a banner in a parade. *Blake?* As soon as she thought of him, she reprimanded herself. *But I told him not to contact me.* She hadn't received flowers from Blake since he'd left. So why would he send any now?

"Good morning." The delivery driver grinned at her. "Mrs. Robertson?"

"Um, I'm sorry. Who did you ask for?"

"I have a delivery for a—" the driver paused and glanced at his clipboard "—a Mrs. Sylvia Robertson." He smiled and waggled the bouquet of yellow roses in his hand.

"Oh." Ava's heart dropped. "No, I'm sorry you have the wrong house." Her cheeks prickled with warmth, as if the delivery man could sense her regret. "Mrs. Robertson is my neighbor across the street." Ava pointed toward the large brick home facing hers about an acre away.

"Oh, I'm sorry to bother you. Have a nice day." The man pivoted on his heels and took off toward his truck.

A weight of sorrow wrapped itself around her. Fighting back the unwanted tears, she stepped inside and shut the door. Ava leaned her forehead against the frame, closed her eyes, and steadied her breathing.

Ava, I've fallen in love with you. The unwanted memory called out to her like a ghost from the grave. Turning, she leaned her back against the door and lifted her hand to wipe away a few stray tears. *I need to stop thinking about him.*

Dylan released a small cry, and Ava blinked. Angry she'd let her mind wander down that path again, she shook her head and made her way to the kitchen. "I refuse to think about you, Blake." She picked up Dylan and brought him in for a tight squeeze. He gurgled and cooed against her shoulder while she sniffled. "We don't need his chaos in our life, do we, buddy?" Tiny fists grabbed her hair as another lump formed in her throat.

"Da-da."

Ava stiffened and closed her eyes as the baby-sized syllables fell from Dylan's lips. She brought him forward to look at him. His expression resembled his father when he lifted an eyebrow and smiled. Her heart ripped in two.

She planted a quick kiss on his cheek and with a forced joviality she asked, "Can you say Ma-ma?"

"Da-da. Da-da."

Sorrow wrapped around her heart and squeezed. Feeling torn between the pull of two men—one who was gone and one she'd sent away—her soul screamed. *God, are you trying to tell me something?*

Had she been too hasty to cut ties with the man He'd sent to heal her broken heart? And if she had, would Blake be willing to give her a second chance?

CHAPTER THIRTY-NINE

23:30 Baghdad, Iraq

The aircraft's wheels skidded as they touched down on the sweltering runway. Outside the windows, the velvet sky resembled a massive canopy draped over the darkened desert landscape. *It's been a while since I've been on a mission in the sandbox.* His heart tightened as his thoughts drifted to Benjamin. *I miss you, little bro.*

The plane taxied a short distance then came to a complete stop. Energy rippled through the aircraft as everyone unbuckled and stood.

"You two better get some sleep." Adams snorted as he jerked his duffle onto his shoulder.

Jacob glanced down at his watch. "What's the point?"

Blake shook his head as he grabbed his own bag.

"The point is you've been up for twenty-four hours, and I need you bright-eyed and bushy-tailed for your trek in the morning."

Blake guffawed at Adams's answer. The description made

him sound like he should be reclining in his rocking chair, whittling wood by the light of a candle instead of leading a mission.

"Bushy-tailed. I like that one." Jacob slapped Blake on the shoulder. "What do you say we go grab a few sets of cards before calling it a night?"

Adams cursed and shoved a toothpick between his lips.

"Team lead says we need sleep." He nodded toward their scowling leader. "We better obey with that look."

Adams sneered at them, and Jacob laughed.

"Okay, but I'm driving tomorrow."

Adams pulled out a coin. "Let's say you and Martin call for the driver's seat."

Blake laughed and pointed at Adams's hand. "It's a double-headed coin, and I always call heads."

Adams's smirk stretched further across his face. Then, after he paused a second, he flipped the coin up in the air.

Blake grinned. "Tails."

Jacob chuckled. "Heads."

Their sole intent was to crawl under Adams's skin.

The coin landed, and he and Jacob stared down at it.

Heads.

"I don't care what you called, Armstrong. Martin's driving." Adams turned in a huff. "I know Martin will try to get some shut-eye."

As Adams trudged off the plane, they doubled over in laughter.

"I'm going to go find a card game."

Blake shrugged. "You heard him. I'm driving." He stepped off the plane not bothering to look back. "I'm going to catch some shut eye." *Or try to.*

"Hey." Jacob caught up to him. "You want to talk about it?"

"About what? Me driving?"

Jacob grabbed his arm and yanked him to a stop. "No. About you and blue eyes."

Blake curled his hand into a fist. Part of him wanted to throw a punch. His partner would understand, right? "On second thought, I'm going to get a workout in. Want to join me?"

A slow smile crept across Jacob's face. "So no talking?"

He shot Jacob a glare. "You won't be able to breathe after we finish."

"Now that's what I'm talking about."

Blake pivoted on his heels and stalked toward the barracks. He'd push himself until he passed out if it would guarantee Ava wouldn't visit his dreams tonight.

CHAPTER FORTY

Ava laid Dylan down in his crib for the night and sighed, still thinking about her morning. The visit from the flower delivery driver had meandered around her mind all day. After she and Dylan had taken their walk, she tried to pull her focus off Blake and work on some room layouts. Then, finding herself distracted with thoughts of the brawny soldier and his intense jade eyes, she opted to clean out a few closets and organize her pantry. With little Dylan by her side "helping," the day quickly morphed into nightfall.

She glanced one more time at her sleeping child. His eyelashes rested like angel's wings against his soft cheeks. *Lord, thank You for my little boy.*

Turning, she tiptoed into the hallway and checked her watch. *Nine-thirty.* It was late, but the anxious pulse in her temples told her she wasn't even close to settling down. After flopping on the couch, she flipped through a few channels before deciding on a home decorating show. *How cliché.* Ava laughed as she listened to the host rattle on about the difference between wainscotting and shiplap.

"You should try building with mud." She voiced the statement aloud to the empty room, recalling some of the more rustic homes in Uganda.

After a few lengthy commercials, the show returned, and the host enthusiastically chatted to the homeowners about filming in *The City of Trees*. A lump formed in Ava's throat as she watched a sweeping drone shot of Atlanta.

I'm from Atlanta.

She shook her head, clicking off Blake's words and the television. *Nope, not going there.*

Shutting off the lights, Ava strolled to her bedroom and quietly pulled the master closet door shut behind her. Her heart pounded as she fished a keepsake box from the top shelf. Hesitating only a second, she lifted the lid.

Inside the box, next to her battered pink tennis shoes, was Blake's thread-bare fatigue jacket. Her mouth dried and she tried to swallow. *Oh, Blake, what are you doing right now?* She picked up the coat and traced the name tape with her fingers. *Maxwell.* Lifting the tattered fabric to her nose, she inhaled a long, deep breath. It smelled like dirt and sweat—and him.

Her eyes welled with tears. "I miss you."

CHAPTER FORTY-ONE

15:24 Baghdad, Iraq

Searing pain racked Blake's body as he fought to remain conscious.

"Get him in the chopper."

"He's seizing."

Anxious voices pushed through his thoughts like a crowbar penetrating a metal door. The wind picked up, and he inhaled tiny particles of sand and dust.

"He's secure."

Sharp electrical pulses shot through his veins, and his limbs shook as if he'd been thrown into a rock tumbler. *What's happening to me?* Unable to fight for control, he allowed the loud hum of the engine to lull him into darkness.

"Stay with me, buddy." Jacob's voice floated through his ears and dragged him back to the present.

Blake tried to open his eyes. One lid lifted, the other was pasted shut.

"I need to get this debris out of his eye."

Through the hazy lens of his left eye, the pale green uniforms danced like ghostly mirages hovering over the desert sand.

"His heart rate is spiking."

A second flash of pain traveled through his body, and his teeth chattered uncontrollably.

"He's having another one. We need to get the IV hooked up and stop the bleeding."

This time, a female voice drifted across his ears. "That one lasted just under a minute."

Someone tugged at his sleeve, and then ice-cold liquid cascaded over the inside of his elbow. Across his vision, everyone in the chopper continued to move like swirling vapors. He closed his eyes. *I'm going to be sick.*

"Get him on his side."

Several pairs of hands grabbed him and rolled him onto his side. A flash of blinding light erupted across his mind as he emptied the contents of his stomach.

"Leroy."

Blake tried to open his eye again as more confusion set in. *My name isn't Leroy. Is it?* He tried to move his lips, but they were swollen and dry.

"Is this your first trip, Leroy?"

Someone wiped off his lips while they repositioned him. Blake strained to focus. A young man in uniform unrolled a package of gauze. The kid's face was ashen as sweat dripped off his brow.

"Yes, ma'am."

"Can you hear me, Maxwell? My name is Sergeant Lyn. We're going to get you out of here."

Maxwell? A flash of light ignited past his temples. *I like Maxwell better.* "Ava." The word floated out just shy of a whisper.

"His name isn't Maxwell." Jacob's voice sliced through the chaos.

I like Maxwell better. "Where's Ava? Is she safe?" He closed his left eye, feeling numb. *Legs, arms, toes...*

"That's what his name tape says." Sergeant Lyn's voice cut through his fog.

"His name is Martin. Blake Martin." Jacob continued but his partner's words turned fuzzy.

My name is Blake Martin. His body jostled as if suspended in a hammock during a tornado.

"We weren't with the rest of them. Just make sure you write it down."

Chilly moisture hit his forearm, and the pungent smell of permanent ink floated up to his nostrils.

Is she writing on my arm? My name's Blake Martin.

"His head is bleeding, and there's a lot of swelling. Was there anyone else on your team?"

"Just us two."

"Where's his family located?"

Texas.

"Georgia."

Someone scribbled across the inside of his forearm again. *Why are you writing on my arm? I'm not dead. Am I?*

"He took the hit from the right. We need to get his boots off and check his feet."

"Come on, Blake, this is not the time to go see *your* maker." Jacob's voice echoed in his ear.

Jacob? Where am I?

"If you care anything about this man, don't let him die."

Jacob, I know where I'm going. Do you?

CHAPTER FORTY-TWO

Ava rolled over to shut off her alarm and groaned. The red numbers told her it was six-thirty. But instead of feeling rested, she felt like she hadn't slept a wink. Her thoughts scurried back to yesterday when her heart betrayed her, and she'd given in to thinking about Blake. She cringed. The tears she shed while sitting on the floor with his uniform shirt still haunted her.

"Don't go there, Ava." Throwing back the covers, she listened for sounds coming from Dylan's room.

Relieved he was still asleep, she shuffled to the master bath and started her morning routine. With a quick splash of cool water, Ava told herself to focus on the day and stop lingering in the past. *What's on my schedule today? A quick lunch with Caroline then a meeting with a realtor.* Mentally, she tallied her to-do list. She'd been running her business from her home office and wanted to expand into a larger space. So today, she'd planned on touring several office buildings downtown.

She threw on a navy-blue pantsuit and a pair of tan flats. She needed to look professional, but hauling around a baby on her hip, she'd learned to ditch the heels. With a few turns of her curling iron, she twisted a handful of curls around her face before she opened her jewelry box to grab a pair of earrings. Her heart did a cartwheel as she zeroed in on the delicate tennis bracelet lying unclasped in the center of the box.

You're going to need someone to help you with that.

Blake's terse words were born out of her rejection.

Ava picked up the bracelet and sighed. She didn't know what he was doing or what time zone he was even in, but she couldn't deny the gentle pull drawing her heart to him. After yesterday with the misplaced floral delivery and now the bracelet, she wondered why. *Maybe I never stopped thinking about him.* Pushing away the thought, she laid the bracelet across her wrist, performed a couple of perfectly timed finger acrobatics, and closed the clasp. She lifted her arm to examine the inscription on the charm. *Little things.*

As she lowered herself onto the side of the sunken tub, she once again permitted her thoughts to return to the morning Blake left. *Please don't contact me again.* Her throat tightened as she rehashed the final words she'd said to him.

He'd done his part. The flowers stopped coming, and there were no more phone calls.

"But wasn't that what I wanted?" Her heart sank. *I thought it was.*

While he'd been gone, she'd focused on learning how to balance being a single mom and resuming her career. Ava's stomach coiled into knots. *I still miss him.* Fiddling with the bracelet, she replayed the mantra she'd repeated for months. *It's better this way. He's off saving the world, and I don't have to worry about him.*

Quiet babbles floated down the hall from Dylan's room and tugged her away from her melancholy thoughts. She'd made her decision, and she needed to make peace with it.

Ava glanced back down at the bracelet. The charm dangled in the air as if waving to her, trying to catch her attention one more time. *Oh, Blake. Where are you today? Are you safe?* She'd always believed when someone lingered on a person's heart, it meant they needed prayer. Maybe that's what this was now. Maybe wherever he was, and whatever mission he was on, he needed her prayers.

She turned her wrist, examining the details of the bracelet. Reflecting the morning light, the intricate row of diamonds cast tiny prisms over the bathroom wall. "Dear God, please be Blake's rearguard and keep him safe." She whispered the prayer, and her voice hitched.

Today, and only today, she'd leave the bracelet on as a reminder to pray for Blake.

CHAPTER FORTY-THREE

15:31 En route to the Field Hospital,
Baghdad, Iraq

Blake moaned as a sharp prick drove through his hand. *Glass. I'm on glass. I need to move.* Ice clawed its way up his veins. *God—help me.*

Immobilized, darkness fell. Then a burst of light. Haze rolled across his mind like the ocean.

"Stay with me."

Jacob? His body dipped and swayed. *I need air. I'm drowning.* Suspended in time, yet still holding on, Blake's pulse thumped in rhythm with the blades. *Why are we slowing down?*

"His pulse is dropping."

Struggling to remain tethered to the world he tried to harness the voices floating through his brain unattached to their speakers. *Where am I?*

The right half of his body pulsed with pain, and his skin burned beneath his clothes. *Why can't I open my eyes?*

"How long until we reach the field hospital?"

The metal beast dipped. Burning acid coated his throat. Again.

"Twelve minutes."

A thick blanket of darkness crawled over his mind. *I can't breathe.* Then, like a rising earthquake, his body trembled. Electrical pulses on repeat. *Please, God, not again.*

"He's not going to make it."

I'm so cold.

"What's our ETA?"

"ETA five minutes."

"Martin. Martin. Stay with me." Jacob rested a hand on his shoulder.

"Are you a praying man?" The medic threw out the question.

"Not really. Do you pray?"

"I do. Some nights more than others."

"He's a believer. Maybe you can say one for him?"

"Already done."

His eyelid yanked open. Prisms of light shot across his brain. Diamonds. *Ava.*

CHAPTER FORTY-FOUR

Ava's cell phone vibrated on her bedside table. The sound pitched her into a panic. Through blurry eyes, she peered at the screen. Two-thirty in the morning. Who's calling this early? The phone vibrated again.

"Hello?" Her voice came out raspy, and she cleared her throat.

"Ava?"

"Yes?" She sat upright, her heartbeat thumping like a kick drum against her ribcage.

"It's Brent."

Her stomach sank.

"Blake's injured." Brent took a deep breath before continuing. "He was on a mission."

The last five words pierced her soul, and her hand clutched the phone tighter. *So this is what it feels like to have my world fall apart. Again.*

"It's bad, but they've managed to stabilize him."

She understood stable was a kind word for saying it could go either way.

"What happened?"

"You know his job." Brent's voice hitched. "It happened hours ago. There aren't many details right now."

She looked down at her hand, fingering her nightgown as a multitude of fears washed over her.

"Ava, are you still there?"

"I am."

"He's in Germany."

She stood and paced the room as Brent continued.

"They put him on a hospital transport after they pulled him off the medivac early this morning. I'm on my way to Atlanta right now. I took the next flight out to be with Mom."

She blew out a breath to stabilize the frantic beating of her heart.

"I didn't know if I should call you. I know things were tense between you two after he left."

"I need to see him. I can't let our last conversation be ..." She swallowed back the expanding lump in her throat. "Be the last thing we say to each other."

Brent hesitated. "Ava, from what I've gathered, he's in bad shape. Are you sure you want to see that?"

"I've seen him in bad shape before." As the words tumbled over her lips, time slowed and her thoughts returned to Uganda.

"Okay. You can fly out with me." A tremor wrinkled Brent's voice. "We'll need to go soon. Do you have a passport for Dylan?"

"I don't." She pinched her eyes shut, stopped, and thought about what she should do. Opening them, she slipped into a chair in the corner of her room and blew out an exasperated breath. Leaving the country was the farthest idea from her mind after she'd returned from Uganda.

"Mom and Dad would love to take care of Dylan. If you feel comfortable with that?"

Barbara Martin was a kind and God-fearing woman. She'd reached out to Ava after she'd returned from Africa. But could Ava really ask the Martins to watch Dylan while she left the country? "Do you think they would?"

"They love kids, and neither Blake nor I have given them any grandkids to spoil." Brent laughed. "She reminds us often."

She stilled. Jake and Barbara Martin would be in Dylan's life if she—she shook off the thought. "I don't know, Brent. It's a lot to ask." Every minute she hesitated was another minute Blake lay alone in a hospital. Of course, Caroline would watch Dylan, but she had a full-time job and four kids of her own.

"Ava," Brent's voice deepened. "Mom asked me to call you."

"She did?"

"Yes. She told me Blake mentioned how much he still cares for you in his last email." For a moment, he was silent, then as if sensing her internal question, he said, "She heard from him a month ago, before he went dark."

Ava sighed. He still thought about her. She looked down at her wrist and fiddled with the bracelet she'd neglected to take off. If she was honest, she'd never stopped thinking about him, either.

"Okay, tell Jake and Barbara I'll tie up a few loose ends and catch a flight to Atlanta later this morning."

"Sure thing."

"Brent?"

"Yes?"

"Thanks for calling me." Did Brent know she'd been the one to end the relationship with Blake? It didn't matter. Did it?

"Of course. How could I keep the love of my brother's life from him at a time like this?"

Ava's cheeks blazed with heat. "Did he tell you that?"

"He didn't have to." Brent paused. "But yes, he did."

Warmth wrapped around her like a memory. "I'll see you in a couple of hours." When she hung up the phone, queasiness sprouted in her belly. *I know you care about me.* Blake's words trickled through her mind, along with the memory of the wounded look in his eyes. Not only did she care about him, she'd fallen in love with him.

Releasing a pent-up breath, Ava forced back a tidal wave of grief. She needed to keep it together. At least long enough to see Blake and tell him how sorry she was she'd pushed him out of her life.

Dallas to Atlanta would be a direct flight, easing her mind about at least the first half of the trip. However, the haste in Brent's plans worried her. *Does he know more about Blake's condition than he's letting on?*

She walked down to Dylan's room and peeked at her son. As he stirred in his crib, her baby's big, hopeful eyes looked up at her. Ava picked him up and gave him a gentle hug. "I love you, little man." He leaned on her shoulder and gave her the best baby hug he could squeeze out with his tiny arms.

She carried him back down to her room, lowered herself to the side of her bed, and situated Dylan to face her on her lap. "Mommy needs to go on a quick trip. You're going to stay with Barbara and Jake. Okay, little man?" He giggled and slobbered, oblivious to her breaking heart.

"I need to see Blake, sweetie." She pulled Dylan in for another hug. He relaxed at her embrace and made sweet, contented humming noises. "Blake's hurt, and your mommy needs to speak to him before …" She couldn't finish her sentence, but her mind raced ahead with fear. *Before I lose him.*

Grabbing her phone, she pushed away her sad thoughts. Opening the travel app, she made a quick airline reservation and scheduled a taxi to pick her and Dylan up a few hours before the flight. Maybe Dylan's wakefulness now would let him sleep on the plane later.

"Let's get you and Mommy packed." She carried Dylan to her closet and placed him on the floor at her feet. Dylan cooed and smiled as a weighty turmoil swirled inside of her. *Please, God, let me speak to Blake before it's too late.*

CHAPTER FORTY-FIVE

The burden of jet lag and fear hung on Ava's shoulders like a weighted blanket. After over twelve hours in the air and several more hours of driving, she'd reached her breaking point. She needed rest. And a coffee. More than that, she needed to see Blake. A shiver walked down her spine. Was she cold? Or just dreading what she was about to see?

She tugged her sweater tighter around her midsection and shadowed Brent through the halls of the hospital. Silence walked between them. No doubt he dreaded the same thing.

Still in a fog, Ava followed Brent into Blake's room. Her breath hitched. Blake lay deathly still. Ensconced in blankets, unmoving and attached to machines, the scene stole her breath. Brent murmured something and reached out to steady her.

Ava shivered again. *What happened to him?* She walked forward, reached out and took Blake's hand, expecting him to respond. When he didn't, her stomach twisted into a knot. "Oh, Blake."

A soft patch covered one eye, and she could barely make

out his angular jawline hidden beneath the swelling in his face. She glanced down at the rest of him. His right leg hung in a sling and a bulky cast encased it from his toes to his thigh. As her eyes roamed over his still body, sadness permeated every crevice of her soul. Brent hadn't exaggerated when he said Blake wouldn't resemble the man she'd said goodbye to months ago. As she stood there, with his limp palm in her hand, the realization of what he'd been through became horrifically real. *God, please help him.*

Closing her eyes, she attempted to push back her grief. It was no use. Tears cascaded over her cheeks and her nose dripped. Sniffing, she reached for a tissue off the bedside table. Catching her reflection on the metal lamp, Ava cringed. With no makeup on, and her hair tied back in a haphazard ponytail, she looked like she hadn't slept in weeks. Swiping the tissue across her upper lip, she slipped back into the hard plastic chair. It didn't matter. She'd looked worse—when she wore the same clothes for weeks and slept on a dirt floor.

You fix this man. The guard's words from her first night with Blake echoed in her mind. Her pulse jumped as she glanced back at Blake's battered body. *I can't fix this man.* It was as true then as it was now—only God could.

Ava sighed, then whispered, "I'm so sorry, Blake. So very sorry." She wouldn't deny her feelings any longer. This broken man in front of her held her heart in the palms of his scratched and battered hands. *I should've allowed you into my life instead of turning you away.* Ava sniffled again. *I should've pushed through my fears and told you I'd wait for you. Forever.*

Irritation rose to the surface. Instead, she'd wasted months of communication with him, and now she didn't know if she'd ever get to hear his deep, tender voice say her name again.

Ava leaned in and whispered in his ear. "I love you." She

prayed he'd hear her, and it would give him the strength he needed to fight.

Brent moved behind her, and the weight of his sorrow hung like a death veil in the room.

"What's he dealing with?" She dreaded the answer.

"He suffered a bullet wound to his side, a broken eye socket, shrapnel in the right half of his body, and skin damage on his right leg." He laid a hand on her shoulder. "His ankle's broken in two places, but the foot is intact."

Ava closed her eyes, trying to process the information Brent hurled at her.

"The blast caused him to hit something or be hit by something. There's bruising and swelling over much of his body." Brent walked to the other side of the bed and kept his gaze leveled at Blake. "No doubt he looks better than when they first found him."

Better? A burning ache crawled across her chest. How could he look worse?

Brent gripped the bed rails. His knuckles turning white. "He needs eye socket surgery, but they saved his eye."

"Will he be able to see out of that eye?"

"They're hopeful, but we won't know until after the surgery."

Nodding, she said another whispered prayer for Blake's healing.

"He's already had one emergency surgery before we got here. They want to do the eye surgery here before transporting him back to the States."

"How did it happen?"

Brent's grave expression sent a cool shiver through her.

"I guess it doesn't matter."

"Car bomb." He paused then added, "This wasn't a dangerous job, Ava."

"But it was a dangerous location, wasn't it?" She cut him off, exasperated and tired.

"Yes, but the detail was easy, and that particular location had been secure for weeks."

She looked back down at Blake, trying to understand what Brent was telling her.

"I spoke to his partner. He's already back in the States." Brent raked a hand through his hair, reminding her of Blake. "Jacob said Blake turned off the car, exited the vehicle, and it exploded."

The details of Blake's last mission were becoming increasingly harder to hear. "How does that explain the gunshot wound?"

"Someone showed up to finish the job." Brent snapped his answer. "His partner suffered a concussion but took out the two men attacking Blake."

"Two men?" Ava swallowed back the bitter taste rising in her throat. The idea that Blake laid injured on the ground while these men abused his body made her want to lash out at someone—anyone.

"It's a miracle he survived." Brent slid into a chair next to the hospital bed.

Silence hung in the air for a few seconds.

Glancing back at Blake, she asked, "How long will they keep him like this?"

He looked peaceful in spite of all the tubes snaking out of him, but she needed to talk to him.

"The doctors want to see the swelling go down." Brent straightened his posture and stretched his back. "They told me it could be several weeks before they even attempt to transport him back to the States."

Ava leaned forward and fiddled with the blanket draped over Blake's body. The idea of leaving little Dylan for such a long time made her uneasy. She closed her eyes, and took a few deep breaths, trying to slow her anxious thoughts. "I need to be here when he wakes up." She hesitated. "I need to tell him—"

"Ava, listen—"

"No. Brent, listen to me. I can't—" *There's always a risk I won't come back from a mission. It's something I've found peace with.* Ava shuddered, recalling Blake's words. Clearing her throat she forced herself to press on. "I can't leave him."

When Brent caught her gaze, grief marked his expression.

"I don't know how long I can leave Dylan behind. I need to see if I can get him a passport so I can bring him here." She drew in a quick breath hoping to hold back another rush of tears. "I have plenty of money set aside for emergencies. This qualifies."

"Ava."

She tore her gaze away from him, not wanting to hear any more objections.

"I don't know how this is all going to turn out, but—"

"Brent, don't. I can't think about that." She looked back at Blake. The machines next to the bed hummed as his chest rose and fell in a rhythmic motion. *Sometimes, we can't stop bad things from happening.* Her own words rolled through her mind, and she refused to linger on them. "I need to believe he can survive this."

As she glanced back at Brent, he nodded.

Gripping tighter onto Blake's hand, she silently begged God to help him make it out of this battle alive.

"We need to pray that God will provide a miracle for Blake." *And for me.* "He's done it before. He can do it again."

CHAPTER FORTY-SIX

Ava finished paying for her coffee at the hospital java bar, then made her way to the elevators. She'd been in Germany for fourteen days. These last two days had been the longest.

Stepping onto the elevator, she checked her phone and read the text from the Martins.

> Dylan is doing great. Thank you for the
> update on Blake.

Her stomach clenched. It wasn't much of an update. Two days ago, Blake had undergone eye surgery. She'd told the Martins he'd come through surgery, but he was still sleeping. She wished she had more to tell them.

When the elevator came to a halt, she stepped out and took another sip of her latte. She hated hospitals. With rattled nerves and little sleep, her diet had reverted to her college days —coffee, granola bars, and kettle corn popcorn. The popcorn she'd stumbled upon at the base gas station when Brent made a quick stop for a soda. The crunchy goodness reminded her of carefree days and all-night study sessions. That seemed like a lifetime ago.

She continued down the long hallway to Blake's room, but when she turned the corner, she stalled. Blake's doctor and Brent stood in the hall, conversing. Still feeling in limbo between the girl who called it off and the one who wanted a second chance, she didn't want to interrupt.

As she gulped down the rest of her coffee, she studied Brent's face. He'd also been keeping odd hours. His hair needed a cut, and he'd consumed enough free coffee from the USO that he'd grown immune to the caffeine.

Ava scrunched up her nose and tossed her empty cup into the bin. She'd offered to grab him a latte, but he'd declined.

"I like my coffee black. Just black."

Another quirk Blake and Brent had in common. She frowned. How could anyone drink black coffee?

After a few more moments of deep conversation, Brent's brows pinched together and formed two lines across his forehead. He shook hands with the doctor, then headed in her direction. *Please, God, let there be good news today.*

In three quick strides, he reached her.

"Any news?"

A heavy breath fell from his lips. "He's going to be okay."

Relief crashed over her. After two weeks of riding a rollercoaster of emotions, tension fled from her shoulders. "Thank God."

Gripping the back of his neck, Brent added, "Despite how he looks, Blake's doing well. He's breathing on his own now."

Ava pressed a palm to her heart. *Thank You, God, for answering our prayers.*

"They don't want him flying right away. The plan is to transfer him back to the States in six to eight weeks."

Her chest constricted. Eight weeks? She missed her little boy. How could she be gone another two months?

"God's working, Ava. It will be a long road ahead, but God's working."

Brent's words snapped her out of her thoughts. "I know He is."

"They want to do surgery on his ankle next, but the doctor is confident by this time next year, Blake will be his old self—with a couple of hurdles to navigate."

Next year? "Hurdles?"

Brent nodded. "He'll need extensive physical therapy to strengthen everything they had to put back together." He snorted a laugh. "If I know Blake, his primary goal will be to get cleared for duty."

Ava's stomach curdled. How could Blake even consider going back after this?

Brent continued, without missing a beat. "The nurse will come get us as soon as he's ready for visitors this morning."

"Will he be able to see when they take the bandages off?"

"I don't know. The doctors will know more about his eyesight in about a week." A shadow traveled across Brent's expression before he glanced at the floor.

Her chest twinged. "Is there something you're not telling me?" She'd grown accustomed to reading Brent's moods after hours together in the hospital. Today he looked distracted.

Brent's head jerked to attention. Dark circles cradled his eyes.

"Brent? What happened?"

"The doctor mentioned Blake had a rough night last night." Brent straightened his thin tie. His typically crisp shirt hung untucked and wrinkled.

"What do you mean?"

"The doctor lowered his pain meds, and he's struggling."

Sorrow filled her. The healing process would be long and arduous, but to hear how much pain Blake grappled with made her heart ache.

"There's something else that you need to prepare yourself for." Brent ran his fingers along his jawline. A five-o'clock shadow shaded his ordinarily clean-shaven face. "Blake's confused, Ava. It may take him a while to make sense of what happened to him. To understand he's no longer in danger."

"But," her voice trembled. "He's been injured before."

The muscle in Brent's jaw jumped. "This is different."

"Different?"

"Living through an explosion is bad enough." Brent tossed his empty coffee cup into the trash can with more force than necessary. "To be attacked like he was—it's not something he'll easily forget." Brent crossed his arms as worry blanketed his expression. "I just want to be straight with you, Ava. My brother's going to have a lot to work through when he gets back to the States."

"I understand." *Do I?*

A nurse stepped out of Blake's room and motioned for them. "He's ready for a quick visit. He's still groggy, so we'll keep it short."

Ava's stomach sank as questions swirled in her mind about Brent's concern. *He's confused, Ava.* Did that mean Blake wouldn't recognize her voice today?

Brent held the door open, then followed her into the room.

"We're keeping his eyes wrapped, so he doesn't strain them." The nurse smiled. "His other eye is perfectly fine, just a handful of scratches across the cornea."

Ava listened in a haze as the nurse rattled off the details of the surgery.

"He can hear you, so make sure you talk to him." The nurse

flashed Ava an encouraging smile. "His mind and body feel like he's walking through a thick fog."

Ava rounded the bed and reached for Blake's hand. Holding her breath, she waited for him to respond. When he didn't, she blew out a sigh and fought to hold back the tears. "Hey Blake, it's Ava."

Blake's fingers fluttered against hers, and he released a low groan.

What do I say to him? Ava glanced up at Brent. He threw her a reassuring look, then lowered himself into the seat on the other side of Blake. A heaviness fell over the room as the whirring and beeping of the machines marched in time with Blake's breathing.

Brent laid a hand on Blake's arm. "Hey Blake." His voice hitched. "You got this, buddy. You just need to rest and heal."

Blake gripped Ava's hand and released. His touch shot a wave of heat down her arm. *God, please help him know I'm here.*

When Blake's mouth curved into a grimace, the nurse offered him some water. He swallowed, then huffed out a breath. With his free hand, Blake curled his fingers around the blanket and bunched the fabric into his palm. Turning his head toward Brent, he tugged harder on the blanket.

"You need to take a few long breaths." The nurse laid a steady hand on Blake's shoulder.

Blake turned toward her voice. The beeps on the machine upped their tempo.

Ava's heart sank. *He's scared.*

Blake's breathing escalated as he tugged at the covers and expelled another agonizing groan.

Unable to hold back a sob, Ava bolted from her chair and stepped back into the shadows of the room. *I can't watch this.*

"I'm going to give him something so he can rest." The nurse scurried beside Blake and flipped the knob on a tube snaking out of his body. Turning to face Brent, she said, "It's been a long couple of days. Let's give it a few hours and you can visit with him again."

Ava stood rooted to the floor.

Brent walked over to her and held out his hand. "Let's go take a walk."

After a few seconds, his words registered, and she robotically nodded. As Brent led her out of the room, cold shivers racked her body. They continued down the hallway to a small sitting area. He directed her to the row of chairs in the corner.

Ava slipped into a seat and hung her head in her hands. Exhaustion and worry engulfed her as waves of nausea churned in her belly. *Blake's hurting, God. Please help him.*

Brent laid a hand on her shoulder. The warmth of his touch pressed through her shirt and seared her skin. "I'm sorry, Ava. I shouldn't have brought you here."

No, he shouldn't have. *I can't stay here.*

Launching to her feet, she ran for the elevators. With trembling fingers, she punched the down arrow several times. *Stop shaking.* Brent sidled up next to her, and like a watchful guardian, he waited silently as the numbers counted up to their floor.

When the doors opened, Ava stepped inside and shoved a finger at the first-floor button. *Keep it together, Ava.* Clammy perspiration dotted her forehead as panic clawed at her mind. Wrapping her arms around her body, she counted down to the lower floor. When the doors finally opened, she darted out of the hospital and into the cool morning air.

By the time she reached the sidewalk, tears were cascading down her cheeks. *God, help me. Help Blake.* Brent's footsteps followed in cadence with hers. She didn't know where she was going, but she was afraid to stop her momentum.

After several steps, Brent's hand gripped her elbow and steered her toward a bench near a copse of trees. "Ava, sit down." His deep voice cut through her confusion.

She stumbled over her feet and flopped onto the seat. *God, I can't do this. Not again.* Pulling her knees up under her chin, Ava pinched her eyes shut. *I can't watch another person I love struggle in the hospital.*

The images of Evelyn fighting for her life flashed across her mind. Terror curled around her heart and squeezed. Following those memories, the picture of her mother, unresponsive and hooked to a ventilator. *No. It's too much. God, please help me.*

Snapshots of Blake, battered and thrown at her feet in Uganda, rose to the forefront of her mind. Ava shook her head. A vision of the last time she'd seen her husband, lifeless on a gurney, in the ER. *We did everything we could to save him, Mrs. Stewart.*

"I can't do this." The words fell off her lips in a sob.

Brent wrapped his arms around her. "It will be okay."

Wave after wave, tears flowed as sorrow mingled with her fear. "I can't bear to see him so hurt."

Brent held her tighter and her muscles fought against his grip. "He's going to get through this, Ava. I promise."

"Stop saying you promise. Nobody keeps their promise." Ava's body ached as she prayed for God to heal Blake and calm the fear racing through her.

Minutes passed, and as her sobs quieted, Brent released her. "I want you on a flight back to the States. Tomorrow."

"What?" She jerked her head up. "No! I can't leave him."

"You're not leaving him. You're going home and waiting for his return."

"But, I ... you brought me ..."

Brent's jaw hardened. "No buts, Ava. Blake will need 'round-the-clock medical care. And you"—he raked a hand across his disheveled hair—"have responsibilities. Back home."

Gut-punched, she turned away. "You think I'm a coward. Don't you?"

"What? No!"

She wrapped her arms tighter around her middle and another tremor rippled through her. If she left, she was admitting she wasn't strong enough. Strong enough to be a part of this world.

Brent punched a fist into his thigh. "I didn't think this through." His voice lowered as he added, "You miss your son. There's nothing more for you to do here. Blake needs time to heal. How is he going to react to you seeing him like this?"

She turned to look at Brent. Fear laced through her. "I need Blake to know I didn't abandon him."

"You didn't abandon him." His voice softened. "You have a duty back home. Blake will understand that. Just like my brother, you need to take care of yourself. He needs you to be strong while he's weak."

Ava's heart tore in two. Brent was right. But she'd already pushed him away once because of her fear. Was she doing the same thing now? She swallowed past the lump forming in her throat. "I was the one Brent. The one to call it off. Did you know that?" Ava searched Brent's face, anticipating his disappointment. "I told him not to contact me again. I ended it between us because I was afraid."

Brent didn't respond, but his eyes filled with compassion.

"I'm not afraid now. Not to be with him. But I am afraid I won't be what he needs."

"Ava, I know you love my brother. And he—well, he's head over heels in love with you." He leaned back on the bench and stretched out his legs. "If you decide to join him in this life, you need to prepare yourself for hard days and tough decisions.

Blake will rest easier knowing you're safe, taking care of Dylan." He turned to face her. "Holding down the fort so he'll have somewhere secure to land when his world is off kilter."

Ava's heart gripped. She wanted to be that for Blake. A refuge in the storm.

Brent rubbed his palms down the front of his chinos and said, "Blake will be back in the States in six weeks. He'll have made progress and had some time to process what he's just walked through." Staring out over the parking lot, sadness shadowed his expression. "He wouldn't want you to see him like this Ava. Not if he had the choice." When he faced her, his gaze sliced to the marrow of her soul. "I brought you here for one reason. So you could ..." He hung his head and released a long breath. "I saw what it did to Ben's fiancée. She didn't get to say goodbye. I thought ..."

Ava's breath hitched. *Brent brought me here to say goodbye.*

Brent lifted his head and faced her. "If my brother thinks I kept you here, to watch him struggle ..." He shook his head. "The doctor reassured me he's out of the woods. Six weeks isn't even enough time for you to file for Dylan's passport and return. Go back home, Ava. Rest." A smile tugged at his lips. "You'll need it. My brother's going to be a handful when he gets home."

Ava's thoughts turned to her son. He was safe and being well cared for, but he needed his mom too. For two weeks, their lives had turned upside down. Blake was no longer knocking at death's door. For that, she was grateful, but it was time for her to go home. Her pulse quickened. *Am I making the right decision?*

She took a deep breath, then released it. "Okay."

Brent nodded as relief raced across his features.

"You're right. I need to go back home and prepare for Blake's return."

"I'll book a flight." Brent stood, then turned to face her. "Just because you're emotional about this doesn't make you weak, soldier." He grinned and flashed her a wink. "It means you're all in."

Ava's skin tingled. As she watched Brent walk away, her pulsed skipped a beat.

She was all in. She just wasn't sure what she'd signed up for.

CHAPTER FORTY-SEVEN

A wave of heat flooded his body. *Wasn't I just in the hospital? In Atlanta?* Pebbles and dirt clung to his hair as he tried to roll onto his side. *This isn't a dream.* Blake frowned as a putrid, burnt chemical odor permeated his nostrils. *What's burning?*

He opened his eyes and held his hands out in front of his face. *No bandages.* Looking past his hands, through the haze of smoke, he caught a sinister pair of fiery red eyes glaring back at him. He reached for his firearm. Nothing. Lowering his hand to his thigh, he grasped for his knife but instead fingered a loose cut of fabric. *My uniform? No. A sheet?*

The glowing eyes pressed closer. Instead of one set, now there were two. Panic surged through him with the force of a tsunami. *I need to get out of here.* Leaping flames reflected in the rage-filled eyes as they looked at him. No—looked through him.

God, help me. The plea evaporated in the air as his arms fell limp to his side. *Why can't I move my arms?* Blake looked up. Two shadowy figures jeered at him and shouted profanities.

One of them reared back to kick, then pain exploded across his midsection.

"Jacob?" No response. A flash of white traced across his vision, then a hard crack to his ankle shot a searing pain up his leg. *I need to get off my back. I need to be ready for the next blow.* Despite the urgency, his lifeless muscles refused to respond.

Like a star burning out, the eyes vanished, and for a moment, the terror fled.

Then, he heard a click.

His body stilled.

Gasping for air, Blake rocked from side-to-side as every muscle in his body fired into action.

"Mr. Martin." An anxious female voice broke through the fog of his terror.

No! Get back! It's not safe. The urge to fight overwhelmed him as wires sprouted from the ground and draped over his arm like a thousand fingers trying to hold him in place. *What's at the other end of these wires?* Flashes of an explosion streaked across his thoughts sending spikes of white-hot adrenaline through his veins. Panicking, he tore at the wires like a rabid dog caught in the jaws of a snare

"Mr. Martin, wake up!"

His chest constricted. Burning liquid bubbled in his throat. Opening his mouth, he gulped and struggled for air. "I can't breathe."

"Blake, it's me, Brent. Wake up!" A male voice pushed through the haze shrouding his mind.

"Brent?" His breathing continued in short, erratic pulses as a distant rhythmic beeping increased its urgency.

"Blake! Wake up!"

His eyes shot open. Above him, Brent hovered like an apparition. The uneasy sight chilled his blood. "Brent? What's going on?" Blake wiggled the fingers on his left hand.

A cast covered his arm past the elbow. "Is something burning?"

Brent stepped back and shook his head. "No, nothing's burning."

The door opened and a soft light floated in from the hallway, along with a hint of charred food. A nurse stepped through the door and Brent shot her a look. "What's burning?"

"One of the night nurses scorched a bag of popcorn. But that was hours ago."

Brent peered down at him and patted him on the shoulder. "Everything's okay, just some popcorn."

Brent's eyes swam with concern as he slid into the chair next to his bed. Blake followed the nurse as she checked his IV. Catching her look, he tried to read her expression. Frustration? Pity? Maybe a hint of both? She pulled out a drawer next to the bed and replaced the tubing leading onto the top of his right hand. After several changes, Blake no longer noticed the pain from the needle pricking his skin.

The beeping from the heart rate monitor slowed its pace while the other nurse wrapped a cuff around his bicep, and started the BP machine. The cuff squeezed his arm as his pulse throbbed through his veins. After a few seconds of pressure, it beeped then released its grip.

"BP's a little high." The nurse released the strap with a rip and patted him on the hand. "Let's have you take a few deep breaths, and I'll come back and recheck it."

He nodded. After the nurses lifted the rails of his bed, they turned and filed out of the room.

"You want to talk about it?" After a long minute, Brent's deep voice sliced through the lingering silence.

"Not really."

Brent laid a hand on his shoulder. "Another dream?"

"I told you ..." Blake stopped. It wouldn't do any good to keep anything from his brother. If anyone understood what he'd gone through, Brent would. "It didn't feel like a dream." He huffed out a breath. "At the onset of the nightmare, I could use both of my arms." Blake lifted his bandaged arm and scowled.

"Did you see *them* again?"

"Yes." Blake took in a few more long, cleansing breaths before he relayed the rest of his dream. "Their eyes were on fire." He paused before adding, "I was in hell. Again."

Brent sat back in the chair. "As they keep backing off the meds, you're going to have more of them."

"I know." The sounds on the monitor leveled off to a normal rhythm, and a soft, recurrent beep filled the room. "Did I rip out my IV?"

"Just about." Brent bit back a smile. "You're keeping the nurses busy."

Fidgeting with the sheet he asked, "Is Ava in town?"

"No."

Blake pursed his lips together. According to Brent, Ava had been by his side in Germany for two weeks. Now that he was Stateside in Atlanta, she flew in from Dallas whenever she could. Their visits had been short, and with the constant cycle of medical procedures and interruption of hospital staff, they'd not had much time to talk. Up to this point he'd evaded the subject of his nightmares. After today, he feared he'd no longer be able to hide what he was dealing with.

"I don't want her to witness one of these." Pushing out a frustrated breath, he glanced up at the ceiling. Miraculously, he'd progressed faster than most of his doctors expected, but he still had a long way to go. Now, while his body worked to put itself back together, his mind wanted to fall apart.

"Do you want me to tell Ava to stay in Dallas?"

Blake's heart constricted. The last thing he wanted to do was make Ava believe he didn't want her around.

When he didn't answer, Brent spoke up. "You need to think of your recovery. It won't do anyone any good if you try to hide this from her. You can try to lock up those emotions, but the only way to harness them is to walk through them."

The harsh reality of Brent's words weighed heavy on him. "I don't want to hide it from her." He turned his head back toward Brent. "I just don't want to scare her off—for good this time."

Brent nodded. "Understood."

"What do I do?"

"Start by being honest. Until Ava sees it happen in person, she may not understand the extent of what you're dealing with."

He considered Brent's advice. Ava struggled as well. She'd told him she still woke up sometimes, in the middle of the night, with flashbacks of the explosion and her time in Uganda. She'd understand. Wouldn't she?

"Ava's fought for you ever since she heard of your injury—with prayer and support." Brent stood and paced around the room. "I think she only pushed you away because she wanted to protect Dylan and give him a stable home. She has no experience with military life." He paused. "Or these kinds of injuries."

Blake's jaw tensed at the mention of young Dylan. The thought of trying to be a father to a little boy, while broken, rattled him. "I wonder if this might be too much to ask of her."

"I don't think so." Brent halted and turned to face him.

Neither of them said anything for a moment. Then, cutting through the stillness, Blake said, "Do me a favor?"

"What's that?"

"Let Ava know about the dreams." He paused, feeling

unsettled. He didn't want her to be surprised by one of his nightmares, but he didn't want to hide it from her either. "And the next time she and I have a few moments alone, I'll try to fill her in on the details."

"Will do." Brent nodded then walked toward the door. "Why don't you get some rest?" When Brent glanced back, a pensive expression blanketed his face. "Be completely honest with Ava. She needs to know what she's signing up for." Reaching for the door handle he added, "Then you need to let her decide."

After Brent left, he considered what his brother said. Hadn't he already tried to explain his chaotic life to her? Hadn't she already turned him down?

A picture flashed across his thoughts of Ava and Dylan. His fear of being unable to move freely in his own body while undertaking the job of husband and father sent a tremor of apprehension through him.

If she didn't want him in her life before, what would make her change her mind this time?

CHAPTER FORTY-EIGHT

Ava stretched her neck to work out the kinks. Her plane landed in Atlanta earlier that morning, and the pumpkin chai latte she'd picked up on the way to the hospital had done little to energize her.

Glancing over at Blake, who slept peacefully, her heart did a mini somersault. She hadn't seen him in weeks. There were so many things she wanted to say to him, but she didn't know when the right time would be. After Brent told her about Blake's nightmares, she was hesitant to be open with him about her feelings. But lately, an urgency to speak to him grew inside her like fuel to a fire. Nothing could deter her from wanting to share the rest of her life with him. Nothing.

"I'm not leaving here until I tell him how I feel." The whispered words brushed over her lips like a prayer. He needed to know everything. She wasn't only here to support him in his recovery—she was here because she loved him. Body, heart, and soul. And while he'd still been thinking of her on his last mission, she'd never stopped thinking about him, either.

Why did it take almost losing him to admit this? The question zig-zagged through her mind, and a smile formed on her lips. *It's because you're so stubborn, Ava.* She hoped Blake wouldn't sense the nervous energy bouncing around inside her when he woke up.

After she'd spent months praying for his recovery, Blake's determination to get well still astounded her. What he'd been through was awful, but God had performed another miracle in his life—and hers.

Ava walked over to the window. The sun's morning rays filtered through a copse of trees. Their long, bulky branches swayed in the wind, showing off tawny orange and fiery red leaves. Wrapping her arms around her body, Ava sighed. She'd turned the page on several seasons since she lost her husband, flew to Uganda, and met Blake. Thinking about the changes in her life made her pause. *Am I doing the right thing?* The question ran across her mind, forcing her to contemplate another one.

"Dylan, would you approve of this?" Her body stilled. She wanted to believe he would.

Watching the sun filter through the trees, she recalled quick snapshots of her life with her late husband. Then, like a refreshing spring breeze, a sense of peace washed over her.

Dylan wouldn't want her to be alone forever. And he also wouldn't want her to try and raise his son without the direction of a strong, godly man. He'd want what was best for her—and young Dylan. Lifting her fingers to the window pane, she touched the glass. The gesture was more about treasuring a memory than letting go.

"I'll never forget our time together." The words wrapped a comforting balm around her heart. The life they'd enjoyed was forever marked in time, and she believed Blake would understand keeping Dylan's memory earmarked in her heart. As a burden lifted, anticipation bubbled in her soul. *A new beginning. A new season.* Letting her hand fall from the glass, Ava turned from the window just as a nurse entered the room. The older woman nodded at her, then mulled over Blake's chart and made some notes.

In a whisper she asked, "Did his procedure go well?"

"Yes, it did." The woman glanced up and smiled. "He'll be released today."

"That's wonderful news."

The nurse did her final routine checks, flashed Ava a smile, and hurried out the door.

Alone in her thoughts once more, she lowered herself into the chair next to Blake's bed and reached out to take his hand. His warm palm filled her with joy as she remembered his motionless body only months before.

Like she'd done so often while he slept, Ava closed her eyes and prayed. She prayed for his healing and encouragement for his family. She prayed for the doctors. And although she couldn't turn back the clock, she also prayed for an opportunity to blot out the moment she'd asked him never to contact her again. *God, please help us to redeem the time we lost.*

After a few seconds, she looked up and studied Blake's face. Several scars stretched across his temple from the eye surgery, but to her, he still resembled the handsome and the *good man* who'd stolen her heart on a dirt floor in Uganda.

"God, please give Blake the strength he needs to continue his recovery." Finishing with an 'amen,' Ava leaned in and whispered, "Blake, I love you. If it means you're only home a few months a year, I'll be satisfied with that. But I want you in my life. Forever."

Blake's groggy voice broke through her confession. "Are you asking me to marry you Ava Marie?"

Ava's head shot up, and her cheeks heated.

His eyes were still shut, but his lips curved into a lazy smile.

"I ..." Stammering, she laughed. "Well ... I ..."

Keeping his eyes closed, he broadened his smile. "So how much would a Southern girl pay for a broken-down soldier these days?" He opened his eyes, and a spark of energy traveled across his expression.

With joy spiriting to life inside of her, Ava laughed, then started to cry. "Well, you know how designers like antiques." The replay of their conversation warmed her from the inside out. She stood and moved closer to him, not wanting their private time to be invaded by anyone or anything. "I love you so much, Blake Martin." Her tears continued to mingle with her words—words that relieved her to finally say them.

Blake lifted his hand and caressed her cheek. "Don't cry, sweetheart." He kept his gaze trained on hers. "Everything's going to be okay. I promise."

She sniffled. "Can you ever forgive me?"

"Forgive you? For what?"

Ava wiped her face with the back of her hand. "For telling you I didn't want you in my life. For letting you go."

He closed his eyes and took a quick breath. "I don't think you didn't want *me* in your life. It was my job." He paused, then he looked at her again. "I'm sorry I made you feel bad about that."

"I don't care about that anymore."

"What do you mean?"

"I mean, I don't care what you signed up for." She sniffled again. "I want you in my life."

A weariness filled his expression. "Even after this?" He used his hand to motion down the length of his body. "I don't know how well they put me back together. I don't know if ..." His breath caught, cutting off his thought.

"It doesn't matter." Ava smiled through her tears. "Even after all of this. I want you in my life—and Dylan's life —forever."

The creases in his brow wrinkled into a scowl. "I don't even know if Uncle Sam will take me back after this."

Frustration encased his voice, and she didn't respond.

Part of her would be relieved to know the military wouldn't take him back, but the other part knew she'd never want his calling forced from him before he felt ready. "Why don't we worry about that later?"

He took a deep breath as he lifted his hand to his face. His fingers moved across the scars around his eye, and he frowned. She bit her lip while he explored the wounds along his cheeks, then let his hand travel down to his chin.

"I can only imagine what I look like right now." He turned his head back in her direction. "This can't be easy for you."

Her heart gripped. Even while injured, he still concerned himself with her feelings. "It's not." Her fingers traced the fine contours of his jawline. "But only because I have this urge to make everything all right."

"To somehow barter my release and get me out of here?" His lips bent into a grin and she fought the urge to kiss them.

"Exactly."

For a few moments, neither one of them said anything. Grateful they'd finally had a chance to speak privately, she wished she could bottle this time and keep it forever.

"I dream about that night." Blake's admission hung in the air like a dense fog.

Ava slipped into the chair next to the bed, then reached out and took his hand again. "You don't need to talk about this now." She paused, then added, "Brent told me not to—"

"I've already told Brent I want to be transparent with you." Blake cut in. "I won't hold anything back from you about my injuries." His voice lowered as he continued, "Physical or emotional."

She nodded. She had so many questions, but she'd wait and let him take the lead.

"I'm having a hard time putting this behind me."

Her heart broke. She could relate to being haunted by a traumatic event. "You've been through so much."

"I've been through things before ..." His body tensed. "I've never felt so helpless in my life as I did that night."

Ava said nothing. She just let him unpack what he was feeling.

"The nightmare of it all, I understood everything they said while they—well, it's like they had a personal vendetta against me." Fighting to steady his voice he added, "It was as if the explosion wasn't enough for them. They wanted me to suffer. They wanted me dead."

Her stomach coiled with fury. How she'd wasted so much time pushing him away. Time she should have spent supporting him.

"As my mind cleared through the fog of my injuries, I wanted to hunt them down." Blake tilted his head and stared out the window. "When I found out my partner took them out, I saw red." He stared at the morning light for a few more seconds, then blinked. "What kind of person does that make me?"

Ava took a moment before responding. "I think it makes you human."

Blake inhaled and exhaled another long-labored breath. "I don't know if I'll ever be able to forget."

Her heart broke at his words. If she was honest, she wanted his attackers to have suffered as well. *Revenge isn't worth it.* Ava pushed back the memory of her own words. "I meant what I said."

"What?" He turned.

"I want you in my life. No matter what." She laid her hand on his cheek, and his five o'clock shadow prickled against her palm. "If it takes a lifetime to get through this, I'm in."

Lifting his hand, he laid it on hers. "This might be the longest mission I've ever been on, Ava Marie."

"What's that?"

"Recovery."

"That's true, but you're strong, and we'll rely on God to help us through this—scars and all."

"I'll understand if you need to sit this one out."

"I don't think so, Maxwell." Ava smiled as she said the name that brought her back to when they first met. "You asked me several months ago if we could make a go of this relationship—"

"And you turned me down."

Ava laughed. "I did." She held up her other wrist and motioned toward the delicate bracelet with the African charm. "It's the little things in life. The time we have together is more important than me trying to control every outcome."

"You kept it?"

His question melted her heart. "I did." Leaning down she brushed her lips against his. Lingering for only a couple of seconds, the warmth of Blake's exhaled breath brushed against her mouth. "My eyes are wide open this time, Blake Martin."

He sighed when she straightened. "I'm not sure if you know what you've just signed up for, sweetheart."

"Oh, really. What's that?"

"For one thing, as soon as possible, I'm getting down on one knee, and I'm going to make this official." He grinned. "I already have the ring."

"What?" Her heart galloped to life. *When did he buy a ring?*

The question lingered in her mind as she searched his face for an answer.

Blake shot her a fervent look. "I wish I could get out of this bed right now. I'd take you in my arms and never let you go."

Warmth pooled in her belly. She wanted the same thing.

Several loud beeps cut through the room as Blake's heart rate monitor registered a step faster. He chuckled. "Looks like I should get some rest before we alert the nurses."

"I, uh ..." She stammered out a response, glad a machine wasn't measuring her heart rate. Lifting her hands to her cheeks, she attempted to cover her blush.

"That won't do any good. They've trained me to be hyper-observant." He threw her another look—one that held a promise. "That color in your cheeks tells me I won't be disappointed when I get released."

When a nurse pushed open the door, Ava dropped her hands to her side.

The nurse glanced at her then back at Blake, arching her eyebrow. "Looks like you're wide awake, Mr. Martin." The stout woman pulled a cuff from a hook on the wall. "Time to get a BP reading."

As the nurse wrapped the cuff around Blake's bicep, Ava nibbled on her bottom lip and tried not to picture his strong arms wrapped around her.

The nurse studied the machines. "Your heart rate is a little high."

Blake laughed. "Is it?"

Another layer of warmth forced its way over Ava's cheeks.

"I'm not sure what happened." Glancing past the nurse's grey curls, Blake threw her a wink. "Maybe the machine's got a glitch."

A tingled swept over her skin. It was good to see him

teasing again. *He's getting better.* As the nurse finished her notes the same thought sprouted a web of fear.

In a few hours, Blake would be released. After today, he'd begin physical therapy.

How long would it take until he was back on active duty?

CHAPTER FORTY-NINE

Ava pulled into the parking lot of Zoo Atlanta and flipped down the visor to check her lip gloss. A flutter walked its way around her middle. Today was their first outing since his injury. Blake had chosen the zoo. A pang of guilt gripped her heart. *My first date with Dylan was at the Dallas Zoo.* Ava scowled at her reflection. "This isn't a first date." And Blake didn't know that detail.

"Ma-ma." Dylan's voice floated up from the back seat.

"Are you excited, little man? We're going to see the animals with Blake."

Pushing the visor up, she rolled down her window and breathed in a deep breath. The crisp fall air circled around her and a light breeze rustled the leaves. This week was going to be a great week.

After a quick early morning nonstop from Dallas to Atlanta, she'd picked up her rental, then headed directly for the zoo. When she'd suggested Dylan and she visit for a week, Blake was overjoyed.

A text came in on her phone.

I'm on my way.

Her four favorite words.

Stepping out of the car, Ava stretched her legs, then popped the trunk and pulled out the stroller. Pushing down the mesh basket, she took stock of what she needed for the day —sippy cup, snacks, diapers. She opened the backseat door and Dylan flashed her a goofy grin.

"What animals do you want to see today?"

Dylan waved the helicopter he fisted and pointed to get out.

"I bet we'll see some monkeys and tigers. Oh, what about the elephants?" Ava reached in and unsnapped his belts, her throat tightening. "Elephants are Mommy's favorite." She brought Dylan in for a quick embrace as she suppressed the painful memories of Uganda. *Thank you, God, for bringing me home safely. Please encourage the families of the missionaries who didn't make it back. Watch over Andrew and the hidden church.*

She blew out a breath. Prayers and scripture, over time, had lessened the sting of her grief. They'd also given her a sense of purpose. Each time a distressing memory bombarded her mind, she remembered to pray for Uganda. What the enemy had purposed for evil, she'd determined, would be for good.

"Dylan." She pulled Dylan back and looked him in the eye. "Can you say *zoo?*"

He giggled. "Doo."

"That's right. Zoo." Ava did a quick diaper check before she slid him into the stroller and strapped the buckles. Turning back to the car, she grabbed his striped blanket and tucked it into the basket. With all the excitement, by the afternoon, Dylan would be ready for his nap.

Closing the trunk, she finger-combed her hair and checked

her reflection in the side mirror. Jitters rippled in her belly. *I can't wait to see Blake again.*

A soft horn beeped behind her, making her jump. She turned and laughed. Blake pulled his car into the adjoining parking spot and giddy energy shot through her veins. *He's here.*

He flashed her a smile as he put the car in park and turned off the engine. Something about him looked different. Was it the hair cut?

Blake stepped out of the car, and Ava did a double take.

He grinned.

No beard. Fresh haircut. And—glasses?

"What do you think?" Blake waggled his eyebrows and pointed to the thin, black-framed glasses sitting on the bridge of his nose. "I need to strengthen my eye and these will help."

"Wow." Her heart did a little flip. The bookish look suited him. Goodness. "They look great on you."

Blake leaned against his SUV and pulled her into his arms. "I feel like it's been forever since I held you like this."

She stepped back, and a flashed him a flirtatious look. "It's only been two weeks."

"That's two weeks too long."

Warmth traced through her. Behind it, a cold shadow of sadness. Could she handle being separated from him again for months when he went back to work? She quickly chased away the thought with a smile. "Can't you do physical therapy in Dallas?"

He laughed. "I wish." Glancing down at the stroller, he said, "How have you been, little man?"

Dylan looked up from his activity toy and flashed a wide grin.

Ava stepped out of Blake's arms, and he grabbed his cane

from the back seat. He still used it to keep his balance as he regained his strength in his right leg.

Checking his watch, Blake scratched at his non-existent beard, and said, "The zoo just opened. Let's head in." When his eyes met hers, his expression brightened. "It's going to be a great week."

"It is." Her skin vibrated from the heat of his gaze. As if reading the excitement stirring inside of her, he leaned in and cupped her cheek with his hand. When his lips met hers, her body hummed with contentment. *I love him.*

When they separated, he brushed a thumb over her bottom lip. "I've missed you."

"I've missed you too."

Dylan released a high-pitched squeal as a couple walked by with their dog.

Blake laughed. "We should get the little man inside. Has he been to the zoo before?"

Grief gripped her chest as she looked down at Dylan. "No." She couldn't go back to the Dallas Zoo. Not just yet.

Blake ran a finger down her arm. "Hey." She glanced up. Concern blanketed his face. "Everything okay?"

"Yes." This was a new chapter. With Blake. "Everything's perfect."

"Good. We're going to have a great time—the three of us." He blew out a breath, then threaded his hand through his short hair. "I need to grab something out of my car."

Ava watched Blake dig through a duffle bag, then send a text on his phone. She slid on her sunglasses, locked the car, and did a quick once over of Dylan's back pack. Pulling out his pint-sized safari hat, she secured the strap under his chin. "There. Now you look official."

After Blake tossed his new specs into the car, he slipped on his shades. As he checked his watch again, his brow crinkled into a line.

"What's on your mind, soldier?"

He jerked his head up and smiled. "Nothing."

Ava laughed at his startled expression. "Are we on a schedule today?"

"No. Not really."

She shook her head as the three of them walked toward the entrance. "So, what's the plan this week?" Nodding toward the gate, she added, "Besides a day at the zoo."

"You'll have to wait and see."

After he bought the tickets, he opened the zoo map, and it flapped in the breeze. "What do you say we check out the tigers and pandas?" He smiled at Dylan. "We can hit the petting zoo before lunch."

"Sounds like you've got this mission all planned out."

"I do. The panda feeding is in ten minutes. Dylan will love it."

"He will. Pandas are adorable."

After they visited the pandas and the large cat exhibit, they took Dylan to the petting zoo. Ava couldn't tell who was having more fun—Blake or Dylan.

"Here you go, buddy." Blake balanced Dylan on a rock while the goats scurried around their legs. "From up here, you can see all of them."

Dylan giggled and reached out to pet the goats as they jumped up on the rock and searched for snacks.

Blake held out a few chunks of kibble he'd bought from the coin machine. "I think Dylan likes goats."

"I think he does too."

"The boy needs a farm to grow up on."

"You think so?"

He shrugged and flashed her a boyish look. "It's just a thought."

After lunch, Dylan's eyelids drooped. Ava motioned toward her drained toddler. "I'm going to go change him. He's all tuckered out." She scooped Dylan out of the stroller and grabbed the diaper bag. "Now that his belly's full, he's probably ready for a nap."

Blake leaned in and gave her then Dylan a quick kiss on the cheek. "Sounds good."

When she came out of the bathroom, Blake was standing across the pathway talking to an older couple. She loaded Dylan back into the stroller, reclined his seat, and handed him his blanket.

When the couple turned, her heart lightened. It was Blake's parents.

"Hey, Barbara and Jake." She pushed the stroller next to the three of them and looked at Blake. "Did you know they were coming to the zoo today?"

Barbara opened her arms and brought Ava in for a quick hug. "We heard from a little birdie you flew in this morning." She winked at Blake, then glanced back at her. "Blake mentioned you and Dylan Maxwell are here for an entire week."

"Yes, ma'am."

"Oh, that's wonderful." Barbara's face beamed with delight.

Ava looked from his parents back to Blake. Blake glanced at his phone, then looked up and held out his hand to her. "I have a mini field trip for us."

"At the zoo?"

His eyes lit up as he nodded.

Ava glanced in the stroller. Dylan curled an arm around his blanket and nuzzled his head into his stuffed helicopter.

Barbara patted her arm and smiled. "It looks like the mister and I are on babysitting duty."

Blake winked at her. "Look at that—babysitters."

Had he set this up? She glanced back at Barbara and Jake. "Are you sure?"

Barbara leaned closer and whispered, "Why do you think we're here, sweetheart?"

Warmth filled Ava's cheeks. No wonder he kept checking his phone. "Thank you." Turning to Blake, she said, "I'm all yours."

He squeezed her hand, pulled her toward him and planted a quick kiss on her temple. "You promise?"

A cool shiver traveled down her spine. *I promise.*

They gave a quick wave to his parents, then Blake tugged her toward the front of the zoo. The area opened up into the African plains exhibit. He paused and turned to face her. Nodding his head toward the map of Africa, he asked, "What do you say? Want to go back?"

She wrinkled her nose as she studied the map. When she looked back, butterflies hatched in her belly.

"Shouldn't be too many bugs and we smell better." Blake threw her a flirtatious look. "And they have elephants." He checked his watch again, then gave her hand a tug. "Let's go."

Anticipation buoyed inside of her as they walked hand in hand to the elephant house. Blake opened the door then followed her inside.

"Hi, can I help you?" The young woman behind the counter smiled at them.

"We're here for the elephant experience at two o'clock."

Ava's eyes widened. The elephant *experience*?

"For a Mr. Blake Martin?"

"Yes."

The young woman glanced up and looked behind them. A

confused expression traveled across her face. She checked the schedule again. "It says here you bought ten slots for the elephant experience. Will the rest of your party be arriving soon?"

"Nope. It's just us." He turned to face Ava and his smile widened. "I wanted it to be a private event."

Ava's heart galloped like a spring pony. He'd purchased the whole time slot for just the two of them. Tears gathered in her eyes and she quickly blinked them away.

The young woman smiled. "Of course, sir." She pulled out the release form for them to sign. "You only need to fill out one form since you're a couple."

He winked at Ava, grabbed the pen and filled out the form. After he signed it, he handed the pen to Ava and said, "It's not an African reserve, but will it do—for now?"

For now? She didn't think she'd ever want to go back to Africa, but with him looking at her the way he was now, she would've followed him anywhere. "It will do." She nudged his arm. "For now."

His eyebrows shot up. Laughing, Ava signed the form.

The woman tossed their form into a wire basket. Moving around the counter, she motioned for them to follow. "Right this way. My name is Jenny and I'll be leading your experience today." As Jenny escorted them behind the building, she rattled on about what to expect and the safety procedures.

Ava leaned into Blake. "Thank you for doing this."

He wrapped an arm around her and squeezed.

When they reached the holding area, Ava gasped. A massive elephant stood only a few feet from them, behind a row of thick iron bars. She looked into the animal's gentle eyes. They radiated intelligence and beauty.

The zookeeper turned and introduced the other two workers who had joined them. "Ava and Blake, this is Jack and

Paul. They'll be assisting us today." Jenny explained the zoo's elephant program, then said, "This is one of our rescues from Africa. She's been with us for a few years."

Ava's heart lodged in her throat. A rescue from Africa. She could relate. As she studied the beautiful creature, flashes of her time in Uganda rolled through her mind like a silent film. She glanced up at Blake. His gaze said he understood where her thoughts had traveled.

As Jenny moved the animal closer, she motioned for them to reach out and touch the gentle beast. Ava's hand glided along the rigid folds of its skin.

"Although their skin is rough, they actually are very sensitive to touch." Jenny smiled, then added, "Elephants can even feel when an insect lands on them."

Ava chuckled. "We have something in common."

Blake shook his head as he reached out and touched the rough exterior of the animal. Leaning forward, he whispered in her ear. "You both are sensitive to touch."

Heat wrapped around her neck. That was true. His touch.

Jenny held out the elephant's ears like a sail on a ship. "African elephants also have more wrinkles in their skin and have larger ears."

Blake bit back a laugh.

Ava rolled her eyes. "Don't you say it."

"I wasn't going to say anything."

Jenny led the animal to another portion of its pen and explained how elephants loved to splash and play in the water. They took a few turns scrubbing the animal and watched as it moved to the center of the enclosure, dipped its trunk in a bucket of water, and sprayed.

Jenny blew her whistle, and the elephant approached the gate. "A couple of last notes before we feed her some snacks.

The elephant is the world's largest land mammal and can weigh up to over six tons."

"Wow, that's amazing." Ava studied the elephant's feet as Jenny gave the command for the elephant to lift one of them.

"If an elephant becomes pregnant," Jenny patted the elephant's midsection. "She'll carry her baby for twenty-two months."

Ava's eyes widened. "That's entirely too long to carry a baby."

Blake snickered.

"For our last activity, we'll feed her some snacks."

Paul brought out a bucket full of green leafy vegetables and placed it between her and Blake.

"Elephants eat bushes, and they love leafy snacks. As you pick up the leaf bundle, hold it out, and she'll take them from you with her trunk."

Ava held out the bundle of fronds, then looked at Blake. "This is wonderful."

"I'm glad you're enjoying it."

She reached into the bucket and continued to feed the elephant. When Ava came to the last serving, she asked, "Do you want to feed her this last bunch?" When she didn't hear a reply, Ava looked beside her. Blake was gone.

Turning to find him, she gasped. Blake was behind her, kneeling on one knee.

Ava glanced at Jenny, whose face beamed with delight as she held up the camera on Blake's phone. She turned back to Blake. He'd pulled out a ring and held it out to her.

"Ava. Sweetheart." He inhaled a deep breath, then let it out slowly. "My heart has been yours since the first day we met in Uganda. The day you flew back to Texas, I didn't want to let you go."

A soft sigh rippled from all the zookeepers.

Blake continued, "I love you. You hold my heart and always will. I don't know what the future holds, but I want to spend the rest of my life with you. Will you do me the honor of becoming my wife?"

Her eyes welled with tears. "Oh, Blake. Yes. Yes!"

Using his cane to balance, Blake rose to his feet and slipped the ring on her finger. She leaned into him as he wrapped an arm tight around her and nuzzled his face into her neck. "I love you so much, sweetheart." His whispered words tickled the soft skin behind her ear.

"I love you too." When she tilted her head back, Blake cupped the back of her neck and brought his lips down to hers. Ava's legs filled with jelly and she swayed. He let the cane fall as he circled his other hand around the curve of her lower back, pulled her closer, and deepened the kiss.

Several heartbeats passed before his mouth lifted from hers. "Forever, Ava. I promise."

"Forever." She leaned forward and pressed her trembling lips back to his. *I could do this forever.*

Jenny blew her tinny whistle twice, and the elephant trumpeted.

Blake pulled back as a fire sparked in his gaze. "I forgot we had an audience."

Ava giggled, then tucked her head into his chest. Her cheeks smoldered with heat. "Me too."

He brought her chin up with the crook of his finger. "Let's go tell my parents." Blake picked up his cane and reached for her hand. "And Dylan."

Her blood raced through her veins. *This is really happening.*

Jenny handed Blake his phone. "Congratulations, you two."

"Thank you!" They answered in unison and followed their words with a laugh.

Ava's cheeks ached from smiling. *Mrs. Blake Martin.*

When they walked out of the elephant house, Blake paused and pivoted to face her. "Are you ready for this adventure, Ava Marie?"

Her heart thudded against her ribcage as a slew of concerns flooded her mind.

He was staying in the military.

Was she ready for this adventure? Ready or not.

CHAPTER FIFTY

Brent walked into the physical therapy room with a paper bag. Blake lifted an eyebrow. "Sneaking in contraband? It better be a pulled pork sandwich from Larry's food truck."

"Sorry, no food. Don't you get enough of that at home?"

He patted his midsection. "I do." He'd gained a few pounds being immobile, but it wasn't anything he couldn't work off in the gym. "More than enough food."

Brent shot him a look. "Must be nice."

Their parents lived in a suburb of Atlanta, and while he finished his last few months of PT, he'd stayed with them, enjoying his fill of Southern cuisine.

Brent handed him the bag, and he opened it. "What's this?" Inside was a block of basswood and a pocketknife.

"I remembered as a teen you were always doing something with wood." Brent slid into the chair opposite him and smiled. "The doctor said you need to work on your dexterity, so I thought this might help get your mind off things."

Blake pulled out the simple three-blade knife with a dark cherry wood handle and opened it. He turned the handle over and ran his hand across the inscription—*Joshua 1:9*. He recognized the verse immediately. *Have I not commanded you? Be strong and courageous. Do not be frightened, and do not be dismayed, for the LORD your God is with you wherever you go.* It was the same verse he'd written inside his first pair of military-issued combat boots when he was eighteen. "Thanks, I appreciate it."

"Sure thing." Brent paused for a moment, then he moved his gaze toward the window.

Giving it a few seconds, Blake said, "Out with it."

"Out with what?"

"You have that look."

"What look?" Brent turned and threw him an innocent smile.

"That look you get when you don't want to tell me something." He punched Brent on the shoulder. "It's the same look you had when you stole the model ship I made and gave it to an eighth-grader named Jenny Garland."

Brent snorted. "You worked hard on that model."

"I did, and it took me weeks." Grinning he added, "And you told Jenny *you* were the one who made it."

Brent's face lightened, obviously recalling the middle school debacle. "I did." He paused. "She never did agree to go with me to the eighth-grade dance. Even after I gave her the model ship."

"Your ruse might have worked if Benjamin hadn't told her you stole the ship out of *my* room."

Brent groaned. "You're right. Benjamin was in what? Elementary school?"

"Yep." An ache wrapped around Blake's heart and compressed. "Mom dragged him to the middle school play where he blabbed to everyone about your thievery."

"The play Jenny Garland played lead in."

Blake added weights to his machine. "If I remember correctly, she played Gretel."

"I tried out for Hansel." Brent sighed. "I wasn't much of an actor back then."

He laughed, remembering how Brent had dressed the part to try out.

Brent flashed him a rueful look. "After Jenny found out I took it from you, she smashed it on the playground."

"Hours of work down the drain."

Brent poked a finger at his chest. "Hey, wait a minute. Didn't she decide to take you to the dance?"

He shoved Brent's hand away then waggled his eyebrows. "She did." He was only in sixth grade, but he'd never forget the one awkward, slow dance with Jenny Garland. "She even apologized for smashing my ship."

"But you got to dance with Jenny. I'm sure it was worth the loss."

Blake chuckled but didn't want to let him off the hook. "So? What did you do this time?"

Brent's brow creased with a scowl. "It's not really what I did. It's a hunch I'm batting around."

"What's that?"

"I think the car bomb might have been personal."

Blake stilled. "What? You think I was the target? Are you talking enemy vendetta?"

"Worse—treason."

Gripping the ringed apparatus suspended above the chair, Blake slowly lifted the weight attached to it. "An inside job? That doesn't even make sense." After ten reps, he switched arms and began again. For weeks now, he'd pushed through the rigorous physical therapy training the military deemed necessary for him to complete. It was working. His muscles grew stronger every day. Blake let the weight down in an unhurried, deliberate motion, pausing his exercise. "Have you tracked everything you know about Rideau? It's plausible we're on his radar."

"Yes."

"And?"

"I don't have a solid answer."

"That's comforting." Blake kneaded the sore muscles in his forearm.

"I find it odd you've been hitting brick walls ever since you started chasing Rideau." Brent picked up a circular band and handed it to him. His brother had almost memorized his entire routine since he graduated to the last level of his therapy. "And I find it ironic your partner, Jacob Armstrong, is conveniently absent when you're in harm's way."

Blake blew out a quick breath. "Jacob? That's not possible."

"Maybe not, but it leads to a lot of questions. At least on my end."

"What would Jacob have to gain?"

"Not sure. I'll look more into his past and see what connections I might find in his family. There must be something we've missed."

Shaking his head, Blake asked, "Is that legal?"

Brent didn't respond.

"Look, we stay above board on this. If we go after people for no reason, then we aren't any better than the bad guys we're chasing."

Brent shot him a hardened look. "I hardly think that's fair."

"Sin is sin, brother." Blake hung up the exercise band and stretched his aching arms. "Is it possible I'm just in the wrong place at the wrong time?"

"Of course, anything is possible."

"It seems a little farfetched to believe everything's been

orchestrated against me. And why? To what end?" He lifted his arm and grasped the ring again. "To have me dead?"

"Maybe."

"That makes no sense. What about Africa?"

"What about it?" Brent arched an eyebrow punctuating the frustration in his voice.

"You think someone organized a group of men to come into the same village we were in, separate me from Jacob, and send a teenager out to draw me down to the river. And then what? Kidnap me so they could do some tests on me like a human lab rat?"

Brent pursed his lips together.

"I mean, I've organized strategic plans before, but that would be impressive."

As Brent handed him a bottle of water, Blake continued his train of thought. "What about Paris?" He ran his hand over his jawline after he took a swig and swallowed. "A car bomb took out an entire apartment building. For what purpose? To eliminate me?"

Brent tapped his fingers on a weight stand but didn't interject.

"Baghdad, another car bomb."

This time Brent interrupted. "In which Armstrong conveniently got out of before it exploded."

"He did, but he shot the men who were trying to finish me off," Blake smirked. "That would've been counterproductive to wanting me dead."

Brent leaned back in the chair and lifted his hands behind his head.

"Why Jacob? Why are you pinpointing him?" He threw out the question trying to draw out whatever else ran through Brent's thoughts.

"Isn't it obvious?"

"No, it isn't."

"Well, he doesn't hide the fact that he doesn't agree with your beliefs."

"Wait, you think because I'm a Christian, he's out for me?"

"Stranger things have happened in the name of religion. Believe me, I've seen them." Brent dropped his hands and leaned forward. "He's got close family members who disdain the mention of God in any setting. They use their money and influence whenever they can to eliminate the footprint of any organized religion. He's got family in politics and business."

Blake knew about his partner's beliefs, but it wasn't a crime in the United States to rally behind convictions. "I think you're reaching."

"Religious differences have caused a lot of chaos in the world. Don't discount that."

He understood Brent's concern. Unfortunately, with the world's current climate, radical religious extremism was a day-to-day occurrence in Brent's line of work.

"How do you explain the fact he never seems to be hurt when you are?"

"He got hurt in Iraq."

"He did, but minimally."

"We're close, Brent, and despite our different beliefs, I trust him with my life." A sinking feeling pressed against his chest. "We've spent hours out in the field. I'd like to believe I would've detected something duplicitous in him by now."

"I did some digging into his family."

Blake held up a hand, cutting him off. "That's done every five years when his clearances are renewed."

"Things change."

"What things?" A coil of uneasiness twisted in his gut.

"His mother just recently divorced—a third time."

"So? That's nothing spectacular."

"She's dating again."

Blake stilled, waiting for Brent to elaborate.

"She's in SoCal with someone on our radar."

"For what?"

"Writing bad checks."

"When? Years ago?"

Brent didn't answer.

Blake took another drink of water and contemplated Brent's concern. After the bombing in Paris, he questioned if maybe someone knew they were shadowing Rideau, but he didn't believe he was the sole target. If anything, someone wanted to throw the mission off Rideau's tail.

He grabbed the dangling rings with both hands. Tiny beads of sweat gathered on his temples as he lifted himself off the bench. It felt good to push the limits of his weakened muscles. After a few reps, he leaned back, feeling winded. "What good would it do to put me in harm's way or even get me out of the way completely?"

Brent stood and paced in front of him. "You want my theory?"

"Let's hear it."

"Maybe Rideau's paying someone to keep *you* off his trail."

"That's definitely a reach. I'm one person in a whole mess of people with Rideau on their radar." Blake rubbed the stubble on his jawline. He'd wasted precious time being injured when he could've been tracking down Rideau. Hopefully, the rest of the team had made progress in his absence. "And besides, up to this point, I've done little more than put kinks in his supply chain."

"And almost get yourself killed. Several times."

"Yes. Thank you for reminding me of that."

Brent laughed.

There was a long pause as Blake picked up the small hand weights.

"I don't know all the answers." Brent shrugged. "I'm just following a hunch."

He thought about it for a few seconds, then sighed. "Okay, follow your hunch, but check every angle, not only Jacob." Shooting his brother a stern look, he added, "But keep the research aboveboard." Intelligence agencies had their own way of doing things, but he didn't want Jacob to be the target of pointless scrutiny. Brent was just being protective. He could check the backgrounds of everyone on his team, including him, but until he had a stronger hunch, he wanted to keep Brent on a tight leash.

An unspoken warning hung between them, and Brent nodded. "Aboveboard. Aye aye, captain."

Blake laughed at Brent's veiled reference to his boyhood obsession with model ships.

After a few seconds, Brent sank back in the chair. "On to another subject. When were you going to tell me about the upcoming nuptials?"

Blake chuckled as he replaced the weights on the rack. "Well, about that ..." Glancing up, he caught his brother's challenging look. "I'd already decided once I could get down on one knee, I would ask her to marry me." He picked up a rubber band and pulled it taught for a deep stretch. "Granted, I've been up and around for a while, but I couldn't find the right time." He threw his brother a wide grin. "I asked her yesterday. At the zoo."

"I heard."

"I even got down on one knee."

"Ouch."

Blake dropped the band, picked up a heavier set of weights, and did some curls. After a few more arm exercises, he could move on to his lower body. "I was on my way to physical therapy. I'd already mentally prepared myself for the pain."

Brent stifled a laugh.

"We've already set a date."

"Wow." Brent shot him an older-brother look. "So, you're really going to do this?"

"I am."

"This should be interesting."

"What do you mean by that?" He frowned, halting his exercise.

"Does she know you're going back?"

"She does."

"Really?"

Blake switched arms and continued to lift. "She doesn't like it."

"I wouldn't think so." His brother's eyes narrowed. "But she knew before you asked her, right?"

"She knew it was a possibility." Blake set the weight down and leaned his head against the wall. Brent's questions weren't helping with his own reservations about returning to work. "I'm going back in a supporting role. I won't be going out in the field."

"Is that so?"

He straightened his posture and scowled at Brent. "Yes."

"Glad to hear it." Brent lowered his chin and gave him a pointed look. "You have a family to raise now."

"That's the best thing I've heard you say all day."

Brent paused for a moment, then jumped to his feet. "I'm heading out tonight, but I should be back in town in a few weeks." Before he moved toward the door, he patted Blake on the shoulder. "Make sure you keep yourself out of trouble."

"Will do."

"And Blake?"

"Yeah?"

"I'm happy for you and Ava."

"Thanks, I appreciate that." They both were quiet for a few seconds as undoubtedly both their thoughts returned to Benjamin and the void his death had left in their family.

"Benjamin would be happy too." When Brent spoke up, there was a catch in his throat. "He always believed love conquered all."

Nodding in agreement, Blake somberly remembered Benjamin's fiancé.

After Brent grabbed the doorknob, he glanced over his shoulder. "I'll look into everyone in your unit, but I want you to consider what I've told you about Armstrong."

"I will."

After Brent exited, Blake was left with a mountain of questions. Had the car bomb been aimed at him or his partner? Could someone from the unit be working for Rideau? He quickly pushed the disquieted thoughts out of his head. Only one thing was more important right now than the mission—Ava. And little Dylan.

Blake stared down at the weights. With a May wedding on the horizon, he needed to focus on his next goal—rebuilding his lower body strength, so he could walk down the aisle without a cane.

CHAPTER FIFTY-ONE

"May I cut in?"

Blake stilled as Jacob approached Ava and him on the dance floor.

"Looks like my partner could use a few minutes off his feet." Jacob winked at Ava and then looked back at him. "Don't worry, she's in safe hands."

Blake had walked unencumbered down the aisle that morning, but the endless time on his feet made his muscles scream with fatigue. He flashed Jacob a tight-lipped smile. "Sure." Near the door, Brent stood like a sentinel, scowling at the crowd. When Brent caught his gaze, he shot him a questioning look. Blake shrugged.

They'd grown no closer to finding any solid facts about the traitor in his unit—if there even was a betrayer among them. Brent remained convinced everything pointed to Jacob, but until he had proof, Blake refused to believe Jacob was complicit in anything.

Walking over to the table at the front of the room, he lowered himself into the groom's seat. As Jacob moved effortlessly across the dance floor, a rush of discouragement washed over him. His body was healing, but he hoped after a few more months of PT, he'd be able to move like that again. When the song ended, Blake stood and waited for Jacob to return with his wife.

"Congrats on your big day, brother." Jacob leaned in and shook his hand.

Ava moved in close to his side and smiled up at Jacob. "Thank you for coming today."

"Of course. And if I haven't said it already, you look beautiful, Mrs. Martin. Every bit the blushing bride." Jacob looked up and flashed a good-natured wink in Blake's direction.

Ava's cheeks pinked. "Please call me Ava."

Ava's hand encircled his, and Blake's heart snapped to attention. Mrs. Martin. It had a nice ring to it.

"Blake's told me a lot about you."

Ava's words pulled him out of his thoughts.

"All good, I hope." Jacob grinned like an ornery schoolboy.

She chuckled. "All good. I've heard you're an excellent partner."

He kept a steady gaze on Jacob as he listened to the back and forth. Nothing about his partner's demeanor struck him as nefarious.

Jacob nudged him. "Did he now? Well, that's good to hear. Of course, Martin's not so bad himself. We've kept each other out of a few scrapes over the years."

"It's good to know he has someone he can trust when he's out in the field." Ava looked up at him. Worry flashed across her expression and just as quickly vanished. They'd already discussed him going back out if he physically met standards, but he knew she still struggled with his decision.

"There you two are."

The three of them turned at the sound of the sing-song voice floating across the reception hall. Then, as only Southern mamas from Georgia could do, Blake watched as his mother gracefully parted the sea of people on the dance floor and glided in their direction.

"Blake dear, do you mind if I steal your bride away for a few minutes?" His mother glanced between the three of them. "There are a few people I want Ava to meet before," she leaned in and whispered, "before the bride and groom make their exit."

He caught Ava's glance, and a fresh wave of soft pink flooded her cheeks. How could she look even more beautiful than she did moments ago walking down the aisle? Ava blinked, and he realized he was staring at her. Clearing his throat, he checked his watch, more out of something to distract his thoughts than needing to know the time.

"Sure, but don't keep her for too long." He leaned down and whispered in Ava's ear. "Remember, we have a plane to catch, Mrs. Martin."

When she smiled back at him, anticipation crackled between them like lightning in a Georgia storm. She turned, and he watched her walk across the crowded room with his mother and sighed. *She said yes.* The flurry of wedding activity hadn't given him much time to contemplate the decision they'd made before God, and because of his mother, nearly half of Atlanta. He was a married man now. In a few hours, they'd board a plane for their honeymoon. And finally, after months of waiting, it would be just the two of them. No doctors. No schedules. No Rideau. Just his bride, a campfire and a well-stocked cabin in Fairbanks, Alaska.

Looking back at Jacob, a lump wedged in his throat. He didn't want his partner to be the reason for the glitches in their mission since they'd started tracking Rideau. *How could I have missed something like that?* Despite Brent's accusations, his gut told him the common denominator was Rideau, not Jacob. The thought of doubting his partner did not sit well with him.

"I'm glad you made it to the wedding." Blake took a quick drink of water, praying the uncomfortable questions racing through his mind would soon be answered. "I know you have an adversity to churches."

"Of course." Jacob smiled animatedly. "Besides, I had to see for myself if you were actually tying the knot."

Glancing past Jacob, he watched as Brent leaned stoically against the arched doorway leading into the courtyard.

Jacob followed his gaze. "Your brother Brent is looking more irritable than usual. It's been ages since I've seen him."

"He's been busy. You know, it's the job."

"Right. What does he do? Work with one of the intelligence agencies?"

"Yeah, something like that."

Jacob laughed as he gave Blake's shoulder a push. "Suits, that's what I call them. Not like us, huh? Getting dirty and part of the action."

His muscles strained at the good-natured shove.

Jacob winced. "Sorry, man, I forgot about your shoulder."

Clenching his jaw, he waved him off. "It's all good." The physical ache had nothing on the internal tension sparking inside of him. He scanned the room again. Like a shadow, Brent had moved to another location.

Turning to face Jacob, he asked, "So, what have you been up to? While I've been in recovery?"

"Not much. They had me sit out for about six months. You know, work on communications and paperwork. All the sleepy stuff."

Blake nodded, and there were a few seconds of quiet between them.

A woman sashayed past them and Jacob winked at her. Her face brightened and she threw him a flirtatious parting wave.

"The best thing about weddings—plenty of opportunities."

Blake laughed. It was one of Ava's single designer friends from Dallas. "I'll be sure and warn her about you."

Jacob held up his hands. "What's there to warn about?" Altering his expression into a mock innocence, he said, "I'm only in town for one more day."

Blake shook his head. "Always the chivalrous one."

"Of course." Jacob bit back a laugh. "How much longer will you be Stateside? Or is this the one that will finally take you out of the game?"

Blake wasn't sure if he alluded to the injury or marriage. It unnerved him to think he might have to leave his job before things with Rideau were finished.

"Not sure."

Jacob nodded toward Ava, who stood across the room in a huddle of women with his mother. "Marriage. That's a big jump, brother. I can tell by the way you two look at each other, it's the real deal."

Still contemplating when he'd be back on mission, Jacob's change of subject caught him off guard.

"How does she feel about you going back?"

He blew out a breath. "She's okay with it." He knew Ava would never ask him to leave his job. She might not have to. Considering the ache lingering on his right side, he wondered if his injuries might not be so easy to bounce back from. He'd gladly retire today if he could be sure all the hours spent tracking Rideau across two continents hadn't been in vain.

Breaking the contemplative moment, Jacob nodded toward the exit. "I think I better head out."

Blake stuck out his hand. Jacob sidestepped the handshake,

moved in for a quick embrace, and slapped a hearty pat on Blake's back.

"Been too long in church, my friend?" He stepped back and forced a smile, feeling traitorous with his suspicions.

Jacob laughed. "I guess you could say that."

"Again, thank you for coming. I appreciate it."

"As I said, that's what partners are for."

Blake nodded.

"I head back out in two weeks." Jacob ran a hand across his jawline. "I won't be out in the field, but I'll go through the intel we've gathered and see if we can finally put this mission in the rear-view."

Jacob had an uncanny way of reading his mind. Blake just hoped he couldn't read the uncertainties threatening to push their way to the forefront while he questioned his loyalty.

"I'll give you an update when I have one." Jacob let out a long breath, appearing hesitant to leave.

He looked his friend over, trying to ascertain any disloyalty in his behavior. He identified nothing other than the normal comradery they'd always shared.

Jacob took a step toward the exit and Brent glanced in their direction.

"Hey, Jacob?" His jaw tensed. He needed to get some answers before Jacob walked away.

"Yeah?"

"Can I ask you an odd question?"

"Sure."

"I know it's been a while, but did you notice anything off that day in the desert?"

Jacob paused for a moment. "No, why?"

"I just wanted to piece together a timeline."

Jacob shrugged. "Not sure I can recall anything odd." He laughed. "Other than the obvious, of course."

It was a long shot. He was grasping at anything to clear Jacob's name to Brent.

Jacob turned to leave again, then paused mid-stride and turned to face him, looking reflective. "There was one thing now that I think about it."

"What?"

"I was supposed to drive."

"What do you mean?" Blake tilted his head, trying to push through the foggy details of that night.

"Remember? We flipped for it."

He let out a breath as the memory came back to him. They always flipped a coin to see who would drive.

Jacob's face twisted into a cocky grin. "You always call heads, but we wanted to mess with Adams, so you called tails."

"So, you were supposed to drive?"

"Yeah."

"I guess it's a good thing you didn't." Blake's heart thudded against his ribcage as a wave of anxiety washed over him.

Jacob glanced down at Blake's injured leg. "Yeah, I guess it is."

"Hey Jacob, one more thing." Blake shifted his weight from one foot to the other, stretching his tired muscles. "When did we do the coin toss?"

"In the plane. Why?"

He tried to recall all the details and then asked, "Did we use Adams's coin?" Adams always carried a two-headed coin with him—said it was good luck.

"Yeah, Adams flew in with us. He stayed back at the Army post about a hundred miles south of where we were heading."

Blake angled his gaze toward the window. The wedding reception sounds faded to the background as Jacob finished laying out the events of that night.

"We picked up the SUV, nothing out of the ordinary. Adams

threw you the keys and told you I didn't sleep a wink and shouldn't drive."

Blake smirked. After their workout, he'd slept like a baby. "It was more of an order than a suggestion I drive." He brought his gaze back to Jacob.

Jacob nodded. "Yep. You know how Adams can be."

"The job was supposed to be a cakewalk."

"It was. We were going to shadow two curators from the Smithsonian. They were trying to piece together artifacts at the Mosul Cultural Museum." Jacob shook his head. "Terrorists had ransacked and looted the place a couple of years ago."

"Right."

"It was a cushy two weeks for the four of us."

"The four of us?" Blake's chest tightened. *There was a fourth person.*

"Yeah, you, me, Adams, and Warner."

A flash of recollection traced across his thoughts. He'd forgotten about the newest member of their unit, Allen Warner. They'd met him when they landed in Baghdad. "Why didn't Adams stay in Kenya?" Blake threw out the question, forcing his voice to sound nonchalant. "He never travels with us. He always stays behind, chained to the intel desk."

Jacob shrugged. "Not sure."

"Adams wasn't in the SUV when we were ambushed?" Blake knew the answer but was thinking out loud.

"No, and Warner wasn't either. They stayed behind at the Army post."

"No Rideau, no African rebels, just driving around an expensive SUV in the desert."

"Like I said, nothing to it."

Speaking up, he continued to untangle his thoughts. "These curators were harmless. Nobody wanted them dead. The Smithsonian's presence made both sides happy."

"You got it, cushy." Jacob sighed. "Except someone forgot to warn us about the ambush fifty miles into our journey."

"We never made it to the museum."

"Nope."

"Guess that's a plus."

"True."

"Two US soldiers and a car bomb barely make the headlines these days."

Blake's jaw clenched as he finished Jacob's thought. "But take out a crew from the Smithsonian, and that would've been an international disaster."

For a brief second, silence passed between Jacob and him.

Breaking through the quiet, he asked, "Ever get the idea *we* were the target?"

Jacob's features flashed confusion, then fury. "Well, now that you mention it ..."

Releasing a frustrated breath, he said, "Maybe I'm reaching?"

Jacob's body went rigid. The way it did when he wanted to pick a fight.

"When do you head back out?"

Jacob scowled. "Two weeks."

"Just stay low and watch your six. Got it?"

Jacob's expression hardened. "Sure thing."

He nodded, and they shook hands again. As Jacob exited the door, Brent walked in his direction.

"He cut in to dance with Ava. Did you have a problem with that?"

"No, not anymore."

"What do you mean?"

"Jacob's not the traitor." Blake kept his voice tight and controlled.

"How do you know?"

"I just do."

Brent scanned the crowd of happy wedding attendees. "Then who is, brother?"

His gut clenched under the jacket of his dress uniform as his mind raced ahead with a torrent of questions. "I don't know, but I intend to find out."

CHAPTER FIFTY-TWO

13:13 US Air Base, Kenya

Blake leaned his head against the stiff office chair and sighed. It had been precisely twenty-six days, eight hours, and—he glanced up at the ticking clock—thirteen minutes since he'd kissed his wife goodbye. *I can't wait to get back home.* He glanced out the single window of the temporary office building as the hot July sun poured in and heated the room. *I can't wait to get back to central heat and air.* He shrugged off his uniform jacket and hung it on the back of his chair.

Yanking off his glasses, Blake rubbed his temples then flipped through the block calendar on his desk. The desktop novelty, a throwback to a TV show that poked fun at dry office humor, was a gift from Brent. He smiled. Brent was never one to pass up a laugh. As he read the one-liner, his thoughts lingered on the date. He'd be home in less than a month if the mission went as planned.

Sliding his glasses back onto the bridge of his nose, Blake read through the rest of the documents. After this week,

Jacques Rideau's track of destruction would come to an end. According to the data they'd collected, he'd resettled since the Paris attack. And seventy-two hours ago, he arrived in Uganda to meet with his buyer.

Watching the team gear up earlier that morning sparked a longing in Blake that he wrestled to snuff out. He'd done his part. He was satisfied with that. But when his replacement and Jacob's new partner arrived two weeks after he did, the finality of it all hit like a ton of bricks.

Releasing a quick breath, Blake's thoughts returned to his wife. He assured her the mission would take less than two months, and he'd be out of harm's way the entire time. For the first time in his career, he'd sit back and watch computer screens while the other, younger versions of himself got their hands dirty. *I have a little boy to raise. A new mission.* This time, his boots would stay clean, and his uniform would be in one piece when he completed his assignment and returned to his family.

Tapping on a few more keys, Blake opened another file— his retirement paperwork. Scanning the details, a sense of peace flooded his soul. God had answered his prayer and brought Ava and him back together. The pull to be with his unit was strong, but the tug on his heart to be with Ava was stronger.

A blip on the screen made him blink. As he closed the document, the screen bounced again, then went blank. He groaned. "Great. Looks like the network's down. Again." Murmuring a complaint, Blake pressed on a few unresponsive keys, trying to elicit a reaction.

"Martin." Glancing up, he noticed Adams standing in the doorway. "You trying to break the computer?"

"Nah, just trying to reboot it."

"Technology. Never works when you need it to."

Blake laughed. "No, it sure doesn't."

"I volunteered us for a pickup."

He waved to the blank screen, then down at the files piled in front of him. "I have some paperwork to finish."

"Well, I penciled you in. I thought you could use a change of scenery."

Glancing at the clock, he frowned. He'd been sitting in front of his computer for hours.

"I'm sure whatever you've got going will hold, and as you said, the network's down." Adams shot him a scowl sending the weather-beaten creases of his forehead into a folded ripple. "I doubt it will be up any time soon. You know how the government works."

Blake leaned back in his chair and tilted his head from right to left, hoping to stretch out the kinks in his neck muscles.

"You can't tell me these four walls aren't making you crazy." A deep chuckle escaped Adams's lips. "Besides, how much trouble can a couple of old guys like us get into driving less than a hundred miles?"

Blake laughed as he looked back at the unmoving screen. "When do we leave?"

"Thirty minutes."

Glancing back at Adams, he said, "Okay, let me gear up. I'll be out in a few." He'd not kept a weapon on him while he sat chained to the desk, but there was no way he was leaving the base without one.

"Roger that." Adams nodded stiffly, then retreated down the hallway.

After grabbing his uniform jacket and hat, Blake grabbed a cold water from the fridge. Taking a quick swig of the refreshing liquid, an icy shiver ran up the back of his neck. *Don't go there. Now is not the time to feel panicky.* Ever since he'd returned to Africa, uneasy thoughts consumed him.

He'd checked, and double-checked, every angle for a traitor among them and found nothing. Jacob had put his feelers out before he'd arrived and had also come up empty-handed. *Maybe Brent's just being paranoid. Catastrophes happen all the time in our line of work.*

Blake thought back to the information they'd received. *If someone was trying to throw off our operation, then why did we get the intel?* Rideau had grown bold enough to travel to Uganda to meet with his buyers. He'd put the final touches on his deadly drug, and someone from another unit intercepted the chatter. Now, two teams worked in tandem on one mission. If someone was shielding Rideau, they'd done a poor job.

Blake pushed through the clunky metal door of the armory and retrieved his firearm. After a quick check of his side holster, he made his way to the hangar, where Adams leaned against a truck.

"What took you so long?" Adams glowered and another wave of uneasiness walked across Blake's thoughts. *What if Jacob runs into trouble? Maybe I should stay behind to help run comms.*

Shaking off the thought, he slapped on his hat. With two groups in play, there was plenty of over-watch back at the base. He wouldn't be needed. Blake pushed away the morose thought. "I had to swing by the armory."

"You want to drive?" Adams shoved a toothpick in his mouth.

Sweat bloomed across Blake's brow. The last time he sat in the driver's seat on duty, he'd been on a mission in the desert and almost died. "Nah. You can." *Just breathe, Martin.* The last thing he wanted to do was have a panic attack out in the middle of nowhere.

"You know my leg sometimes gives me trouble," Adams smirked and pointed to his knee. "Besides, its heads." Lifting his hand, Adams revealed the coin he'd just flipped in the air to Blake. "You always call heads."

Not always. Blake kept his thoughts to himself and reluctantly took the keys. He said a quick internal prayer and slid into the driver's seat. *Ignore the click.* It wasn't the driving that bothered him as the click of the ignition. Thankfully, his new SUV back in Dallas didn't need a key.

"Something the matter?" Adams cut his eyes in his direction. "You seem a little jumpy."

"No. All good." His throat constricted. *Keep it together, Martin.* As his heartbeat quickened, the tension squeezed around his throat like it had sprouted hands.

"The pickup is up here about seventy-five miles." Adams huffed out a curse. "Two Airmen got stranded when their vehicle broke down."

Blake couldn't remember if there was much of anything seventy-five miles ahead. Then again, he'd been out of the country for months. No doubt things had changed since he'd left. Straightening in his seat, he jammed the key into the ignition. *God has not given me the spirit of fear...* Repeating the Bible verse, he blew out a breath and started the truck. Thankfully, his heart maintained its calm rhythm. Blake gave the pedal a gentle push.

Adams let out a hoot. "You're driving like an old lady, Martin. What's the deal?"

Ignoring him, he pushed the pedal down farther.

They drove in silence for thirty minutes before Adams spoke up. "So, you think they will finally wrap this up?"

From his peripheral, Blake watched Adams shove the toothpick back into his pocket.

"Wrap what up?"

"This thing with you and Rideau?"

He glanced at Adams. "It's not really personal."

"It isn't?" Adams chuckled. "Sure seems like it is."

"How so?"

"Well, you were nearly blown to bits, and here you are, back on a mission to apprehend Rideau."

Cutting his eyes back to the road, he asked, "What's that supposed to mean?"

"I mean, you would've thought you might have taken the hint by now." Adams snorted a laugh. "I can understand it, though."

"Understand what?"

"The vendetta."

His jaw tensed. "It's not a vendetta. He's a bad guy. That's what we do—we take out the bad guys."

"Is it?"

He didn't respond. He wanted to see where Adams went with his questioning.

"Is that what we do? Take out the bad guys?" Adams shifted in his seat to face him. "It seems so cut and dry. Doesn't it?"

Blake's gut threw out a warning shot. "So, where are we heading exactly?"

"Should be close." Adams grabbed his phone to check the location.

Something didn't feel right. *I can't believe Adams is the traitor. It doesn't make sense. Why feed us the intel if he's working for Rideau?* He'd been out of the field for months, but he learned never to ignore his instincts. Shoving aside his anxiety, Blake quickly ran through different scenarios in his mind. *Could Jacob be in danger? Am I?* He lifted his foot off the pedal and the vehicle slowed. He'd been here before—threatened and alone—but this time, he refused to be caught off guard.

Adams's body tensed beside him. "What's with the slowdown, Martin? We don't have all day out here."

"Oh, you know, it's been a while since I've been behind the wheel. Just being cautious." He shot Adams a narrowed look.

Adams's expression darkened. "Is that so?" Adams nodded to the abandoned shanty, jutting out from the trees. "This is the stop."

Blake scanned the secluded area. He had about three minutes to make a decision. *What if I'm wrong?* Taking a deep breath, he ordered his thoughts. *But what if I'm right?* The only thing he carried was a loaded 9mm on his hip. If he was going to make a move, it needed to be now.

"Just pull up to the front, and I'll go have a look around." Adams's stoic voice pulled him out of his internal battle.

He pulled up to the front of the dilapidated building, and his thoughts turned to Ava. He'd lied to her. This mission would be his last. But he'd most likely not return to her in one piece.

Taking another quick breath, Blake tried to decipher the warnings screaming inside of him. Finally, he decided to gun the truck as Adams exited. If his gut was right, Adams would want to be far away in the event of an attack. *But what if he rigged the truck?* His blood iced. *Don't turn off the ignition.*

Adams slapped his shoulder and he flinched. "Just wait here and give me five."

Turning, Blake tried to read his expression. Nothing. Adams's face remained as indifferent as his military training had taught him to be.

"Turn off the engine, son. I know it can't be easy for you, sitting behind the wheel after what you've been through."

The hairs on his neck bristled. *Gun it.*

Adams barely had two feet on the ground before Blake slammed his foot on the pedal, jerking the truck forward. A shot rang out from the south, then a high-pitched clang echoed in his ears. The bullet had hit the vehicle. He jammed the truck into park, kept the engine running, and rolled out of the seat, taking cover behind the massive tree he'd nearly catapulted into. Yanking his firearm out of its holster, he aimed and pointed it in Adams's direction.

"Adams, put your hands—" Before Blake finished his command, Brent darted out from behind the run-down building, followed by four other agents dressed in full tactical gear.

"Get on the ground, Adams."

Anger and shock spread over Adams's face.

Trying to make sense of what had just happened, Blake scanned the area where the shot aimed at him had come from. "Brent, you need to get back. Someone took a shot at me from the south."

Brent looked up. "Are you hurt?"

"No, but you need to get back." Blake yelled louder as adrenaline pulsed through him.

Brent nodded, then ordered his team to move back. They complied and took cover behind the trees near the shanty. Brent searched beyond the tree line, his gun still fixed on Adams's chest. Adams stood unmoving, a smug smile pasted on his lips.

"Get down, Adams. I won't hesitate to shoot." Brent remained in the open, as he continued to scan the outlying area.

Adams held up one hand, balled into a fist, then lowered himself to his knees, favoring his weak leg.

"Brent!" Blake hollered again, his sidearm still fixed on Adams. "Get back. I've got him."

Brent's torso was thick and bulky with an armored vest, but there were other places to shoot a man that could still be fatal.

Adams glared at Blake while he continued to hold up one

hand, fist closed and poised in the air. *Something's off.* He studied the scene unfolding between Brent and Adams. If Adams was the traitor, who was hiding in the tree line?

"Adams, it's over, and you know it." Brent's words sliced through the tepid air.

"Is it now?" Adams glanced back at Brent and an icy shiver worked its way down Blake's spine.

"We have enough evidence to put you away for the rest of your life. Plus some."

"I don't think so." Adams jerked his head and shot Blake a heated look. "And you. You just won't die. Will you?"

White-hot fury filled him as he glared at Adams. *It's been Adams this whole time. How did I miss it?* "Brent, something's off."

"Raise both your hands and lower your face to the ground," Brent shouted another command at Adams.

"I haven't had the pleasure of meeting you, Brent, but it seems as if we have some unfinished family business to hash out."

Blake studied Brent's expression. *What does Adams mean by that?*

"I said, put your hands up, or so help me, I *will* shoot you."

He didn't like how Adams appeared to be stalling. Blake looked out over the clearing, trying to decipher any unwanted activity. Without his glasses, most of the terrain resembled a blurred painting.

"You're so much like your brother, aren't you? Brent, was it?" Adams looked over at him and kept his hand raised in the air. "It's too bad little Benjamin couldn't be here today."

Fury ignited inside Blake at the mention of his younger brother, and he lifted his 9mm a few inches higher, zeroing in on Adams's forehead. *It would only take one shot.*

"Hey Martin? Did you know I had a cousin. His name was

James. James met little Benjamin in the Marines, but James didn't quite make the cut."

Confusion coiled inside of Blake. *What is he rambling about?*

Adams turned his head and looked at Brent. "Looks like all the Martin boys have a little unquenched fire in them. Don't they? Too bad my cousin couldn't be here today. We'd all have a little family reunion."

Blake noticed the connection register in Brent's expression.

"James paid a dear price for his poor choices." Brent took a step toward Adams.

Don't do it brother. Don't move any closer. Blake willed Brent to read his mind. Something was off with Adams, but he couldn't pinpoint what.

"You made sure of that, didn't you?" Adams barked out a scornful laugh.

Blake looked from Brent to Adams, trying to unravel what the two were saying.

Adams spat on the ground. "James did right by his family." Adams turned his head and looked at Blake. "And isn't family all that matters?"

An uneasy hush filled the air.

Blake moved his finger along the trigger and steadied his breathing.

Adams shifted on his knees. *What's your game, Adams?* Brent cut a glance in his direction, and a be-on-your-guard look passed between them.

Several seconds ticked by, then like a jet tearing apart the silence, Adams's bellowing scream filled the air.

"Brent, watch out!"

Adams lifted his left arm in the air with both hands tightly gripped into fists. He followed it up with a slew of unrecognizable commands. As fast as he rattled them off,

Blake struggled to translate. Who were the instructions directed to?

Brent took another step forward, his finger curled against the trigger of his firearm. Blake's forefinger pulsed. Both brothers prepared to take a shot.

Adams opened his fist and time leapt forward as a blast from inside the shack rocked the ground. Brent dove for cover behind a low hedgerow as Blake leaned his body against the tree for support. *God, protect us.* Peering around the trunk of the tree, Blake kept his gun aimed at Adams's temple.

Adams turned and drilled a look in Blake's direction. "I wanted all of you to pay for my cousin's death." Adams's voice slurred, and spittle mingled with blood flew from his mouth. "See you on the other side, partner." He lifted both of his hands in the air and a gunshot rang out from the trees.

Adams's body slumped to the ground as blood flowed from a single shot to the back of his head.

Brent tried to push himself up.

"Brent, stay down!"

Groaning, Brent fell prostrate onto the dirt.

Blake darted behind trees, scanning the direction of the shot, until he reached Brent. "Are you okay?"

Brent rolled on to his back and groaned as blood trickled down the side of his temple. "I'll live. My team?"

Brent's team rushed in around them, weapons drawn and pointed at the tree line.

"They're here." Glancing at the group, he asked, "Is anyone hurt."

Several responses assured them everyone was accounted for. Blake eyed the leveled shanty. It was now a smoldering pile of charred wood and dirt.

"Adams?"

"Gone." His blood heated. Someone he'd trusted with his

life wanted him dead. He glanced back at Adams, lying motionless in the dust. He'd be lying if he said he was sorry Adams was dead. And for a fleeting moment, he was sorry he'd not been the one to take the shot.

"We need to get out of here." Blake looked over at Brent. "How did you and your team get here?" Scanning the area, he hoped to see another vehicle close by.

"Jumped."

"What?"

Brent spit out dirt from his mouth and pulled himself up so he leaned against a tree.

"You mean to tell me—"

"Yep."

"Wait until I tell mom." Blake's lips tugged into a grin as he recalled a memory from their childhood. Brent, Benjamin, and he had climbed onto the roof of their house, so they could jump onto a pile of cardboard boxes. It horrified their mother when she'd found them. Laughing, they'd reassured her it was safe. They were learning how to parachute out of airplanes. She scolded them and told them they could never jump out of planes. Ever.

"No, I take that back." Blake shot Brent a cockeyed grin. "I'm not going to tell Mom. You are."

Brent chuckled then groaned. "Don't make me laugh. It hurts."

Blake rolled his eyes and scanned the tree line again. "We better call in our location."

"My team already did." As Brent answered, two armored military vehicles sped toward them kicking up dust.

"That didn't take long."

As soon as the vehicles pulled up, Blake informed them there could be shooters to the south. They gave a thumbs up and pointed overhead as two faded green helicopters moved in that direction.

"Ah, they brought in the cavalry. That was nice of them." Brent glanced up at the metal birds in the sky.

"Very nice of them." Blake blew out a breath as relief swept over him. God had spared his life. Again.

Now, if Jacob's team captured Rideau, he'd push the button on his retirement paperwork—tonight.

CHAPTER FIFTY-THREE

B lake walked into the hospital room and grabbed the folder in the plastic bin by the door. They'd been back at the base for several hours, and he was eager to have a sit-down with Brent.

"Let's see, Mr. Martin, you have a few bumps and bruises." He opened the file, pretended to scan the documents, then glanced at Brent.

"Did you forget about HIPAA?" Brent shot him a scowl. "Don't make me call the FBI."

Adjusting his glasses to appear more astute, he ignored Brent and glanced back down at the file. "It looks like they're keeping you overnight to observe your brain activity." He smirked and shot Brent a look. "That observation should be short and sweet."

Brent picked up a pen and flung it at him.

"Hey now. No weapons until they evaluate your head."

"You're enjoying this, aren't you?"

"You mean, you being in the hospital bed instead of me for

a change?" Blake pulled up a chair and tossed the file on the side table. "Immensely."

"Did you call Ava?"

"I did." Warmth traced through him. It felt good to have someone back home to check in with.

"What did you say?"

"What do you mean? I just told her 'Hi.'"

Brent rolled his eyes.

"What can I say? She thinks I'm chained to a desk." Blake looked at all the files lying in front of Brent and shrugged. "This is all classified, isn't it? I can't tell her anything."

"So you lied?"

"I didn't lie. She asked how my day was, and I said—well, I told her it was uneventful."

"I guess you left the part out about unchaining yourself from the desk."

"I did." He grinned. "I told her you dropped in."

"Funny."

"Speaking of jumping out of planes or helicopters or whatever it is you do," Blake leaned back and put his hands behind his head. "Are you going to fill me in? Or is this above my pay grade?"

"I tried to warn you this morning, but the network went down at the base."

He shrugged. "It happens."

"I didn't think you'd leave the base." Brent tapped his fingers on the table, looking annoyed. "When I heard you were on your way to pick up the airmen with Adams, I had to move quick."

"So, you decided the best way to intervene was to jump out of a plane?" Blake punched Brent on the shoulder.

Brent winced. "It was a helicopter, and it was going this way."

"You should've never put others in danger to save me."

"I didn't."

"What do you mean?"

"A man by the name of Hakeem Abdul Aldanna became a person of interest last week."

Blake raised an eyebrow, confused. "I thought we were tracking Rideau?"

"Well, you are, but today has nothing to do with Rideau." Brent paused. "Well ... not exactly. A first-year analyst connected the dots."

"Let me guess, a relative of Adams?"

"On his mother's side." Brent shifted against the flat pillows on the hospital bed. "But the major connection is Adams's cousin."

Blake folded his arms and waited for Brent to explain.

"Adams's cousin—also a US citizen—is James Omar Sandalwood."

The name didn't ring a bell. Brent fingered through the files sprawled out next to him on the small rolling table. Obviously, Brent's brain worked just fine if he worked on the case from his bed. After finding the one he wanted, he handed it to Blake.

As Blake scanned the documents, Brent explained. "Adams's mom sought refuge in America following a turf war that took out most of her family's village. She was pregnant with Adams, but she died in childbirth."

"Really?"

"Yes. In one day, Adams became an American citizen by birth and an orphan."

A tinge of empathy for his now-deceased unit leader trickled through him.

"Adams's adoptive family raised him in an affluent neighborhood in Baltimore, sending him to the finest schools and handing him the American dream on a silver platter."

"So, what went wrong?"

"There was another child."

"His mom had two children?"

"No, there was a child we traced back to the Sudanese refugee transport his mother was on." Brent pulled out another file with a child's picture on it. "He'd been adopted and was living thousands of miles away in California."

Blake opened the file and studied the picture of a man in his twenties.

"Is this him?"

"Yes, James Sandalwood, a resident of Los Angeles." Brent sat back and released an exasperated breath. "It's the tale of two completely different childhoods."

Blake continued to leaf through the file while Brent explained.

"James's parents divorced six years after his adoption, and as a family, they struggled with the loss of income in a declining job market. His last two years of high school had him tossed between two unstable homes where money was scarce, and violence was plentiful."

Blake closed the file, placed it on the table, and folded his arms.

"Trying to escape from the life of a poor, displaced teen, he enlisted in the Marines at eighteen." Brent's brow furrowed. "He couldn't hack answering to authority, and the military kicked him out, after a DUI and a handful of other issues. After that, James took a job as an unskilled construction laborer in Los Angeles."

"So, he got restless and reconnected with his family in Sudan?" Blake threw out the question.

"James fit the orphan profile. He was lost, alone, and disillusioned by life. He went looking for a connection with anyone who understood his plight."

"Sounds like many people in the world."

Brent nodded in agreement. "He left the United States, went to Sudan to look for his relatives, and immersed himself in his family's politics. He was old enough when he fled Sudan to have seen some of the worst aspects of his home country's civil unrest."

Blake shook his head, trying to put all the pieces together in his mind.

"He joined Hakeem." Brent's tone turned terse.

"How did Adams find him? I knew Adams was adopted, and a car accident tragically took both of his parents shortly after he enlisted in the military. All of this was common knowledge."

"True. On paper, he'd been a clear patriot for the US government, dedicating his life to the military."

"What was it then?"

"I don't think we will ever know the answer to that." Brent shrugged. "Could be several things. Maybe Adams felt unfulfilled, or something was missing."

Blake knew Adams's leg injury hit him hard. He'd lost partial use of his right leg following a mission that both he and Blake were involved in. After his injury, he got transferred to a support position in the unit. He missed being a part of the team, but Blake didn't think that would be a reason to throw away everything he'd worked so hard for.

"How did Adams find James?"

"One of those mail-in DNA tests."

"You're kidding."

"No." Brent looked up. "We have access to it. Sometimes the information is useful, sometimes it's not."

"Is that even legal?"

Brent shrugged. "Under certain circumstances. You have to make sure you read the fine print."

"So, Adams gets injured, decides he needs connection, and goes looking for his mother's family?" He rubbed his hand across his beard as he tried to untangle the story. "But why go after me? Does this have anything to do with Rideau? Did Hakeem want Rideau's drugs?" Blake rattled off his questions in rapid-fire. "It would have been so easy to feed Hakeem the intel, and we'd be chasing our tails." Brent said nothing, and Blake cut a glance in his direction. "Am I missing something?"

Brent tapped his fingers on the files. "James."

"What about him?"

"He's dead, and I pulled the trigger." Brent scowled. "He gave me no choice. He forced my hand."

Blake understood. Neither one of them took a life unless absolutely necessary.

"Adams must have found out I fired the shot that killed his cousin." Brent looked up at him, and fury flashed in his eyes. "That must have initiated the blood lust against you."

His hands clenched at his side. He'd always believed Adams to be rigid and standoffish, but he chalked it up to his battle-hardened personality. He never considered him buried underneath the burden of such a ruthless grudge.

"Do you think he had anything to do with Benjamin's death?" Anger twisted in Blake's gut like a rattlesnake threatening to strike.

"There is no way to know for sure."

He tried to temper his anger. The answer wouldn't matter now that Adams was gone. "So, what about Hakeem? What's he have to do with this?"

"Hakeem is Rideau's buyer." Brent looked down at his watch. "If all went as planned, he's already in custody. Adams pushed out a warning when Rideau landed in Uganda, but after my hunch, everything got siphoned through our channels."

Releasing a pent-up breath, Blake ran his hand through his hair. Nothing about this mission unfolded as he'd expected, but he was relieved to hear it would soon be over. In a few days, he'd be on a plane back to Dallas, and he could put Africa behind him.

Forever.

Please, God, let it all have gone according to plan. Retirement never sounded so sweet. And he was more than ready to get back to his wife.

CHAPTER FIFTY-FOUR

"Happy anniversary, my love." Her words came out barely above a whisper as she snuggled closer to Blake.

Blake stirred, but didn't wake.

Gliding her fingers over the scars on his back, she recalled the night they first met. The marks weren't painful, but they were a constant reminder of the danger he put himself in every time he'd gone out on a mission. Thankfully he was done with that part of his life. He was safe now—at home, with her.

My team leader betrayed me. Resting her palm on his warm skin, Ava closed her eyes. *Thank You, God, for keeping him safe.* The memory of Blake's words still lingered in her mind. The idea that someone he worked with had double-crossed him made her stomach clench in anger. He'd not told her any of the details. He couldn't. But she suspected this person may have been involved in the car bomb that almost ended his career. And his life.

Sighing, Ava let her hands linger on Blake's body for a few moments longer, then she climbed out of bed. A shiver tickled a path down her back as she grabbed the thick terry robe and draped it tight around her body.

The sun's rays peeking over the mountains beckoned her, and she slipped on a pair of fur-lined slippers, opened the French doors, and stepped out onto the deck. The view from their Alaskan lodge looked like a panorama of a picture-perfect painting.

Breathing in deep, Ava relished the spring mountain air filling her lungs. Sensing she was no longer alone, she smiled and leaned back. As the heat of Blake's body steadied her, goosebumps rippled in waves across her arms.

"You're up early." Wrapping his arms around her midsection, he nuzzled into her neck and placed a trail of kisses across her cool skin.

She giggled as his prickly beard tickled the nape of her neck. "The chill in the room must have woken me up."

Blake spun her around and pulled her in for a long, tender kiss. When they parted, he nodded toward the bed, then looked back and flashed her a roguish grin. "It looks like we misplaced a few blankets last night."

Ava's cheeks filled with warmth recalling how they spent most of the evening in a heap of covers in front of the fire.

When Blake pulled her in close again, she closed her eyes and melted into his arms. "Happy anniversary, my beautiful wife."

Ava glanced up and his green eyes flashed with a spark of energy. Heat traveled through her body as she anticipated another lengthy kiss. Without warning, angry butterflies danced in her stomach and her insides swayed. As Blake tilted his head toward her, she took a step back, brought a hand up to her lips and swallowed back a moan.

A worried expression replaced his smoldering one. "Everything okay?"

She wasn't sure. Shaking her head, Ava rushed toward the bathroom. Blake turned and followed, but she closed the door before he could enter. "Oh, Blake, don't come in. How embarrassing."

"It's not like I haven't seen you sick before."

Ava groaned, recalling their time in Uganda. She splashed some water on her face and prayed her stomach would settle.

"Could have been the salmon they brought to our cabin last night. You mentioned you weren't feeling seafood." Blake's muffled words floated through the closed door.

As she studied herself in the bathroom mirror, she tried to recall what she'd eaten. "I only ate a few bites of my salad and some bread." A few seconds passed as another wave of nausea burned in her belly. "I don't know what it is." Feeling lightheaded, she ran cool water over a washcloth and wiped her clammy brow.

Blake pushed the door open as she lowered herself to the side of the tub. Taking in a few long breaths, a thought popped into her head. *No, it couldn't be.* "Blake? I think maybe ..."

"What is it?" He sat down beside her and took her hand.

"I can't imagine ..." She couldn't link the words together as her heart skipped a beat. Finally, she lifted her other hand to her abdomen and shook her head. "No, it can't be. It doesn't make sense."

"What can't be?" Blake glanced at her midsection, then a look of understanding stretched across his face. "Is it possible?"

She shrugged. "Well, anything is possible, I guess."

"I mean, *is it* possible, Ava?"

She thought for a moment, going back over the calendar in her mind's eye. Her face warmed. "Oh, my."

"What?"

"I don't think I paid much attention. We've been so busy

lately." After Blake's retirement, they purchased a large farmhouse on several acres. Ava planned to work from home and was busy setting up her new design studio. They wanted more room for Dylan to roam, and maybe even adopt a few farm animals for him to play with. Glancing up at her husband she said, "I would say it's very possible."

Blake took her in his arms and held her close.

She pulled back and tried to read his expression. "Are you excited?"

"Yes!" He cupped her cheeks and placed a gentle kiss on her lips. "How close is the nearest pharmacy?" Jumping to his feet, he bolted out of the bathroom. After a few seconds, Blake peeked around the corner. "I just checked. About twenty minutes away."

Ava laughed as she strolled out of the bathroom and watched him race around the room, throwing on sweatpants and running shoes.

"Are you planning on running to the pharmacy?"

"Of course not." He grabbed the keys, shot her a quick smile then moved toward the door. "Need anything else? Have any cravings?"

A giggle escaped her lips as she shook her head. He acted like a kid going to the county fair. "You're something else, Maxwell." She threw out his nickname as giddy excitement raced through her entire body. Could God really be blessing her with another child? They'd discussed adoption. Agreed they didn't want Dylan to grow up alone. She'd already prepared to open her heart and her home to a couple of more children in need of a family. But this—this was something she'd not planned on.

"I'll be back." Blake glanced over his shoulder, winked at her, then bolted out the door.

IN LESS THAN AN HOUR, Blake pulled up to the cabin and turned off the engine. "Is this really happening." *A baby?* The little girl from the river flashed across his mind's eye and he struggled to breathe. This world was a dangerous place and they were about to bring another child into it. *God, I can't forget her.* Blake pinched his eyes shut. *Or my failure to keep her safe.*

Opening his eyes, he blew out a breath and grabbed the pharmacy bag. He needed to have faith.

He hopped out of the car and took the stairs to the door two at a time. When he walked into the cabin, Ava, sat reclined on a chaise, freshly showered, and wrapped in a robe.

"Was your mission successful, Martin?"

"Yes, it was."

She smiled up at him then stretched like a lazy cat in the sun. "I think I need a nap. Care to join me?"

He blinked, almost forgetting why he'd gone to the pharmacy. "Stop trying to distract me." His voice dipped into a commanding tone as he handed her the bag. "Your nap will have to wait."

She took the bag and her lips bent into a pout. "I'm feeling much better now. Maybe I was just hungry."

Reaching for her hand, he lifted her slowly to her feet. When she stood, the soft fabric of the robe slipped off her shoulder. Blake groaned. "Why are you torturing me, woman?"

She giggled, playfully batted her eyelashes, then turned and sauntered toward the bathroom. Before she stepped through the door, she looked over her shoulder and blew him a kiss.

The blood pulsing through his veins heated. "Don't be gone too long."

After a few long minutes, Ava opened the bathroom door.

"Well?" Blake pushed himself off the wall he'd been leaning on and wrapped his arms snug around her.

Pulling him closer, she pressed her lips against his in a lingering kiss.

When she pulled away, he asked, "Is that a yes?"

She nodded.

Blake picked her up off her feet, kissed her again, and lowered her gingerly back to the ground. They both laughed.

"This is crazy." Her eyes sparkled with joy. "I can't believe we're going to have a baby."

"I know." Blake drew her in for another kiss. When he pulled back, a hint of concern shadowed her expression. "What's wrong?"

"What about adoption?"

His heart galloped ahead. They'd already decided to adopt and were prayerfully asking God for direction. "We can still adopt."

Tears gathered below her lashes as her face brightened. "Are you sure?"

"Definitely."

"Well give it a few years."

He laughed and nodded toward the living room. "So, what were you saying earlier about taking a nap?" Before she had time to answer, he scooped her up in his arms and carried her over to the chaise.

Heat flooded Blake's body as he cradled Ava close. Their family was growing. How big? He wasn't sure. *Have I not commanded you? Be strong and courageous.* As he finished repeating the verse a peace washed over him.

However many children God decided to bless them with, he needed to trust that God would equip him to be the father they needed him to be.

And to keep them safe.

CHAPTER FIFTY-FIVE

Nineteen Months Later

Blake leaned over the cold granite counter and studied his reflection. It was January, and the long winter months of beard growth lay thick along his jawline. He fished through his drawer and grabbed for his trimmer. *If I'm heading to warmer weather, I'd better cut some of this off.* After a few quick swipes of the blade, he hung his head and blew out an exasperated breath. *Ava will be home in an hour. Please, God, help me explain.*

He didn't finish his petition as he flipped on the shower and went back and forth in his mind about how today's conversation would play out. He didn't have a choice. He needed to go back—back to the place where their story began. Back to Uganda.

Flipping on the spray jets, Blake stepped into the palatial shower, and waited for the steam to drape a thin film of humidity across the glass door. "If only I could tell her what I know." Muttering under his breath, he argued with himself. "Maybe I should tell her about Andrew?"

As his frustration mounted, he leaned his body against the cool, wet tiles, and thought about the moment he'd uncovered Adams's betrayal. Thankfully, over time, the sting of disloyalty had receded into a dull ache.

You want to drive? Blake shook off the memory, and the water clinging to his hair sprinkled around the shower. Time healed his aversion to driving, but that day—that day was different.

The sound of the ignition.

The smell of the blast.

The sick feeling of helplessness as someone shot him at short range while lying on the ground.

Getting behind the wheel that day, he'd pushed through the torturous images of his assault in Baghdad. Adams knew what he was doing. The rest of that day tumbled through his mind like a storm, and the rage gathered in him like a cluster of darkening clouds.

As the steam lifted around the shower stall, Blake's back muscles tensed. Most days, the memories stayed inside the mental boxes he'd shoved them into. But other days, his leader's deception ached more than any of the physical wounds he'd suffered during his entire career.

You're driving like an old lady, Martin. Another trace of Adams's mocking voice trekked across his thoughts. Blake forced himself to concentrate on the stream of water beating down on his skin. The tropical heat wrapped around the enclosed space, soothing his stiff shoulders and the tight scars that crisscrossed his back.

How could I have missed it? "He wasn't in the field much. We weren't that close." Blake answered his question aloud to nobody but the stone walls and himself.

Brent had discovered only minutes before he'd left the base with Adams that the notorious human trafficker from South

Sudan was Adams's distant relative. Blake slammed an angry palm against the shower wall. Adams had turned his back on his country and his mission, lured by the prospect of money, power, and, more importantly, a sense of belonging.

As the water cooled, Blake switched off the faucet. Noticing the time, he towel-dried with the pace of a newbie at bootcamp, then slipped on his boxers, a fresh pair of jeans, and a crisp white T-shirt. *This conversation won't be easy.* A text alert from his phone jarred him out of his internal war. Slinging the wet towel over the shower door, he left the bathroom as he read the text.

Everything's in play. Are you in?

Without hesitation, Blake confirmed his decision.

Make the plans, and I'll be there.

Sighing, he lowered himself onto the bed and picked up the sterling silver picture frame. Dylan, and the twins, Benjamin and Andrea, all stared back at him with joyful, bright smiles while Ava looked content and peaceful.

His eyes darted to the clock on the wall as it chimed a quarter past the hour. *Please let her understand.*

Blake glanced back at the picture. Dylan would start school in the fall, and the twins were just over a year old. His life since he left the military ebbed and flowed into a domestic calendar of bliss and joy. "Retiring was the best decision I ever made."

After he put down the picture, he ran his hand along the curves of the bedside table and smiled. Through Ava's prodding, he took his love for carpentry and built a business of specialty crafted, high-end furniture. Together, they created an interior design and furniture empire that surpassed anything either of them had ever dreamed of—*Martin Interiors and Design.*

An incoming message on his phone jolted him out of his thoughts. Running his finger across the screen he scanned the text.

Plans made. You leave in the morning.

The muscles along his jawline tightened like a drawn rubber band. "Lord, give me the right words."

Standing, Blake paced the floor, and minutes later, he heard the familiar chime of the front door. Releasing a pent-up breath, he glanced at the clock. Thankfully, Caroline offered to watch the kids for the evening so he could have some time alone with his wife.

Soft footsteps carried across the entryway tile. Blake heard Ava plunk her keys into the basket hanging on the wall. He glanced down at the items on the bed, then added two more pairs of socks to the pile. God willing, he'd only need one week's worth of clothing. He hoped even less.

The doorknob turned, and a current of tension shot through the room like a runaway firework on the Fourth of July. Blake took a deep breath and hesitated only a second before turning around.

"BLAKE?" Ava glanced at the bed then back at her husband. A rugged, black military-issue duffle bag sat unzipped, filled with clothes and a few other pieces of gear she'd not seen out of storage in months. "What's going on?"

He ran a hand through his hair, and a lump wedged in her throat.

"Sweetheart." The low timbre of his voice was soft and steady. "I need to talk to you about something." He led her to the end of the bed and motioned for her to sit down. "There's been a development."

When he stepped back, she tried to read his expression.

"I need to leave for a little while."

"What? What are you talking about?"

Blake crouched in front of her and reached for her hands. "I need to go back to Uganda."

"What did you say?"

He stood, leaned against the wall, and folded his arms. "The mission I was on in Uganda before I was—"

"—Captured and nearly killed."

"Ava, please listen to me. I need to go back. Something has come up, and it's my duty to see it through."

"Your duty is here. To our family." A shiver rippled through her body, and she fought the urge to cry. *I can't go through this again. What if he gets hurt? Or worse? What if I lose him?*

"Remember how I told you someone betrayed me on my last mission?"

His words snapped her back to attention. Ava nodded while her eyes pooled with tears.

"That man is gone. No longer a threat. But he put something in motion he knew would torment me, even from beyond the grave." Blake paused for a moment. "I've lived with the memory of what I couldn't change—until now."

"What do you mean?"

"I can't—"

"Wait, don't say it. You can't tell me, right?" She cut him off as a fire burned in her belly. "This was supposed to be over, Blake. This part of your life wasn't supposed to interrupt ours anymore."

He didn't respond.

"I thought you put all this behind you for good." Ava

glanced over at the items on the bed. His tactical jacket and pants sat rolled in neat, orderly bundles.

"I did, and I am, but—"

"But what?"

"I have an opportunity to right some wrongs."

"You can't just up and leave. We have a successful business now. I thought you were satisfied with that."

His phone buzzed to life in his pocket. He took it out and answered it. After a few yeses, no's, and okays, he finished the call. The tension in the room grew thicker.

"Who was that?"

"Brent."

She folded her arms.

"I'm duty-bound to go back."

Narrowing her eyes at him she said, "You're retired."

"I'm going back as a civilian." He gripped the back of his neck. "I need to finish this, Ava."

She opened her mouth, then bit back her protest. She wanted to say something about the fact that he'd retired, and he should never consider leaving his children—or her. Ever again. But the resolute look in his eye told her all her objections would be in vain.

"I promise I will explain everything when I get back."

"How do I know you're coming back?"

He blew out a breath. "I promise you. I'll come back."

"You'll tell me everything?"

"Yes, everything. From the beginning."

"The beginning?"

"From the day we met in Uganda."

Ava pursed her lips together.

"I can't give you names or anything, but I can give you the timeline."

"What if ..."

He sat beside her. "Don't say it."

"Why, Blake?" She stood and moved away from him. "Why can't I say it? Uganda was a dangerous place for—" she hesitated and waved her hand in the air. "For whatever you did there." The fears she'd tamed years ago catapulted to the surface and threatened to strangle her sanity.

"It's not the only place I've been in danger, Ava."

"That's not helping."

He stood and wrapped his arms around her, pulling her in to the warmth of his chest. "Adams had a personal vendetta against me, but he's gone."

She glanced up, still enveloped in his embrace, and met his gaze.

"You need to trust me."

"I trust you." She answered him in a whisper. "It's the rest of the world I don't trust."

"I promise to be as safe as humanly possible." He pulled her forward and placed a gentle kiss on her forehead. "Besides, I'll be with Brent."

Ava scowled and stepped back. "Somehow, that doesn't relieve my fears very much."

Blake chuckled, and she deepened her pout.

"When do you leave?"

"In the morning."

"What?" He'd not even given her time to digest what he was telling her. She pushed away from him and catatonically walked into the master bath, where the fresh smell of his shower still lingered in the humid air. Lowering herself onto a bench, she removed one of her ankle boots. Blake walked around the corner. Ava sensed his gaze but refused to look in his direction.

"Ava?"

She kept her lips pressed together as she yanked the second

boot off with a jerk. Releasing a heavy breath, she stood, sidestepped around him, and stomped to the closet.

"Ava, look at me."

She turned and blinked back the handful of tears threatening to fall. Blake took a few quick strides and stood in front of her. With a gentle motion, he lifted her chin and she caught the determination in his jewel-green eyes. "I promise, you *will* understand when I get back."

She wanted to be strong, but a bevy of questions swirled in her mind, taunting her. Ava only gave voice to one. "Do you know how long you'll be gone?"

"A week. At the most." He leaned in and kissed the top of her head. "I don't plan on being separated from you or our children for longer than I absolutely need to be."

She nodded as he pulled her toward him. This time his lips pressed onto hers and she almost forgot why she was angry. Stepping back out of his arms, Ava tried to make sense of her tangled thoughts. She believed what he promised, but she still worried about what he was heading into.

The gear on the bed reflected the harsh reality that he wasn't flying to Africa for a vacation. She sensed a shadow over this trip. Was it unfinished business or regret? Or both. But it wouldn't help to wallow in her anxiety. The conversation was over. Long ago, she'd promised to support him until death do they part, so right now she needed to have faith in his decision.

"I love you, Ava."

"I love you too."

She leaned into him and he held her for several minutes.

"Thank you for trusting me."

She sniffled. He hadn't really given her a choice.

CHAPTER FIFTY-SIX

Uganda

Blake glanced around at the group of armed men and women fanned out along the hill. Some of them situated themselves behind trees, and others lay on their stomachs, their weapons resting on tripods.

"How did I end up back here?" He shook his head. It wasn't the first time he'd asked himself why he'd decided to lace up his tactical boots and fly back to Uganda.

"Well, I'd like to say it was by the grace of God," Brent answered him with a grin.

"How's that?"

"I've been able to work with some of the best analysts in the business, and if they weren't able to put this puzzle together, then we"—Brent motioned to his team—"wouldn't be here at all."

"Here seems like a bad place to be." Blake had only been in the country twenty-four hours, and the memories of his tumultuous time in Africa hung like a weight across his shoulders.

"Maybe." Brent pointed behind him. "But we have a hundred good guys on our side, and there are only twenty bad guys in that valley below. Those are good odds."

He swiped at the sweat beading his forehead while staying safe for his wife and children dangled at the forefront of his mind. "True, but there are twenty fully armed adults. And I counted just over fifty children." He glanced down at the row of dilapidated mud buildings with corrugated roofs. "I don't like it."

"Look, after this is over, your life can go back to normal."

Normal? What's normal? Blake bit back a laugh. "I sure hope so, brother."

Brent slapped him on the shoulder. "Don't worry, you haven't died yet."

"It's not like I haven't had the opportunity."

"That's true. God must have kept you alive for something."

He laughed. It was true. God had always been his refuge in times of trouble. Shifting his position on the hill, Blake scanned the shadowy valley below them. The small makeshift compound was home base to the most horrendous of crimes— child trafficking. Rage coiled in his gut. Days before he'd landed on the continent, the report he'd been given mentioned ninety-six children. Forty-six of them had already been taken, and two trucks were on the road to transport more.

"You've already lost over forty kids. What are we waiting for?" He gritted his teeth as frustration buoyed to the surface. The waiting game was not one he played well.

"They aren't missing."

"What?"

"Like I said this morning, there's been a team working this for months." Brent's lips curved into a cat-that-ate-the-canary smile. "We only brought you in for the finale." Nodding toward the trucks, he continued. "While you were back in the States building your furniture empire, the rest of us were here wrapping up loose ends."

Looking through his binoculars, Blake asked, "Where are they?"

"Our guys, disguised as buyers, picked up the children a few days ago. They'll be reunited with relatives or one of the agencies set up to rescue trafficked children."

He breathed a sigh of relief. If he could do nothing more this week, he needed to know he'd helped a few of the innocent. That's why he was here.

As he scanned the area again, his relief was quickly replaced by a gnawing in his gut. *I have to find her.* He'd made a promise to someone the last time he was here, and he'd do whatever it took to fulfill it.

Find my sister. The plea danced in his memory, threatening to stir up an ample supply of anger and regret. Weeks after Ava and he escaped, he'd gone back to the village looking for Andrew. He wanted to retrace his steps so he could unearth the location of his abductors. However, when Jacob and he approached the village, it had been decimated. Guilt had torn him up when he found Andrew beaten and scarcely alive.

"Soldier. They'll go after my sister. Find her. Please." Andrew's sputtered words fell over his parched lips. Then, lifting his hand to the symmetrical lines carved into the dark skin of both of his cheeks he added, "Amara Rose has the same."

Pinching his eyes closed, Blake pushed the recollection of the heart-wrenching final moments with Andrew back to the recesses of his mind. *God go with you, soldier.*

Andrew also explained how little Amara Rose had a distinct birthmark on the bottom of her foot—a large faded splotch of skin shaped like a rose. But that had been years ago, and now little Amara was no longer a baby. What are the odds she'll still have that mark? Blake sighed. Until he could find Andrew's sister, he'd never be able to quell the uneasiness in his soul.

He surveyed the landscape of the buildings again. If ever there was a model of hell on earth, this was it. Several children sat in rows on the dirty ground, their faces downcast and sullen. Most of them wore rags and looked as if they hadn't bathed in weeks. The spectacle sparked a reaction in him to advance. "How much longer?"

"Eleven minutes."

Good, he was done waiting for something to happen.

"Our guys are in place. Those trucks belong to us, and the adults are all accounted for."

"Looks like you have it all under control."

Brent shrugged. "As I said, I brought you out of retirement this week for one reason only."

"Amara Rose."

"Yep."

For a quick, heartbreaking second, he wondered what he'd do if Amara wasn't among this group of children. He trusted Brent's intel, but if they'd already lost her in the network, finding her would be nearly impossible.

"Nine minutes."

As he peered through the binoculars, his heartbeat slowed to the rhythm of his breathing. In his line of vision, several children clung to each other in groups under leafless trees, and others splashed in murky puddles. An ache clawed its way into his heart. *God, please help me find Amara.*

When he shifted his view, a child tucked away behind a tree caught his eye, and he froze. The little girl sat alone, on a broken log, wearing a soiled sack dress with her knees pulled up under her chin. "It can't be." He studied the girl a moment longer.

"What?" Brent lifted his binoculars and followed his gaze. "Something the matter?"

"Please God, let it be her." As his plea lifted, a lump formed in Blake's throat.

"What do you see?"

Closing his eyes, he unearthed a memory he'd tried for years to bury. A child down by the river. Her parents dead at his feet. A needle plunged into his arm. Fiery lava coursing through his veins. Blake glanced down at the broken log again, not wanting to lose sight of her. "It's her, Brent."

"Who?"

Turning to face Brent he said, "The little girl from the river." *The one I couldn't save.*

"Are you sure?"

"Yes. It's her. I know it is." He studied the little girl's features once more. On the right side of her face stretched a prominent burn scar from her eye down to her chin. The shape reminded him of the letter *J*.

"Are you positive?"

"I am." Her hair had grown in, but he'd recognize those haunted, deep-set amber eyes anywhere.

"What do you want to do?" Brent checked his watch.

Blake leaned against the craggy tree stump jutting out of the ground. "I don't know."

The weight of seeing the girl, sitting alone, filthy and abandoned, sent a surge of adrenaline through him. *I have to do something.* He wanted to take off down the dusty hill, scoop her up into his arms, and tell her how sorry he was. Sorry he couldn't save her family. Sorry he'd not protected her. Sorry he'd failed. The wind picked up but the only sound he heard was his heartbeat pounding in his ears.

"Was her family killed the day she was taken?" Brent's question pulled him out of his remorse filled thoughts.

"Yes."

"What about the teenagers who alerted you?"

"They weren't family."

Blake leaned his head back and tried to think. With less than six minutes until the raid unfolded, he needed to make a decision. *God, please tell me what to do.* The plan was for him to go in and get Amara Rose to safety. Keeping her in her home country and reuniting her with her family was plan *A*. A trickle of warmth filled him. If there were no living relatives, he and Ava were ready to adopt.

"We have safe houses all over the world for these children. I can make sure the other little girl gets somewhere secure and has a chance at finding a loving family."

Brent's words hung in the air while a list of scenarios bombarded his brain. *What do I do?* This decision didn't involve procedures and tactics—it involved his heart.

"Blake?"

"Yes?"

"We have about four minutes. What do you want to do?"

"Can you fast-track the paperwork?" As he blurted out the question, peace replaced his unease. It was simple. He and his wife wanted more children, and they both agreed they wanted to adopt. The little girl he'd agonized over for years sat in front of him, alone and in need of a family.

Brent shot him a questioning look. "Are you sure?"

"Definitely. I can't let her end up in an orphanage. Not when she's sitting right in front of me." He looked down at the delicate little girl, skinny and frail from malnourishment. "This world isn't kind to children with scars. I need to give her a chance at a good life with a loving family."

"What about Ava?"

"I haven't even told her about Amara Rose. I planned on surprising her."

"Oh, you're going to surprise her all right."

Blake smiled. Brent was right. "I didn't want to get Ava's hopes up about Amara. I told her I had one last mission, that I wouldn't be gone long, and I would be safe."

"Safe is subjective in our line of work."

"Remember, I'm not in your line of work anymore."

Brent looked him over. "Looks like you are today."

He glanced down at his clothes. A bulky body armor vest wrapped around his torso, and a 9mm hung snug against his hip. Underneath the rugged tactical pants, a knife was strapped to his calf. And the boots—the boots he hadn't worn in years—were covered in dust and loose grass.

Blake gave Brent's shoulder a quick punch. "Only for this week, then I'm done." He paused. "For good."

Brent's lips pulled at one corner. "Right. That's what they all say." Nodding toward the valley below, he said, "Two-minute warning."

"Copy that."

One hundred and twenty seconds passed, then Blake watched as the team moved in and systematically took control of the compound. As he waited for them to secure the area, a passage from the book of Psalms flashed across his mind. *Even though I walk through the valley of the shadow of death, I will fear no evil, for you are with me; your rod and your staff, they comfort me.*

This, indeed, had been the valley of death for those innocent children. Had they not been rescued today, they would have endured a life of terror and abuse until the day they escaped or perished.

Blake glanced up at the clear Ugandan sky and thought about Ava. It was the same sky they met under, and even then

God had been working behind the scenes, preparing both of them for this journey. A journey that involved opening their hearts to love and a lifetime of God's grace. Like a much-needed rain covering a thirsty land, peace flooded his soul.

Finally, his mission in Africa was complete.

"Let's go." Brent stood and motioned down the hill. "It's time to go rescue your children."

Blake's pulse quickened as he strode down the hill and watched as the hand of justice reached out to gather the innocent to protect them. At one time, he and his younger brother Benjamin stood shoulder to shoulder with them. Glancing at Brent, Blake wondered what the future had in store for him. Would Brent one day find the love of his life to walk through this journey with? He hoped so.

"I'll go get Amara." Brent laid a hand on his shoulder, then nodded toward the little girl hiding in the copse of trees. During the raid, she'd not moved. She'd only tucked herself up smaller and buried her face in the tattered fabric of her dress.

He studied the girl for a moment, then glanced back at Brent. His heart tore in two. "I don't know if I ..." Blake's voice hitched. The failure and guilt he'd carried for years twisted through him, choking back his words.

Brent gave his shoulder a squeeze. "It wasn't your fault. But you're here now. God has given you a second chance."

Swallowing hard, he turned and walked over to the cluster of trees. When he reached the broken log, Blake crouched in front of the little girl. She kept her chin tilted into her chest. The faint sound of her sobs carried through the tepid breeze and up to his ears. Taking a deep breath, he whispered, "Hello."

Her body stilled.

Closing his eyes, Blake begged God for His mercy and grace. When he opened them, he said, "You're safe now, little one."

After a few seconds, the girl raised her head. As a

questioning look flashed across her amber eyes, she glanced past him and stared at the bustle of activity weaving in and around the makeshift compound.

"You're safe." Blake said the words again hoping to ease her fears.

She brought her gaze back to his then glanced down at his vest and the weapon on his hip.

His chest tightened. "I won't hurt you."

She blinked and several loose tears rolled down her cheeks.

"I'm so sorry, little one." As the words fell off his lips, the weight he'd been carrying began to lift. "I'm sorry I couldn't save your parents." He doubted she understood him, but as he said the words a wave of release fell over him. Only God could've brought him to this place. Full circle. To make amends. To redeem the time. "I'm sorry I couldn't protect you."

More tears curled down her cheeks as a hint of recognition traced across her expression. "Soldier?" Her eyes widened.

Nodding, he did the only thing that felt natural to him. He held his arms out.

And when she leaned forward and snuggled into him, he cried.

EPILOGUE
ONE YEAR LATER

Kampala, Uganda

Ava stepped out of the double doors of the hotel, and a blanket of heat draped around the cool flesh on her naked arms.

"Good evening, Mrs. Martin. Can I call you a taxi?"

She glanced at the young man, who smiled back at her, and her heart leapt. *He looks like Andrew.* The concierge stood a few inches taller than her, and with his lanky body and wide, hopeful brown eyes, he reminded Ava of the man who'd once risked his life to save her.

"No—no, thank you." Shaking off the pang of loss, she slipped on her sunglasses, then motioned toward the semicircle where taxis and cars dropped and picked up. "I'm meeting my husband in a few minutes."

The man nodded. "Very good."

Gliding down the tile steps, Ava reached into her canvas bag and fingered the two tiny stuffed animals she'd brought with her—a bunny and a lamb. Both she'd spent hours picking out and both a motherly gesture she hoped the girls would enjoy. She pulled the furry creatures out and studied them, releasing a silent plea. *Please, God, let everything go as planned today.* Tucking the soft toys back in her bag, she thought back to a year ago, after Blake left for Uganda on what he called an 'unfinished mission.' When he returned, he explained how he'd been part of a rescue and her well-ordered world turned upside down—again.

You won't believe it. We found her. She smiled, recalling the passion in Blake's voice as he described how he'd found Andrew's little sister, Amara Rose. The story he unfolded progressed from good to miraculous when he told her he'd also found the little girl who'd haunted his dreams since the day he was ambushed by the river.

She was there, all alone, sitting on a log, and I knew then that God had heard my prayers. For years Blake prayed for the little girl—the one he'd been helpless to save. And for years, distress over her kidnapping had seared an agonizing wound through his soul.

A taxi pulled up in front of the hotel, and her pulse quickened. They're here. When the car rolled to a stop, Blake jumped out of the passenger seat and she rushed into his open arms. "How did it go?" Stepping back, she glanced up at him, trying to read his expression.

"Seamlessly." He smiled down at her, and the windswept sound of giggles floated out of the car and circled through the balmy air.

Ava laughed and waved at the two little girls in the back seat. She'd met them a handful of times over the past twelve months while the agency checked into every potential lead for the girls to be reunited with family. After several dead ends, they'd finally received the call—they could adopt the girls and bring them home to Texas.

A row of tiny fingers wiggled out of the rolled-down back seat window, and Blake pretended to grab for them. More snickers bubbled out as he blew them a kiss, then leaned against the taxi and folded his arms. "All the paperwork's buttoned up. It's time to take Faith and Amara Rose home to meet the rest of the crew."

"I can't wait. They'll be so excited." They'd already introduced Dylan and the twins to their new sisters via video calls. Overjoyed, the Martin kids had made sweeping plans to introduce them to all their friends at school and church.

Blake pulled her close and kissed her forehead. "If we keep adding to our family like this, we'll have our own kid-sized platoon."

Ava shook her head and laughed. Shifting her gaze skyward, she watched as fleecy puffs of clouds drifted across the bright azure backdrop. Warmth dappled her cheeks. She recalled the day she crawled into a battered truck with a handful of missionaries, and the trajectory of her life changed forever. She breathed deeply, lowered her eyes, and caught Blake's contemplative look. "You were right, you know."

"About what?"

"The memories."

He nodded, and a hint of understanding marked his expression.

"I never thought I'd want to come back to Uganda." She blinked back the tears threatening to gather in her eyes. "But now, with these girls—" Her voice hitched, and she swallowed back a torrent of tangled emotions. "I mean, the fear still lingers, but the awful images are slowly being replaced with happy ones."

Blake lifted his thumb and swiped away the tears just below her lashes. "God's redeeming the time."

She blinked past her tears, then nodded. "You're right. He is." For a breath of a second, clarity overshadowed her anxious thoughts. Despite all the heartache and fears, she'd never reverse her decision to join the mission trip to Uganda.

"I love you." He mouthed the words in a whisper, then placed a soft, pillowy kiss on her lips. Hearing the rush of giggles in the back seat, he pulled away. "I think we're being watched."

"What are they saying?" Ava looked at the smiling girls, then at Blake. She'd been studying their language but still struggled to decipher the words in flowing conversation. "I picked out the words goat, chickens, and water."

Blake laughed. "Let's just say it's a good thing we bought some land." His lips curved into a satisfied grin, then he turned and winked at the girls.

She smiled as he rattled off a few more sentences that sounded like a promise to go fishing and camping under the stars. Ava laughed after he turned to face her and waggled his eyebrows. After she married him, she realized somewhere deep inside hid a giant kid who craved fun and mischief.

Before she could ask Blake more about the translation, a man dressed in a colorful shirt approached them with a luggage cart. "Mr. Martin, would you like me to put these in the back?"

Blake nodded, then reached out to shake the man's hand.

After he loaded their luggage into the trunk, he opened the back door of the taxi so she could slip in. "It's time to go home."

Both girls clapped their hands together in delight.

"Mrs. Martin."

Hearing her name, Ava glanced over her shoulder before she slid into the backseat.

"Someone left a note for you at the front desk."

The concierge she'd spoken to earlier threw her a smile, then thrust a small envelope into her hand. Ava opened the envelope and pulled out a leather bookmark. As she traced the painted lion's head and the row of tiny sunflowers with her forefinger, a warm shiver walked its way down her spine.

"Who left this?" Glancing up, she looked at the young man.

He shrugged. "A woman." He lifted his hand to below the level of his shoulders. "About this high." After he explained a few more details, he turned and bolted up the steps.

A small piece of paper inside the envelope caught her eye, and she lifted it out.

Remember, today ALL is good.

Ava's heart constricted. *The hidden church.* For so long she'd tried not to think about her time in Uganda, but reading those words sent waves of emotions flooding through her.

"Is everything okay?"

Blake's voice yanked her out of her memories, and she blinked. *Breathe, Ava. You survived.* Overwhelmed by the onslaught of emotions, she turned into Blake's chest. Taking a few deep, measured breaths, she inhaled the refreshing scent of his recent shower and the light trace of sweat now covering his skin.

"It's okay, sweetheart. I'm here."

The encouraging words of the kind African woman who'd tended to her circled back through her thoughts. *Today, all is good.*

On the night she almost collapsed from exhaustion, God had provided a place of refuge, reminding her that even in her darkest moments, He never left her side. She released a sigh and with it, a silent prayer of thanks. Stepping out of Blake's embrace, she slipped the bookmark and the note into her purse.

"I'm okay." She glanced up at her strong, and fiercely loyal husband—the good man who God had brought to her while she was frightened and alone. "In fact, today—" Her voice hitched, and she swallowed back the lump threatening to expand in her throat. "Today, and every day, with you by my side, *all* is good."

ACKNOWLEDGMENTS

First and foremost, I thank Jesus, the author and finisher of my faith, for the gift of imagination.

Thank you, Steven, my rock. Your love and support for my writing dreams have kept me forging ahead. I'm glad we share an office because, without your constant tech support and lunch dates, I'd be lost.

I'd like to give a shout-out to my critique partners, Shelley, Richard, Nelda, Anna, and Susan, for taking me under their wing and helping me fine-tune the details of this story.

Finally, I'd like to thank Laurel Thomas for being a mentor and friend.

ABOUT THE AUTHOR

Author Christina Rost is a mother to three amazing children and is married to her high school sweetheart, Steve.

An avid reader, she can still remember the first box set of sweet romance stories her mother bought her as a young teen —*The Canadian West Series* by Janette Oke. Reading about the rugged landscape of the west and handsome Canadian Mounties, Christina daydreamed about writing her own love stories.

After spending twenty-four years as an Air Force wife, her husband retired, and they settled in Oklahoma. Seeing this as an opportunity to pursue writing full time, she jumped in with both feet and in 2020, she attended her first writer's conference—WriterCon in Oklahoma City. That weekend confirmed she'd found her people and writing was a part of her soul.

In 2021, one of her unpublished romantic suspense novels took first place at WriterCon, and in 2022, the same story was a finalist for the ACFW Genesis Contest. She's also won several awards in Flash Fiction.

Writing inspirational romance has always been Christina's passion, and she loves to craft relatable characters with redemptive qualities that reflect the importance of her faith.

Her literary hero is Jane Austen, and like Jane, she hopes her own contemporary romances can sweep her readers away for a swoon-worthy, enjoyable experience.

When she isn't spending time with her family or writing, you'll find Christina chatting with friends over creamy cups of seasonal coffee or perusing antique shops for tattered books and hidden treasures.

YOU MAY ALSO LIKE:

Death in High Places by Sara L. Jameson

An Interpol agent with a deadline he can't miss.

Urgent intel warns of terrorist cells planning coordinated attacks throughout Europe. Special Agent Jacob Coulter of Brussels Interpol is assigned to find the terrorist financiers supporting these groups and shut down their funding operations.

An opera singer's life and career hang in the balance.

The Queen of the Night's vocal pyrotechnics have launched many a soprano's international career. But Riley Williams, Jacob's fiancée, is terrified of heights, and her Antwerp Opera debut as the evil queen requires her to sing from a hydraulic lift forty feet above the orchestra pit. When newspapers cite Riley's recent unmasking of an international terrorist plot and the lift malfunctions, Jacob suspects terrorist sabotage.

He encourages Riley to accept her BFF's invitation to stay the Savoy

Hotel in London where she'll be out of danger. Or so he thinks ...

A series of murders connected to a notorious terrorist financier known as the Priest leads Jacob across Europe. When the victims' deaths point to London, his Interpol partner convinces him London is a haven for terrorist financiers.

But the clock is ticking and what Jacob uncovers is more devastating than anything he could have imagined.

Get your copy here:

https://scrivenings.link/deathinhighplaces

Strong Currents by Delores Topliff

Columbia River Undercurrents Series—Book Two

Erica Hofer, a young German Christian woman opposes Hitler and flees to her uncle in America but encounters suspicion, rejection, and attempts on her life.

Josh Vengeance, a pastor's son joins the US Navy to become a hero but gets invalided home, crippled in body and spirit.

During world war, is any price too great to pay for love and freedom?

Get your copy here:

https://scrivenings.link/strongcurrents

Scrivenings
PRESS
Quench your thirst for story.
www.ScriveningsPress.com

Stay up-to-date on your favorite books and authors with our free e-newsletters.

ScriveningsPress.com

9 781649 172938